An old, familiar ache tried to work its way into Sarah's chest.

She sure wished she could make Gregory see what his extra job was doing to his son, Hunter. Surely if he saw the effect, he would quit. Why waste time working for gifts that would mean nothing to the boy after the first five minutes? What was truly important was time with family. Because it could be taken away at any moment.

She looked at her calendar and counted dated blocks. Twelve days until Christmas Eve and their pageant.

Twelve days… An idea began to blossom.

She took a deep breath as she envisioned those empty blocks on her calendar and began to brainstorm ideas. But could she pull it off? It would take a lot of strength to spend that kind of time around Gregory.

Strength she might not have right now.

Hunter's sad, angry face flashed through her mind.

Yes, she had to do it. For Hunter.

Born and raised in Kentucky, **Missy Tippens** met her very own hero when she headed to grad school in Atlanta, Georgia. She promptly fell in love and has lived in Georgia ever since. She and her pastor husband have been married over twenty-five years and have been blessed with three children. After ten years of pursuing her publishing dream, Missy made her first sale to Love Inspired in 2007.

Lorraine Beatty was raised in Columbus, Ohio, but now calls Mississippi home. She and her husband, Joe, have two sons and five grandchildren. Lorraine started writing in junior high and is a member of RWA and ACFW, and is a charter member and past president of Magnolia State Romance Writers. In her spare time she likes to work in her garden, travel and spend time with her family.

Their Hometown Christmas

Missy Tippens

&

Lorraine Beatty

2 Uplifting Stories

A Forever Christmas and *A Mom for Christmas*

LOVE INSPIRED
INSPIRATIONAL ROMANCE

LOVE INSPIRED®

INSPIRATIONAL ROMANCE

ISBN-13: 978-1-335-42997-1

Their Hometown Christmas

Copyright © 2022 by Harlequin Enterprises ULC

A Forever Christmas
First published in 2009. This edition published in 2022.
Copyright © 2009 by Melissa L. Tippens

A Mom for Christmas
First published in 2016. This edition published in 2022.
Copyright © 2016 by Lorraine Beatty

For questions and comments about the quality of this book, please contact us at CustomerService@Harlequin.com.

Love Inspired
22 Adelaide St. West, 41st Floor
Toronto, Ontario M5H 4E3, Canada
www.LoveInspired.com

Printed in U.S.A.

Recycling programs for this product may not exist in your area.

CONTENTS

A FOREVER CHRISTMAS

Missy Tippens

To my sister, Mindy Conley Winningham, for forgiving all the mean big-sister things I did throughout our childhood and for being my friend anyway.

To God, for giving me the stories and for allowing me a career doing something I love so much.

Acknowledgments

Thank you to Michael House, Robyn Fogarty and Debra Marvin for research assistance.

I'm grateful to Margaret Daley and Camy Tang for your help and support.

A big thank-you to the members of the Faith, Hope and Love Chapter for sharing your knowledge when I have questions.

I love and appreciate my sisters in Christ from the F.A.I.T.H. blog and the Seekerville blog. You make me look forward to getting online each and every day.

Maureen Hardegree, grammar queen, thank you for always answering your phone!

A special thank-you to Emily Rodmell for always going above and beyond in helping me make the book the best it can be.

For as high as the heavens are above the earth,
so great is His love for those who fear Him.
As far as the east is from the west,
so far has He removed our transgressions from us.
—*Psalms* 103:11–12

Chapter One

Sarah Radcliffe forced one foot in front of the other, up the front steps of her parents' church—her childhood church home—with her insides churning. She'd come as a favor for her friend, Donna Rae Durante. And though it wasn't time for a worship service, she really didn't want to go inside. She'd been angry with God for weeks. Hadn't been able to bring herself to even enter a church building.

Which was sad, because normally, walking inside gave comfort—a feeling of warmth, of peace. All of which she really needed at the moment.

But instead, the pervasive grayness wrapped around her as she took the last step leading to the church door. The cold December wind gusted as she flung it open. A cacophony assaulted her ears, reminding her of the school hallways at the end of the day. She entered the sanctuary, and saw kids swarming all over the place, yelling and laughing.

All except for a little boy over to the side, taking it all in. Her heart immediately hurt.

The boy's straight, dark hair reminded her of her former student, Peter, but she closed off the line of thought before it got out of hand.

"Oh, Sarah, I'm so glad you came!" Donna Rae hollered from where she sat on the front pew.

Sarah waved and proceeded down the center aisle. A carrot-topped little boy zoomed across and almost tripped her.

"Sowwy," he called, then continued on his race.

Donna Rae stood and hugged her. "You're such a lifesaver."

"It's great to see you, Donna Rae." She glanced down at her friend's very pregnant belly. "You look fantastic. As usual."

Donna Rae rubbed her protruding abdomen, and worry furrowed her brow. "I'm feeling pretty good, too. But I'm swelling, and the doctor is worried about my blood pressure. Didn't have any trouble on the first four kids."

"I'm sorry. Anything I can do to help?"

She cackled. "Oh, boy, is there. That's why I asked you to meet me here."

From the looks of things—boxes of costumes lying off to the sides of the church and pieces of the set for their annual Christmas pageant—she suspected Donna Rae was fishing for volunteers to help with the play. "Uh-oh. I'm afraid I'm going to regret my offer."

"Come over here. I need to stay off my feet." She grabbed Sarah's hand and pulled her down on the pew beside her. "As you can tell, I'm the director of the pageant this year. And I'm finding out just how much Lindsay Jones Wellington always did around this place."

"Mother told me she got married and moved to Boston."

"Yes." She leaned in conspiratorially. "She and Bill held hands around The Forever Tree, you know."

How could she forget the local legend that said a couple who holds hands around the tree would have forever love? "Yes, I'd heard that." Sarah's breathing stuttered as she remembered the time she'd held hands around the tree. With Gregory Jones.

I'll love you forever, no matter what happens, he'd said to her as they circled the huge pecan tree in the park in downtown Magnolia, Georgia. She'd been so young. So trusting.

So naive.

"Well, I've been trying to fill Lindsay's shoes," Donna Rae said. "And I'm afraid it wouldn't be possible in even the best of circumstances. And now my doctor is talking about putting me on bed rest."

Sarah shook off the remnants of her trip down memory lane. "What?"

"I'm showing signs of preeclampsia. The doc said to get my life in order. He'll probably stick me on bed rest till the baby comes."

"Oh, no, Donna Rae. Is the baby okay?"

"She's fine. It's just a precaution. I've asked five different people to take over for me, and although they all said they would help, not a one would agree to head it up. When I heard you were back in town, I knew you'd be perfect."

Sarah took a deep breath.

"Oh, please say you'll do it. You have so much experience with kids."

The dark-haired boy caught her eye once again, as if she had radar for detecting lonely children. "Honestly, I don't know if I can handle being around kids right now. I'm home because one of my kindergartners passed away from cancer, and they closed school early for the holidays."

"Oh, you poor thing." Donna Rae wrapped her arms around Sarah again. "Well, you can think about it before making a decision. My last resort is to ask Bea Kennedy to do it."

"Do you think she could handle it?"

"Well, she's working with kids at the community center now."

Guilt gnawed at Sarah. Would she make a woman in her eighties take over just because it was painful for her to be around children?

Her gaze darted to the quiet boy again.

She was home from Nashville for the holidays with absolutely nothing to do. And her parents had more social engagements than she could shake a stick at—none of which interested her. How could she refuse Donna Rae? Surely she could find several volunteers to help her. Maybe it would help her to heal. She took another deep breath. "I'll do it."

Donna Rae grabbed her in a huge bear hug. "Bless you!"

Sarah looked around the room at the children playing in pairs or small groups. A couple of teenagers had come in and seemed to be helping corral them. The quiet little boy was still off by himself, his face the picture of misery. "Why isn't that boy playing?"

"He's having a tough time with Lindsay's marriage and move." She leaned in closer as if watching Sarah for a reaction. "That's Hunter Jones."

Sarah tried not to let the shock show, but she knew she couldn't hide the surge of emotion battering her already-tender heart. "Gregory and Delia's son," she whispered. "I haven't seen him since he was a baby." Since the time she came home for a visit and Delia brought the baby over to show him off. Of course, that was before she abandoned him a year later.

"He's five now. And the energetic little angel with the bright red hair is Chase Jones, who's four."

The cute little one who'd nearly run her down when she came in?

"I don't think Delia has any contact with them anymore," Donna Rae whispered behind her hand.

"I've heard that. I just can't believe it."

"The boys really miss their Aunt Lindsay. She'd been their mother figure pretty much since Chase was born. Now Gregory has to do everything."

Sarah pressed her hand to her chest. This wasn't going to be easy. How could she not be over Gregory's betrayal even after so many years? The stuffy sanctuary closed in, forcing her to breathe deeply. "Do you mind if I step outside for a minute?"

"Sure, take your time." Donna Rae pointed to the pile of halos in the pew beside her. "I still need to get these untangled and bent back into shape."

"Thanks, Donna Rae." She wanted to race up the aisle but instead controlled her pace.

She could do this. Pouring herself into the pageant might help to take her mind off Peter's death. Might help her climb up out of the smothering grief. She'd just take it one step at a time.

As she reached out to grab the door, it swung open.

And she stood toe-to-toe with six feet of ruggedly handsome man.

The last person she wanted to see right now.

She froze.

He didn't move either, except for his dark blue eyes, which blinked, then widened. "Sarah."

The way he said it, so deep and raspy…so familiar… sent her stomach on a nosedive to her feet and back. "Hi, Gregory."

Gregory could not believe he was face-to-face with Sarah Radcliffe. He'd done well to avoid her through the years on her rare trips home.

And now he'd practically run into her. The closest they'd been in a decade.

"Are you in town for the holidays?" he asked.

"We, uh…yes, school got out earlier than usual this year. So I decided to do Christmas here instead of in Nashville." She gestured to the sanctuary, her hands all fluttery like a nervous bird. "And now Donna Rae has asked me to take over as director of the pageant."

He studied her for a couple of seconds, stunned by the news, yet trying to hold his stiff smile in place. "Oh. That's…nice."

He tried his best not to stare. To act as if it were no big deal to see her again. But he couldn't help it. Beyond all reason, she was even more beautiful at thirty-two than she'd been as a teenager. Her hair was still long and blond, her eyes that warm, light brown. He had once thought they seemed to have light behind them.

He used to wonder if God gave her that glow. Used to resent it at the same time he wanted it.

But now, the light wasn't there. She seemed…sad.

"Gregory, what are you doing back so soon?" Donna Rae asked as she lumbered up the aisle.

He slowly dragged his attention to Donna Rae. "I'm

actually here to beg you for a favor." He held up two car booster seats, one in each hand. "Can you take the boys to my dad's house after rehearsal? I just got a call to meet a potential client and won't be back in time."

"Sure. Just put the seats in my car for me."

"Thanks. I owe you one." He scanned the room for his boys. Chase was fine, playing with friends. But Hunter sat alone. It killed him to see his son so unhappy.

Donna Rae shooed him out. "Go ahead. We'll take care of him."

He glanced at Sarah, then nodded, his mind racing.

Sarah Radcliffe. Here in Magnolia.

Directing the Christmas play.

Unbelievable.

As he installed the booster seats and then drove to his meeting, he tried not to think about her or the sadness clinging to her.

They'd had such a roller-coaster past. He'd been crazy about her from the moment he laid eyes on her. He'd had big plans, including marriage. But then she'd dumped him—because her judgmental parents had thought he wasn't good enough for their little princess.

She had no idea what that rejection had done to him.

And then there had been all that stuff with her dad. Gregory still prayed no one would find out about it.

But he couldn't dwell on it. He had work to do. He padlocked all thoughts of Sarah. Relegated them to the painful past. The better-left-unopened past.

Before Sarah could fully comprehend that Gregory had been there, he was gone, leaving a vacuum that wanted to suck her out the door after him.

But then, it had always been like that between them.

He was every bit as gorgeous today as he had been the first day of her sophomore year in high school, the day he, a senior, first noticed her and leaned against her locker to talk. Blue eyes twinkling. Turning on that bad-boy charm. He'd been like some kind of powerful magnet, and she hadn't stood a chance.

But she'd grown up. At thirty-two, she was a far cry from that starry-eyed teenager. She was much wiser, with lots of experience under her belt. No way would she fall for his charm again. Besides, he didn't look quite so confident now that he had responsibilities—a business to run and children to care for. "So does Gregory still have his landscaping business?" she asked Donna Rae.

She nodded. "Yeah. But I just hate all the hours he works."

"I imagine it's slowing some for the winter."

"You'd think it would. But he seems to always be full throttle no matter the season. And with this being his first Christmas to do everything without Lindsay, he's putting pressure on himself to make it the best Christmas ever."

Sarah could see the worry on Donna Rae's face, could hear it in her voice. As she looked across the sanctuary at Hunter, sitting by himself on a pew, she wondered how Gregory would be able to do it all. And wondered what kind of man he'd grown up to be.

She couldn't shake thoughts of him as Donna Rae gathered the children and led them through the rehearsal. Distracted and scattered, Sarah started when Donna Rae introduced her as the new director.

The precious four-to-six-year-olds stared up at her expectantly. A few even clapped, so she waved to them.

"Thank you. I used to be in the Christmas play when I was a child, so I know we're going to have a good time together."

Donna Rae sat down, and Sarah could see she was in pain. Donna Rae waved her away when she tried to help. "I'm fine. Just a contraction. Go ahead and hand out the schedule."

All eyes were on Sarah. It was the first time she'd been around children since Peter's funeral, and she found it difficult to go on. But she had to. Too late to back out now.

When she finished passing out the papers, she said, "Well, I see some parents gathering in the back. So I guess it's time to go. I'll see you at the next practice."

Though it demanded more energy than Sarah had at the moment, she made a point to meet each parent. As stragglers arrived late to pick up their children, she kept a close watch on Donna Rae. "Do you want me to call the doctor?"

"No. Really, I'm fine. But I probably need to go on home and put my feet up. Make Vinny pamper me." She smiled, but it was tinged with worry.

"Go."

"Can you take Hunter and Chase to Harry's house for me?"

Gregory's father wouldn't hold any fond memories of Sarah. She dreaded facing him. "Of course. I'll walk you to your car and get their seats." She knelt in front of Hunter and Chase. "I'm Miss Sarah, and I'm going to give you a ride to your granddad's."

"Let's go, boys," Donna Rae said as they turned off the lights and headed out the door.

Hunter followed obediently, but he didn't appear

happy. Sarah couldn't help but wonder if he was angry about something. In contrast, Chase slipped his little hand into Sarah's and looked up, his sweet cherub face all smiles. He chattered a mile a minute, with a lisp that seemed to be caused by his chubby cheeks, as they walked to her car and installed the seats.

When she and the boys arrived at the Jones house, Chase raced ahead. Sarah, even weighed down by the car seats, had to slow to wait for Hunter, who dragged his feet as if they were in blocks of cement.

She kind of felt the same way having to face Harry Jones.

Two hours ago, she couldn't have imagined this turn of events even in her wildest dreams.

"Hunter, do you think you could carry your booster seat for me?"

He nodded, then he wrapped his arms around it and picked up the pace a little.

"So, it must be fun to get to stay with your grand-father," she said.

He shrugged. "I guess so."

"You don't sound excited about it."

Hunter shook his head. "I wish Dad could pick us up."

"Oh, I see."

"Huwwy up," Chase called from the front door be-fore he disappeared inside.

A few seconds later, Harry appeared on the front porch. But he jerked back a step when he saw her. "Sarah?"

She tensed and forced her leaded feet forward. "Hello, Mr. Jones. I'm helping Donna Rae with the pageant, and she wasn't feeling well. She asked me to bring Hunter and Chase by."

"I appreciate it." He didn't look too thrilled, but he was the consummate Southern gentleman.

Not only had *her* parents objected to Gregory and her dating in high school, but Harry had also discouraged it. He had told Gregory from the beginning not to fall for Sarah, that he would be setting himself up to get hurt.

The relationship hadn't stood a chance.

"Well, I should go." She handed Chase's seat over, then squatted down to Hunter's eye level. "I'll see you at the next rehearsal, okay?"

He shuffled his feet. "I guess."

Chase ran out the door and hugged her neck. "'Bye."

"'Bye." The pressure in her chest sent her quickly toward her car. She needed to back off a little. Getting involved with Gregory's kids was not a good idea. Her heart couldn't take it.

After dropping the boys off, Sarah walked into her parents' home. She could almost still feel Chase's tiny arms around her neck from where he'd hugged her goodbye—a gesture so sweet it was almost painful.

Harry had been polite, if a bit cool. But she couldn't blame a protective father.

"I'm home," she called, then located her mother and father in the family room, sitting by the fireplace reading. Even with the fire, the room had never felt warm to her. The huge old house had always seemed drafty and a little empty.

"That took a while. What did Donna Rae need?" her mom asked.

She plunked down in an oversized leather chair, her favorite spot to curl up and read whenever she came home. "She's had a complication with her pregnancy and will probably be put on bed rest."

"I hope the baby's okay," her dad said.

"Yes. But she recruited me to take over the Christmas pageant."

Her mother put her book facedown on her lap and appeared distressed. "Oh, sweetie, can you handle that right now, so soon after Peter's death?"

As long as she remained strong where Gregory's boys were concerned. "I'm going to give it a try."

"Well, I think it'll be good for you." Her dad folded the newspaper. "It'll get you out of the house. Take your mind off the boy. You need to get over him."

As if she could just snap her fingers and be all better. "There's a little boy at church who reminds me of Peter." She steeled herself. Her parents wouldn't want her near anyone connected to Gregory.

"Who?" her mother asked.

"Hunter Jones."

As expected, her dad scowled. "You don't need to be around that man or his family. Call Donna Rae and decline."

"Winston, she's already agreed to help," Katherine said. Then she turned back to Sarah. "Just be careful, dear. Gregory always did seem to hold some special power over you, and you're still so vulnerable."

Sarah looked at her dad. "That was years ago. We've both moved on. It sounds like he's been very busy. I guess his business has been doing well?"

He rose, set the paper aside with a slap. "I don't keep tabs on Gregory Jones." He walked out of the room.

She looked at her mom with a raised brow.

"There's no love lost between the two of them."

"Dad never has forgiven him for hurting me."

Katherine stood and patted Sarah's cheek. "Neither of us could ever stand to see you in pain. So be careful."

"I'll be fine."

"Well, keep your distance. Simply put the play together, and then back away. You'll be back in Nashville soon enough."

Yes, Sarah decided. She could do that. She could direct the pageant and return to her normal life. But she doubted the look on Hunter's face would ever leave her.

Chapter Two

At nine o'clock that night, Gregory headed toward home. He parked in his driveway, then made his way across the street to his dad's. He slipped quietly into the house.

His father was snoozing in the recliner with the television turned down low. Gregory touched his shoulder. "Dad. I'm here."

Harry jumped. Then he rubbed his hand over his face, brushing against whiskers. "Chase cried for his Aunt Lindsay again tonight. And then for you right before he fell asleep."

"I'm sorry to put you through that again."

"You need to be home at night, son. No need to work yourself to death."

"I don't want to miss out on a potential new customer. I'm trying my best to keep my seasonal workers busy through the winter. Or at least through Christmas." And he needed to grow his business to be able to buy a bigger house before the boys were grown and walking all over each other. And so each could have his own bedroom.

And then there was the fact that he wanted to provide a perfect Christmas so maybe Hunter and Chase wouldn't be so upset by Lindsay's absence this year. "It's just hard right now because they still miss Lindsay. They'll adjust."

"You know, son, it's past time to move on and start dating. Molly Patton seems to be interested, and those boys need a mother."

"Dad…"

He waved and headed toward his room. "Think about it."

Gregory slipped into his old bedroom and found Hunter and Chase huddled in the bed, Hunter on his side in the fetal position, Chase plastered up against Hunter's back as if he'd snuggled there for comfort.

That certainly didn't help with the guilt.

He picked up Chase, then nudged Hunter awake. Hunter usually complied, then didn't even remember it in the morning. But this time he seemed more alert as he followed Gregory down the hallway.

"Where have you been, Daddy?" *Daddy*. He never called Gregory that unless he was upset or scared.

"I had a late meeting."

"But I don't want to have to wake up and move to my bed," he whined.

He wished the boys could be at home every night. But he hated to ask his dad to come there. He was already imposing by asking him to babysit so often. "I'll see what I can work out with Granddad."

When they got to their house, a shivering Hunter threw off his jacket and fell into bed. He started to doze almost immediately. Chase cried when Gregory laid him down in his own twin bed, so he took him and put him in Hunter's bed, where he slept every night, anyway. Then Gregory watched as the two settled in.

Keeping up this kind of pace wasn't easy. He was worn-out after twelve hours on the job. But it would be worth it to see the look on the boys' faces on Christmas morning when they discovered the new game system, then looked outside and saw the huge trampoline— the exact one they'd circled in the toy store wish book.

He'd make it up to them by providing his sons with the best Christmas ever.

The next day, Sarah's father left early for the office, and her mother tried to persuade her to attend a luncheon at the country club with her. Sarah had no desire to go, smile and make small talk with a group of her mother's friends, so she declined. Instead, she ate a quiet lunch alone in the echoingly empty house. She didn't so much mind being alone. But she had to battle her thoughts. About Peter. About his parents and their regret.

About Gregory…and Delia.

Delia had been two years older than Sarah, more mature, more experienced. Her father had been in the same firm as Sarah's dad, so they'd grown up together at parties and social functions. They'd even spent the night at each other's houses a few times.

And Delia had always had a thing for Gregory. She said she liked to go after guys who drove her dad crazy. Guys who presented a challenge.

Gregory had told Sarah he loved her. But apparently, love hadn't been enough. Because when she'd broken off the relationship and asked him to wait until she graduated and finished college, he'd ignored her plea and moved on. Then within a few short weeks, he'd been dating her supposed friend—seriously.

Very seriously.

Seriously enough that he and Delia were forced to get married right after they graduated, because she was pregnant.

Recalling it made Sarah sick. Still to this day.

And then when Gregory and Delia lost that baby, Sarah wondered if she'd lied about the pregnancy to trap him. But somewhere through the years, Sarah concluded the suspicion had been a way to try to ease the sting of rejection. She'd asked him to wait for her, but he'd chosen Delia, plain and simple.

Not pleasant memories, so she puttered around the house trying to forget, wondering how she was going to fill her day.

The phone rang. "Hello?"

"Well, it's official. I'm stuck on the couch until this baby gets here," said Donna Rae.

"Is everything okay otherwise?"

"Yes, so far. But I promised the doc I would be good. Vinny's trying to farm out the younger kids for me during the day."

"Let me know if I can help."

"Well, you can. I was supposed to go to a meeting at the church tonight as director of the play. Seven o'clock. Can you go and be me?"

"Of course. What do I need to do?"

"Just tell them about our progress. Let them know if there's anything you need for the lighting and sound. And give them a copy of the rehearsal schedule so they'll know when you'll be at the church."

"You've got it." She'd have to sit down and come

up with a plan. "Maybe I can go over early to look at what's available for sets."

"They're in the basement storage closet. The custodian will help with setting up the stage area. Oh, and call Gregory if you need anything made. He's pretty handy with tools."

Her heart fluttered. "Okay."

"Thanks a million. I really owe you."

As soon as they hung up, Sarah grabbed a notebook and her copy of the script. Maybe she could put some sort of new twist on the play this year. For variety.

The one thing she wasn't going to do, though, was ask Gregory to build any props.

That evening, Gregory whipped into the church parking lot and nabbed the closest spot to the back door. "Come on, boys. Hop out. I'm late for the meeting."

"Do we have to come?" Hunter asked.

"Yes, you do. I'm sorry, but Granddad is on this committee, too."

"I'm hungwy," Chase said in a pitiful little voice.

They'd come straight from the day care center where Chase spent each day and Hunter went after school. Why hadn't Gregory thought to bring a snack? His sister would have. "Hang in there, guys. We're going to eat dinner as soon as we finish."

Work boots and two pairs of tennis shoes clomped and squeaked down the long hallway. When they reached the door, he held his finger in front of his mouth to quiet them. Then he stuck his head in the door to see how badly they were interrupting.

Sarah—handing out papers?

"Come on in, Gregory," Pastor Eddie said. "Sarah was just telling us about the Christmas pageant."

She stood motionless as if shocked to see him, then all of a sudden jerked into motion and continued distributing papers.

He walked in with Hunter and Chase in tow. "I'm sorry I didn't think to get a babysitter."

"It's okay. Come on in, boys," Pastor Eddie said. "There's a box of crayons and some paper over there on that table."

Gregory smiled his thanks. And thanked God for crayons.

He ducked into a chair as he watched the boys get settled across the room. Sarah started to place a sheet of paper on the table in front of him, but it slipped off, and they both reached for it. Their hands touched, and it was like a shock wave streaked from his hand to his heart.

She looked into his eyes for a split second and appeared alarmed. "Oops. I'm sorry," she said as she handed him the paper and moved on.

She was still in his space, though. Smelling as good as she always had. In fact, she might wear the exact same perfume she did in high school. Clean, fresh… classy.

His mind made a lightning flash trip back to high school. *Sarah in his arms… Sarah in his car, scooted up beside him…*

Sarah dumping him.

Yeah, that was the sticking point. She'd said she wanted to break up because he didn't understand her goals. But he knew the real reason was because she'd let her parents get to her. And that because he wanted to stay in Magnolia and start his own business, he wasn't good enough for her.

She continued with her presentation about the pageant. But he barely heard a word until she moved away from him.

Once she reached the other side of the room, he came back to his senses and noticed her smile at his sons.

Hunter dropped a crayon.

Sarah picked it up without missing a beat. Just kept talking about sets and lights. Like any good kindergarten teacher could do.

"Miss Sawah, I'm hungwy," Chase said as he continued to scribble on the page, forgetting where he was and seeming to think he was in her classroom.

She looked over at Gregory, expecting him to produce a snack.

"I'm sorry, son. We'll get you something as soon as we're through."

Sarah quickly finished up and asked for any questions.

"We really appreciate you taking over for Donna Rae," Pastor Eddie said. "Especially during your vacation."

"I'm sure I'll enjoy working with the children."

"Well, let's move on to the next item on our agenda. Sarah, there's no need to keep you. You're free to go."

Hunter raised his hand like he would do at school. "Can I leave, too?"

All the adults around the table chuckled.

Gregory's dad raised his brows and looked a little concerned that the boys were starting to get vocal. Not a good sign.

"Maybe I should go," Gregory said.

"No, stay," Sarah said. "I don't mind taking them to the kitchen and seeing if we can find a snack."

Before he could say no thanks, Pastor Eddie said, "That's a nice offer. We won't be much longer. And I'm sure it would help Gregory."

He didn't want to look at her. He nodded his gratitude as he wondered what she thought of him bringing children to a meeting with empty stomachs.

She gathered a bundle of crayons and stack of paper and placed them in her leather bag. Then she reached out a hand for each of the boys. Chase hurried to take her up on the offer. He grabbed her hand and grinned up at her. It hurt Gregory to see his eagerness.

Hunter, on the other hand, didn't get up. He heaved a sigh and looked at Gregory as if he'd let him down once again. Gregory nodded his head toward Sarah, so Hunter followed her obediently. But he rejected her hand and shoved his into his pockets. Chase's chatter faded as they squeaked down the hallway toward the church kitchen.

Assuming the boys already had dinner, Sarah searched through the cabinets until she found two un-opened boxes of cookies. "Chocolate chip or oatmeal and raisin?"

"Chocolate chip!" Chase answered as he danced around the kitchen, hopping from one foot to the other.

Hunter, who'd been dragging along behind her, seemed to perk up. "Cool. We get cookies for dinner?"

Dinner? "You haven't eaten yet?"

"No. Dad was late picking us up again." He sighed, and it occurred to her that he seemed to sigh a lot more than a typical child.

She couldn't help wondering what was going on. Could it all stem from Lindsay's absence?

She pointed to a table in the fellowship hall. "Come on. Cookies will be your appetizer tonight. And if your dad doesn't like it, we'll tell him it was my fault."

Chase giggled.

Hunter looked at her as if he didn't know what to make of her.

She settled them at the table and gave them each two cookies. Enough to hold them over, but hopefully not enough to spoil their appetites. She couldn't find any drinks other than expired juice, so she got them each a cup of water.

How could Gregory not plan better? They wouldn't get dinner until after eight o'clock.

Once they'd started on their second cookies, she sat beside Chase. "So, Hunter, are you in kindergarten?"

He nodded.

"Do you like it?"

"Yes, ma'am."

"Chase, where do you go while your daddy works?"

"Day care," he said, blowing crumbs out of his mouth. "And Hunter comes, too."

"After school," big brother added.

"I see." She watched as they finished eating. Then the silence became awkward. For her, anyway. "Guess what my job is."

Hunter shrugged.

"Ummm…teacher!" Chase hollered.

"How did you guess?"

He climbed into her lap and knelt so that he was face-to-face with her. "Because you're nice like my teacher."

Sarah's bruised heart gave a quick stutter. Then she

couldn't help brushing a piece of cookie off his cheek. "You're absolutely right." She looked around Chase to catch Hunter's eye. "I teach kindergarten."

"Cool," he said without much enthusiasm. "When will Dad be here?"

Her heart sank. For some reason, she wanted badly to connect with him. "Well, I don't know. Soon, I'm sure."

Chase settled into a sitting position in her lap. His carrot-colored curls brushed her chin, tickling, so she smoothed his hair.

"Here, I brought the crayons." She pulled the supplies out of her bag and divided them between the boys.

Chase jumped right in and started to color. Hunter simply stared toward the door, waiting.

A few minutes later, voices sounded in the distance making her stomach do a dance of nerves. She glanced at Hunter, and it seemed he'd heard too. He sat up straighter. Watching.

A moment later, Gregory filled the doorway. His gaze zoomed straight to hers.

"Boys," he barked. "Time to go."

Hunter bolted as if his dad's voice had shot him out of a gun. He hurried over and glued himself to Gregory's side.

Chase nuzzled closer to Sarah. "Hey, Dad, Miss Sawah gave us cookies!"

"I hope you told her thank you."

"Thank you," he said, looking up at her with his gorgeous blue eyes, so much like his dad's.

"You're welcome."

Gregory nudged his oldest son. "Hunter?"

"Thank you for the cookies."

"You're welcome."

Chase still didn't seem inclined to leave, so she set him on his feet. He turned and gave her a quick hug before running across to join his family.

"I appreciate your help," Gregory ground out as if every word cost him.

Would they ever be able to get over their past?

She watched as they walked away. Sometimes relationships were too complicated, too painful to move beyond.

Friday was nothing but frustration for Gregory. First, he had to run a new blower out to one crew. No sooner had he gotten the broken one back to the shop, than the other crew called about a broken-down trimmer. Then a customer complained, so he had to ride by and check that out, to see what kind of job the guys had done.

Sure enough, they'd forgotten to mulch the back of the bank.

He didn't want to lose the bank's account, so he got on the phone to talk to the crew and tell them to go back and finish. Then he followed up by doing a ride-through to check all their jobs for the day.

Once everything checked out, he finally had time to hit the two job bids he'd planned to do that afternoon. But he was behind.

He dialed his dad.

"Can you pick up the boys for me? I really can't be late again this week."

"Sure. How about we meet you at Minnie's for dinner?"

"Thanks, Dad. I owe you."

"You know, I'd be glad to babysit anytime you plan a date."

"Yeah, yeah. Keep wishing."

"It's time."

He refused to have this conversation again. "See you at Minnie's," he said and disconnected the call.

Why wasn't he ready to date again? Surely he wasn't normal. Didn't most men remarry pretty quickly after losing a wife or after divorce? And even though his wife had deserted him, it had been four years. Surely that was long enough to heal and to move on.

But for some reason, he couldn't bring himself to take that step.

Maybe it was the pool of eligible women. There wasn't a soul in town who appealed to him. Although Molly had made it clear she was interested.

She was a gorgeous woman. Sweet. Fun. Talented. Would make a great mom. Why didn't he jump at the chance?

Sarah's face flashed through his mind. Just like it always did when he let himself think about women. No one ever seemed to measure up to his high school sweetheart.

No wonder he didn't want to date again.

Sarah ran a hand over the freshly laundered costumes, stacked and ready to go back to the church. She'd spent the day drawing up a plan for the set. And she'd gone to the church for a lesson on how to operate the sound system. She appreciated the distraction while her mom and dad went about Christmas-as-usual.

As if there could be Christmas-as-usual this year.

Anything joyful or celebratory seemed almost obscene to her. A child had died, and yet the world seemed to go on. She was trying hard not to let her distaste show.

She struggled with the dissonance. She knew she should probably be praying about her grief over Peter, praying for his family, but she couldn't. She just couldn't.

Peter had been her favorite student—a sweet, affectionate, lonely little boy. He depended on her for support while his parents worked all the time, leaving him in the care of a nanny. Sarah had probably been too attached.

Then he'd become sick. And afterward, the cancer diagnosis.

God had ignored her desperate pleas on Peter's behalf. Why would He listen to her now?

Anger bubbled deep inside, but she tamped it down. Being mad at God was a scary thing. Something she didn't want to dwell on.

Yes, she should go out to eat. Get out of the house so her mind wouldn't work overtime.

She called Donna Rae, but they'd already eaten, since little children needed to eat early.

Like Hunter and Chase should have yesterday.

She grabbed her purse and keys. Maybe she'd run to Minnie's and get some of her famous fried chicken.

She drove into town and lucked into a parking spot on the downtown square, right in front of Minnie's Meat And Three. She'd loved to hang out here with her friends in high school. To order a good old-fashioned chocolate milk shake and a side of French fries.

Bells jangled as she walked inside, the sound reminding her of better times.

"Well, if it isn't Miss Sarah Radcliffe," Minnie said

in her deep, raspy voice. Sarah and her friends had always thought she sounded like a frog.

"Hi, Miz Minnie. How are you doing?"

"I'm doing as well as can be expected. Are you eatin' in tonight?"

"Um…" Should she get it to go? But she'd wanted to get out of the house. For the distraction. But now that she was here, she—

A familiar voice grabbed her attention. A little voice.

She quickly scanned the restaurant in her peripheral vision. Harry, Hunter and Chase sat at a table in the corner. And there was a menu in front of the empty fourth chair. For Gregory?

"It's to go."

"Well, whataya have?"

After she placed her order, Minnie said, "A milk shake and fries too?" She gave a rattling laugh, followed by a couple of hacking coughs.

Sarah found herself smiling. "Um, I could go for that milk shake."

"There's Miss Sawah," the little voice called from across the room.

Distraction couldn't work if the subject of her thoughts sat in front of her. But she walked over to them, hoping she'd get her food and get out of there before Gregory arrived. "Hi, Chase. Hunter." She nodded at Harry. "Mr. Jones."

"Hi, Sarah. Care to join us?"

She could see that he didn't really want her to. And it hurt for some silly reason. But in his mind, she was the bad "guy."

"Thanks, but I've ordered mine to-go."

It appeared they were nearly finished eating. Maybe Gregory wasn't joining them, after all.

"I ate four green beans," Chase said proudly as he held up all five fingers. Then with his other hand, he pushed down his thumb.

"Very impressive. You're going to be so healthy. Hunter, what about you?"

He shrugged. "Don't know. I didn't count." He finally looked her in the eye. "But I ate some."

She wanted to cry. To hug him to her. He was so serious for a child. "Good for you."

"Well, boys, it looks like your dad got tied up and isn't going to make it," Harry said. "Why don't I take you to your house and you can get going on your homework."

"I have homework, just like Hunter," Chase bragged.

She gasped. "You do?"

"Yep. I'm a big boy."

"You sure are." She patted his back. Then Minnie held up a to-go container. "It looks like my food is ready, so I better run. Hunter, good luck with your homework. I can help if you ever need it." Now why had she said that?

"Really?"

"Yes, remember? I teach kindergarten."

"Oh, yeah. Okay." His eyes brightened in what appeared to be a true flash of interest.

"Thank you for offering," Harry said.

"I guess I'll see you tomorrow." She gave a little wave and went to get her food.

It looked like Gregory was having a hard time leaving work on time that week. First, too late to feed his sons dinner before the meeting. And now, missing dinner all together.

She couldn't help but wonder if all was well in the Jones household. Didn't Gregory realize these days when his sons were young were precious and fleeting?

Chapter Three

$\sim$

On Saturday morning, Sarah quickly finished setting up for rehearsal. And not a minute too soon. Children started arriving early.

Hunter and Chase included. *Wow. Gregory's on the ball today.*

But then she looked up and saw Harry walking down the aisle. "Good morning, Sarah."

"Good morning, Mr. Jones."

"Gregory's working right now. But he's supposed to pick the boys up."

"Okay."

"Call if you have any problems or if he doesn't get here in time," he said as he waved and walked out the door.

Problems?

Someone tugged on her sweater. "Hi, Miss Sawah."

"Hi, Chase. How are you?"

"Good. It's Saturday! Dad is home on Saturdays."

"No he's not," Hunter said sounding as bitter as a little old man. "He'll have to work."

Chase's smile dropped into the most pitiful frown.

"Well, it sounds like today he'll have the afternoon off," she said trying to cheer them up even while wondering if she should speak with Gregory.

No, Sarah. Do not get involved with this. She smiled and walked away.

Yes, that was good. Smile and walk away. Her new mantra.

She gathered the children and teen helpers. She even found a couple of parents had stayed to help.

"Okay, boys and girls, let's all try standing in place where you'll be at the beginning. I need to make sure you'll fit on the stage." Sarah took the list Donna Rae had given her and began to call out names, assigning each a part as a shepherd, Mary, Joseph, animal or angel. She placed the children and hoped they would stand still long enough for her to see the whole group.

"Now, I want my angels to come down to the very front."

Chase jumped right in front of her and yelled, "I'm an angel!"

He was so precious it made her want to grin every time she looked at him. It seemed like it had been weeks since she smiled a genuine smile. Yet his excitement was contagious. She couldn't resist—the smile or the warmth that seemed to try to seep into her bones.

Once she had placed all the angels, she said, "Now, I need the speaking shepherd." She glanced at her chart. "Hunter Jones."

"I don't want a talking part," he said from the perimeter of the group.

To push or not to push? Some children just needed a bit of encouragement. Hunter didn't have the look of someone seeking that little nudge. "Okay. But could you stand here for me until I can get someone else?"

He nodded and then let her lead him to his spot.

Once she had him all set, she patted his head and thanked him. His hair was like silk. Dark and straight, just like his mother's. He had her hazel eyes as well.

A pain she'd pushed into submission for so long tried to work its way into her chest, but she wouldn't let it. How could looking at Hunter, a reminder of Gregory and Delia's betrayal, possibly hurt her over fifteen years later? She should have been over him years ago.

By the time she finished posing the children and working to teach them several songs, the parents started to arrive. "Children, thank you so much for working so hard today. I'll see you next time."

The kids played while waiting for their parents. Of course, Hunter stood off by himself. And she realized she needed to talk to Gregory about encouraging Hunter to keep his speaking role. Maybe if she kept their conversation strictly pageant-related, she could remain objective. Could remain personally uninvolved.

By the time twenty minutes passed, though, she was quickly becoming personally involved.

"See, I told you," Hunter said.

"Come on. I'll call your granddad." Since Hunter didn't know Harry's phone number, she had to go find a directory. When she told Harry what had happened, he sighed and apologized, then said he'd be right there.

It was a sunny day and fairly mild for December, so she locked up the building and waited out front with the boys.

Harry pulled up to the curb in a couple of minutes. She walked the boys to the car. "Hi, Mr. Jones."

"I'm sorry to delay you."

"Oh, it's no problem at all." The waiting wasn't a problem, at least. But Hunter's disappointment was.

Hunter climbed in the back of the car and buckled himself in his booster seat. "Where's Dad?"

"I just talked to him. He got a call about taking down a dead tree."

"But he said he would get us today."

Sarah helped Chase in the other side and tried to guard her heart against the dejection on Hunter's face.

"I know, son," Harry said. "Your dad is a busy man, trying to make a living to take good care of you boys." He twisted around to look back at Hunter. "And hey, guess what? We get to hang out together today. And you're going to spend the night with me, so you don't have to wake up and go to your house tonight." Harry made a big production of looking excited.

Hunter didn't buy it. Tears welled up in his eyes. "But I want to sleep in *my* bed," he yelled, then turned his head into his seat and cried.

His pain was palpable, and she wanted more than anything to just smile and walk away. But she couldn't do that any more than she could have walked away and skipped Peter's funeral like her mind had screamed for her to do.

She reached across Chase to rub Hunter's back.

"It's okay. I'll take care of him," Harry said. "He's having a hard time since Lindsay moved to Boston. She was like a mother to the kids, and we're muddling our way through."

"I'm sorry, Mr. Jones. I wish I could help."

As they drove away, heaviness settled over her. A feeling of helplessness like she'd felt as Peter declined so rapidly.

But what could she do to help Hunter and Chase? Volunteer to be their mom?

Gregory needed to know what was going on. Surely he didn't have any idea what his absence was doing or he would make more of an effort to be at home.

Of course, in her experience, he wasn't very dependable. He'd flitted from her to Delia in the blink of an eye. But she liked to think he would have grown up by now.

As soon as Harry's car turned the corner, she dug her cell phone out of her purse and called Donna Rae. "How are you feeling?"

"Bored."

"Well, try to rest and enjoy the break."

"Yeah, right."

Though she didn't want to worry Donna Rae, she knew she had to bring up the incident with Hunter. "Hey, I had a little problem with Hunter today. He refused his speaking part. Then when he found out Harry was taking him home to spend the night, he threw a fit and cried."

"Poor little guy."

"Do you think it's the fact that Lindsay is gone, or is it the time Gregory's away because of work?"

"Both, I imagine. He needs Gregory now more than ever."

Yes, Gregory needed to know what his overtime was doing to his son. Maybe it would help if she told him about Peter. About how he'd spent most of every day at school or with a nanny. How his parents had provided all the best, but he'd had no interest in the "stuff," had wanted only time with his mom and dad. And how his parents learned the hard way—after it was too late.

"Donna Rae, could you give me Gregory's phone number? I think I'm going to have to talk to him."

"Sure, hon. That's probably a good idea."

She jotted the numbers on a slip of paper, then after hanging up, programmed them in her cell phone.

Money, or the lack thereof, had always been important to Gregory. But it seemed he was doing fine now. Why work all that overtime for gifts that would mean nothing to the boys after the first five minutes when what was truly important could be taken away at any time?

She climbed into her car, pressed a hand against her thumping heart and forced herself to dial his cell phone.

"Gregory Jones."

Oh, my. His deep, baritone voice had always done crazy things to her stomach. "Hello, Gregory. This is Sarah."

"Hey, I'm sorry I was late. Did Dad get there yet?"

"Yes. But we had a little problem today, and I thought you'd like to know about it. That is, if you have a minute."

"Can't right now." He huffed as if he was lifting something. "But I've got to run to town in an hour."

She could visit Donna Rae and gather her thoughts. "Okay. How about meeting in the church parking lot in an hour."

"Fine." He cut off the connection.

Gregory found her lone car in the back parking lot. He hopped out and went around to her passenger side, opened the door and climbed into the pure luxury.

The car wasn't brand spanking new, though. He'd heard that her dad bought it for her when she graduated from college. Or maybe it was when she got her master's degree. He'd tried not to listen to town gossip through the years.

Especially when it had to do with Sarah. It was too painful.

"So Hunter gave you a hard time?" he asked.

"No, he didn't act out. He just didn't want to have a speaking part." Then she described his refusal and the fit he threw for his granddad.

He ran a hand through his hair. "He's been like a different child since Lindsay moved. Quiet, sad…"

"Donna Rae told me it's been hard on them. Is he usually as sunny a personality as Chase?"

"Well, no. He wasn't so affectionate. But he was very active and talkative."

And now he walked around like a pitiful, quiet little thing. And Gregory had no idea what to do about it.

Could Sarah, with her experience, maybe help?

Was he desperate enough to ask?

Even though the car was off and she wasn't driving, she gripped the steering wheel tightly and faced out the front window. "I hate to seem like I'm prying, but I'm wondering if there's more to it."

"Like what?" he snapped.

"I'm not trying to be accusatory. I'm just concerned."

"Well, they've had a rough few years."

She faced him, but still didn't quite meet his eyes. "Has Delia had any contact with the kids?"

What a question for her to ask. How could he tell Sarah, of all people, that he'd failed as a husband? That no matter what he'd done—including marital counseling—he hadn't been able to keep his wife happy, because she knew he only asked her out because Sarah hurt him. That no matter how hard he tried, he'd never love Delia like he'd loved Sarah.

It might help Hunter. She might have advice.

"No contact at all for the last couple of years. And she's been gone since right after Chase was born. So he doesn't even remember her." He sighed as he shook his head. "But Hunter does. And now with Lindsay—married and living far away, he's had a terrible time."

"Your dad told me Lindsay was like a mother to them. I imagine it'll take a while to adjust."

"I knew it wasn't good to depend on my sister so much, but she was single and had the time. And she loved them like they were her own. When she left, they both cried every night, so we'd have to call her and have her tell them good night. But then it got better. Briefly."

She looked right at him with her gorgeous brown eyes. "Have you been working more overtime lately? Maybe it would help if you spent more time with them."

He saw it then. The pity.

He hated pity. "My work schedule has nothing to do with it."

"Well, I think maybe it could. Please just think about it."

Of course, she'd only seen the worst—hungry kids at a meeting and him standing up his family at Minnie's. He slung open the car door. "Why do you suddenly seem interested in my life, anyway? You haven't been around in years."

"I, uh…well, I've had students with parents who work all the time. I've seen them regret it later."

If there was one thing he'd learned from his past, it was to not let Sarah's opinion sway his decisions. But it galled him to have her think badly of him. "My boys aren't your students. So leave them well enough alone."

He got out and closed the door nicely when he wanted to slam it off the hinges.

He steamed all the way to his truck and indulged in slamming his door. But once inside, he realized he was steaming mad because she'd pretty much hit the nail on the head.

He had been working a lot of evenings lately. But there wasn't a thing he could do about it. He had employees to take care of. Customers to take care of. A business to run—and to grow. Not to mention a household to run.

He was doing the best he could for his boys, and he didn't need his ex-girlfriend telling him how to raise them.

Sarah's hands shook as she drove home. Was she meddling as he'd insinuated? He was right that she hadn't been around or involved in their lives.

So why did she care what he did?

Hunter's dejected expression plastered itself in her mind, and she couldn't shake it loose.

Miss Radcliffe, why do Albert's and Tyrone's and a bunch of other moms and dads come to our class parties but mine don't? Peter's little voice echoed in her head.

She'd tried to explain how they were working to give him the best of everything. But he never could get past the fact that his mom and dad were absent parents.

Miss Radcliffe, I sure do need a hug today, he'd said at least once a week. At first, the comment cracked her up, because it was not the request of the typical kindergartner. But the more she hugged him, the more she'd grown to need the hugs.

And now she felt like she was watching a replay, watching Gregory and his sons travel down that same road. Even though Harry was in the picture and was family, it apparently wasn't enough for Hunter. He wanted more time with his dad.

Was there anything she could do? To somehow bring Gregory and his boys together before Christmas? If she did, Gregory was certain not to like it.

Yes, she had to do something. Her conscience wouldn't let her do otherwise.

She looked at the calendar in her cell phone and counted dated blocks. Twelve days until Christmas Eve and their pageant.

Twelve days…. An idea began to blossom.

She took a deep breath as she envisioned those empty blocks on her calendar and began to brainstorm ideas to fill them with activities for Gregory and his sons. But could she pull it off? It would take a lot of strength to spend that kind of time around Gregory.

Strength she might not have right now.

Thank you for bringing my mom and dad here. They even spent the night. We pretended we were staying in a tent. Peter had smiled at her from his hospital bed, happy even while needles and tubes stuck into his body, so sure she'd had something to do with his parents' change of heart. But, no, a terminal diagnosis had seen to that.

Hunter's sad, angry face flashed through her mind.

Yes, she had to do it. For Hunter.

For Peter.

Though she'd been powerless in Peter's situation, at least she had time to try to make a difference in Hunter's and Chase's lives. To make sure Gregory spent time with his sons. Every single day. For the twelve days till Christmas.

Chapter Four

The next morning, Sarah woke and got ready for church. Though she wasn't on great terms with God, she knew her parents would expect her to go. As she suspected, they didn't seem at all surprised.

But when they got to the front door of the church, she hesitated. It was different from going in for a rehearsal. No longer a theater, the prospect of entering the sanctuary felt intimidating, suffocating. "I'll be in in just a minute," she whispered to her mom, then hurried down the steps to the front sidewalk. *Okay, I'm just going to walk around for a moment to catch my breath.*

She steeled herself. She could do this. Simply walk in. Sit down in their regular pew. Appreciate the nice music.

She yanked her coat tightly around her and marched right back up the steps. She plowed through the door and walked down the aisle as if she owned the place.

Once seated, she searched to see if any of the Jones men were there yet. Only Harry and Gregory's younger brother, Richard.

A minute later, it sounded as if a herd of horses had entered the back of the church. Little footsteps stomped down the aisle.

"Hi, Miss Sawah," Chase called out too loudly. He grinned at her, his bright blue eyes shining so much like his dad's.

She wiggled her fingers at him.

Then a big hand lighted on his shoulder.

She scanned upward. Gregory, of course. Looking so handsome in khaki slacks and a long-sleeved button-down shirt. No coat. No tie. It wouldn't be Gregory if he dressed up any more than he had. Of course, he looked amazing no matter what he wore.

Hunter stood behind his dad, but she caught him take a quick peek at her. She waved, and he gave a halfhearted wave back. No smile. No sparkling eyes like his brother.

If she was going to help Gregory and the boys, she was going to need access to Hunter and Chase. And she was afraid she would have to enlist Harry's help to do so.

Since the man blamed her for hurting his son, he was sure not to trust her.

She had to find a way to persuade him to help.

After lunch at his dad's, Gregory spent the afternoon in his home office working on billing. Or *trying* to work on billing. His thoughts kept wandering to Sarah, and how beautiful she looked that morning in her soft, blue sweater. And those pearls—the real thing. Necklace and earrings. He assumed they were the same ones she'd gotten for her sweet sixteenth from her parents.

The boys darted in and out, playing, fighting, trying

to get his attention. He needed at least another hour of relative peace to finish up.

He made a note on the calendar to follow up on a delinquent account. As he did so, he saw December 25 circled. Alarmed at how soon it was coming up, he did the math and saw he had only twelve days before the *big* day.

"Man, I need to make a list and get on it."

First on the list: buy the trampoline. The boys needed a good outlet for all their energy. Once that was done, he would spend a day putting up the outside lights and decorations.

It was going to be tough. There were only so many hours in a day. He'd have to plan carefully. And he needed to start ASAP.

Using the notes he'd jotted, he marked everything on the calendar showing what he needed to do each day to finish all the preparations in time.

He wanted so badly to do all Lindsay had always done to make the holidays so special. He realized now that he'd taken her for granted. Or maybe it was more a case of just not knowing how much work it was to pull off a big Christmas. But his boys deserved it.

Beyond the gifts Lindsay was sending, he wouldn't have any help from her. She and Bill were flying to Europe to be with Bill's brother, Drake, this year. He couldn't blame them for going. Bill didn't get to see Drake often since he traveled the world for his photography. He hadn't even made it home for the wedding.

But the timing couldn't have been worse.

So not only did he have to pull off Christmas, he had to fill Lindsay's void as well.

His heart raced, and his chest tightened, a feeling that

was getting a little too common lately. Stress-related, he was sure. Nothing to worry about. He just needed to get a grip.

Maybe his dad was right. He needed to date a nice woman. Go out. Have some fun.

But if all he could think about was Sarah, he was better off at home. Focusing on his kids. He could do this. He could be father and mother—and Santa—to his kids.

Yes, the big Santa gifts would definitely take their minds off any disappointment over Lindsay.

Christmas and all the trimmings, coming right up.

He'd give anything to see a smile on Hunter's face again.

Later Sunday afternoon, Sarah decided to go to Harry's house to speak with him.

As she pulled in the driveway, she heard a screen door slam. Harry had walked out to the front porch.

She couldn't blame him for his surprise at seeing her at his house for no apparent reason. But he quickly masked the surprise and waved her over.

She parked, climbed out, then walked up the sidewalk. "Hi, Mr. Jones. Could I speak with you for just a minute?"

"I guess. Come in."

She couldn't remember ever being inside Gregory's childhood home. Their dates had all been on the sly since her parents had been so adamant that he was too old and too wild for her. She'd rebelled for a short while, but when he started talking marriage and about her going to college locally, despite her dreams of an out-of-state private women's college, she told him she couldn't see him anymore.

Harry eyed her cautiously. "So what did you want to discuss?"

"I came to ask a favor." She was surprisingly nervous, but she rushed on. "This is about Gregory. I'm worried about him and the boys. I've seen a few issues with Hunter, and I'm afraid his sons need more of his time if they're going to get over Lindsay's leaving."

A frown was his only response.

She swallowed and decided to plunge in. "I'd like to help him see that time with his children is more important than making extra money for gifts. And I need your help."

"And you'd like to do this because…?"

"I, uh… I've seen parents of one of my students make a similar mistake."

"You do realize his working overtime has as much to do with him looking out for his employees as it does with him buying nice gifts?"

"Well, no. I didn't know that. But either way, the outcome is the same. Hunter misses his dad. He's sad. Withdrawn."

Harry rubbed his chin. "Have you talked to Gregory about this?"

She recalled the awkward conversation and the not-so-satisfying result. "Yes. But he ended up angry with me."

He studied her. "I'm still trying to figure out your motive, here."

"I guess it's the teacher in me. I see a problem with a child, and I try to fix it."

"You know, as long as Gregory thinks you're trying to *fix* him, he's not going to cooperate."

She had a feeling he wouldn't cooperate simply because she was Sarah Radcliffe. "I just want to present opportunities for him to spend time with his boys. That's all he needs. The rest will happen on its own."

Harry nodded. "Makes sense." He continued to nod as if assimilating all she'd said. "Okay. I'll help. As long as you don't hurt my son."

"No. Of course not." She wouldn't let herself get involved enough for either of them to get hurt.

"Well, what did you have in mind?"

"I was hoping I could pick the boys up at school and day care tomorrow to take them to buy a Christmas tree."

"How will that involve Gregory?"

"We'll need him to bring the truck to haul it home. And then he'll have to help put it up. And decorate it." Just telling of her plan made a grin twitch at her lips.

One side of Harry's mouth lifted into a crooked smile. "Leave the details to me."

The next afternoon, Sarah arrived at the Jolly Time Day Care Center after picking up Hunter from kindergarten. Hunter remained silent as they drove to pick up Chase, but he hadn't complained.

"Come on, let's go get your brother." She held out her hand to him, trying to act as if she wasn't anxious. After all, she hardly knew these children. And they didn't really know her.

"What are we going to do?" Hunter asked, ignoring her outstretched hand.

"That's a surprise. I'll tell you once we get Chase."

"Hi, Miss Sawah," Chase called as soon as they walked in.

"Hi, Chase. I'm here to pick you up today."

She was relieved to see the day care center was bright, cheery and clean. The children seemed happy and well cared for.

"I'll get my book bag." He ran to his cubby while she provided her driver's license to the worker and signed Chase out.

"So why didn't Granddad pick us up today?" Hunter asked.

"Well, I asked him if I could take you shopping for a Christmas tree." She clapped her hands together, hoping they'd get excited.

Chase didn't disappoint. He hopped up and down, clapping his hands as well. But then he noticed his brother's lack of reaction.

Hunter stood stock-still. "I thought Dad would take us."

She hadn't expected Hunter's reaction. Had assumed he'd be thrilled. "Well, would you mind if I take you? I thought we'd pick it out, then call your dad to help us take it home and decorate it."

He shrugged. "He won't come."

"Why don't you let me worry about that part, okay?"

He shrugged again. "Okay."

She buckled them in the car seats provided by Harry and drove to the tree farm outside of town. She'd always bought trees shipped in from North Carolina, but this was a cut-your-own tree place, her excuse to get Gregory involved. She'd call him to ask him to come help. How could he resist?

"There's one!" Chase yelled as soon as they walked up.

"That's tiny," Hunter said.

"Let's keep looking and see if we can find one you'll both like."

They tromped through row after row of Leyland cypresses and Virginia pines. The boys couldn't agree on a tree at all. Hunter liked the tall fat ones. Chase liked the short, scrawny ones. As the light started to fade, she looked at her watch. Time to call Gregory.

"Gregory Jones," he answered, sending her pulse into overdrive.

"Hi, Gregory. This is Sarah."

After a two-second pause, he said, "What's up?" He sounded wary.

"Well, I have your boys with me, and—"

"What? Why do you have my boys with you?"

Her pulse continued to race. Only this time it wasn't due to the familiar sound of his voice. Now she feared she'd made a mistake. "I asked your dad if I could bring them to get a Christmas tree. But they can't seem to make up their minds. And now I've realized it won't fit in my car trunk, so—"

"Hold up a second. I'm still trying to figure out how you got my kids out of school."

"Your dad gave permission for me to pick them up. I showed my driver's license."

"And took them tree shopping."

"Yes."

He sighed. "So now they've picked out a tree?"

"Well…no. Not exactly. They can't seem to agree. Hunter likes tall and fat. Chase like short and skinny. So, what do you say you come with your truck, help pick one out, and then haul it home?" She smiled, because she was doing a great job of sounding cheerful. Maybe he would get in the spirit.

"But I have an appointment in…forty-five minutes

and need to make a quick shopping trip on the way. Just get them to strap it to the top of your car."

Chase started jumping up and down, excited that his dad might be coming. Hunter fidgeted as he tried to listen to the phone call. Of course, they hadn't heard Gregory's response.

Hunter tugged her arm down to move the cell phone closer. "Hey, Dad!" he yelled.

"Hey, Dad!" Chase echoed.

She put the phone back to her ear. "The boys really want you to come help pick it out. I know it would mean a lot to them."

He sighed—an angry sigh. "I had set aside a day this week to go get the tree. It's on my calendar."

Her heart pounded. What if she'd gone too far? What if he wouldn't come? "We're here already. Come on over and help. It'll be fun."

"Pleeease," Hunter yelled. And of course, Chase echoed. She almost said the same, but instead prepared to watch her plan crash and burn.

"Okay. But make them pick one before I get there. I won't have time to shop."

She smiled and gave the boys a thumbs-up. They whooped and danced around the trees while she gave Gregory directions to the farm.

After the celebration, they walked two more rows of trees. Still no consensus.

"Okay, you two. I have a solution. One wants tall and fat. One likes short and skinny. So how about we get a tall, skinny tree."

Hunter looked at Chase. Chase looked at Hunter. Both smiled. Then Hunter held up his hand for a high five from his brother. *Success.*

A good while later, way back on the property, about as far as they could go from the parking lot, the boys found their tree. Most of the surrounding trees had been cut, and there stood their perfect tree. Well, perfect in their eyes anyway. Sarah tried not to laugh.

It was tall.

It was skinny.

It was pitifully scraggly.

"That's kinda holey," Hunter said as he shook his head, a gesture so like his dad that it made her heart lurch. "But it looks lonely. Can we take it home, please?"

Lonely? Her heart hurt once again. Hunter...so sweet, so tender, so...lonely.

"Pwease," Chase added, sealing the deal.

She pushed aside the ache for Gregory's children and grabbed the saw. "Let's get started." She made the boys stand back as she attempted a couple of passes of the saw. Not easy work. Maybe she would wait for Gregory to—

"Need some help?" he asked from behind her, his deep voice a rumble she could feel as if it were wrapping around her, enveloping her.

Chase squealed, and Hunter actually smiled, both excited that their dad was taking part in getting the tree. Once he'd patted their heads, he rubbed his hands together and reached to take the saw from her.

He'd always been the opposite of the men of her childhood dreams. Way back then, she'd imagined her perfect husband in a suit and tie like her dad—a slick businessman. But here he was in his boots, khaki work pants and polo shirt embroidered with the Jones logo, his auburn hair a little too long, his face scruffy with a five-o'clock shadow. And so very appealing.

Before sawing, he stood back and really looked at the tree. He shook his head, just like Hunter had done.

Please brag on it. Please don't say anything negative.

"Why on earth did you pick out a Charlie Brown tree?" he asked.

"A Charlie Brown tree?" Hunter asked. "What's that?"

He gave Sarah a look. "I guess if you've already started cutting, we have to buy that one."

"It's perfect. And it needs love," she said, daring him to say another word.

"A tree needs love?" he said quietly for her ears only.

His whisper rustled the hair by her ear and caused chill bumps to travel down her arm. A hint of clean, crisp, manly fragrance teased her nose, and she breathed in deeply. She couldn't quite bring herself to move away. So she leaned in closer.

"According to your son, the tree is lonely," she whispered. "So watch yourself."

Gregory couldn't look away from Sarah. Her nearness. Watching her with his kids. Seeing her protect Hunter. It was overwhelming. So he tried to focus on the tree. He was not at all surprised the tree looked lonely. It had been left behind for a reason.

Forcing thoughts of Sarah from his mind, he made quick work of cutting the trunk, then carried it to where he'd parked his truck. Once he had paid, he said, "I've got to go. I'll bring the tree home with me tonight."

"Ah, man. I wanted to decorate it now," Hunter said.

"Can we, Dad, pwease?"

He'd already had to move buying the trampoline back one day. They could decorate the tree later. "I'm sorry, boys. I have some shopping I have to do before my meeting. And I'm probably going to be late as it is."

"Stupid job," Hunter mumbled as he kicked at the truck tire.

"Gregory, do you think you could help us just get the tree in the house? You could decorate it another day."

Hunter looked at him, a hopeful expression on his face. Sometimes it took so little to satisfy them.

He glanced at his watch. "I guess I could do that. But we'll have to hurry." And he could forget shopping.

The boys hopped in the backseat of his king cab truck to ride with him.

"Sowwy, Miss Sawah. You have to wide all alone."

"That's okay, Chase. I don't mind," she said as she buckled him in.

"We've gotta go." Gregory turned and leaned over the seat. "Sarah, can you follow us home, then take them to my dad's?"

"Of course. See you there."

He wanted to rush home, sling the tree into a bucket of water, then zip to the toy store, all in about five minutes. But he drove safely, making sure Sarah stayed behind him, safe as well. When they got home, he suggested the bucket of water.

Hunter leaped over the seat of the truck and tumbled into the front. "But, Dad, we've got to take it in the house so we can decorate it later."

"We won't be able to do it for a couple of days." He tried to remember which day he'd set aside to do the tree. "I think I planned for us to do it Wednesday."

"Let's do it tomowwo," Chase said as he carefully tried to tumble where his brother had just done so effortlessly. Instead, he ended up stranded, hanging on the seat back.

Gregory gave him a tug to pull him the rest of the way. "Okay, guys. We'll take it inside now, put it in the stand, then decorate tomorrow."

Sarah stepped up beside the truck. "Do you have a tree stand?"

How come she had to keep popping up? It was as if she was trying to torment him—drawing him to her with her silky hair, sparkling eyes and sweet nature. She reminded him of the good parts of their past. When in reality it was a past that was best forgotten.

He sucked in a breath as a thought hit him.

Would Winston Radcliffe expect him to honor their agreement even after all these years?

"Gregory? A tree stand?"

"Oh, uh, check the attic. Pull down ladder's in the hallway." He handed her the house key.

It had been over fifteen years ago that he'd made the stupidest bargain of his life. Surely Sarah's father wouldn't hold him to it now.

While Sarah went on a mission to find the tree stand, he trimmed off the lowest branches as Hunter and Chase looked on. By the time they got the tree up and tried to find one decent side, it was six o'clock and time for him to be at his new customer's office.

"I've got to go. You three can try to find a side that doesn't have too many gaps in the branches."

He rubbed Hunter's head. And started to rub Chase's. But Chase launched into his arms and gave him a quick hug and sloppy kiss.

He started to thank Sarah. But for what? Throwing

his whole schedule off and making him late? "I appreciate you taking the boys to Dad's for me," he said.

"No problem. Thanks for coming to help get the tree." She gave him a big smile.

Did she feel it too? Or were his feelings one-sided. "Hey, boys, you two run outside and get your book bags out of Sarah's car so you don't forget them."

Both obeyed and headed out the front door.

"I hope you don't see Hunter and Chase as some sort of mission project," he said voicing the fear that had been nagging him for the past few hours.

She looked surprised. "Oh. No, of course not." But she seemed uncomfortable, as if he'd hit at least on some bit of the truth.

"So why'd you want to spend time with them?"

"They're in the play. I wanted to get to know them."

"And you're going to get together with each of the children in the play?"

She didn't say anything.

It made him sick to think her kindness to his boys was nothing more than feeling sorry for them. "My kids aren't neglected. They're not needy. I do a perfectly fine job providing for them." He paced across the living room, wishing his house were bigger so he had decent room to work off the aggravation.

He'd been a fool to let her get to him. "You know," he said as he approached her once again, "I think this is because of our past."

She flinched. "Why would you think that when I'm just trying to help?"

He'd hit the nail on the head, and it made him angry. "I was never good enough for you. And now, you're trying to prove— What are you trying to prove, anyway? That I'm a horrible dad?"

"I'm not trying to prove anything. I just want you to spend time with your kids."

"Don't bother again." He grabbed his keys out of the front door. "I've got to go." He walked out the door and waved to the boys as he climbed into the truck.

He tried to smile at them, but it was hard when the one woman he'd always wanted to impress had basically indicated he was a failure as a dad—just as he'd been a failure as a boyfriend.

Well, now that he was on to her, maybe she'd leave him alone.

The next morning, Sarah went to visit Donna Rae. Her friend's house reminded her of Gregory's—warm, inviting, homey. The aroma of coffee nearly lured her straight to the kitchen.

Donna Rae had been relegated to the couch for four days, and seemed stir-crazy.

"I miss my babies," Donna Rae whined. "They're at my mom's. It's totally quiet. And I'm sick of daytime television."

Sarah clicked the remote to turn the TV off, then relaxed in a well-worn recliner. "Well, I'm here to entertain you. Let's talk."

"Has seeing Gregory been difficult?" Donna Rae blurted so quickly that she had to have been thinking about it for a while.

Sarah had tried to focus on the sons so she wouldn't think about the dad. But she hadn't been very successful. "Yeah. There's still some old baggage there."

Donna Rae strained, trying to rearrange her pillow. "Do you have a new guy in Nashville?"

"No. I'm single. Haven't dated in ages."

"You never did tell me what happened with Ted."

Sarah popped up out of the chair. "Boring story. Unhappy ending. How about I make us some coffee or tea?"

"Give me the Reader's Digest version."

Sarah hadn't talked about it with anyone. She hadn't even told her parents the full story. But she sat back down. "Ted and I dated four years. He talked about marriage, but I wasn't ready to commit—thanks to Gregory, who'd left me gun-shy. So I wanted to wait. Ted got impatient, ditched me, then married someone else less than a year later." Further proof that there was just something wrong with her when it came to long-term relationships.

"Oh, hon, I'm sorry."

"It was for the best. Obviously, he didn't love me. Just like Gregory couldn't have loved me like he said he did."

"Oh, I think Gregory loved you all right. He just couldn't stand the fact that you listened to your parents and broke up with him."

"You know, Donna Rae, maybe my expectations are too high, but I have this dream that if love is real, then it's strong enough to withstand a few obstacles. It's not something you toss aside when things get tough, as if it's yesterday's news."

"Amen to that. And if it makes you feel any better, I think Gregory regretted what he did. Of course, I know he loves his boys and wouldn't trade them for anything. But he has to know Delia was a mistake."

Sarah raised one corner of her mouth in a smirk. "No comment."

Donna Rae laughed. "He's learned something, I guess. He hasn't given any woman a look since Delia divorced him. Although he's definitely had opportunity."

"Oh, I'm sure. He's a very attractive man."

"Molly Patton's had her eye on him. You remember her? She's in my quilting group, the Quilting Beas, and talks about him all the time. I think they'd be good together if he'd give her a chance."

A pang of jealousy hit so strongly that light flashed behind her eyes. "Yes. But didn't she have a thing for Gregory's brother?"

"Yeah, I think she did have a crush on Richard in high school. But now she's got her eye on Gregory—and his sons." Donna Rae observed her for a reaction.

Sarah smiled to hide the nasty feeling eating at her insides. It made no sense, and she couldn't believe she could possibly be jealous after so many years, when she had no relationship at all with Gregory. It wasn't as if she had a claim to stake. "Well, I wish her well. She would probably make a great mom for Hunter and Chase."

"She loves them already. Teaches them in Sunday school, asked specifically for their class."

Even though they'd been apart for years, Sarah couldn't bear to talk about Gregory and another woman. She had to change the subject, or at least turn it away from Molly. "You know, since Hunter's been crying a lot, I'm trying to help Gregory spend more time with him and Chase—trying to help him see what's truly important this Christmas. And I've got Harry helping me."

Donna Rae grinned. "Well, good luck with that. It'll

be a challenge for sure." She reached out her hand and wiggled her fingers. "I think we need to pray for it right now."

Sarah still didn't want to pray—wasn't sure she could without railing against God for failing Peter. And she didn't want to talk to Donna Rae about the anger, the disappointment. Because the woman had more faith in her pinkie finger than Sarah had ever had. So to keep off Donna Rae's radar, she stood up and clasped her outstretched hand.

Donna Rae launched into a minute-long prayer. The words were beautiful, and in the past, Sarah would have been very moved, would have felt God's presence. But not today. She was somewhat stunned that she still didn't feel the slightest stirring. It was as if God was a million miles away. As if He didn't care about her at all.

"Amen," Donna Rae said. "Now, be sure to let me know if I can help with your plan."

"I called Gregory to come help us cut their Christmas tree yesterday. But I ended up making him late for a meeting."

Her friend laughed. "I bet he wasn't too happy."

"Not at all. And now Harry asked me to pick up the boys today, so I plan to make sure Gregory helps them decorate the tree."

Donna Rae's grin morphed into a worried frown. "I love that you're doing this. He sure needs a wake-up call. But don't you end up getting hurt."

"How could I get hurt?"

"You could fall for him again."

She waved away the thought. "Are you crazy? Sure, we had feelings in the past, and sure his kids are cute. But I know better now."

"He's changed. He'd be a good catch."

Was any man truly trustworthy and a good catch? "For Molly. Let her have him."

"And that wouldn't bother you?"

What? Had Donna Rae seen the green-eyed monster a minute ago?

Sarah pushed the notion aside. The jealousy was just an old feeling resurfacing. Not something new and real. "No. I'd be happy for all of them."

"Just watch yourself. I'd hate for you to return to Nashville with a broken heart."

She nodded. Yeah, she would hate it, too. That's why she wouldn't let that happen.

Chapter Five

Gregory left his crew to finish blowing leaves as he headed home. He planned to stop on the way to buy the trampoline—finally. Dad was going to pick up the boys and meet him back at the house. He would get all the ornaments out, then hope to at least get lights on the tree before heading back to the shop to meet his crews.

His cell phone rang. An unknown number with a 615 area code. But for some reason, familiar.

"Gregory Jones."

"Hi, Gregory. It's Sarah."

Note to self. The 615 area code is Nashville. "What's up?"

"Hunter and Chase and I are at your house. We have all the lights and ornaments out of the attic. By the time you get here, I'll have the lights on the tree. So you can spend the evening decorating the tree and the house with your sons."

For the first time in his life, he was speechless.

The woman had some nerve.

"Gregory? Are you there?"

"Did you not hear what I said last night?"

"I'm just trying to help. I have a lot of time on my hands."

Apparently, too much time. Time enough to mess with his schedule again. He clenched his teeth to keep from telling her to go bother someone else. He could at least be civil. So in a very calm voice, he said, "I'm on my way to buy the trampoline. And then I was going to help the boys put up the lights."

"So that's the big gift?"

"One of them."

"But, Gregory, they're dangerous."

He sucked air in through his nose...*slow breath in*...

She was at it again. Just like old times. Wanting to change his plans—which were never lofty enough to suit her. Wanting to change *him*.

...*slow breath out*... Finally, he was calm enough to speak. "And since I'm a responsible adult, I'm also buying the safety net. So no need to worry. If you want, you can help them decorate the tree until I get there after my shopping."

"No. I can't stay. I, uh, have plans."

Yeah, right. "You started this. You finish it."

"I really can't stay. I'm taking dinner to Donna Rae."

"Then please call my dad."

"He asked me to pick up the boys, said he'd be home by six. He remembered he had a meeting at church this afternoon."

Oh, man. He probably did. Maybe Gregory should give Sarah the benefit of the doubt this time. "Okay. I'll be there in a minute."

When he pulled in the driveway, he made sure not to block Sarah's car. Before he got out of the truck, she came out the door. She had on dressy jeans and a nice sweater. And her pearls.

Not exactly what someone should wear while digging through his attic.

But definitely Sarah. Classy. Expensive. In a different league from him.

"Hi," she said, all perky and cheerful, even though he'd just been a grouch on the phone. "The boys are inside. They're so excited you're home."

"So what did you cook for Donna Rae?"

Her cheeks turn pink. Or maybe he imagined it. "I'm going to go buy…something. Maybe pizza. Maybe chicken."

"Does she know you're coming?" he asked just to see if she would turn redder.

She didn't disappoint him. "Well, no, if you must know. I thought I would surprise her."

"And if she's already cooked?"

"She can't cook. That's why I'm taking it. It'll help Vinny."

"Uh-huh."

She wouldn't look at him, and she fiddled with her earring. Both telltale signs. But for some reason, despite the frustration, he wanted to smile. Because no matter how irritating she could be, she was so nice it made it difficult to stay angry.

"Well, I've gotta run. Have fun." She waved and hurried to her car.

He stood and watched as she drove away in her expensive sedan that even years ago probably cost more than his big work truck.

He sighed. *Lord, help me not resent her or her money. Or her degrees. Or her fancy car. And, Lord,*

I ask that You keep me strong where she's concerned. Don't let me be sucked in by her pretty blushing or sweet smile. She's right. I need to focus on my boys.

When he walked in the house, the boys came flying down the hallway, begging him to help with the ornaments. They grabbed his hands and pulled him to see the tree with the lights.

It didn't look half bad with the lit strands of tiny multicolored lights. Didn't seem quite so scraggly.

"Okay, guys. We have a lot of work to do." He discovered Sarah had laid all the boxes of ornaments around the tree. "Pick a side and have at it."

"Chase can't reach," Hunter said. Of course, he couldn't reach much farther than Chase.

"You're right. I'll take the top. Hunter, you fill the middle. And Chase, you put stuff on the bottom."

As the boys reached into the boxes, he said, "Watch the hooks. No poking eyes out today."

Hunter started to giggle—a rare sound lately. Then Chase got tickled, too. Soon, they were both laughing as they worked to fill their pitiful tree with decorations.

They managed to finish with a few minutes to spare. Just enough time to take them to Dad's before heading to the shop to meet back up with his crew.

"Wow," Chase said as he stood back and stared. "It's so pwetty."

"You boys did a nice job. It turned out to be a great tree."

"I like it." Hunter walked from one side of the tree to the other as if checking it out further. "So, can we stay home tonight? Please?"

"I'm sorry, son. I have to go back to the shop." He

unplugged the tree. "In fact, let's get you ready to go to Granddad's."

"What good's a stupid tree if you never get to look at it?" Hunter ran out of the room, crying.

Gregory sighed. Sarah might think she was helping. But so far, she'd only made everything worse.

Sarah laughed as she dialed Donna Rae.

"Hello?"

"So, how does pizza sound for dinner tonight?"

"Awesome! The kids would love pizza."

"Great. I'm on my way."

She called Harry as she pulled away from the pizza place and headed to the Durantes.

"Hi, Sarah. How's your plan working?" he asked.

"Well, so far so good, I think. Although Gregory's pretty aggravated with me right now."

"I hope he'll come around before the holidays are over."

She did, too. And she hoped she hadn't ruined it by being a little pushy that day. "I wanted to see if I could pick up the boys after school tomorrow and take them to my house to help them make gifts for their dad."

"Are you sure you don't mind doing all this?"

"I don't mind at all." *As long as I can stay objective and aloof.*

"I know Hunter and Chase will be thrilled. I'll let the school and day care know."

A few minutes later, she arrived at Donna Rae's house.

"You're a lifesaver," Donna Rae said as she let Sarah into the house. "Vinny will love you forever."

"I'm happy to do it. Now go back and lie down." After she made a tray for Donna Rae, she marshaled the kids to the kitchen to feed them.

After she located paper and plastic products for easy cleanup, she made eleven-year-old Nora and eight-year-old Neal's plates. They were pretty self-sufficient, so they were easy. Next, she cut pizza into small bites for three-year-old Ruthy and pulled out a jar of baby food for Nancy. She poured everyone milk, the youngest two getting theirs in a sippy cup. Then she fed Nancy while chaperoning the others as they ate. She didn't even have a chance to eat and wondered how Donna Rae didn't just waste away from lack of time and energy to take care of herself.

Was this how Gregory felt raising his boys? Was she merely adding to his angst by insinuating herself into their lives?

By the time Sarah arrived home, her parents had already eaten dinner.

"There you are." Her dad met her in the foyer as she came through the door. He stared at her as if examining her for evidence of where she'd been, who she'd been with.

"We made you a plate and kept it warm," her mom said. "Where have you been?"

"Out doing good deeds." She hung her coat in the closet. "Helping Gregory and the boys decorate their tree and feeding Donna Rae's family."

"That's nice, dear." Her mother motioned her to come to the kitchen. "Let's feed you now."

"Good. I'm starving." As she sat down to eat, and her mom bustled around to make her a glass of iced tea, her dad joined them at the table.

His brows pulled together, worry adding to his wrinkles. "I've told you already, I don't want you spending so much time with that man."

"It's not as if it's a social get-together, Dad. I'm trying to help the boys."

"How?"

"Gregory spends all his time at work. Hunter and Chase miss him. I'm trying to help him see how important it is to spend time with them while they're young."

"It's his responsibility to take care of his family," he said. "You should stay out of it."

She scooted the pasta around on her plate. The tension with her parents was getting tiring. "Peter's parents worked all the time, and I saw their regret after he was diagnosed with cancer and then died so quickly. It broke my heart. I can't let that happen to someone else. Especially someone I once lo—had feelings for."

She thought her dad might growl at her near slip of words. He refused to consider that his daughter had ever loved Gregory Jones. And it was almost unnatural how much he resented him.

Katherine patted her hand. "Honey, that's not going to happen. Don't let your fears send you into a relationship that could end up hurting you."

Relationship? No way. But she would be forced to spend some time around Gregory. "There's not any kind of relationship. I'm just trying to help two little boys have a merry Christmas. I would do it no matter who the family was."

Her assurances didn't change the expression on her father's face. And not on her mother's either.

"Come on, you two. It'll be fine."

"You watch yourself. I don't trust Gregory Jones," her dad said before walking out.

"Well, if it makes you feel any better, I don't trust him either," she called after him.

And she didn't. No matter what Donna Rae said about him changing.

After school on Wednesday, Sarah picked up Hunter and Chase and took them to her house.

"Wow. You have a giant house," Hunter said as he stood on the front walk staring up at the front porch with its two-story columns.

"It's about a hundred years old. They used to build them really big." She hoped he didn't say anything about the house to Gregory. It used to bother him that her family owned one of the larger houses in Magnolia, and his family owned a modest home on the other side of town. He used to talk about living on the wrong side of the tracks. "But you know what," she whispered to the kids. "I like your house better. This one feels too big sometimes. Feels kind of empty."

"You can come stay at our houth anytime you want," Chase said, so sweet and generous.

"Thank you, Chase. I appreciate that."

She took their hands and walked them inside, straight to the kitchen. Her mother met them there, and Sarah introduced them.

Acting like an eager grandmother, Katherine set a platter on the table. "I baked you some cookies."

Interesting. She seemed as excited as the boys.

"Yum!" Hunter yelled and raced to grab one.

Chase was close on his heels.

As they finished their snack, Sarah pulled out a box of craft supplies that had been in her car from when she'd left school for the holidays, and also some items she'd picked up that morning.

"I thought you boys could make your dad a gift for Christmas."

"Cool," Hunter said. And Chase echoed him.

"Does he drink coffee?"

Hunter rolled his eyes. "Yes. Every day."

"Good. I thought you could make him a coffee mug and decorate it with paint."

"We can put his name on it!" Hunter jumped out of his chair and started digging in the box.

She laid out the supplies, giving them each a paintbrush.

"Can I paint 'Dad' on it?" Hunter asked.

"Great idea. You go first. Chase, let's work on an ornament while he does that."

As they worked, it pained her to see how much her mom wanted to help. It reminded Sarah that she wouldn't be providing grandchildren any time soon.

It also reminded her of all the holiday fun she would miss in her own life…making crafts, decorating cookies, decorating the tree with kid-made ornaments, attending parties at school as a mom and not a teacher… watching the Christmas pageant with a camcorder in hand, zoomed in on her own little angel.

She let out a sigh that seemed to come from the deepest part of her—the place inside that used to hope and dream.

"What's wrong, Miss Sarah?" Hunter asked.

"Oh, nothing. I was just thinking that you're two special boys. And I'm having so much fun."

"Me, too!" Chase shouted.

In less than an hour, they had finished the mug and had each made several ornaments to put on the tree.

"You know, we made so many ornaments, it might be nice to share some. Would you like to take one to your granddad, and maybe take another to Bea and Jasper Kennedy?"

"Yeah. But can Dad go with us?"

She'd hoped he would ask. "Hunter, you're full of great ideas today. I'll call and ask him. Or better yet, why don't you call?" She grinned as she punched in Gregory's cell phone number and handed Hunter the phone.

"Hi, Dad. We're at Miss Sarah's house, and we made some stuff to put on the tree." He grinned at her. "And we made you a surprise."

He paused as Gregory spoke.

"We made ornaments for Granddad and for Granny Bea and Mr. Kennedy. Can you take us to deliver them?"

A second later, his smiled dimmed. He looked at Sarah and said, "He wants to know how long it'll take. He has shopping to do."

Shopping. The trampoline they didn't need. "Here, let me talk to him." She took the receiver from Hunter. "Hi, Gregory. The boys have worked really hard, and I'm sure it would mean a lot to them to have their dad help them deliver the gifts."

"Why are you doing this?"

She smiled at Hunter and Chase. "You have a couple of artists on your hands. Very talented children. I can't wait for you to see their work."

"I still haven't been by the store to buy the trampoline. And you have rehearsal at seven."

"Christmas is about sharing gifts of love," she said in a sappy voice that she was sure he would perceive as patronizing. But how else could she speak with Hunter and Chase staring at her expectantly? She sure wasn't going to be the one to dash their hopes. "So how soon can you be here to pick them up?"

He sighed.

And she almost laughed, because she had him.

Gregory pulled into the Radcliffe mansion drive-way. Well, it wasn't really a mansion, but it had always seemed like one to him. Like a place far out of his reach. Something he could never offer Sarah.

Even though he'd been crazy in love with her, he'd always known he'd never be able to provide for her like her dad had. But in his stupidity, he'd thought maybe that wouldn't matter.

To this day, he didn't know why he'd ever gone after her in the first place. The spoiled princess, apple of her parents' eye, Miss Goody-Goody, Miss Obedient... going out with the town bad boy, her parents' worst nightmare for their baby. No wonder she'd dumped him.

Sarah and the boys walked out the front door, spar-ing him having to ring the doorbell and risk a run-in with her parents. As they came closer to the truck, he climbed out. The boys ran ahead of her, and she fol-lowed at a slower pace, smiling down at them.

She didn't know he was watching her, so he had a moment to look his fill.

And it took his breath away. She had always done that to him, from the first time he'd seen her at school.

There was just something about a blonde with brown eyes...

"Hi, Dad!" Hunter called as he ran around to the passenger side of the truck. He seemed so happy. A rarity these days.

Chase grabbed Gregory around the legs and gave him a hug. He patted his son's head, then lifted him into his seat.

"Miss Sawah is so nice."

He looked into her eyes—couldn't have stopped himself if his life depended on it—as she helped Hunter into his seat. "I know, son. I'm glad she helped you make Christmas presents."

How could he calmly say that as if she hadn't thrown his world into chaos the last few days? And not only his schedule.

"I put the gifts back here between the boys," she said. "There's something for the Kennedys and for your dad."

"What about Dad's?" Hunter whispered.

Gregory acted as if he hadn't heard.

"I wrapped it and put it beside your seat," she whispered back. "Hide it when you get home."

"'Kay."

"Well, thanks for coming," she said. "You guys did a great job."

"But, Miss Sawah, you have to go, too!"

"Oh, you and your dad can deliver these just fine. You don't need me."

"Please come," Hunter said.

The quiet, simple request was like a gunshot through the car. Gregory knew it was his move. He should go ahead and invite her. But he wasn't so sure he could handle being around her tonight.

"Dad, can Miss Sawah go with us?"

Well. "Um, sure, Chase. If she'd like to come."

Once again, he couldn't keep from looking at her. She appeared torn. He was sure she didn't really want to go. But she probably realized Hunter never asked for much. And hadn't cared about too much lately either.

"Come on. Hop in," he said against his better judgment. "The kids won't enjoy it as much if you're not along." There. He'd done what was right, even though he hadn't wanted to. *Give the man a medal.*

"Okay. I wouldn't want to miss it."

The boys whooped and cheered.

She climbed in the passenger seat as he got behind the wheel. It was strange having her in his vehicle, riding along beside him as if she belonged there.

The last time she'd ridden with him, she'd been plastered up against his side, with her head resting on his shoulder, telling him how much she loved him. He'd basked in her declaration and felt like the king of the road.

During this drive, though, she sat as far away as possible. Was probably hanging on to the passenger door. Neither of them spoke, and you could cut the tension in the air.

Of course, the backseat occupants didn't notice. They chattered and laughed as if they were on some grand adventure.

"Are we going to Granny Bea's first?" Hunter asked.

"Yep."

"I called and told them you and the boys would be coming," Sarah said. "So they'll be expecting visitors."

When they pulled up to Bea's house a couple of minutes later, an extra car sat in the driveway.

"Look," Hunter said. "There's Miss Molly's car."

Sarah wanted to just wait in the truck. But how rude would that be? So she trudged up to the front door with the Jones family.

Bea and her new husband answered the door before Sarah had time to prepare to face Molly.

She did *not* want to see Gregory and Molly together.

"Merry Christmas," Hunter yelled and hugged Bea. Apparently, she was close to them.

"Oh, look. Sarah is with you!" Bea said. "It's so good to see you're home, dear." Then she introduced her husband.

As they walked inside, Bea said, "Molly just happened to drop by, too." It seemed she watched Gregory as she said it. Then she glanced at Sarah and winked.

Of course. Sarah should have known, after all Donna Rae had said, that Bea would be playing matchmaker.

Molly walked over. "Hey, everyone."

Then she spotted Sarah. "Oh, Sarah! I'm so glad you're home this year."

They hugged as they greeted each other. Molly acted so happy to see her that Sarah felt like a heel.

"Hunter and Chase made something for you. Boys?" Gregory said.

Hunter handed Bea a gift bag. She and Jasper opened it together.

"Oh, how beautiful," Bea exclaimed.

"It'll be perfect on our tree."

Mr. and Mrs. Kennedy seemed thrilled. And Sarah found she was envious of the sparkle in their eyes as they smiled at each other.

Did Gregory and Delia ever look at each other that way?

Molly looked over Bea's shoulder at the ornament. Then she looked up at Gregory. "Oh, how sweet. 'Our First Christmas'. And they even put the date. Your boys are precious. And so talented."

Will Gregory and Molly ever look at each other that way?

"You boys *are* precious," Bea said to Hunter and Chase.

"We'll treasure it every year as we put it on our tree. Thank you." Jasper said, and then went to hang the ornament on the already-full Christmas tree.

Sarah happened to look in Gregory's direction. He was staring at her. And he had the strangest look on his face. Almost…as if he was wondering something.

She stared back, because she couldn't look away. She wanted to know what was inside his head. Wanted to know what his thoughts were—about her, about life.

About his hopes and dreams. Whether they had changed.

No, no, no. She did not need to be thinking about his hopes and dreams. That was dangerous territory because it would mean she was getting involved. Too involved.

"Ta da! Perfect." Finally, Jasper had made a space and hung the ornament front and center.

It broke the connection between her and Gregory. She owed Jasper big-time.

As they said their goodbyes, Bea whispered in her ear, "It was me who asked Molly here tonight. But it looks like I may be barking up the wrong tree." Then she backed away and snickered, leaving Sarah to wonder just what she'd meant.

As Gregory pulled away from the Kennedys', he said, "Sarah, we're running a little behind. I'll drop you off, then take the kids to Dad's."

"But we want Miss Sarah to go with us to give

Granddad his present. She helped make it." Hunter rocked back and forth in his booster seat as if he was trying to launch out of it. "Please."

What could he say? Hunter was enthusiastic about so few things lately. "If it's okay with her."

"Of course," she said.

"I'll drop you back at your house on my way to the job bid." He looked over to the passenger's seat and realized she'd been observing him. But as soon as he looked her way, she jerked her head back to facing out the front window.

When they arrived at his dad's house, the kids tore inside with the gift. He hadn't seen them so excited in ages.

Hunter had made progress after spending only a couple of afternoons with her. Gregory should be grateful. But the more time his kids spent with her, the more time *he* seemed to end up spending with Sarah.

He worried how Winston would react.

"Here, Granddad. We made it for you for Christmas!" Hunter handed over the gift bag.

His dad looked up, surprised. Then shot a questioning glance at Gregory.

He assumed it was over Hunter's exuberance.

Chase had to get a hand on the gift, too, and helped shove it toward his granddad. "You can open it now, though."

"Why, thank you boys." He gave each child a hug.

Then he smiled at Sarah. A very friendly smile. Not one Gregory was used to seeing on his dad's face where Sarah was concerned.

Odd.

Harry pulled out the tissue paper and carefully lifted out an ornament. "It's beautiful. I love it."

"We made it ourselves," Hunter said as he bounced around like a jumping bean.

"Yeah. Ourselfs," Chase added.

Gregory found himself smiling. "Time for me to take Miss Sarah home. What do you boys say?"

"Thank you for helping us," Hunter said.

"When can we make one for Uncle Wichard and Aunt Windsay?"

"Oh, I think Miss Sarah has helped plenty already," Gregory said to thwart another day at the Radcliffe house.

"I'll tell you what," Sarah said. "How about I give the supplies to your dad, and he can help you make the other gifts?"

Great. He knew nothing about crafty things. How was he supposed to help make them? "I guess it can't hurt to try."

Both boys agreed, then ran off to put their grand-dad's ornament on his tree.

Harry walked them to the door. "Oh, Sarah, I'm going to Atlanta for the next couple of days to help Richard finish packing for his move on Saturday. If you don't mind, I may be calling on you to help some with Hunter and Chase."

What? When did his dad decide this?

"Sure. Anytime."

Gregory hurried her out the door, even as he wondered what universe he'd plopped into.

A few painfully quiet minutes later, Gregory parked in the Radcliffes' driveway. Such a contrast with the rowdy drive earlier. But they didn't really have much to say to each other.

She turned sideways in her seat to totally face him.

He wasn't sure he wanted to be the center of her attention, but he forced himself to turn and look her in the eye. He blew out a nervous breath.

"I know I'm only a visitor here in Magnolia. I'm just home for the holidays. But I hope you don't mind me helping with your kids."

"Because I'm such a failure as a father?" He hadn't been able to keep the bitterness out of his voice.

As if without thought, she put her hand on his hand. "Oh, no. I didn't mean that at all. I—" She pulled her hand away and clenched it in her lap. "I just…well, I want you to understand why I'm doing all this. It's because I recently saw someone close to me, one of my students, wish for more time with his parents. And they were working all the time, trying to provide all they thought he needed."

Did she think he pawned his kids off on everyone else? "I have time with them. And they have time with my dad. It's not like they're at day care all the time."

"My student had a wonderful nanny. But he told me he wanted time with his mom and dad."

Why was she like a dog with a bone? How could he make her understand? "I know Lindsay's leaving took a toll on them. And now she's in Europe for the holidays. That's why I'm trying to make this the perfect Christmas."

"My student, Peter…he died."

He jerked back in his seat as if she'd socked him in the gut. He hadn't seen that coming in a million years. *A kindergartner died?* "How awful."

Her lip quivered. "Cancer. And it took him quickly. We closed school early because of the funeral. And the other children needed counseling."

Poor thing, she probably needed it, too.

Before he could stop himself, he took hold of her hand. At least he hadn't hugged her like he wanted to do. "I'm sorry."

She held tight. "I just can't bear to see any child missing his mom or dad. And Peter's parents… The regret. Just too painful for anyone to have to bear."

Well, no wonder she'd been hounding him. At least he understood better now.

He wanted to hold her in his arms. To comfort her like he had so many times before. But he couldn't. It wasn't his place now.

Gregory turned off the truck. "Come on. I'll walk you to the door."

She seemed disappointed. "Okay."

When they reached the front door, he couldn't help glancing in the direction of her upstairs bedroom window. Where years ago, he had tossed rocks to get her to sneak out to meet him. Which, of course, reminded him that her parents never approved of him.

Never would either.

Then why do I want to get closer to her? To breathe in her fragrance? To remember holding her close? To remember kissing her?

To remember all the big dreams I had when I was with her?

Before he knew it, he had moved closer. He took hold of her hand again. "You know, I should thank you for spending time with Hunter and Chase. They seemed to have a good time. Seemed happy."

"I had fun, too."

Frustration. Gratitude. Attraction. They all warred, yanking his thoughts all over the place.

But one thought dominated.

He wanted more. More than the touch of her hand. He wanted to look into her eyes and see that she cared. He wanted to know if she felt anything for him now.

His gaze slid from her eyes to her lips...

He took a step back to fight the temptation. He couldn't look at her right now—too many emotions swirling around. So instead, he let go of her hand and looked up the length of the big white columns, took in the expensive furniture on the porch, to remind himself whose house he stood in front of. Then he nodded. "Good night."

She started to unlock the door, then turned quickly, nearly running into him. "Oh, wait. The craft stuff."

He had to get out of there before he did something stupid. "I'll get it later."

He hurried to the truck. As he started the engine, he noticed a shadowy figure standing at the side of the house. Just outside Winston's home office.

Even with the sun setting, and the shadows on that side of the house, he could tell it was him.

How long had he been there? How much had he seen or heard?

His stance—legs spread wide, arms crossed in front of him, his head following Gregory's truck as he backed out—said everything. *Stay away from my daughter.*

Apparently, Winston expected that the agreement *was* still in effect.

No threat was needed. If Gregory wanted to keep his shameful past a secret, he needed to stay away.

Chapter Six

Sarah closed the door behind her and leaned against it in the cool, dark entry hall. She heard the television off in the distance. A door closed. Then indistinct words of her parents talking.

She closed her eyes and imagined being sixteen once again, slipping inside the house after her parents were in bed. Not wanting to leave Gregory. Wishing she could spend every waking moment with him.

He'd made her feel so loved, so cherished. Every bit of his attention had been focused on her. They talked about what he would do after he graduated. About his goals. And then about her wanting to go to college and to become a teacher. He'd told her she could do anything she put her mind to. That he would be here waiting for her once she graduated. Of course, he said he hoped she would go to college nearby so he could go ahead and start his business. That way, as soon as she graduated from college, they could marry and start their lives together. He'd even hinted at marrying sooner.

They'd had such big dreams. Silly dreams, because her mom and dad had forbidden her to see him. After a few weeks, she just couldn't stomach the lies anymore, and Gregory was pressing her to marry earlier than she was ready for.

So she'd broken up with Gregory. But asked him to wait for her. Told him that once she was older, she could make her own decisions. That once she was eighteen and had graduated from high school, they could officially date and eventually follow through on all those plans they'd made.

But then he hadn't waited. And everything in her world seemed to go crazy as she watched him start seeing Delia. And he avoided her like the plague, so she couldn't even get close enough to him to talk. He ignored her calls and her letters.

A light flashed on in the hallway, calling her back to the present.

"Sarah, honey, is that you standing there?" Katherine asked.

"Yes."

"Are you okay?"

"I'm fine. Just enjoying the quiet. A moment to think."

"You didn't spend the whole afternoon with the Jones boys, did you?"

Trying to be patient, Sarah said, "Yes, I did. But the important thing was that Gregory spent time with them."

Her dad's footsteps sounded, coming from the direction of his study.

"Be. Careful," Katherine said, stressing each word.

Sarah sighed. "I am. So quit fretting."

"Come on, you need to hurry and eat before your rehearsal."

As her mother walked ahead into the kitchen and pans started banging, Sarah trudged along behind.

If only Gregory had waited. How different her life could have turned out.

"Okay, children. Let's line up in your places and try saying your lines again. This time without my help," Sarah said.

They all moved to their places. But then Hunter raised his hand.

"Yes, Hunter?"

"Do I have to do it again? You said someone else could do the talking part."

"Oh, I'm sorry. I completely forgot." She'd been amazed that he'd attempted *reading* his lines. At how well he sounded out the words for a child not quite halfway through kindergarten. He was extremely bright. She walked up to him and quietly said, "But don't you think you can do it? You've read the lines just fine using your script."

"No, ma'am." Big greenish-brown eyes stared back at her.

She could tell he was scared. But she also knew he had the capability. "I know you can do this." She smiled to encourage him. "Please?"

Big tears welled up in his eyes. "No. I don't wanna do it!" He ran up the aisle and out the front door of the church.

She asked one of the mom volunteers to continue with the rehearsal, then followed him outside. He was nowhere to be found. But he couldn't be far.

She took her cell phone out of her pocket and dialed Gregory. "Hi, Gregory. We have a little problem at the church."

"Are the boys okay?"

"Yes. But Hunter just had a meltdown. He's refusing to do his lines. And he's upset."

"Excuse me a minute," he said to someone he was with. Then to Sarah, "Put him on the phone."

"I can't." She scanned the front sidewalk. Looked up and down the street. "He ran outside, and I haven't found him yet."

"Check in the back. He likes the prayer garden."

"Hang on." She took off at a brisk pace, searching as she walked around the side of the church. When she got to the little courtyard, she heard sniffing, then a whimper. "I think I found him. He's still crying."

"Put him on."

"Hunter, honey." She approached and put her hand on his shoulder. "I have your dad on the phone. He'd like to talk to you."

He jerked his shoulder away and turned his back. "You can't call him. He's *busy.*"

She ached for the boy as she tried to rub his back to console him. But he refused any affection, so she stepped away.

"Gregory, he won't get on the phone."

"I heard him."

Silence. And she had no idea what to say.

Hunter whimpered and sobbed some more.

His crying spurred her into teacher mode. "I'm afraid you need to come get your son. He won't let me near him."

"Can't you just reassign his lines to someone else?"

"Maybe if we had more than two rehearsals left. Besides, I believe he can do it. He just needs some support and encouragement."

More silence. "And what's that supposed to mean?"

She could imagine his quandary. But it was of his own making. So she steeled herself to say exactly what was on her mind. "I think this is more important than work right now."

"I believe that decision should be mine. I'm his father."

She huffed. "I'm sorry. But I'm angry. Hunter needs you, and I don't know what else I can do."

"Go do what you think Lindsay would do. He'll be okay. He's a real trouper."

"So you're not coming?"

"I don't see how I can for another half hour or so. I'm sorry. Tell him—" He exhaled a long breath. "Tell him I'll see him later tonight." He hung up.

Well.

She slowly approached Hunter. "Hunter, do you think you're ready to come back inside now?"

He shook his head, then sniffed.

She sat on a marble bench near where he stood picking berries off the holly bush. "You know, you're such a big boy now. And I can tell you know most of your lines. I could really use your help showing the younger shepherds what to do."

He plunked himself down beside her. "I mostly know it."

"See? I can help you finish learning the lines."

He looked up at her with big tears pooling. "I can't."

"Are you scared?"

He nodded. Then he blinked, sending the pooled tears down a path along his cheeks. "I might mess up."

"Oh, Hunter, that wouldn't matter." She pulled him into a hug. "We all mess up sometimes."

He wrapped his arms around her waist and held on for dear life. Sobs tore through his body.

"Oh, baby. It's okay. You don't have to do it."

"But I waaaaant tooooo," he wailed.

The poor thing really wanted to have the part, but he was too scared to do it.

She pulled him into her lap and let him cry. He had a lot of tears for someone who was just scared of forgetting a few lines in a church Christmas pageant.

Maybe it was about his mom. Or about Lindsay leaving. Or about his dad being gone all the time.

She rubbed soothing circles on his back. "Everything will be okay. We'll work it out."

In a while, about the time he started to calm, she heard a vehicle pull in the back parking lot. A moment later, footsteps approached.

Gregory couldn't believe he'd done it. But he had abruptly walked away from a potential customer.

He only hoped the guy had kids and would understand.

When he walked into the courtyard garden, he saw her. Sarah. In the moonlight. Holding his son in her lap. Hugging him. Crooning something.

The scene stopped him in his tracks.

He couldn't budge, couldn't manage to put one foot in front of the other. Because fear rooted him to the stone walkway. Fear at how the scene playing out in front of him left him shaken. Left him…wanting…he wasn't even sure what.

But then he heard Hunter sniff and whimper as if

winding down from a good cry, and it prodded him back to reality and into action.

"Hey, buddy, you okay?" he asked.

Hunter pulled away from Sarah's embrace. He sat up straight and scrubbed his fists over his eyes. "Yeah." Trying to look like a tough guy.

"I hear you don't want to do your speaking part."

Hunter didn't say anything as he squirmed out of Sarah's lap.

Sarah said, "Well, I think he does want to do it. He's just a little afraid of messing up."

"Is that so?"

Hunter nodded.

"I imagine your dad can help you," she said. "Gregory, maybe you can work with him on his lines. And make plans to stand offstage and cue him if he forgets."

Trapped. She'd trapped him. What could he say?

And now she'd gotten Hunter's hopes up. Gregory could see it in his eyes. "Would you like that, son?"

He nodded. Then fought a smile.

Lord, what have You gotten me into?

Sarah beamed a smile at Gregory. And it was as if the sun had started to shine right along with the moonlight.

He was toast.

"Okay." He jerked his head toward the church building. "Come on, big guy. Let's go show 'em what a shepherd's really made of."

"All right!" Hunter pulled up his shirttail and wiped his face. Then he dashed ahead of them and into the back door of the church.

It left them alone in the quiet coziness of the prayer garden.

"So can you stay for the rest of rehearsal?" She stood

and smoothed the front of her dress pants. Then she tugged at her earring.

"I guess so."

"You know, I just discovered that I need someone to help with the sets. And if you're going to be at rehearsals anyway...." She grinned at him. "Please say you'll help."

She'd railroaded him again. How did she do that?

Because in five minutes and with one smile she has me wrapped around her little finger all over again. "I don't know." Could he do it without spending time around her?

"Please. You'll have quality time with your children as you serve your church."

Only Scrooge could say no to that. "I'll think about it."

She put her hand on his arm. "Thank you."

Her hand was cool, and for the first time he realized she'd hurried outside without a coat. "You need to get inside. You're freezing."

She led the way back into the church.

Right before they entered the sanctuary, he stopped her. "Thanks for helping out with Hunter."

"You're welcome. I just automatically go into teacher mode and—"

"No, it's more than that. You really care about the children. They're lucky to have you direct the play."

She looked up into his eyes, and he felt as if she was looking straight through to the inside of him. He wanted her to see who he really was. To see the good, not the failings. To see a dad who was trying the best he knew how.

Lord, I want her to see me, the man, too. And that's not good. Help me to quit thinking about what might have been.

"Thank you," she said, and then she walked into the sanctuary and gathered the children.

When Chase saw Gregory, he jumped up and down, waving his hands. "Dad!"

"Hey, buddy. I'm going to stay and help."

"Yay!"

Sarah tried to regain control of the practice. Gregory put his finger over his mouth to quiet Chase while she talked.

"Go stand with the angels," he whispered.

Chase complied with a huge grin on his face. He kept looking over at Gregory and fighting giggles.

The older children stood in place, and each said their lines. When it was Hunter's turn to speak, he only bobbled one little sentence. Gregory cued him, Hunter grinned, then he finished his part beautifully. When he finished, Gregory gave him a thumbs-up.

After the rehearsal, he gathered the boys.

"Are you going home with us?" Hunter asked him.

"Yes. I'm not working anymore tonight."

Hunter and Chase both danced around in celebration.

"Miss Sarah, we get to sleep at home tonight, in our bed!" Hunter shouted.

She smiled at the boys. "That's great news."

But then she wouldn't look at Gregory. And he knew it was because she couldn't. She probably knew her disapproval would show. And right now, he didn't need to see it, because he felt horrible that his boys celebrated over sleeping in their own beds.

Maybe she was right about his working overtime.

But the image of that wish book with the trampoline circled, with the new game system circled, flashed into his mind.

"So, do you think you'll be able to help with the sets?" she asked him.

He had to give her credit. She certainly had perfect timing.

He shook his head at her tenacity and couldn't help but laugh.

She smiled, her eyes twinkling with what appeared to be mischief. "All I need is a new manger. And a hanging star. And maybe a couple of other little things."

"By Christmas Eve—how many days away?"

"Seven more days till Christmas Eve. I'm sure the boys will help you."

Of course they would. More quality time. More *quantity* time. And they could work on it at home— away from Sarah. "Okay."

She jerked up straight. "Really? You'll do it?"

"Yes. How big do you want the manger?"

Still surprised, she hesitated. Then she held out her arms to show the size. "And I'd like the star to hang right there if possible." She pointed to the right side of the choir loft.

"I'll see what I can do. Come on, guys. Let's go home."

"Oh, and can you come to rehearsal on Saturday morning?" she asked.

"I'll see what I can work out." It would be tough. But even though he usually worked Saturday mornings, he could make the time to be there. Hunter needed his help.

And now Sarah was counting on him.

When Sarah walked in the house, her mom met her at the door.

"Hi, dear. I was just heading to bed but wanted to let you know Bea Kennedy called to invite you and me to a Christmas luncheon. For her quilting group. And I accepted."

"Mother, I told you I don't want to go to any parties. I just don't feel like celebrating."

"Well, honey, this is different. This will be laid-back and fun. With some of your old friends." She kissed Sarah's cheek. "Tomorrow at noon."

Great. Donna Rae couldn't be there, and other than Bea, Sarah had no idea if she would know anyone.

Wait. Molly Patton? Hadn't Donna Rae said Molly was in the group?

She would have to prepare herself. She didn't need a reappearance of the strange jealousy she'd felt the other day. In fact, if she could work it out, Donna Rae would be the perfect defense. She could offer to take her to the party. That way Sarah would have someone to talk to and to worry about.

There wouldn't be any opportunity for thinking about Molly and Gregory.

Chapter Seven

The next day, Sarah and her mom picked up Donna Rae, propped her in the backseat, and took her to Bea's house. They'd called ahead and had Bea prepare a place on the couch. So when they arrived, they walked her to her spot, helped her lie down on her side, and wedged a pillow between her knees.

"I can't believe y'all did all this," Donna Rae said. "But I'm glad you did. I'm so sick of the four walls of my living room."

"We're glad you made it, dear," Bea said. "It wouldn't be a party without you."

"I'm sorry I didn't bring any food."

"Yes, you did." Sarah winked at her as she held up a picnic basket. "You brought deviled eggs and a pecan pie."

Donna Rae shook her head. "You're too good to me."

Sarah and her mom greeted a few other ladies she vaguely recognized but couldn't quite place the names.

"Helloooo," someone called from the front porch. "Can you get the door?"

"Oh, that's Molly. I bet her hands are full," Bea said as she went to let her inside.

Donna Rae looked straight at Sarah.

Oh, brother. Was she obvious? Or was Donna Rae just overly sensitive to Sarah's feelings?

"Hi, everyone," Molly called in her cheery voice as she walked in carrying two dishes. She'd also handed a basket to Bea.

"Goodness, Molly. What all did you bring?" Donna Rae asked.

"Well, I brought extra, just in case." She laughed. "You know me. I never know when to stop cooking." She turned. "Oh, Sarah, it's so good to see you here. You too, Mrs. Radcliffe."

"Hi, Molly."

"We're all here now, so let's eat!" Bea said.

Sarah and her mom helped lay out the food on the kitchen table while Bea made Donna Rae a plate. Molly was in the midst of everything. Sarah couldn't turn around without nearly bumping into her. But she was so doggone nice, Sarah couldn't dislike her.

All the ladies filled their plates, then joined Donna Rae in the living room.

"I'm sorry I'm causing such a ruckus," Donna Rae said as she tried to make room for someone else to sit on the couch.

"We're just glad you're here, baby," Bea said. "Thanks to Sarah."

"Sarah, I hear you've been helping Gregory with the boys," Sandra, Bea's next-door neighbor, said.

"Oh, just a little. I've got a good bit of time on my hands."

"He's having such a tough time since Lindsay moved away," Molly said. "Those precious boys need a mom."

"Yes, ma'am. And we know who wants to be that lucky gal," Sandra said with a grin.

Sarah's stomach dropped, but then she noticed Sandra wasn't looking at her. She was looking at Molly.

Molly, with her fair, freckled skin, turned all shades of red.

Sandra laughed and turned to Sarah. "We've been pushing Molly to take Gregory over to the park."

"To hold hands around The Forever Tree," another of the women said.

"That's nice," Sarah managed to say.

Molly stared right at Sarah. "He's such a charmer. I imagine he's already held hands around it with someone before now."

Sarah suspected Molly was fishing for information. And Sarah sure wasn't going to bite and share the fact that she and Gregory *had* held hands way back when. She kept her mouth shut and looked to Donna Rae for help.

"He's a good-looking man with two cute little boys," Donna Rae said to Molly. "So if you're interested, don't dillydally." The last was said while looking at Sarah.

Molly waved her hand. "Oh, he never notices me."

Bea got up and walked toward the kitchen. "Honey, you've gotta make your move and be straightforward about it. Men can be thickheaded sometimes." She came back a minute later with a pitcher of sweet tea and refilled all the glasses. When she filled Sarah's, she raised her brows and gave her "a look" as if maybe that comment had been for her.

Apparently, Bea still had the mistaken idea that Sarah was interested in Gregory. Or that she should be.

Thankfully, Sarah's mom changed the subject to the decorations downtown.

"Speaking of men," Sandra said, not sticking with the subject change, "do you have any prospects up there in Nashville, Sarah?"

"Uh, not at the moment. I'm so busy with work."

"You still teaching?"

"Yes. Kindergarten. And I love it."

Sandra tsked. "Well, you need to find yourself a man before you hit thirty."

"Too late for that," Donna Rae muttered.

Sarah had to laugh. "I think I'm going back for seconds on the excellent fried chicken."

"Got it at Minnie's," one of the ladies said. "She makes the best around."

"Speaking of Minnie…" her mother said.

Bless her, she'd changed the subject again. And this time it stuck. The ladies all went on to other subjects as Sarah grabbed another piece of chicken she didn't really want.

As she puttered around, trying to kill time in the peaceful kitchen, Molly walked in.

"Do Hunter and Chase really seem to be doing okay?"

"I think they're doing better now that Gregory is spending a little more time with them."

"Yeah, I wish he didn't work so hard. But you can't tell him anything."

She'd said it as if they had a relationship, as if she'd been telling him to ease up. Which made Sarah's insides churn. She stared at her plate. "So, have you two been dating?"

Molly sighed. "No. But not from lack of trying. I've offered to babysit. I've taken them meals. I've—" She stopped in the middle of shaking a bottle of salad dressing. "Is this awkward for you? I know you two used to date…well, not really date. But to see each other."

Apparently, not everyone had guessed how serious they'd been since they'd snuck around all the time.

"No, not really awkward." Although it made her stomach hurt. "We don't have a relationship at all now. In fact, until I ran into him at the church the other day, we hadn't talked in years."

Molly fanned her face. "Oh, good. That's a relief. It's just that…well… I love his kids. I would love to be a part of his family. I'm just kind of waiting and praying, hoping God will show me what He wants."

Sarah felt about an inch tall. Because here Molly was being so faithful, praying for God's will. And Sarah was doing anything but praying, avoiding a conversation with God that she knew would eventually have to happen.

Instead, she focused on Molly. Which, of course, led to Sarah feeling jealous, thinking of Molly being Hunter and Chase's mother. And even more jealous thinking of Molly being Gregory's wife—of her being in his arms. Kissing him. "Gotta get back to the party!" she said, a little too cheerfully as she stepped out of the kitchen.

"Donna Rae, do you need more food?" she asked, interrupting a chat in the living room.

Donna Rae looked startled by her rudeness. "Uh, no thank you."

Sarah stared at her friend, trying to plead with her eyes. *Get me out of here.*

"You know, Sarah. You could do me a favor. Can you call Vinny to check and see how the kids are doing?"

She beamed a grateful smile. "Of course. I'll step outside and use my cell phone."

Sarah walked to the front porch and plopped down in Bea's swing. She launched herself into full swing, grateful for the cold breeze that hit her in the face as she dialed Vinny.

Jealousy was such an ugly thing. So how could she possibly feel it? There was nothing between her and Gregory. And there never would be.

Gregory finished work early, about four o'clock, and dialed his dad. "Hey. I can get the boys today."

"I'm glad to hear it, son. But Sarah's already picked them up for me. I'm about to head to Atlanta to help your brother pack."

He shook his head and sighed. "Where's she taking them?"

"Your house. I gave her my key. She said something about a surprise."

"Thanks." He hung up and drove home, thinking maybe he could use the time to shop, if she didn't mind babysitting. That way he could definitely stay away from her.

Then he wondered if Winston knew where she was. If Gregory were to hang around the house for a while, would he find out?

When he arrived, he found Sarah on a ladder hanging lights on his house. She was reaching out way too far.

He hopped out as fast as he could turn off the truck. "Hey, watch it!"

She wrenched around at the sound of his shout, and the ladder wobbled.

He raced across the yard to stabilize it. By the time he got there, it had righted itself.

"Gregory, you scared the life out of me."

"You shouldn't be up on a ladder with no one else around."

She jammed a hand on her hip, making the ladder wobble again. "I was fine till you yelled at me. I'm not even up that high."

He put both hands on the sides of the rickety wooden ladder. "You could still fall and break something. Now come on down and let me finish it. I had planned to do it myself anyway."

"When?"

"Well, we can go inside and look on my calendar. Of course, you've thrown my whole schedule off by plunging me into the middle of a different activity every day this week."

She jammed her other hand on the other hip, but the ladder stayed firmly anchored in his grip. "Well, pardon me, but I think maybe you've had a good week with your children."

He held out his hand to her. She took it and started down the rungs. When she got to the last rung, she stopped, since he stood in the way.

How was he supposed to stay away from her? If she was arranging time with his children almost every day, Winston couldn't expect him to.

Yes, he kind of liked where he stood at the moment. For some reason, he didn't want to move. Maybe because they were eye to eye, about six inches apart. So close....

"So, will you admit you've had a good week with your boys?"

He leaned in closer. "Well, I've had an unusual week, to say the least." He zoomed in on her lips. "With a blast from the past showing up and butting her way into my schedule."

She laughed—and it sounded nervous—then grabbed his chin and lifted it, dragging his gaze away from her lips. "Time with your boys? Focus, Gregory."

For the last week, she was all he'd been able to think about. "Believe me, I am focused." He smiled at her, hoping to win her over. Of course he had no idea why he wanted to. But he did.

"You are so bad," she said, biting her lip. Trying not to smile. But she smiled, shining sunshine on him, warming him.

"I have had a good week with my boys. I like seeing them laugh and have fun."

She pushed against his chest. "Good. Now let me down."

He refused to budge. How had everything changed so quickly? How could he feel happy for the first time in ages?

All of a sudden serious, he stared into her gorgeous brown eyes. "Thank you."

She swallowed, as if having difficulty. "You're welcome," she whispered.

He moved in slowly, testing the waters, afraid she would disappear into thin air as he neared his target. His lips brushed hers, but she turned her head, dragging his lips across her cheek.

"Don't do this, Gregory. We can't just go back to how we once were and act like nothing happened." She pressed her back against the ladder, trying to retreat further. "You went out with Delia—my friend. And then married her. I can't forget that."

He breathed in, knowing he might never be this close again, wishing he could bottle how good she smelled.

What had he been thinking?

He stepped back and offered his hand to help her down the last step. "I apologize. For everything."

What else could he say? He couldn't begin to explain himself. Then or now.

"The boys are inside untangling the rest of the lights. Let's go check on them," she said as if the kiss or their past had never happened.

What was it his friends used to tell him? *She's out of your league, man.*

Yeah. And she still was.

Sarah led the way inside as she tried to conceal her struggle to pull in enough air to feed her fuzzy brain. She also worked to make sure her knees didn't buckle.

He almost kissed me.

She mashed both hands against her chest as she forced herself to speak. "Hey, guys, look who's here."

"Dad!" they both yelled as they hopped up to greet him.

"Hi, guys. Nice job decorating the house."

"We wanted to 'pwize you," Chase said.

"You sure did surprise me. I found Miss Sarah nearly on our roof."

The boys giggled, thinking their dad was hysterically

funny. They were clueless that he'd trapped her on the ladder, making her weak in the knees and leaving her to wish she were sixteen again.

"How are the rest of the lights coming?" she asked.

"Almost ready," Hunter said. "You can take this bunch." He handed her one large strand of icicle lights.

Gregory snatched them out of her hand. "I'll get those. You're not going back up that ladder."

"So you can climb up there without anyone around, but I need a babysitter when I climb it?"

"I'm used to being on a ladder."

"You can't risk your neck. You have two little ones depending on you."

"And you don't have anyone depending on you?" he said as if he didn't believe it.

But honestly, when she thought about it, she didn't. Sad, but true. "Well, I do have my students," she said so she didn't seem quite so pitiful.

He smoothed a hand over the bundle of lights. "And maybe a special man in your life?"

When she looked up from where his hands tinkered with the light cord, three pairs of eyes met hers. All seemingly waiting for her answer. "No. Not at the moment."

"What does that mean, Dad? Does she have a husband or not?" Hunter asked, so serious.

She burst out laughing, all tension eased. "No, Hunter, I don't have a husband. Or a boyfriend."

Chase looked confused. But when he saw his brother smile, he smiled too.

"Let's get these lights finished," Gregory said.

"You mean you don't have to go back to work?" Hunter asked.

"Not tonight. I took off early to do some shopping. But it looks like we're decorating today instead."

"Yeah." Hunter pumped his fist in the air.

Chase tried his best to do so, too.

She just shook her head, too pleased to even know what to say. Could things be looking up around the Jones household? "Come on. If we hurry, we can finish before dark."

They went back outside and left the boys untangling strands of lights across the living room floor.

She held the ladder still while he climbed up and began clipping lights to the gutter. She said, "So, have you bought the big you-know-what yet?"

He glared at her mid-snap of the light clip. "For some reason I haven't had a spare moment to do it."

She gave him a sassy smile. "Good. There may be hope for your Christmas yet."

Once Sarah and the boys put a wreath on the front door and all the lights were up at Gregory's house, she couldn't see a reason for staying. In fact, she probably should have left as soon as he arrived. But…well, she had no excuse.

She frowned as she realized she'd enjoyed being there with him. She'd started looking forward to spending time with his family.

But, she was pleased, anyway, because as she was leaving, she overheard him tell the boys he needed their help building the star and manger that evening.

Rather than head straight home—which was sure to include a lecture from her parents about staying away from the Jones family—she detoured to Donna Rae's house.

Once inside, Sarah asked her friend, "How are you feeling?"

"You and Gregory held hands around The Tree, didn't you?" she said without preamble.

"The tree?"

"Oh, come on, Sarah. Drop the clueless act."

She'd been hoping for a distraction, and Donna Rae had zeroed in on the exact topic she needed to stay away from. "Yes, we did. Now can we change the subject?"

"You do know I believe in the legend, don't you?"

"I've heard that." She couldn't sit down. Talking about The Forever Tree always set her on edge, because she also believed in the legend. Or at least she used to.

Still wanted to.

Yet she knew it was childish hopefulness.

Donna Rae struggled to sit up. "Well, you need to admit it and start praying about you and Gregory. He may just be the one God has picked out for you."

Sarah grabbed Donna Rae's hand and helped her upright. "I'm not praying too much right now. Not since Peter's death. I'm too angry." Just saying the words out loud to someone helped ease the fear and tightness in her chest just a little.

"Understandable. But don't shut God out. Tell Him you're mad."

"Oh, I can't do that." The thought of doing that gave her a heart palpitation. She envisioned getting struck down by lightning.

Donna Rae patted the couch beside her for Sarah to sit. "God knows how you feel, so you might as well talk with Him about it."

"Please don't push me on this. I'm not ready."

Donna Rae rubbed Sarah's back like her own mom

would do. "Oh, hon, it'll be okay. He wants to ease your pain. Give it all over to Him."

The urge to cry—no, to wail—nearly suffocated her. Her breathing quickened. "I need to go home. I'm sure they're waiting for me for dinner."

"You know me. I can't hold my tongue. Sorry if I'm running you off."

"No. It's okay."

"One more thing. And then I'm going to stay out of it, because you and Molly are both my friends. But if you have feelings for Gregory, then you need to do something about it. Otherwise, Molly will eventually make a move. And you might be too late."

She immediately thought of the near kiss. Of how badly she'd wanted to just forget all that lay between them and to jump right in. But she couldn't just indulge in a stolen kiss or two when there was no way they had any hope of a relationship.

"No, Donna Rae. I can't let myself have feelings for him. I can't trust him." She wasn't sure she could trust any man, for that matter.

"You've got first dibs in my book, what with holding hands around The Forever Tree and all. But those boys need a mom. And if Molly steps into that role first.... That's all I'm sayin'. Just think about it."

She gave Donna Rae's hand a squeeze. "Thanks. Duly noted."

She left and drove home.

After a quick change of clothes, she joined her mom in the kitchen to finish preparing dinner, her mind still on the near kiss.

Well, technically, he had kissed her. For a split second. But of course, she had freaked and turned her head.

Not easy to do when her heart was screaming for her to kiss him back.

"What's wrong?" her mother asked. "You've been distracted since you got home."

"Nothing." She spooned rice out of the pan into a serving bowl, trying to focus on the yummy jasmine aroma that was making her stomach growl.

Katherine narrowed her eyes. "You saw Gregory today, didn't you?"

"Yes, out front of his house, while on a ladder putting up icicle lights."

"And now you're acting all dreamy and preoccupied."

Sarah added a tad of milk to thin the gravy as she considered how much to disclose since her mom had always disapproved of Gregory. "I'm just a little confused right now. I'm happy to help him and the boys, but…well, it's making me crazy, too. Because I enjoy being around him, too."

In a flash, Katherine took the spoon out of Sarah's hand and turned her so they faced each other. Then she grabbed both of Sarah's arms and gave her a gentle shake. "Well, don't. Strengthen yourself with the knowledge that he left you for a fling with Delia. He got her pregnant, Sarah. Right after telling you he loved you."

As if she needed a reminder. "You don't have to throw that in my face just because you're scared I'll fall for him again. I won't." She grabbed the spoon once again and stirred the gravy. "You'll be proud to know I turned away when he tried to kiss me today."

Katherine gasped. "Sarah…."

"It's okay, Mother. I just want you to know I can

resist him." She smiled really big. "See, I'm fine now after talking about it. You helped clarify everything."

"Well, I certainly hope so. You can't risk becoming attracted to him again."

No, she couldn't. And she wouldn't.

The next morning, Sarah got a call from Harry in Atlanta. "Sarah, I'm sorry to call at the last minute. But I need a favor—if it's not too much to ask."

"Sure, anything."

"Hunter and Chase have Christmas parties today. And I'm worried that Gregory might not make one or both, so…" He trailed off as if waiting for her response.

She took the bait without missing a beat—and with a little leap of joy inside. "Say no more. Tell me when and where." *How pathetic am I?*

Once he relayed the information, she hung up. She turned and found her mom eavesdropping. "So you've resorted to snooping?"

"Just watching out for my daughter. What are you doing with Hunter and Chase today?"

"Christmas parties at school. Then I was hoping you wouldn't mind me bringing them over to bake cookies."

She sighed. "Honey, Gregory is dangerous enough without you falling in love with those cute boys."

"I'm not stupid. I know I need to be careful."

"Especially with Hunter reminding you of Peter."

"Actually, the more I get to know Hunter, the less I think of Peter. And I'm not going to give up on my plan now. Gregory is spending more time with his sons, so I'm succeeding. It's helping to ease the pain over Peter's death."

"And once Gregory and the boys seem to be doing okay?"

She understood what her mother was intimating. Would she be able to stand aside and let father and sons move on with their lives?

Of course she would. "If he scales back on his time at work, we'll all celebrate that he's seen the light. Then I'll relax and enjoy my Christmas."

"And then you'll head home to Nashville without looking back?"

Even as her stomach did a panicky flip-flop, she nodded, a decisive bob of her head. "Just like I always do."

"If you can promise me that, I'll quit snooping and pestering. And you're welcome to invite Hunter and Chase over to bake cookies."

She held her hand up as if in a court of law. "I promise."

Gregory hurried to the Jolly Time Day Care Center. He was late, and couldn't find a single spot to park. Thankfully, with a truck, he could go just about anywhere, so he bumped up over a curb and parked partially in the grass.

He ran through the front door, signed in, and rushed toward the sound of someone reading a story. He stopped at the door to check out the situation.

A group of parents and children sat on the floor while the teacher stood up front holding up a book, showing the illustrations.

Where was Chase?

He scanned the room, looking for a little boy by himself, but didn't see his son. So he started scanning for red hair.

Nothing.

Assuming someone was blocking his view, he walked around to the side of the room. A little carrot-top immediately caught his eye. But Chase was sitting—

He was sitting in Sarah's lap. How in the world…?

Chase leaned back against her, totally relaxed. Totally comfortable. As if he belonged there.

She rested her cheek against the top of his head, as if she, too, belonged right where she was. A motherly gesture that tore at his heart. His kids hadn't had that kind of tender affection since Lindsay moved away. Sure, they enjoyed the wrestling and tickling, the tossing them up in the air. But how often did he sit with them in his lap? How often did he hug and kiss them?

An old, familiar ache hit him, the pain he had after his mother died, while his dad pulled away and grieved. Even though Gregory had been sixteen at the time, he remembered missing her soft touch.

Dear Lord, I need Your help here. This scene looks a little too good to me.

As if she sensed him staring, Sarah looked up and met his eye. She sat up straighter, surprised maybe, then smiled at him. But as soon as she did it, she checked her smile and seemed to withdraw. As if the first reaction to seeing him had been a mistake.

He forced his legs to move, to carry him around the back of the room to join Sarah and Chase on the other side.

Gregory sat on the floor beside Sarah. As soon as Chase saw him, he launched over into his lap and grinned up at him.

Would Gregory's lap be enough? What if no matter

how well he provided for Hunter and Chase, it would never be enough?

The story ended a couple of minutes later.

"You came!" Chase said. "Both of you came!"

"Yeah, I told you I would but I might be late."

Sarah looked at him through squinted eyes.

"What?"

"Oh, nothing. I'm just surprised to see you. Your dad told me he didn't think you could make it."

"Now why would he say that? I told him I'd be at the day care party."

"What about Hunter's party?"

"Well, I did say I might not be able to make that one."

"I have something to show you." Chase hopped up and ran across the room to his cubby.

"You have to go, Gregory. You can't make Chase's party but not Hunter's. He might feel cheated."

It grated on his already-raw nerves to have her hounding him. "I have an appointment that I can't miss. A bid for a huge new home improvement warehouse."

"I'll go to Hunter's party. But it would be great if you could stop by for any amount of time."

"Okay. Sure, if I can."

He hated the thought of disappointing Hunter, especially with all the rough times lately.

And he also hated the thought of disappointing Sarah.

"Dad, look what I made." Chase held up a reindeer made from a candy cane. It had pipe cleaner antlers and wiggly eyes. And a red puff nose. "Can we leave now?"

"Not now, son. I have to go back to work."

"I'll be picking you up later, Chase. I have something fun planned."

"Goody!" He ran off to play with a friend.

"So will I see you at the elementary school?" Sarah asked, a smirk on her face.

"You're persistent, aren't you?"

She simply smiled.

"I'll see what I can do."

A few hours later, Sarah sat beside Hunter at a kid-sized table eating Rice Krispies treats, carrot sticks and pretzels.

Hunter seemed despondent that his dad hadn't come. Sarah couldn't quite fill that void.

He poked at his food. "Do you want to see my bag of Christmas decorations?"

"I'd love to, Hunter. Did you make them?"

"Yes, ma'am." He pushed his food aside and stood to look inside the decorated paper grocery bag. He pulled items out one at a time.

"Here's a reindeer made from my handprints. And here's a picture of me sitting in Santa's lap."

"Oh, that's so cute. Did he come to your school?"

"Yes. And here's an ornament I made."

It was made of beads on pipe cleaners. "Oh, I love that one."

"You can have it." He held it out to her and gave her a tentative smile, his first since she'd arrived at the school and he'd seen that Gregory wasn't with her.

Her first reaction was to tell him his dad would want it. But then she realized he was making a genuine offer. A heartfelt offer.

"I would love to have it. Thank you so much." She took it from him and bent one of the pipe cleaners to loop over her pearls. "See, I can wear it now, then take it home and put it on my tree."

Hunter giggled. "You look silly. Like a Christmas tree."

She was so glad to see him laugh that she did a silly dance, acting like a talking Christmas tree.

He went into a fit of giggles and threw himself on the floor laughing, holding his sides.

"Nice dance."

Gregory. Behind her. Watching the whole stupid act.

Her face burned hot, but she placed a cool smile on her face. "Why, thank you. I'm glad you enjoyed it."

He grinned at her as he glanced down at her new necklace charm. "Nice ornament, too."

"Thank you. Your son made it for me."

Gregory bent down and tickled Hunter. Then he helped him up. "Sorry I'm late, son."

"It's okay. We were eating."

"I'm glad you made it," she said, so pleased, yet trying not to grin like a fool.

"You want to see all my decorations?" Hunter asked.

"Sure. Did you make them?"

"Yep. Every one of them." He showed Gregory what was already on his desk, then he pulled several more projects out of his bag. "And I gave Miss Sarah that one with the beads."

He didn't glance at the necklace. He looked her straight in the eye. "Very nice."

Oh, goodness. It felt as if he were talking about her. She clenched her hands together. "Well, Hunter, it looks as if the party is winding down. I should probably go."

"Yeah, me, too," Gregory said.

"I think they'll let you sign me out early. Pleeese, Dad!"

"Actually, they do have a sign-out sheet hanging on the classroom door," Sarah said. "I saw it when I came in."

"I guess all this school stuff is very familiar to you," Gregory said as his son bounced up and down, excited that he might get to leave early.

Very familiar. Except for the fact that her school's Christmas party got cancelled when they closed early. "Yes, like a home away from home."

"So you really like Nashville and your job."

"I do."

"I guess that's home now."

"Yes."

His blue eyes probed. Seemed to be examining her. Then he looked away so suddenly it jolted her. "Son, I have to go back to work. I can't check you ou—"

She stopped Gregory with a hand on his arm. "I can do it if you don't mind. And we could get Chase as well. I know your dad's out of town and…well, you need some help."

Hunter threw his arms around Sarah's legs. "Oh, thank you, Miss Sarah."

"I appreciate it. If you can watch them this afternoon, I'll try to get off work before dinner."

"Well, what a cute family you three make," someone said from behind Sarah.

"Hi, Miss Polly," Gregory said.

Not Polly. Sarah turned. "Hi, Miss Polly. Are you working here again?"

"I'm just subbing these days. The newspaper takes most of my time." She looked through the bottom of her bifocals. "Gregory, I'm glad to see you're dating again. It's time to find a mom for your boys."

Sarah wanted to crawl away and hide. It was obvious Polly had her daughter, Molly, in mind for the job. And poor Hunter stood there listening. Thinking of him cranked her mouth into gear. "I got to have lunch with Molly the other day. It's great to see her again."

"Oh, you went to the Quilting Beas party, didn't you? She told me she saw you. And that you two talked about…well, about a certain person. I guess maybe things have changed since you two talked."

"Uh, not really." Goodness, this talking in code was getting difficult in front of Hunter. And in front of Gregory. "Well, we should go. It was nice seeing you again." She turned to Hunter. "Why don't you get all your things? You won't be back to school until January!"

"So have you two been dating?" Polly asked.

"I've gotta run. Nice to see you, Miss Polly," Gregory said, escaping Polly's snare. "Hunter, you be good for Miss Sarah." He ruffled his son's hair, then strode out of the room with a quick, concerned look at Miss Polly, who just happened to be the gossip column writer for the local paper.

Great. Just what Sarah needed. To worry about her name plastered across the local newspaper's "Who, What, When, Where?" column, tied with Gregory's.

"Well, what have we here?" Sarah's dad asked as he walked into the kitchen that afternoon. He didn't look happy to find her with Hunter and Chase.

"We're decorating cookies," Hunter said, then returned to sticking his tongue out of the corner of his mouth to concentrate on spreading icing.

"See my spwinkles!" Chase said, showing off a cookie he'd piled high with red and green sugar crystals, Christmas tree-shaped sprinkles and nonpareils.

Her dad's face didn't soften one bit. "I see."

"You can eat it." Chase held out his masterpiece, a sweet offering to her dad.

"No, thank you," he said brusquely. He gave her a disapproving glare as he left the kitchen.

She nearly followed him out to give him a piece of her mind. But she couldn't do that with little ears so close by.

Chase looked a little disappointed that her dad hadn't praised his cookie. But the cooling rack drew his attention. "Miss Sawah, can I make another one?"

"Of course. You can decorate as many as you like. We'll wrap them up and take them to some of the homebound people from our church."

"What's homebound?" Hunter asked.

"People who are too sick or too old to leave their houses very often."

"That's sad," Hunter said. "I bet they'll like cookies."

"They sure will. And we'll even take some to Miss Donna Rae if you'd like."

"Yeah," Chase hollered.

As the boys continued decorating, Sarah wrapped the cookies. "You know, your dad is supposed to pick you up in a little while. Maybe tonight he can take you to make your deliveries."

"He has to work tonight," Hunter said, his face drawing downward in a frown.

"No, since your granddad is out of town, he's going to pick you up before dinner."

"Really?"

Oh, please, Gregory, show up on time. Don't make a liar out of me. "Really."

While the boys continued decorating, she slipped off to the dining room to call him.

"Hi, Sarah," he answered as if he expected her call. "So, what do you have planned for me today?" Then he laughed.

The sound sent a frisson of joy—and fear—bolting through her. She'd always loved to hear him laugh. But she didn't want to love it too much right now.

"Your sons have made some beautiful Christmas cookies for you to deliver to the homebound. I just wanted to make sure you'd be on time to pick them up."

"I should be there as planned. I am *finally* at the store buying the big gifts. I have to take this stuff by the house to hide it. I'll be there in a half hour."

Her heart hurt, because now he would feel like he had to work extra just to pay for the gifts. "Okay. See you soon."

"Is Dad coming?" Hunter called from the kitchen.

So much for slipping off to call privately. Not much got by him.

She walked back to the messy kitchen table. "Yes. He'll be here in a bit."

"Woo hoo," Hunter squealed, pumping his fist in the air.

"Woo hoo," Chase mimicked, making a chubby fist and looking at it as he swung it back and forth.

"Now, let's finish up so you'll be ready when he gets here."

* * *

Fighting the temptation to simply honk for Sarah to bring the kids out, Gregory climbed out of his truck, laughing at how that would have gone over with her parents. As he rang the bell, he prepared to face Winston and Katherine. Being in their territory—with the trappings of wealth all around—used to intimidate him. But he refused to give in to old insecurities.

"Hello, Gregory," Katherine said as she opened the door and let him inside. "Your sons are in the kitchen." She wasn't as cool as he'd expected. But then, she'd always been the queen of politeness.

"I appreciate you letting them come over," he said.

"They're a delight. You must be proud."

He looked toward her. She sure was being nice for a change. "Yes, very proud."

"Come this way." She led him through a grand foyer, past an elegant curving staircase, back to a huge kitchen that had obviously been updated since the house was built.

"Dad, look!" Hunter yelled through lips tinted green, apparently from cookie icing. Chase's looked the same.

Gregory laughed. "Hi, guys. Did you eat 'em all, or did you leave a few cookies to deliver?"

"We have lots to deliver," Hunter said. "But here's one you can have." He held out a cookie piled high with icing and sprinkles.

Gregory glanced at Sarah.

She nodded toward the cookie, eyes sparkling, as if she couldn't wait to see what he would do. "It's all yours."

"So generous of you. Are you sure you wouldn't like it?" he asked, smiling.

"Oh, but I already had one. Or three."

He looked to see if her lips were stained green. But they were just rosy and looking all too kissable.

"But, Dad. We made this one just for you."

He turned away from Sarah and looked at Hunter. "Wow. Thank you." He took it from his son's sticky, green-and-red-stained fingers. It wasn't very appealing, but he wouldn't refuse it for the world. Sarah watched with a grin on her face as he bit into it.

While he chewed, he held the rest of the cookie up in a mock toast.

She laughed, probably because she knew how over-the-top sweet it was. And maybe even because she remembered that he wasn't a huge fan of sweets.

"Hello, Gregory." Winston's voice cracked through the kitchen like a lash of a whip against his nerves.

Sarah's smiled died, and she herded the boys to the sink to wash their hands.

Gregory's hands and mouth were coated in cookie. He turned and nodded toward the man as he dusted his hands off and reached out to shake. Why did the man make him feel as if he was eighteen again? As if he were some kind of lowlife come skulking around his daughter.

"Mr. Radcliffe, look how many cookies we made!" Hunter yelled over the running water.

"Very good," he said to Hunter, yet never taking his eyes off Gregory. Then he shook Gregory's hand with an extra-firm grip and an angry glare. Almost as if warning him to stay away.

Gregory kept his grip just as firm, determined not to show a trace of weakness, because the man had the instincts of a seasoned predator.

Once Gregory swallowed the last of the cookie, he said, "Hello, sir." He finally let go and turned to his kids. "Come on, guys. We need to get going."

"They're ready," Sarah said as she dried Chase's hands hurriedly, then snatched up a box from the table. "Boys, you two head on out to the truck. I'll be right behind you with the cookies."

"Thanks for having them over," Gregory said to Katherine. "It seems they had a good time."

"Oh, the boys are welcome anytime," she replied. Had she said that intentionally to leave him out of the invitation?

"I'll be back in a minute," Sarah said to her parents.

Sarah's dad rocked back on his heels as if trying to look casual, relaxed. "Before you go… Gregory, could I have a word with you? In my office?" Even with the casual pose, his body language screamed tension.

Instinct told Gregory to refuse. But he didn't want to make a scene. "Sure. Sarah, could you wait outside with Hunter and Chase?" He handed her his keys.

She didn't say anything, but he could see the worry in her eyes, in her little frown.

He smiled at her, then followed her dad out of the kitchen. They went back toward the foyer, then veered off down a short hallway that led to an office they'd added to the side of the house many years ago.

Gregory had been in this office before.

That one time.

Winston stalked into the dark-paneled room the size of Gregory's office and living room combined. "Have a seat."

Gregory sat in a leather chair while Winston sat behind a huge, formal desk that probably cost as much as a small car.

Time to go on the offensive. "I can't imagine what you would need to discuss with me unless it has something to do with my sons' behavior today."

"Oh, I think you know one other person I might want to discuss with you." He leaned back in his chair and stared at Gregory.

Gregory refused to be intimidated. He was no longer a scared teenager, heartbroken and pathetically in love with the man's daughter. He stared right back. "Why don't you get to the point?"

"You broke my daughter's heart once."

"Excuse me? I believe she dumped me—trying to please you and your wife."

"She still cared for you. Was silly enough to think you two might get together when she was older. But of course, we all know about your indiscretion soon after."

"You have some gall to run me down when it must've fit your plan perfectly."

"Well, I admit the end results pleased me. But I didn't like seeing my daughter suffer. And I won't watch her suffer again."

"You have no reason to be concerned."

"Oh, that's where you're wrong. I've seen the way you look at her. And the way she looks at you. I've seen her smiling all dreamily when she comes home after being with your sons."

Gregory's heart galloped inside his chest. Could it be true? "You're imagining that."

"I won't risk it. We had an agreement."

"More than fifteen years ago. Doesn't apply now."

"And you're breaking it," he said as if Gregory hadn't

spoken at all. He leaned forward once again. "I want you to stay away from her, or I'll tell her about that little agreement you so willingly accepted."

His gut clenched. "You wouldn't do that. It would hurt her."

"No, I don't think it would. I think it would make her see you for the person you are. And she would be glad to know the truth."

Maybe the truth would be a good thing after so long. But it made him sick to have Sarah thinking the worst of him, and having proof he was low-class scum. No, he had to keep her dad from digging up the past. "I don't think you really want to do it. She would be crushed that her father bribed the man she loved to stay away from her."

"But she never really loved you, Gregory. And what feelings she had were killed when you went after Delia."

Chapter Eight

Gregory stormed out of the office and out of the oppressive house. He began to calm as he all but ran down the steps. Then he slowed to try to compose himself before reaching the truck.

Winston Radcliffe was hateful. Vindictive. He would risk hurting his daughter just to make sure Gregory stayed away from her.

But wouldn't she be better off if he stayed away? He couldn't provide for her like she was used to, anyway. And—

How ridiculous could he get? She wouldn't give him a second look. She had no respect for him. And once her dad informed her that Gregory had taken the bribe money, she would hate him for sure. It would be further confirmation that he wasn't good enough for Sarah Radcliffe. And never would be.

He yanked open the door and climbed in.

His main concern, though, was for Sarah. He couldn't stand the thought of how hurt she'd be to find out. He had to stay away.

Sarah closed Chase's door and stepped beside Gregory's open door. "You okay?"

"Yeah. Sure."

She stood with the box of cookies in hand. And he could predict how the scenario would play out if he took them from her. The boys would invite her along.

No way could he do that.

"Hey, guys, with the delay, I can't take you to deliver cookies this evening. It's dinnertime already."

"But Dad, you said you would," Hunter whined.

"Pwease, daddy?" Chase added.

Both pleas highlighted what a rotten human being Gregory was.

"I'm sorry. Miss Sarah will have to do it."

On Saturday morning, Sarah prepared for dress rehearsal, then remembered the box of cookies that she'd been left holding last night when Gregory left so quickly. The boys had been so disappointed. Maybe she could talk Gregory into helping deliver them later in the day.

When she arrived at the church, his truck was already there. The boys hopped out as she was parking.

As soon as she opened her door, Hunter and Chase popped into her space.

"We helped Dad make the manger," Hunter said proudly.

"Yeah," Chase said.

"What a nice surprise. I can't wait to see it." She stood and looked over the top of her car.

Gregory nodded a tentative hello. Then he climbed out of his truck and walked around to open the back. He didn't speak. Didn't look at her. He was in self-protect mode. She recognized it from years before.

What's the deal?

"And we worked on my talking part again last night," Hunter added with a proud grin. "I can do it by myself!"

"You've really worked hard. I'm proud of you." She ruffled his hair as she watched his dad out of the corner of her eye.

Gregory carried the manger to the front door of the church, but then he had to wait for her to come unlock it.

She loaded her arms and handed off some things to Hunter and Chase to carry. When they reached the door, she handed him the key.

"It looks perfect," she said about the manger. "Thank you."

"No problem."

Without saying another word, he hauled the manger to the front of the church and set it on their makeshift stage. "Is there anything else in the car?"

"Yes, in the backseat."

He was like a cold wind blowing past as he headed past her and out the door.

She checked on Hunter and Chase, who were driving little Matchbox cars on the carpet. Then she followed him out.

He lifted up a box. "I see you still have the cookies."

"Yes. I was hoping we could deliver them today after rehearsal."

"I'm sure Hunter and Chase would love to. You can take them."

She walked around to the other side of the car and opened the door. She looked at him across the backseat. "But they'll want you to go, too."

"They'll get over it once you're on the way."

"What's wrong, Gregory? Did my dad say something to offend you last night?"

"He's just worried about you. Seems to think I broke your heart in high school."

That broken heart flip-flopped in her chest. "Well, you did."

He raised a brow and looked at her with his piercing blue eyes. "You do remember you dumped me, don't you?"

She put the doll that would play the Baby Jesus in the pageant into a canvas bag. "I remember that I asked you to wait so we could date freely later. But you couldn't wait and started dating Delia." *Dating.* That was putting it politely.

His hand stilled. "Biggest mistake of my life."

She jerked her gaze to his face. But he continued staring at the stack of items on the seat.

She couldn't believe he'd just admitted that. She waited, afraid to even breathe.

"Of course, I wouldn't trade my sons for anything," he added.

"Oh, I'm sure." She'd been so curious, she had to ask. "So what happened with you and Delia?"

He shrugged, then moved the box of cookies to the floor. "Once we lost the baby, and we realized what a mistake we'd made, we talked about divorce. But Pastor Eddie suggested counseling." He straightened up and walked around to her side of the car. "This isn't easy to talk about."

"I'm sorry. I didn't know—just assumed you were happy."

He shook his head and looked off down the road.

"Nothing helped. We separated a few times over the years. Then she decided kids might help."

"I guess that's never the answer."

"You know, I never could please her. Didn't have a good enough job. Never made enough money. Didn't give her the house she wanted. Refused to let her parents give us money." He shoved his hands into his pockets. "But I could give her children. Thought maybe that would make her happy."

"But it didn't."

"No. And then when Chase came along so quickly after Hunter, she didn't handle it well."

"I heard she deserted you."

"Yes. And you know, Sarah, I think any woman who could leave her children like that has a big problem. I begged her to get some help. But she refused. Then she took up with a man in Atlanta who could offer her the easy life, the best of everything."

"I'm so sorry." She touched a hand to his chest. Right over his heart as if she could ease the pain.

All this time she'd pictured him and Delia so happy. She thought Delia had just stepped into her dream and stolen the life she'd planned.

But they'd been living their own private nightmare.

He put his hand over her hand, squeezed, but then let go and backed away. "Hey, it's all in the past." He pasted on his charming smile. "We survived. Chase doesn't remember her at all. Hunter used to be disappointed when she didn't come visit. And he used to ask for her. But once she lost contact with us, Lindsay took over."

"And now he's missing Lindsay."

"Yeah. But we're doing better." He stared into her eyes. "Thanks to you."

There was something warm in the depths of his eyes. Something…

Man, his eyes really packed a punch.

He suddenly moved into action. "We need to get this stuff inside." He loaded his arms and headed back inside, leaving her with her thoughts.

Leaving her with the stirrings of emotion she wasn't sure she could handle. Maybe she'd been too hard on him through the years.

But why had he given up on her and moved on to Delia in the first place? It still didn't make sense.

It seemed he wanted to let the subject drop, though, so as soon as she walked inside, she asked, "Hey, do you have our nativity star yet?"

He smiled. A relieved smile? "Yep. I'll get it rigged up now."

They worked for a half hour before the children started showing up. Today was dress rehearsal. The last chance to make sure everything would go well on Thursday night—Christmas Eve.

"Look at the cool star," Hunter hollered to a friend. "My dad made it." What a difference from the last practice where he'd cried. Maybe his dad spending extra time with him—helping him with his lines, building sets for the play—had made the difference.

Maybe she'd actually done some good while being home for the holidays. Gregory had said as much. She hadn't been able to help Peter's family in time. But maybe she'd helped one family.

A sense of peace flooded her, peace she hadn't felt in a while. *Thank You, God, for taking care of these precious boys. For working good in this situation.*

As she moved the manger into place, it occurred to

her that she'd just prayed. For the first time in weeks. She smiled as she ran her hand over the rough wood, then placed straw inside. *Thank You for the birth of Your Son, the Baby Jesus.*

And thank You for being so patient with me. So loving. Lord, help me be faithful.

The pain of the last few weeks welled up once again—this time more for Peter's parents than for herself. And it wasn't as overwhelming as before.

Oh, Lord, help me continue to heal. And thank You that it's easing some already.

A light touch landed on her shoulder. "Are you cwying, Miss Sawah?"

She blinked, then turned toward Chase. "I'm fine. Didn't your dad do a nice job on the manger?"

"Yes, ma'am."

"Come on, let's go find—"

She bumped into Gregory. Right beside her. Had probably been there the whole time. "You okay?" he asked.

He wouldn't be as easily distracted as Chase. "I can tell you about it later."

"Chase, why don't you run over and play with Hunter for a minute so Miss Sarah and I can talk."

Chase zoomed to the back of the church toward his brother.

"So what's bothering you?"

"I've been angry at God over Peter. I haven't been able to pray for weeks. But I just looked at the manger and…" Embarrassment made her neck hot. She shrugged. "I was just feeling thankful Hunter seems to be doing better. And because I'm doing better, too."

A parade of expressions flashed across his face—

pain, frustration? Anger, even? Gregory seemed to fight some kind of battle. Then he pulled her into a rough hug. "I'm glad."

Her mind told her to shrug away, but it felt too nice to be circled in his strong arms. "I'm finally able to pray again," she told him, wanting him to share in the wonder.

Gregory held her tighter, and she rested her face against his chest, smelling the clean, fresh fabric softener in his soft cotton T-shirt. For some reason, it made her want to cry, because she didn't like to think of him washing all their laundry by himself with no help from a loving wife.

He drew away, but not too far. He looked at her face, probably to see if she was crying. But she had already cried buckets over Peter. She didn't think she had any tears left.

She stepped back one more step when she realized Hunter was looking their way. "Thank you. Sometimes a girl just needs a hug."

He appeared to tamp down whatever emotions he felt a moment ago. "I guess it's time we get this show on the road." He gestured toward the children, ending their conversation.

It was a good thing she wasn't the type to read too much into a hug.

And it was better that way.

"Time to get started," she called to the children. "Let's get in your places. We'll go all the way through it once, then we'll put on costumes and do it again."

This has got to be the longest rehearsal ever. Or at least it seemed that way to Gregory. He really needed to get away from Sarah. They'd said too much. Or at least he had.

And he'd felt too much.

Vinny walked in. *Good. A distraction.* Gregory waved him over.

He greeted Gregory with a handshake. "Sarah wanted to try something new this year. I'll be reading the Scripture with her," Vinny said.

"Seems like the pageant is going to be good, as usual."

When it was time for the reading of the nativity story, Vinny walked "backstage," which was behind a curtain that the custodian had hung every year for probably a decade. Vinny and Sarah took turns reading from the book of Luke over a microphone as the children reenacted the story onstage. Youth volunteers helped make sure they moved and spoke as needed. Gregory knelt near Hunter and whispered his lines whenever he paused.

Hunter seemed nervous, but he did fine whenever Gregory gave him his cues.

Once the play was over, everyone who was watching clapped. Gregory couldn't have been prouder.

Hunter fought a grin. The grin won.

"Okay, now the fun part," Sarah whispered to Gregory as she walked by. "Full costume."

After a short break for snacks, extra parents arrived to help dress the children.

Hunter's shepherd costume was made from what appeared to be a pillowcase. And there was a bedsheet. And also a towel?

When Gregory found holes cut in the pillowcase, he realized they could put it over Hunter's head. Once that was done, they tied the rope around his waist. But for the life of him, he couldn't figure out what to do with the towel or the sheet.

"I don't think shepherds wore pillowcases," Hunter declared very loudly.

"Probably not," Hunter's buddy, the other shepherd, said as if he were an expert on shepherds.

"What seems to be the problem?" Sarah asked.

Gregory looked around and realized they were the only ones not dressed and ready. "I can't figure out what to do with the towel."

"Miss Sarah, I don't think they wore pillowcases. I think they wore real clothes," Hunter said.

Sarah laughed, but then got control of herself as she knelt down in front of him. "Well, what would you like to wear?"

"I don't know." He looked up. "Dad, can we get online and find out what real shepherds wore?"

"A pillowcase works for me," he said, hoping Sarah would back him up. But she didn't say anything. She stared at him as expectantly as his son did.

"But it's white," Hunter whined. "Didn't shepherds work with sheep? Outside?"

"Yes, Hunter, they did. They lived outside with them," Sarah said.

"Then I bet their dads wouldn't let them wear white or they would get really dirty."

Gregory regretted ever refusing to let Hunter wear white T-shirts. But he'd been so tired of bleaching out grass and red clay stains.

"I'll tell you what. Why don't you wear this today," Sarah said as she adjusted the pillowcase on him. After that, she put the towel on his head, then stretched an elastic band around it to hold it in place. "And you and your dad can do some research and make you something else for Thursday night."

"I wouldn't have any idea how to make a costume," Gregory felt compelled to admit.

"I'm sure Hunter will help you." She winked at Hunter, then walked away.

Great. Now he had one more crafty thing to add to his to-do list. One more thing to make him feel totally inept.

"Places, everyone! We're ready to go through this one more time."

As they worked through the pageant in costume, they had several major goof-ups. Also, his star didn't function properly when they tried to lower it. And Hunter rolled his eyes and sighed through his lines as if wearing a white shepherd robe were too humiliating to survive.

By the time they finished, Sarah, who was normally so calm and cheerful, looked a little panicky.

She gathered everyone in a circle once they were finished. "Well, it looks like we're going to need our optional rehearsal on Wednesday."

The kids groaned.

"I'm sorry. I know you're getting tired of practicing. But we'll just go through the play one time in full costume. That's all. And I'll bring you a treat."

Cheers rose up in the sanctuary.

"Good. It's a plan."

She stood by the door and informed the other parents as they picked up their children.

Once everyone had gone, Chase, still standing there in his little angel costume, said, "Miss Sawah, can we dewiver the cookies today?"

"Well, I brought them, hoping we could. Gregory?"

It would be the perfect time to shop if she took the boys for a while. With the added bonus that he would be following Winston's edict to stay away—and following his own good sense as well. "It's fine for you to take them. I could use the time to get some things done."

"But, Dad, you have to come," Hunter said. "Please?"

"Pwease?" Chase echoed.

"Please?" she added, then grinned because she knew she had him.

It shouldn't take long. And besides, was he really going to let Sarah's dad dictate what he did or didn't do with his own sons?

"Well…"

No, he wouldn't let the vindictive man hurt Hunter and Chase. Besides, he still couldn't imagine Winston ratting himself out.

"Okay. You boys take your costumes off and I'll give you one hour."

They didn't even take the time to celebrate. They moved faster than ever to get undressed so they could deliver those silly cookies.

Lord, am I a bad dad? Should I be more patient and giving? 'Cause I can't seem to get this fatherhood thing right.

Help them to turn out okay despite me.

"Thank you for going with us," Sarah said. "I need to put the microphones away, then I'll be ready."

Within ten minutes, they were all locked up and ready to take cookies to people who, he hoped, had a huge sweet tooth.

Sarah pulled a piece of paper out of her purse. "Okay. I made a list."

They delivered the first three packages to the nursing home in town. The boys were a little timid. In fact, Hunter was downright scared as he walked along the hallway lined with wheelchairs. He gripped Gregory's hand so tightly it started to hurt.

But Chase smiled and waved and said hello to all. And Sarah called people by name that Gregory could barely recognize.

"Oh, there's the famous couple, now," a woman in a wheelchair by the front door said. She waved a folded newspaper in the air.

"Uh-oh," Sarah said under her breath.

As he looked at Sarah for a clue, she put a big smile on her face and approached the woman.

"Hello, Mrs. Buckner. How are you doing?"

"Oh, I'm just fine. I loved reading about you and your handsome gentleman, here." She looked up at Gregory. "Nice to see you, young man."

"Hello, Mrs. Buckner. Nice to see you, too." He couldn't place her name at all.

"Yessiree, it sure is nice to see good news in the paper for a change." She smiled down at the boys. "And these young 'uns need a mom, since—"

"Here you go," Sarah thrust a bag of cookies into Mrs. Buckner's lap, interrupting whatever she was about to say. "Have some yummy cookies the boys made. Boys, why don't you go sit in the rocking chairs on the front porch and wait for us."

Thankful to escape, Hunter led the way at a near run.

"As I was saying, those young 'uns need a mom since their mama lit out on 'em. 'Bout time you found someone, son."

Mrs. Buckner whipped open the newspaper and

began to read. "'A new family seems to be forming in the Gregory Jones household. Sarah Radcliffe, home visiting for Christmas, was seen playing the role of mom for Hunter at—' Which one's Hunter?" She tilted her head as if confused all of a sudden.

Sarah let out a big breath as if relieved. "He's the older one with the dark hair."

"Cute boy."

"Well, enjoy the cookies, Mrs. Buckner," Sarah said. "We have to hurry home."

"Oh, how sweet. Thank you. Good luck with your second marriage, son. I think it'll go better this time around."

"Merry Christmas," he said, trying not to laugh. And at the same time he was mortified that all that garbage would be in the newspaper.

Polly had outdone herself this time.

As they gathered the boys, it hit him that it wasn't a laughing matter. Winston would certainly see the "The Four W's" column.

When he got to the truck, he said, "Any idea how to do damage control?"

"I'm sure most people around here know to take her gossip column with a grain of salt."

As they pulled away from the nursing home, he said, "You sure seemed to know a lot of the residents. Have you been here before?"

"My mom coordinates a homebound visitation schedule for the church. I help when I can."

Of course. He should have known. Her mother also volunteered on almost every committee in town. It seemed she had her photo in the newspaper every other week for one charity event or another.

And now Sarah was following in her footsteps.

He felt his face draw downward into a frown. Though she'd said it wasn't the case, he hated to think that she might feel sorry for him. Or even for his kids.

That thought, combined with the newspaper article, made him start to think he shouldn't have gone along on the deliveries.

He needed to be more careful.

They made two quick home visits where he didn't even get out of the truck, then she directed him to Donna Rae's house.

"She's our last stop," Sarah said.

They rang the Durantes' bell. "Who is it?" a young voice asked from behind the door.

"Tell your mom it's Sarah, Gregory, Hunter and Chase," Sarah called.

The little voice yelled to announce the visitors. Then a pause. Then the door opened.

"Come in," Neal called as he ran toward the family room.

"Well, look who's here," Donna Rae said from the couch, where she lay on her side. "The newest victims of Miss Polly's gossip column."

His stomach clenched with a sense of foreboding. Had everyone in town read the thing?

"We heard a bit of it. I can't wait to read the rest," Sarah said. "But first…" She nodded at Hunter.

"We brought you cookies we made," he said.

Chase presented the bag. "Mewwy Chwistmas."

Donna Rae gasped. "Oh, how sweet of you. Can I open it now?"

"Yep," Chase said.

She peeked inside, pulled one out, then made a show

of tasting a bite. "Mmm. So yummy. Hey, would you two like to go outside and play?"

"Yes, ma'am," Hunter said.

"Well, go right through the kitchen and out that door. Neal was heading to the sandbox."

Once the boys were gone, Gregory said, "Okay, where's your copy of the paper?"

"Here on the table."

"Is it awful?" Sarah asked.

Donna Rae cackled. "Depends."

That didn't sound promising. Gregory snapped open the paper and located "The Four W's."

Sarah, obviously too impatient to wait her turn, hopped up and leaned over his shoulder. How was he supposed to read with her right there, brushing his shoulder, her fragrance wafting up his nose?

He tried not to breathe and focused on the column…

A new family seems to be forming in the Gregory Jones household. Sarah Radcliffe, home visiting for Christmas, was seen playing the role of mom for Hunter at the elementary school party. Though Sarah hasn't acknowledged the relationship, it's clear to see there's something going on there. No word from Gregory yet. He lit out once I started asking questions. Seems maybe this relationship is being kept secret for some reason. Or maybe he's interested in someone else? Only time will tell.

"Unbelievable," he said as the foreboding morphed into full-fledged dread. Winston would be livid. And might fight back.

"That's got to be illegal," Sarah said.

Donna Rae just laughed again. "I guess you could demand a retraction in next week's paper."

Gregory folded the paper closed and dared look at Sarah.

Her face was on fire, and she looked as if she was ready to do battle. "My parents are going to have a fit."

Even with this awful predicament, he had to smile. "That makes me feel really good." Part of him really did feel bad she would say it, though. That apparently they'd been telling her to stay away from him.

But could he blame them?

"Aw, phooey. No one pays any attention," Donna Rae said.

"We just did." He stood and handed her the newspaper. "Thanks for warning us about the article."

"Well, at least she can't do any more damage for a full week," Sarah snapped before walking through the kitchen to holler for Hunter and Chase.

When she returned, Donna Rae asked, "So how did rehearsal go?"

Sarah rubbed Hunter's back. "It was a little rough once we put costumes on. So we're going to have the optional rehearsal on Wednesday."

"That usually happens. It distracts the children to have the costumes on."

"Dad and I are going to make me a new costume," Hunter said with a serious expression. "Because a shepherd wouldn't wear a white pillowcase."

Bless Donna Rae, she didn't laugh. With a very straight face, she said, "Oh, I bet you're right. Thank you for fixing that mistake."

Once Hunter looked away, Donna Rae winked at Gregory. "So, Dad, are you up for sewing a costume?"

"Ha ha."

"I imagine you can find a nice brown pillowcase," Sarah said. Her golden brown eyes sparkled, some of the life back in them, the anger now gone. She apparently got a kick out of his distress over the costume.

He'd be glad to play the fool, though, if it brought the shine back into her eyes.

"Yeah. We'll see about the pillowcase," he said.

"Oh, wait…" Donna Rae squiggled so she was sitting up a little more. Then she reached out with both hands. "Let's say a prayer."

Hunter and Chase moved first. They each took one of her hands. Then he and Sarah met in the middle and joined them. He had hold of Hunter. And of Sarah's soft, smooth, warm hand.

He hoped he could concentrate on the prayer.

He shut his eyes tightly and blocked her out.

"Dear God," Donna Rae said, "I ask that you be with these children and the adult helpers as they work on a program to glorify You. Be with each and every one of them. Touch the hearts of all who attend the performance." She paused and waited.

Gregory jumped in next. "Thank you for all the hard work the kids have done. And please help Donna Rae and the baby to stay safe and healthy until delivery."

"You can take a turn, too, boys," Donna Rae whispered.

Gregory's heart raced. He'd not taken the time to pray with his children like he knew he should have. They barely ever remembered their nighttime prayers. And even when he remembered, he usually did it quickly himself.

"Dear God…" Hunter said loudly, confidently "… please bring us a mom to love us."

Sarah's grip tightened. His racing heart nearly stopped. Did Hunter not feel loved?

Gregory opened his eyes and looked at his son. Hunter's eyes were squeezed shut, and his little face was so earnest.

Lord, help me. I had no idea… What can I do?

Hunter leaned toward Donna Rae. "Can I ask for that?" he whispered.

"You can tell God anything," she whispered back. "In fact, He knows it already."

"Me too," Chase said as if he'd waited for Donna Rae's approval. "I want a mommy."

"Amen," Sarah said abruptly. Probably trying to end the awkward, painful situation. She dropped his hand as if they were playing hot potato. "Well, we should go."

"Yeah, and I have to get over to Richard's to help him. He's moving back to town into Lindsay's old house today."

"It'll be good to have him home," Donna Rae said. "Thanks for visiting. And boys, thank you for the cookies. Come hug me."

They hugged her, then took off toward the front door.

His boys wanted a mom badly enough to pray—out loud—and ask for one. And not just any ol' mom. But one who loves them.

Chapter Nine

On Sunday morning as Sarah got ready for the church service, she still couldn't get Hunter and Chase's prayers out of her head. *Please bring us a mom to love us.*

She couldn't forget her reaction either. As soon as the words left Hunter's mouth, she'd thought *I want to be that mom.*

She mashed her hand against her heart. *Oh, Lord, please help them. I may be way out of my league, here. What if Gregory spending time with his sons isn't going to be enough?*

And what if spending the holidays with Gregory wasn't going to be enough for her, either? She'd been enjoying the time with him a little too much. Enjoying the time with his family a little too much, too. So much so that it was going to be hard to leave and go back to Nashville.

Well, there was nothing she could do about that now, other than to be more careful. To try to remain job-oriented. Her job was to help Gregory spend time with his sons, to help him realize how family was everything.

She was doing her part. Now Gregory would have to do his.

But find a wife?

The name *Molly* reverberated in her mind. Jealousy raged through her system. No, she didn't want it to be Molly.

"I have to think about this rationally," she said to herself in the mirror as she applied mascara. "I have to help those boys in any way I can." *But what if that means stepping aside and watching Gregory make a move for Molly?* She stared at her brown eyes. Her limp, straight, pale hair.

And then she thought of Molly, with her glorious head of curls in the most beautiful golden-red color. Her striking green eyes.

Chase looked like he could be her son.

Sarah slapped on some lipstick, then hurried downstairs to get away from her thoughts.

"Are you two lovely ladies ready?" Dad asked as he offered an arm to each of them. They looped their arms through his and left the house.

As he helped Sarah into the car, he said, "Did you see the local paper yesterday?"

"Yes. It's a total misrepresentation, as you can guess."

"Is it?" He tried to sound casual, but she sensed the underlying anger.

"Yes. She saw me at Hunter's party and jumped to conclusions."

"Why did you go if Gregory was there?"

"Harry asked me to. He thought Gregory couldn't make it."

"I don't like it. It seems like Gregory may be setting up these meetings."

A laugh burst out of her. Because she knew how badly she'd frustrated him lately. "Far from it. I have to force him into every activity."

"Well, maybe it's time to back off. To give him a chance to step up."

Maybe it was.

Then why did the thought leave her feeling edgy? "We'll see."

"I'm afraid I have to insist. Starting today, I'd like for you to back away from his family."

She jerked her gaze to his, not liking his tone of voice.

His stern expression eased…a little. He tried to smile. "Your mother and I want to spend more time with you."

Then quit going to parties every single day, she almost blurted. Instead, she clamped her mouth shut and reached for the door handle.

He took the hint and closed it for her. Then he got behind the wheel and drove them to church.

But in her dad's request, there was still an undertone of something…negative.

Yeah. That was it. It just felt negative. As if it really had nothing to do with whether or not her parents got to spend time with her.

Thoughts of her past with Gregory zipped through her mind. Thoughts also of how her parents had been so involved in trying to control her life, her friends, her boyfriend. Had Dad been so domineering back then?

Well, of course he had. He'd forbidden her from seeing Gregory. And now there was something about the tone of his voice, about the look on his face, which made it feel like more than just a request.

Threatened. She almost felt threatened.

Had her dad bullied her into breaking up with Gregory in high school? Or had she really chosen to because Gregory had been pressuring her to go to college locally when she'd dreamed of attending Wellesley?

When they arrived at the church and walked into the building, it felt different from entering for rehearsal or even for last week's service. A calm assurance wrapped around her, as if God was welcoming her back to His house. It brought a smile to her face as they sat in their regular pew.

The stage curtain was gone. Bless the custodian's heart. He had taken it down for the service and would replace it afterward so it would be ready for their play.

Once again, this time right as the organ music started, a ruckus of footsteps sounded in the back of the sanctuary.

The fact that she recognized them sent a cozy warmth through her system, relaxing her, making her smile.

Even their footsteps are becoming familiar.

"Hi, Miss Sarah!" This time it was Hunter who called out her name as they approached.

She smiled and waved at the boys. "Good morning," she whispered.

"Hi, Mr. and Mrs. Wadcwiffe," Chase added, his eyes bright as he leaned into the pew and flapped his fingers in a little boy wave.

"Hello, dear," her mother whispered.

Her dad stared straight ahead, ignoring them.

How could he ignore Chase's sweet greeting? Sarah

ruffled his hair and smiled at him, hoping to distract him from her dad's rudeness.

Gregory took the hint and moved his boys closer to the front to join Harry and Richard in the Jones family pew.

About the time the Jones family settled into their pew, Molly came in the side entrance with her mom. Sarah looked away so she wouldn't be caught glaring at Polly. She still couldn't believe the two of them were related, because Molly had always been so sweet. She must take after her dad.

Molly left her mom's side and went to sit in the choir loft.

"Why isn't Molly with the rest of the choir?" Sarah asked her mother.

"I think she's doing some special music today."

She was right. Later in the service, Molly picked up a guitar and sang a hauntingly beautiful song. Her voice was soothing, and Sarah could just imagine her singing lullabies to her own babies someday.

Oh, boy. I don't want to go there.

No, she couldn't avoid it. She had to think about Hunter and Chase. And once Sarah left to go back home, it might just end up that Molly would step into the role of mother.

She closed her eyes. *Lord, help me not be selfish. Help me to put the Jones family before my petty feelings.*

After the service, while a good many people were gathered on the sidewalk outside the church, Molly asked for everyone's attention. "I'd like to get a group together to go caroling tonight. I hope you'll all come!"

Sarah smiled. Though the bottom was supposed to fall out on the temperature that evening, and they would probably freeze, it would be a perfect way to get Gregory to spend an evening with his kids. "Great idea, Molly." Her gaze darted to Gregory, who seemed to be ignoring the idea.

"Okay, let's plan to meet here at five o'clock," Molly said in Gregory's direction. "We should be done in an hour or so."

As families headed to their cars, Sarah flagged down Gregory before he could climb into his truck.

His cologne wafted her way, and she had a flashback of being in his arms on the ladder the other day. Of being in his arms at rehearsal yesterday. "I'm sure Hunter and Chase will want to go caroling. I hope you plan to go."

"I usually work on billing and scheduling on Sunday afternoons. Plus, I was planning to help Richard unpack."

"This isn't until five o'clock."

"Pwease, Dad? I like to sing," Chase called from the backseat.

"I can help watch them this afternoon while you do your paperwork if it'll help," she said as the wind whipped leaves around her feet. She shivered.

"No, thanks. But I appreciate the offer." He took a step closer. "I'd give you my coat, but I didn't wear one."

"I'm okay. We do need to dress warmly tonight. A cold front seems to be passing through." She crossed her arms in front of her and rubbed her hands over her upper arms.

His warm hands followed suit. "You're ice-cold."

"So will you come tonight?"

A horn honked in greeting. Molly stuck her head out the window. "See you tonight."

Had she seen him touch Sarah and honked to break it up? Sarah stepped away from him, missing his warmth. "So...?"

Another car pulled up beside them.

Her parents' car.

Well, so what? She was tired of her dad's interference and rudeness. She hoped he'd seen them together.

"Are you ready, Sarah?" Her dad's stony expression didn't bode well. Yet he only looked at her. His gaze didn't stray to Gregory.

"Give me a second."

He rolled up the window but stayed put.

"Please say you'll come tonight," she said to Gregory.

He looked at the car, and even though the windows were tinted, and he couldn't see her parents, it seemed as if he was trying to have a stare-down with her dad. "Yeah. I'll be there. For the boys." He turned his attention back to her and smirked. "And to make you feel better—you know, spending quality time with them and all."

A laugh bubbled out. "You know me too well." As soon as the words left her mouth, she wished she could call them back. She didn't want to think about how well they knew each other. About how much they had shared when they were young and in love—things like the pain of him losing his mother, about his feelings of insecurity, about her desire to get away from her hovering parents and to feel as if she had the capability to make her own decisions, about her dream of being a kindergarten teacher, about his dream of running his own business and of being his own boss....

"Yeah, I guess I do know you pretty well. Or I used to," he said.

Her stomach dropped to her feet, then fluttered back upward. Why did he always make her insides do crazy things?

He climbed in the truck. "See you at five." He drove away without so much as a backward glance.

When she got in the car, her dad asked, "What did *he* want?"

"*He* didn't want anything," she snapped. "I stopped him to make sure he was going caroling tonight."

"And is he?"

"Yes." *Because I asked him to.*

"I see." He was agitated. Angry.

"I'm glad to see him doing more with his boys," her mom said. "So don't scowl so, Winston."

"I'm perfectly fine with him spending time with his family. I just don't want him around mine."

At five minutes after five, Gregory hurried Chase toward the front door.

"We're late." Hunter paced the entry hall all bundled and ready. "Hurry up."

"Okay." He zipped Chase's coat and grabbed his own. "Let's go. And hope they haven't left us."

When they arrived, everyone sat loaded into the van, and it was running. Sarah was standing outside the vehicle, watching for them. As soon as she saw his truck, she smiled and waved.

Knowing she'd been waiting for them made him smile and wave in return, even when he didn't want to be so pleased. Even when he wanted to try to remain aloof.

He really should stay away from her if he didn't want Winston airing his dirty laundry.

But how on earth could he do that if she kept pushing herself on him and the boys? If she kept playing social director of his family?

Hunter and Chase raced toward her and the church van. "Hi, Miss Sarah."

"Hi, Miss Sawah."

"Hi, guys. Hop on and buckle up."

Gregory managed not to run toward her like one of the kids. "Hi. Thanks for waiting."

"No problem. I was worried, though."

"Couldn't find Chase's warm coat." He opened the passenger door for her.

"Hi, there, Gregory," Pastor Eddie said from the driver's seat.

"Hi, Pastor Eddie. You think it's cold enough tonight?"

As the pastor laughed and commented on the weather, Gregory gestured for Sarah to climb in. It was a pretty big step, so he held her hand to assist.

The innocent touch nearly drove him insane. He wanted more. And he couldn't allow himself to want it. So after she was seated he slammed her door to break the connection.

When he climbed in the back of the van, there was only one seat left. Beside Molly.

Great.

"Hi, Gregory." She gave him a cute, freckled smile. But there was something about her smiles that always disturbed him. As if she wanted something in return.

He nodded to her and in the general direction of the van passengers. "Evening, everyone. Sorry to keep you waiting."

"Hey, big brother. Did you lose one of your mittens?" Richard sat in the very back, grinning. Always such a jokester.

It was nice to have him home for good. "Hey, don't make fun. I remember pinning yours to your jacket a few times when you were a snotty-nosed kid."

That prodded a big round of laughter, and it shut his baby brother up.

They drove outside of town to the home of an elderly couple and sang a few carols. Then they drove to Donna Rae and Vinny's house.

They and the four kids listened from the porch as they sang a round of "Silent Night," "Joy to the World," and then "We Wish You a Merry Christmas."

Molly played her guitar and led the singing. Such a beautiful voice. So talented. But he winced as Richard's voice carried to his ears.

Poor Richard was tone-deaf. But at least he seemed to be enjoying himself.

When he looked away from Richard, he discovered Molly smiling at him as she sang. But more than that, he noticed her smiling at his sons. She'd always been friendly with them and was generous with her time to teach them in Sunday school.

Lord, are You making me notice her tonight for a reason?

When they finished the carols, Donna Rae and Vinny's clan clapped and begged for an encore, even though they had to be freezing in the unusually cold weather.

Molly looked directly at him. "Gregory, what's your favorite? I'm taking requests."

"'White Christmas.'"

"That's not real likely in Georgia," Richard jabbed.

She didn't take her eyes off Gregory. "I love that one. Maybe if we sing it, it'll bring some snow our way."

She finally looked away and started the song.

As they were nearing the end, he caught sight of Sarah out of the corner of his eye. She was squatting down in front of Chase, warming his hands between hers, blowing warm air on them.

It was like a jolt of electricity, shocking his system.

He wanted Sarah in his life. And not just for Christmas vacation.

He was starting to want something so far out of his reach. So far out of the realm of possibility.

Having Sarah love him again was about as likely as that white Christmas in Georgia.

Sarah rubbed at Chase's cold, little hands, wishing she'd brought gloves so she could give them to him.

As they climbed back into the van, Molly said, "Here, baby, come sit by me, and I'll warm you up. You can even wear my mittens."

"Me, too," Hunter yelled. "I'm freezing." He barreled up the step and into the seat beside Molly.

Sarah patted Chase's back and nudged him onto the van. She forced herself to smile at Molly, who was simply being helpful. But it pained her to do so.

This was *not* good. She was even getting jealous of Hunter and Chase's attention to Molly.

Time to back off and let nature take its course.

She moved toward the front passenger door. Gregory stood there waiting for her.

Boy, if nature took its course, she'd like to march right up to him, run her arms inside his jacket and around his waist to warm her ice-cold hands, and then kiss him senseless. Senseless enough to forget their turbulent past. And she'd do it right in front of the pastor and Molly and everyone else.

But since that couldn't be allowed to happen, she smiled and said thank you as he helped her into the vehicle with his warm hands.

How could he stay so warm with his coat wide-open and no gloves? Standing there looking so strong, as if even the frigid wind couldn't faze him—rugged face with a hint of whiskers, a hint of laugh lines around his piercing blue eyes, slightly wavy hair whipping in the wind.

She turned to speak to the pastor so Gregory would close her door before she launched herself at him. *I must be going crazy.*

After several more stops to sing for homebound members, Pastor Eddie said, "Why don't we head back? I think we've hit everyone on my list. And it's gotten too cold for the little ones." He turned the van around and drove to the church parking lot.

Once they unloaded, Molly tugged Sarah to the side and whispered, "Did my mom have it all wrong in her column yesterday?"

"Yes. She jumped to some majorly wrong conclusions."

"That's what I figured." She fairly glowed with excitement. "Pray for me. I think it's time to make my move."

"Your move?" Sarah asked, even when she was nearly certain what Molly meant.

"For Gregory and the boys. I think I'm going to ask them out. I mean ask *him* out." She giggled, then pressed her hands to her cheeks. "My face is on fire. If I can just stop blushing, I'll go ask him." She looked heavenward, fanned her face, and then whispered, "Please help me."

And help me, too. Because I don't want her to do it.

Sarah hurried to her car. She couldn't bear to watch. It was like watching him date Delia all over again. Would he choose Molly like he'd chosen Delia?

I want him to choose me.

The realization sucked the breath from her.

Oh, this isn't good. It can't end well. The man practically cheated on me before. I can't fall for him again.

She shook her head, trying to get rid of whatever crazy notions had taken over her normally rational self. Then she started the car. She couldn't help but look for Gregory and Molly as she drove through the parking lot toward the exit. No matter how hard she tried, her eyes would not stay glued firmly ahead.

Molly was beside Gregory's truck. Smiling. Looking gorgeous. And nervous.

Gregory was smiling, too. And since she couldn't stop and stare, she pulled on around toward the front of the church and the main road.

Lord, this isn't good. I had good motives, but now I'm starting to get attached to Gregory. Please help me to do what I can to help him and his family. But protect me as well.

Gregory tried to focus on Molly as Sarah drove by. He really did. But all he could think about was where Sarah was going. What Sarah was doing that evening.

"…and so, well, I was wondering if maybe, well, you know…"

"I'm sorry, Molly. Something across the parking lot caught my attention. What were you saying?"

"Dad, I'm freezing!" Hunter yelled from his booster seat.

Molly laughed. "I was doing a really bad job asking you out on a date."

His eyes flew open wide. "Oh." Boy, he hadn't seen that coming.

"Tomorrow, maybe?"

"Well, I do have some shopping I need to finish."

"Oh, that would be perfect. I could help you." Her smile was so genuine. And she was truly beautiful. Inside and out.

But what he really wanted—

Nope. Don't even go there. Maybe he should give Molly a chance. His dad had even suggested it.

As bad as he hated to admit his dad was right, it *was* time to move on. His boys did need a mom.

One date. That's all it would take to jump back into the dating scene. He could manage that, couldn't he? "Sure. I'd like that. What time do you get off?"

"We close at five. But I can get off a little early if you need more time to shop."

"You know, I need to take the day off to work on Hunter's costume and to fix the malfunctioning star of Bethlehem." He laughed at how silly that sounded. But he was pleased at the same time. Maybe Sarah was getting to him after all. "How about I pick you up at your house at five?"

She grabbed his hands and squeezed. "Perfect. I'm really looking forward to it."

Oh, Heavenly Father, You know Your will for me. I need to know it, too. And fast. Because Molly asked me out.

But all I can think about is Sarah.

Chapter Ten

Sarah faced Monday with a blank calendar. She had absolutely nothing planned. And she didn't need to plan anything because Gregory had called the night before saying he was taking Monday off to get Hunter's costume ready and to make sure the pageant sets were back in place and ready to go for the last rehearsal. And to ask her advice on where to buy a brown pillowcase if needed.

She smiled into her coffee mug, pleased that he would have a whole day with his sons. She could just imagine how excited the boys were.

"What do you have planned with Hunter and Chase this morning?" her mom asked as they sipped coffee together at the kitchen table, taking turns with sections of the Atlanta newspaper.

"Nothing." She puffed up as if very proud of the fact.

"Really? And why is that?"

"Because he's taking the day off to spend with his family."

Katherine nodded. "Well, that's wonderful. It looks like your job is done."

Sarah frowned. Couldn't help it. And she didn't wipe it off her face before her mom saw.

"Sarah, honey, don't get sucked in," Katherine nearly begged.

Sarah plucked at a corner of the newspaper that had gotten folded under. "I'm not," she said, even though she knew it was a fairly high risk at the moment. "Plus, I'm pretty sure Molly Patton asked him out."

"Well, that's good." Her brows crooked in a frown. "Isn't it?"

Sarah patted her mom's hand. "Yes, of course it's good for him and the boys." She couldn't help but wonder when they would have their first date. Where they would go. What they would do.

"Excellent news," Winston said from the kitchen doorway, dressed in a suit and tie, ready to go to work. "The best news I've heard in a while."

Why did her father look so smug? So satisfied? "Are you spying?"

He chuckled, then kissed Katherine's cheek. "Not at all. I was on my way in to say I'd try to come home for lunch, and I didn't want to interrupt."

"It seems that Gregory has learned the value of spending precious time with his children," Katherine said.

"Then, Sarah, it's time for you to step back," Winston said. "You've done what you set out to do."

"You're right," she said as she stood and put her mug in the dishwasher. "That's why I'm free today. I'm going to go visit Donna Rae to see if she has any last-minute advice for the pageant."

"And tonight?" he asked.

She realized what he was doing and shook her head. "I'll be at home."

"And tomorrow?"

Wariness made her say, "I don't know yet." Was he trying to manipulate her?

He kissed the top of her head. "Well, I hope you'll spend some time with your family. We've missed you." Then he kissed his wife and left for the office.

Had she been ignoring her family? Was that why her dad had been acting strangely? Had she gotten so wrapped up in Gregory's life that she'd neglected her own?

Maybe it was time to spend an evening at home.

Gregory was glad he could take a day off when he really needed to.

He was *not* glad he had gotten himself into a jam, forcing him to take a day.

"So can we get online now?" Hunter asked. "Pleeee-ase…"

Might as well quit putting off the inevitable. "Okay, buddy."

While Chase played in his room, Gregory and Hunter moved an extra chair beside the computer in Gregory's office. Then he did a search for shepherd costumes.

"Cool! I like that one." Hunter pointed to a fairly authentic garb from a costume manufacturer.

"I'm afraid we're too close to the play to order one. We need to find out how to make one."

He did another search for how to make a shepherd costume. Several sites that had question-and-answer bulletin boards came up. "Here's one," he told his son.

He read the description out loud.

"Do we have a sewing machine?" Hunter asked.

"No. So let's try one of these other sites." He clicked

another link and read the description. He grinned at Hunter. "This one says to cut holes in a brown-striped pillowcase."

Hunter giggled. "I guess shepherds did wear pillowcases."

Gregory observed his son to see if he was serious. But he quickly noted Hunter was teasing. He hadn't realized his son had such a good sense of humor.

He ruffled Hunter's hair. "It looks like we need to go find us a nice brown or brown-striped pillowcase."

Hunter pointed to the screen. "Can I have one of those hook things?"

"Hmm. I guess you didn't have a staff at practice, did you?"

He shook his head.

"Well, we'll rig something up. What do you think we could use?"

"One of those canes that people use to help them walk."

"That's perfect. We'll see if we can borrow one. Thanks for suggesting it."

"You're welcome." Hunter smiled, very pleased that he'd contributed.

"Come on. Let's go find you a shepherd's pillowcase."

They laughed as they and Chase bundled up to go to the store. The temperature was still dropping. It was gray and overcast. And it smelled like snow.

By the time they left the store after purchasing the supplies, the sky was darkening. "Wouldn't it be something to have a white Christmas?"

"Awesome!" Hunter yelled.

"Awthum!" Chase echoed.

He grinned, happy that Chase loved trying to be like his older brother. Maybe Hunter would always be a good example. He hoped so, since he hadn't been a very good role model for his own younger brother. Though Richard had turned out just fine.

Gregory parked the truck in their driveway and turned it off. "Okay, let's go cut holes in this thing. Maybe we won't mess it up."

"How can you mess it up?" Hunter asked. "You just need one hole for my head and one for my left arm and one for my right arm."

Yeah, simple. If you're a five-year-old.

Ten minutes later, Gregory nearly pulled Hunter's ears off as he tried to shove the thing over his head—again.

"Owwww," he whined. "Take it off. It still doesn't fit."

Gregory tugged it back off and attacked the pillow-case head-hole opening with the scissors. He felt totally inept. How could it be so hard to cut three holes? "I'll cut it big enough for your whole shoulders this time."

"But I don't want my shoulders to hang out."

"I didn't mean that literally, Hunter. I just meant I would cut it plenty big." He made the last snip, then put it over Hunter's head.

It went on with ease.

"Daaad. Look what you did."

Gregory jammed his hands into his pockets. "It's not bad."

"But you can see my shirt underneath."

"Hey, at least you have your ears." He laughed as he tugged on Hunter's earlobe.

Hunter didn't appreciate the humor. "A shepherd doesn't wear a sweatshirt underneath his robe."

"A shepherd doesn't worry too much about fashion."

"But, Daddy, I'll be onstage. In front of *people*." His voice nearly cracked.

Poor thing. He was probably more stressed about being onstage on Thursday than about the costume.

"Come on. We have one more pillowcase in the package. I'll get it right this time."

"Can you make the arm holes a little bigger this time, please? My fingers are asleep."

Gregory yanked the case off Hunter's head as quickly as possible and resisted sighing. It wasn't Hunter's fault.

While he very carefully cut the new neck hole, Hunter said, "So what are we getting for Aunt Lindsay and Uncle Richard for Christmas? Are we going to make ornaments?"

He stopped mid-snip and looked at his son. "Oh, no."

"What's wrong, Dad?"

"I totally forgot their gifts. I never got the craft supplies from Sarah."

"Can we make stuff tomorrow?"

"I have to work tomorrow." And he also had to finish up buying for the boys. He still needed to get stocking stuff and a few little items. "I'll figure out something. And I'm going shopping tonight."

Man, how had Christmas crept up so quickly?

"So, what do you think about the news?" Donna Rae asked Sarah as soon as she walked in the door.

"What news?"

"You don't know?"

She smirked at her friend. "Maybe if you'd tell me what you're talking about, I could give you an answer."

"Molly and Gregory are going out together."

She sucked in a breath but managed not to let Donna Rae see her shock. "Well, I assumed that would happen. She told me she was going to ask him."

"Well, he must've accepted. I heard from Miss Polly."

"You mean you don't know for sure that he accepted?"

"Well, Miss Polly acted like it was a done deal. And she was pretty excited about it. She actually smiled."

The thought irked Sarah. She wasn't even sure Polly had teeth, since all she ever did was frown. And now she was all giddy? Once Sarah scooted a chair beside the couch and sat, she put aside her pettiness. "It's a good move for everyone."

"My foot."

"What's that supposed to mean?"

"I can tell by the look on your face that it's not a good move for you."

The muscles in Sarah's shoulders squeezed with tension. "Hunter and Chase are what's important, here. And it's a good thing for them."

"Granted, Molly would be a good mother for them. But so would you."

"I came here to keep you company. Not to be lectured."

"Oh, hon, I'm not lecturing. But Lindsay nearly waited too late and missed out on Bill. I don't want you to do the same with Gregory."

"So can we change the subject now? I need to think about dress rehearsal." That and about making it through the next few days so she could go back to Nashville and settle into her old routine.

And face the pain of an empty spot in her classroom. Donna Rae just stared at her, then shook her head.

"I've had some success while I've been home," Sarah said. "Gregory's actually taking a day off today. And the boys love the time they're spending with him. Can I just focus on that?"

"Well, that's great news." She smiled as she patted Sarah's hand. "You do what you need to do. I'll butt out."

After lunch, Sarah went out for a walk in the brisk cold to clear her head. The meal with her parents had been pleasant. Her dad behaved. Didn't try to tell her what to do. Didn't talk down Gregory.

But he'd been on edge. And he'd watched her as if afraid she might break or something.

Was he worried because of Peter's death? Did she seem fragile?

The wind kicked up leaves and dirt that swirled around her. Even with the dreary weather, she felt better. She'd felt a little better each day. The constant sadness had lifted. And now Gregory had given her hope for his family.

She could go back to Nashville, secure in the knowledge that his family was healing. And though she had no hope of a future with him, at least maybe now she'd be able to let the past go and move on. To try dating some. And maybe she'd actually be able to risk loving someone again.

She turned around and headed home. She simply hadn't dressed warmly enough.

When she walked in the house, her mom met her at the door. "Gregory asked that you call him. It's urgent."

"Are the kids okay?"

"He didn't mention anything about them."

She popped open her cell phone and made the call. As soon as he answered, she said, "Is everything okay?"

"Oh, we're fine. Sorry to scare you."

She made a growling sound. "Don't do that to me again."

"I said I'm sorry. But it is urgent. I need a babysitter for tonight."

"I thought you were going to spend your new free time with your sons."

"I'm trying the best I can. But I have a lot of gifts to buy. Including—" the phone rustled as if he was looking around "—stocking stuffers," he whispered.

Okay, she was going to try not to judge him. She hadn't been in his situation before, so she couldn't be certain what she would do. "Did you ask your dad to babysit?"

He sighed. "The man is acting so strange lately. He said he has plans. To try asking you."

Perfect opportunity for Molly to step into the role she seemed to be coveting. "Have you thought to ask Molly?"

Dead silence.

"I've heard she asked you out. You don't have to worry about hurting my feelings or anything."

"I don't, huh?"

"No. She would be a good match for your family. You should start dating again."

"Well, thank you for your advice." He sounded angry.

"Fine. So then you don't need me to babysit tonight."

"Yes, I do. I, uh… Molly's my date tonight."

The announcement jarred her. A date *tonight*? So

quickly? Then again, Donna Rae had given warning. But still… Why did she want to cry? Why did being second choice—or no choice, rather—have to hurt so much?

The same reason it had hurt so much before.

"Oh. Well, I guess I can do it. What time?" Her voice nearly cracked, but she forced the sounds past her vocal cords.

"A little before five?"

"Sure. See you then." She hung up before she started blubbering. Apparently she did still have a few tears left.

A hand squeezed her shoulder. Dad's hand.

She blinked and reached for a tissue before turning around.

"What did he do?"

"Oh, nothing. He's just moving on with his life. And I'm being silly." She blew her nose and checked her emotions. She didn't need to get her dad riled up.

"Moved on?"

"He has a date with Molly Patton tonight."

Her dad visibly relaxed—all tension in his posture eased, the disapproval on his face turned to relief. "Well, that's good. They'll make a good match."

Why would he be so relieved? It didn't make sense how much he disliked Gregory this many years down the road.

A good match? "Yeah." She dabbed at her nose with the tissue. "So I'm going to watch the boys tonight."

Sarah had heard the description before, but her dad was truly struck by a thundercloud expression. "Of all the nerve…"

"It's okay. I've repeatedly offered to help. And now he's taking me up on it."

"You should call back and refuse. Just stay away from that family."

She wiped her own feelings of disapproval off her face and laughed. "I know how ridiculous this sounds. But I care about Hunter and Chase, and I'll do the favor for them."

"Stay away. Gregory Jones may have two cute kids, but he's not all he appears to be."

That was a strange thing to say. What, was he some double agent or something? "Dad, I'm smart, I'm independent and I'm not going to fall for him again."

Who was she kidding? She was afraid she already had.

A little before five, Gregory was ready for his date and standing in his office, waiting for Sarah to arrive. Prepared to zip out the door, limiting contact as much as possible. He needed to focus on Molly, to give time with her a fair assessment.

The doorbell rang, and he yanked the door open.

"My goodness, you must've been standing there ready to bolt out."

He had to chuckle, because she'd pegged him. "I was in my office." He stepped back to let her inside.

"Any special instructions?"

"No." He wanted to head right out the door and forget all about Sarah. "Just have fun. Make them behave."

"Okay." She offered some semblance of a smile. But she seemed down.

"Well, I guess I'll go."

"Have fun. And don't worry. We'll be fine."

"Yeah, I know you will." He really needed to leave. Now. Just walk out the door.

But the temptation to stay home, spend an evening with Sarah and his sons, was stronger than his legs at the moment.

"Um, are you supposed to pick up Molly? Or is she coming here?"

"I'm getting her. So, well…bye." He tore away from her and stormed out the door. *I've lost my mind.*

As he drove to Molly's, he tried to switch gears to focus on her. He thought of Molly's smile and cute freckles. He thought of her gorgeous voice. As he walked up her front walk, he thought of the sweet things she'd done for his sons since she started teaching their Sunday school class.

What on earth am I doing here?

Gregory held his knuckles two inches from Molly's front door but couldn't bring himself to knock. What had he been thinking when he'd agreed to go out with her?

With his hand still in the knocking position, he stood like a statue.

The door whipped open. "Oh, I thought I heard something."

She blushed, and it hit him again just how pretty she was.

But instead of her wavy, red-gold hair, he dreamed about Sarah and her silky honey-blond hair. "Are you ready?" he snapped.

Her smiled dimmed a smidgeon. "Yes." She walked out and locked the door.

He really did need to be nicer. He'd agreed to go out with her, hoping he could muster some attraction, could make it work for his boys' sake. He had to at least try, because he needed to get Sarah out of his head.

When they arrived at the huge toy store, she asked, "So, do you have a list?"

A list? Would have been a smart thing to do. "No. Sorry. I just need some small things for stockings. And a few other small gifts." He spotted a familiar sale paper at the entrance. "Hey, this is the wish book the kids looked through at home. They circled items they wanted."

"Oh, good. Grab that and look through it."

He flipped through the pages. Nothing looked familiar. Of course, other than the two gifts he'd already bought. "I tell you what, why don't you make some suggestions?"

She smiled as if she loved being useful. Such a nice person. Efficient. Organized. Friendly.

Not Sarah.

She scanned the pages. "Okay, I see a couple of things I think your boys will love." She flipped the sale catalogue closed and tossed it into a cart. "And they even have coupons."

Nice. She was thrifty, too. He could use someone like that. Not someone like Sarah who was of the same ilk as his ex-wife—pampered, spoiled, desiring only the best.

To be fair, Sarah wasn't nearly as bad as Delia had been. But she was definitely more high maintenance than Molly would be.

He followed Molly up and down the aisles as she tossed toys into the cart. She even had the good sense to pick out items that would be educational or would boost creativity.

When they went to stand in the mile-long checkout line, he said, "This is great. I never would have thought of such good gifts. Thank you."

"Oh, it was my pleasure. I had a blast." She couldn't quite look at him.

Maybe he'd been rude too often that evening. "You know, I bought a trampoline for Hunter and Chase. And I'd like to get it set up so they could play on it Christmas day. But I can't exactly hide it."

"You could set it up at my mom's house, then move it later. I'd be happy for you to bring them by on Christmas day." Her face blazed red.

His cell phone rang—a little too conveniently. *Lindsay.* "Excuse me, Molly." He turned away from her and answered the call.

"Hi, big brother. I hear you're shopping."

"How'd you know?"

"Small town. And a date with Molly Patton, huh?"

"Yes."

"Good for you. And I won't keep you. I just realized I forgot to tell you I mailed all the gifts to Dad's house before we left town. They should arrive tomorrow. I left one of Chase's unwrapped so you can assemble it."

"Okay. I'll be sure I get to it."

"Thanks. I'll miss y'all this year."

"We'll miss you. Tell Bill and Drake hello for me."

"Sure will." She laughed. "Oh, and I'm glad you're finally dating. I'm sure Molly is thrilled to have finally caught you."

"Love you. 'Bye," he said, cutting her off. He was half afraid Molly could hear her teasing.

He put away his phone. "That was Lindsay calling with a Christmas gift update."

"She's so on-the-ball."

"Everything's in the mail. Only one thing to assemble."

"Don't forget my mom's yard's all yours for the trampoline."

"Thanks for the offer. I'll think it over."

"Whatever you decide, you need to do it soon." She smiled, and he didn't feel judged by her. She was only making a suggestion. No big deal.

Why did he always end up in a huff when Sarah suggested something?

Maybe because he was on pins and needles, waiting for her dad to spill the news about the bribe. Because he hadn't quite managed to stay away from her.

And he wasn't sure he could stay away long enough.

Now, tonight, she would be at his house. With his children.

"Molly, would you like to go get some dinner before we hit the next store?"

She put her hand on his arm and looked him right in the eye this time. "I'd love to."

Once Hunter and Chase were ready for bed, Sarah said, "How about some hot chocolate by the Christmas tree?"

Thrilled with the idea, they raced to the kitchen.

"So what's your normal bedtime?" she asked as she heated milk on the stove top.

Hunter muttered something toward the floor.

One glance at the clock told her the time had most likely passed. "I'm sorry, Hunter, I couldn't hear you. Have I let you stay up later than usual?"

"Yes. But can we still have our hot chocolate? Pleeease?"

"Pweeease?" Chase added.

"Well, you don't have school tomorrow, so I guess it'll be fine."

"Can we make some for Dad, too?" Hunter asked.

"I don't know how late he'll be out."

"Oh, he won't be too late," Hunter said, very sure of himself.

"You don't think?"

"No. He'll have to come home when the stores close, won't he?"

Hunter was one smart little boy. But apparently, he didn't realize the shopping expedition was also a date. "I guess you're right. We can make him some, and he can reheat it if he needs to."

"Can we put it in the mug we made for him?"

"Oh, how nice. He'll love that."

"I'll get it," Chase said.

Hunter stuck his arm out in front of Chase to stop him. "No, I'll get it. It's in my top drawer, and you might break it."

"No I won't."

"You might."

"Wait," Sarah said. "Go together to get it. Hunter, you find it. Chase, you carry it very carefully."

They ran off together as she stirred the warming milk and wondered how the date was going. She tried her best to think charitable thoughts.

Were they having dinner at a romantic restaurant? Was Gregory thinking of buying Molly a Christmas gift?

A couple minutes later, Chase came in the room walking like a doddering old man. Holding the mug as if it were a priceless piece from a museum. She was grateful they were back.

Hunter sighed. "That took forever."

"Well, that's fine. The milk is just now ready."

Chase set down the white mug with *Dad* painted on it and with primary-colored thumbprints scattered over the rest of it.

"Your dad's going to love it."

After a quick wash of Gregory's mug, they put the hot chocolate mix into all four mugs. Then Sarah added hot milk.

They each stirred their own cup, and the boys took turns stirring Gregory's.

"Okay, let's go enjoy the fire and the tree."

When they walked into the family room, she set his mug on a table near the tree. A nice warm fire blazed in the fireplace. She'd had to add wood a couple of hours earlier, but Gregory had been thoughtful enough to leave a log on the hearth.

She plugged the tree lights in, and the boys squealed with excitement. "That tree looks good if I do say so myself," she said.

"We did good," Chase said.

"We never get to see it. Dad works all the time." Hunter blew into his mug to cool the drink. "Except for today."

She blew into her own cup, and steam hit her in the face. "Well, your dad has only been trying to do what he thinks is best for all of you. But I think he'll have more time at home before Christmas. And you can enjoy your tree for the next few days."

They sat on the floor around the tree, Sarah leaning against a chair. She observed their sweet faces, lit by the tree lights, as they sipped their hot chocolate. The time with the boys was bittersweet. Because she knew it was probably the only time she would have a chance to do this.

It would be hard to leave them behind. Would be hard to watch as Molly stepped in as their mom.

No way. I'm not allowing that. The thought seemed to reverberate through her brain.

To ignore her own feelings would be a lie. No, she couldn't just stand back and watch Gregory choose Molly. Not without at least telling him she was starting to fall for him again.

She sank back against the chair as if her spine couldn't hold her upright. It scared her to death to realize it.

Could she trust him? She'd thought not. But hadn't she seen a different side of him lately? Hadn't he proven he was a responsible, caring dad? Hadn't he been there to offer support when she'd shared about Peter, and about learning to pray again? Hadn't he followed through on everything for the pageant?

He seemed to have grown up into a dependable man. And had learned from his mistakes.

Against all logic…against her better judgment…she had fallen in love with Gregory.

"I know! Let's sing Cwistmas cawols," Chase yelled as if he'd just had a stroke of genius.

She had to tell Gregory how she felt.

What if I'm too late?

With that depressing thought hanging over her, the suggestion of singing cheered her up. "I'd love to sing carols."

Gregory walked Molly to her front door. He'd had a nice time. But no fireworks.

"Thanks for dinner. I had a great time," she said,

leaning close, smiling up at him, all inviting. Sending all the right signals that she was interested.

What's wrong with me? She's gorgeous. She's sweet. She loves my kids. "I really appreciate your help tonight. I'm totally done shopping now."

She placed her hand on his arm again and gave a throaty laugh. "Hey, I'm a shopping machine. Anytime you need help, just call. I could throw together a good birthday party, too."

"Oh, boy. I haven't even thought of birthdays."

She raised up on her toes, closer. "You can do this, Gregory. You're such a good dad. And if you ever need help, I'm here for you." She put her hands on his shoulders.

It took a full second, but when her eyes fell closed, he realized what she was doing. *She's trying to kiss me.*

I can't do that to Sarah.

He avoided the kiss and gave her a quick hug, then stepped away. "Thanks again. I guess I'll see you at the Christmas pageant." He tried to smile at her. But with her dazed, embarrassed expression, he felt horrible. He had to get out of there.

And he wasn't prepared to see Sarah just yet either. So he drove around the town square a few times. The shadowy outline of The Forever Tree stood in relief against the cloudy night sky.

Forever love. He and Sarah were supposed to have forever love. But could that really happen if God didn't intend for them to be together? Because surely if He did, then both sets of parents wouldn't be against it. And surely if He did, then Sarah would be showing some interest. But all she seemed to remember was their past, and how he had betrayed her. She conveniently forgot that she had ditched him first. That he had been acting out of hurt.

Of course, she didn't know the half of it—about her dad getting involved. About Gregory's shame for taking the offer. And he hoped she never did find out.

Moisture dotted his windshield, so he stopped the car for a moment. Maybe snowflakes?

Still not ready to go home, he drove to his dad's house. After a quick *tap, tap* on the door, he let himself in.

Dad and Richard were watching television.

"Hey, I thought you had plans tonight," he said to his dad.

"I did. I'd invited Richard to go out to eat tonight to celebrate his moving home."

Richard rubbed his belly. "Had Minnie's fried chicken."

"I went shopping with Molly," he said, checking their expressions for a reaction. He remembered that at one time, Molly had been interested in Richard, so he watched him closely.

Richard didn't react at all.

"Oh, you did, huh? How'd it go?" His dad didn't look too pleased. Almost frowned.

"I thought you wanted me to go out with Molly," he said to him.

"I'm fine with whoever you go out with. But I was starting to think Sarah might be a better choice."

Gregory huffed. "You told me to be careful around her."

"Well, I've changed my mind since seeing you two together. You obviously care about her. The boys love her. And she's been good for you."

He *obviously* cared about her? This was not what he needed to hear at the moment.

"Did you have fun?" Richard asked, still looking rather blasé about the whole thing.

"Yes. She helped me finish my shopping."

"Was it a date or a shopping trip?" Richard asked.

"Both."

"You're not just settling for a mom for your boys, are you?"

Starting to feel as if he was being grilled, Gregory asked, "Why the third degree?"

Richard shrugged and looked back toward the TV. "You need to be looking for a wife—someone you love and are attracted to. And I saw how you and Sarah looked at each other while we were caroling the other night."

"Well, Molly is very attractive. She's gorgeous, in fact. And she tried to kiss me," he blurted like a cornered animal.

Richard looked him in the eye once again. "Tried?"

"Don't force anything," his dad said. "Go out. Have fun. See what happens. And don't be afraid to ask Sarah out, too. You're just now getting back into dating and need to keep your options open."

"I'm not going to date Sarah. Her dad would run me out of town."

"Then it's time for Winston to put the past where it belongs. If you're interested in his daughter, you need to go talk to him and set him straight."

Yeah, in a perfect world. But theirs wasn't a normal past. Theirs was filled with shameful secrets.

He told his dad and brother goodbye, then braved going home.

As he stood on the front porch unlocking the door, he heard laughter. Then singing. When he walked inside, the singing grew louder. Sarah and the boys burst into a verse of "Angels We Have Heard on High." When they got to the chorus, Hunter did a solo in a high falsetto voice. Thus, the laughter he'd heard before. Sarah and Chase died laughing at Hunter's operatic rendition of the "Glorias."

He walked to the family room as they started to sing "The First Noel." Sarah and Hunter and Chase sat around the Christmas tree, the fireplace popping, the room toasty warm. They were holding mugs of something, probably hot chocolate. It was the perfect family scene. His kids happy, laughing, singing about the Baby Jesus. Sarah beside them, where a mother should be. Sarah, the first woman he'd ever loved. The only woman he had truly loved.

The woman he loved now, even when he knew he shouldn't. Even when he knew there was no hope of them being together. Winston would see to that.

He spotted another mug on the table. It had Dad painted on it in kid handwriting. Like a starving man drawn to food, he stepped into the room and lifted the mug. It was still warm, and he sipped. Yes, hot chocolate. For him. They'd made it for him. Had expected him soon. Had hoped he would be here, a part of this perfect scene.

"Dad!" Hunter yelled mid-song. "Look, Miss Sarah, Dad's home. Just like I said he would be!"

"Dad!" Chase yelled as he streaked across the room and nearly knocked the hot chocolate from his hand trying to get Gregory to pick him up. Gregory set the cup down.

As he picked up Chase and patted Hunter on the head, he had eyes only for Sarah.

"Welcome home, Gregory. The boys have been waiting."

Have you been waiting, too? he wanted to ask. "I love my new mug. Thank you, guys."

"I wrote on it," Hunter said proudly.

"Those are my thumbpwints."

Gregory tucked Chase on one hip, then held out his other hand to Sarah. "Come on. I want to show all of you something."

She took his hand and let him help her up. She didn't let go, and he didn't either. Tears brightened her eyes, and she smiled at him.

He smiled back. "Thank you for this. It was a wonderful greeting when I came in."

He kept hold of her hand and led them all toward the front door.

"Snow!" Hunter screamed.

"Snow," Chase squealed as he wiggled out of Gregory's clutches.

"It's not much. And it may not stick. But it's fun anyway."

While the boys hopped around the yard in bare feet, trying to catch flakes on their tongues, he held Sarah's hand.

Something about it felt right.

"How did it go tonight?" she asked.

"Fine."

"Only fine? Not good, not great?"

"Yes, only fine."

"No sparks?"

He looked at her though slitted eyes. What was she getting at? "No."

She nodded and faced the boys once again. "That's good to hear."

His heart nearly stopped. "Do you really mean that?"

"I'm scared to admit it, but yes. I decided something tonight."

"And what would that be?" He almost let go of her hand, because he was afraid he might be shaking.

"I decided I don't want to let Molly have you without putting up a fight."

He looked at her, but she was staring at the sky. He swallowed, scared to speak. Unsure how to interpret her comment. "Somehow I can't see you, in your cashmere and pearls, in a catfight."

She laughed and turned toward him. As she stood bathed in the light from the icicle lights, she took a deep breath. He could see her shoulders move up, then down. Could hear the air whoosh out of her. "I've found I have feelings for you again. And tonight...well, once you got here, it was perfect."

Could it be possible after all this time? Even with all the bad stuff in their past?

Lord, what should I do here? I'm not good enough for her. I need to tell her the truth about taking that money.

But it would hurt her. And he couldn't stand to do that. Why hurt her if it wasn't necessary? Maybe his dad was right. Maybe he could try to reason with Winston.

He looked into her gorgeous, shining eyes, and... melted. Just like the snowflake that landed on her cheek. "I don't know what to say."

Her expression dimmed a bit. But he couldn't tell her how he felt about her. Not until he'd talked with her dad.

Not until the man assured Gregory he wouldn't devastate her by telling her about the bribe.

"My feet are frozen," Hunter said as he ran up the front porch steps and leaped between them onto the doormat. He shivered.

"Come on, boys, time to go inside. If the snow is still here tomorrow morning, we'll get bundled up and play in it."

Once inside he sent the kids to go brush their teeth. In the quiet that followed, he stared into Sarah's eyes. She stared right back. But then he saw her wariness. It seemed so much was on the line this time. Not only his happiness, but his sons' as well. And he'd never been more scared.

He wrapped his arms around her waist and pulled her closer—to reassure himself as much as her. She was so small, so delicate. He'd always loved that he could wrap his arms around her and feel like they might go around a second time.

He felt strong. As if he could handle anything. He wanted her to trust him. To depend on him.

He wanted to be the man for her. A man she could respect.

She looked up at him, her face flushed, her eyes serious. He could imagine what she had to be thinking about his evasive comment a minute ago. He couldn't make her any promises in the present. But he could deal with the past.

"I'm sorry I hurt you in high school. I don't ever want to hurt you again," he said, even as he wondered if *he* would end up being hurt.

She looked a little confused, but then she smiled. "I believe you. And it's okay if you don't feel the same for me—yet." A little of the sparkle returned to her eyes. "We can just see what happens."

Although he'd been hugging her, she finally wrapped her arms around him. Then she looked up at him. Grinning. Inviting. The woman that he loved.

This was the real thing. This was what an embrace should feel like.

And even though he had no idea how he was going to convince Winston to let him love his daughter, he kissed her. This time, she didn't turn away. This time she kissed him back, and, once again, he was like a starving man feasting.

"Whoa." She gasped for breath, then laughed. She pushed away from him. "Um, I guess we haven't lost the sparks."

He felt as if he'd been running a fifty-yard dash, too. "You've got that right."

"I should go."

"Yeah, probably best."

She laughed, and the sound soothed his soul. "I'm glad you asked me to babysit. Even if I was mad at first."

"Yeah, I'm glad, too. Walking in that room, seeing you with my sons, knowing you'd made a place for me…" He stopped before he embarrassed himself.

She stepped closer to him once again. Pressed her hand lightly against his chest. "I know, Gregory. I know. I felt it too," she whispered. Then she reached up on her toes and gave him a feathery soft kiss. "Good night."

He watched her to her car, waved, then watched her drive away.

He had no idea what would happen next, but he could try to be patient and just take one step at a time. *Lord, help me be patient. Help me to trust You to work out this relationship.*

He walked toward the bathroom. "Boys, you're taking way too long to brush your teeth."

"We're in here," Hunter called from their room.

"We have a new list for Santa," Chase said.

It was folded up several times until the notebook paper was a little square.

"Okay. I'll make sure he gets it."

"Can we sleep in your bed tonight?" Chase asked.

"No, not tonight. But you can share Hunter's bed."

"Can I, Hunter, pwease?"

"I guess." Big brother sighed as if Chase hadn't been doing it every night since Lindsay moved, as if it were a terrible burden.

But Chase seemed excited once Gregory got them tucked in. "I want to say bedtime pwayers. Miss Sawah said it's a good thing to do."

"Okay, son."

They held hands in a circle and bowed their heads. Gregory opened with, "Lord, please be with those who are out in the cold tonight. Please be with those who are lonely or sad this Christmas." *And thank You for bringing Sarah back into my life.* Then he whispered, "Okay, your turn."

"Dear Lord," Hunter said, "we've been good this year. Please ask Santa to bring us everything we asked for. It's not much. Only three things. Amen."

"Yeah, what Hunter said," Chase added. "Amen."

Sarah nearly floated home, just like one of the little snowflakes, flitting and dancing. When she got out of her car, she wanted to dance in the snow to celebrate this new lightness. This new feeling of joy.

She couldn't believe so much had changed in a few short hours. When she'd left, she'd been hurt and jealous. But as the evening had progressed, being there in Gregory's home, with his sons, just felt…right.

Somehow, she'd known God would make it right.

And then when Gregory had looked into her eyes while holding the mug of hot chocolate, she had seen the naked truth on his face. He wanted it, too. He liked the scene before him. He loved the idea of all of them together. He looked at her the way he used to look at her back when he said he loved her. Back before all the awful stuff happened. Back when things were still simple.

A simple singing of carols around a Christmas tree by a roaring fire, time with family, with loved ones. That's what she'd seen. And then she had this vision of them doing it again and again every year as the boys grew up. And she'd known it was…right.

Of course, Gregory hadn't been able to put his feelings into words yet. But she wouldn't rush him. He might need longer to realize what it meant for their future.

She walked into the house and strolled to the family room. Her mom was snuggled up on the couch reading. Her dad was reading the newspaper in his chair.

"I'm home," she said. And she couldn't help but smile, especially when she noticed how dreamy her voice sounded.

"How did it go?" Mother asked.

"It was perfect. Hunter and Chase were great. We

had hot chocolate by the fire after dinner. And we sang around the tree and had so much fun."

"Was Gregory there?" her dad asked.

"Come on, Dad. Ease up on him some."

"He had you crying before you left. How can you come waltzing in here, smiling as if you're in love or something?"

"Originally, when I was so upset, I thought maybe he was going out on a date with Molly because he cared for her. But he said there weren't any sparks between them."

"Listen to yourself, Sarah. You've fallen for him again."

"Leave her alone, Winston," Mother said. "She had a nice time. That's all."

Sarah was not going to let them ruin her chance with Gregory again. She turned to her mother. "No. It wasn't just a nice time. It was more than that. We have feelings for each other. Strong feelings. And I won't let you make light of it." Then she turned to her dad. "And I won't let you forbid it or disapprove of it. I'm capable of making my own decisions now."

He folded his newspaper slowly and deliberately. After an eon, he stood. "Sarah, it's time we have a talk."

Chapter Eleven

"I'm afraid I have something very difficult to tell you," Sarah's dad said once he'd spent two solid minutes pulling two chairs to face each other in the privacy of his office, as if postponing their conversation as long as possible.

"Go ahead." Somehow she knew she didn't want to hear what he had to say. She wanted to walk out and say forget it. But now she had to listen.

He took hold of her hands. "I know this is going to be hurtful. And I would give anything not to have to tell you. But your change of heart where Gregory is concerned has forced me to."

She ground her back teeth together. "Just spit it out."

"I'm not proud of this. But know that I did what I felt was necessary, what was best at the time." He swallowed. "After you broke up with Gregory, I knew the separation wouldn't last long. I saw how you looked at him at church. You appeared…so fragile. As if you were ready to break. And I knew it was because you still cared for him. I also saw how he looked at you." He rested his elbows on his knees and stared at the floor, shaking his head. "He was still crazy about you. And he wrote you a letter that confirmed it."

"What? I never got a letter from him."

"I intercepted it. I couldn't take the chance, couldn't let him manipulate you again. And when I read it, I was glad I had acted."

"But, Dad, you had no right to do that. What did the letter say?"

"It said that he would wait for you. As long as it took. I couldn't let you give up your future for him. He had no goals. He had no future beyond this town."

She pulled her hands away from his. "How could you? I thought he ignored me. I thought he didn't care at all."

"But there, you're wrong. Because he did care. Just not enough. He cared about money enough that when I offered him some to stay away from you, he jumped at the chance."

Her stomach plummeted, then began to hurt. "You bribed him?"

"To protect you. I offered him the money, and he accepted it and kept his end of the deal—until now."

She tried to scoot her chair back, to move away from this man who supposedly loved her. But it wouldn't budge on the thick carpet. So she stood and shoved it backward. "How could you do that to me? I loved him."

She started sucking in air in short, quick bursts. What if her dad was telling the truth? She didn't think she would be able to breathe if she didn't get out of this hideously stuffy office.

"I'm sorry, baby. I had to think of your future. And look what a great future you've had. You went to your dream college, graduated with honors, got your master's degree. You—"

"Stop it," she yelled, then thought she might faint. She ran out of his office, down the hallway to the foyer. She grabbed her purse and ran out the door.

It was still snowing. Light little flakes. So beautiful.

And she still couldn't breathe. So she fumbled and finally hit the unlock button on her key chain. She climbed into the car, her windows covered in a light dusting of snow. Finally, with the rest of the world blocked out, she gasped for a good deep breath.

Gregory couldn't have done that. Dad has to be wrong. There's some mistake. She'd been so happy just an hour ago.

Surely no money passed hands. Surely her Dad thought they'd made a deal when there really hadn't been one.

But Gregory had stayed away. Against all odds, he'd stayed away. And then he'd asked Delia out.

No. Lord, please no. Please don't let this be true.

She cranked the engine and backed out of the driveway. After circling the downtown square, hoping she could cry and diffuse the tightness in her chest, but finding no release, she drove toward Gregory's house. She had to know the truth.

The light was on in his office. She knocked on the front door rather than ring the bell.

He opened the door. "Sarah? What's wrong?"

"I need to talk to you."

Was that fear on his face? Or maybe resignation?

No, she couldn't read anything into the expression on his face as he motioned her inside.

She walked in and started to pace. The house was quiet. "Are the boys in bed?"

"Yes. Sound asleep."

The smothering feeling hit her once again. She stopped pacing and wrapped her arms around her waist. She turned to face him. "Dad told me something tonight. I need to know—"

His eyes fell closed. He threw his head back and said, "No. Not now."

His reaction poked at her gaping wound. "Please tell me it's not true," she whispered, unable to produce more sound. Afraid she would choke, weep, scream.

"What did he tell you?" Gregory still wouldn't look at her. He stared at the wall now. His jaw twitching.

"That he paid you to stay away from me. That you agreed." She grabbed his arm. "I know you wouldn't do that. Please tell me you didn't."

He jerked away. "Don't you know by now what a loser I am? At least according to your dad."

She stepped back. "Did you take the money?"

He looked her right in the eye and stared as if determined to see this horrific discussion through to the end. "Yes. I made the stupidest mistake of my life, and I've regretted it ever since."

All the blood drained from her face, and she wobbled on her feet. "How could you?"

"There are no excuses. And I've been ashamed of myself since that moment."

"Well, you should be." She yanked open the door and started to walk out. But she couldn't let it go. She turned and said, "You and my dad have both always worried about money and status, but that's not what's important. What's important is honor. And neither of you has it."

As she stepped outside, she wanted to slam the door. Oh, she wanted so badly to slam it. But she didn't want to wake Hunter and Chase.

She knew they didn't need to see their daddy in the condition he was going to be in.

She hoped Gregory felt as rotten as she did.

Gregory sat in his chair, staring at the embers in the fireplace. Staring at the blaring, too-cheerful Christmas tree lights.

Gone. Gone in an instant. What had been a beautiful, homey dream just hours before was…gone.

No more singing carols around the tree with Sarah. No more little family scenes by the fireplace. It had all been just an illusion, negated by one awful decision he made when he was eighteen years old.

Sarah had every right to be angry. He *had* acted dishonorably.

And he would never be good enough for her or anyone else.

Sick. Heartsick. Stomach-sick. Just sick.

It was late the next morning, and Sarah didn't want to get out of bed. Yet she couldn't sleep when what she needed most was to sleep to escape the constant thoughts of this new betrayal.

Sarah tugged the covers over her head. She would give herself one more hour. But then she would have to get up and face the fact that she was in love with a man who was in love with money more than her.

There had to be more to it, a little voice nagged.

Sarah ignored it, threw the covers off and stalked to the bathroom. She glared into the mirror—at her swollen eyes and mess of hair. "Sarah Radcliffe, you will never shed another tear over a man. You will be content being single. And God will help you do it." She nodded her head as if pronouncing it done.

Then she showered and got ready for lunch. She really should stop by and visit Donna Rae, but she wasn't ready to face her yet. Donna Rae would have the whole story out of her in thirty seconds flat.

Then again, maybe Donna Rae could knock some sense into her head.

When she left her room, she found her dad had gone to the office. Even when he hadn't planned to.

The chicken.

She and her mom had a nice lunch, and Sarah tried to act as if her world hadn't split in two. "So did Dad tell you about our talk last night?"

"No. He was rather evasive and hurried to the office. Care to fill me in?"

"I think he needs to."

"Does it have to do with his business dealings with Gregory?"

Shady dealings. "Yes."

"I'm sorry, dear."

"Now I've got a whole day and nothing to do."

"I know, let's go shopping."

What did she have to lose? Maybe the frustration of the hustle and bustle could replace the dogged pain. "Sure. I'd like that."

The next afternoon, Sarah headed to the church early. This time, the peaceful sanctuary failed to soothe her.

The manger reminded her of Gregory. The star hanging above also reminded her of Gregory. Of how he'd come through on making the set for her. On how he'd come through for his boys—albeit unwillingly at first. Still, he'd been coming to practice to help Hunter. And he was making a costume for him, too.

She should call to remind him to bring it.

Nope. Too difficult at the moment. Having him arrive soon would be about all she could handle.

The door of the church opened and in zoomed several children who had apparently ridden together. *Lord, I need Your help today. I don't feel like facing this, but I have to. And I have to do it with a smile.*

"Miss Sarah, I remembered my halo!" one child hollered.

"I'm glad. Did the rest of you bring your last-minute costume items?"

"Yep."

"Yes, ma'am."

"Um… I forgot my donkey tail."

"Well, please try to remember it tomorrow."

They ran off to play while the others arrived.

The door opened again. Something about the footsteps alerted her. So she braced herself, pasted a smile on her face, and waited.

It seemed like forever before Chase shouted, "Miss Sawah, we're here."

Smile frozen in place, she turned. She looked down at the boys. She could see Gregory's feet but refused to look higher than Hunter's eyes. "I'm glad you're here. You can play with the other children while we wait till everyone arrives."

She turned back to her notebook, shuffling through pages, pretending to look for a paper. Gregory's footsteps sounded as he walked away.

She sagged into a pew. Her calf muscles quivered from the released tension. Her thigh muscles ached. If she wasn't careful, she'd end up in full muscle spasms.

And her heart hurt. Physically. Pain in her chest. Could a broken heart really hurt? And why did it hurt more this time?

Sarah hid out with her nose in her notebook until it appeared everyone had arrived, the youth and adult helpers as well.

"Okay, everyone. Time to put on your costumes and get in your places."

"Miss Sarah." Little hands tugged on her sweater sleeve. Hunter's hands.

"Yes, baby?"

His lower lip quivered. "I forgot my new costume."

"That's okay. You can use the same one you wore the other day."

"But I want my brown-striped costume."

"You'll have it tomorrow. Don't worry about the rehearsal."

Two big tears welled up and then spilled down his cheeks. "But Daddy worked really hard on it. I was supposed to put it in the truck. I forgot," he whispered.

She squatted down. "Your daddy will understand. Go tell him right now, and he can help you put on the white shepherd outfit."

He sniffed. "Will you tell him?"

"Sweetie, he won't be mad at you. Go on and tell him."

"Please?"

Lord, is there no end to this? "Okay. Let's find him."

They found Gregory outside on the front steps. He was on his phone. Probably already calling Molly for another date.

As soon as he hung up, Sarah said, "Gregory, there seems to have been a mistake. Hunter forgot his costume."

She still didn't look right at him. She looked more at his shoulder.

"Oh, man. I'm sorry," he said. "I knew I should have had Hunter put it in the truck as soon as we finished. But I let him play in it for a while." He knelt down in front of Hunter. "My fault. Don't worry about it."

"I told him it's okay," Sarah said. "But can you come help him put on the white costume so we can hurry and get started?"

"Sure."

She braved a glance into his face.

And wished she hadn't. He looked bad. As if he'd had a rougher couple of nights than she had.

Lord, I don't want him to hurt either. Oh, please... She couldn't bear to see it. So she hurried back inside.

"Miss Sarah," one of the youth said as she tried to blaze past to put her nose back in her notebook.

"Yes?"

"Mr. Vinny isn't here."

"He's not?" She glanced around. "I thought I'd seen him come in."

"No, ma'am."

As the kids finished dressing and moved into place, still no Vinny. So she called his house. No answer. Maybe in labor?

She tried calling Donna Rae's cell phone.

"Hello?"

"Hey. Is everything okay?"

"Vinny's driving me to the hospital," she said in a strained voice.

"Is it time?"

"I think so."

She laughed. "Well, I'd think you'd know by now."

Donna Rae laughed, but it morphed into a groan of pain. "Gotta go."

"Okay. And tell Vinny not to worry. We'll find someone to read his part. I'll be praying for y'all."

"You will? Oh, sweetie, that's so nice to hear. I'm glad you're all straight with God." She groaned again. "I'll call when baby Durante gets here."

Sarah put her phone away, excitement for Donna Rae making her heart race as she gathered the cast. "Well, it looks like Vinny won't be here. They're on their way to the hospital to have the baby."

The room erupted in cheers.

"Who's going to read his part?" Hunter asked.

"Well, I don't know yet."

"My dad will do it!" Hunter beamed proudly at his dad. "Won't you, Dad?"

"Well, that's up to Miss Sarah. She may have someone else in mind."

She made herself look at him. "No, I don't have any planned alternates. I guess we could use you. Can we depend on you to be here tomorrow?"

Gregory couldn't believe she would say that. He felt the barb like an uppercut to the jaw. Right there in front of everyone. "Of course I'll be here." He shoved his hands into his pockets as he stared into her eyes. "You can count on me."

He wanted to add that she could count on him in all ways, not just for the pageant. But he had no right to promise her anything. And he couldn't expect her to believe him.

"Well, let's get started, then."

The kids went to their places.

"Gregory, we need to be backstage," she told him as she made her way behind the curtain.

Great. He hadn't thought of being in close quarters with Sarah when he'd volunteered.

"We'll be reading out of the Bible here at the pulpit, into the microphone," she whispered. "I have my part highlighted in pink. Yours in blue."

As the children did their parts out front, it hit Gregory that he wouldn't be there to cue Hunter. "Wait, I need to be down there for Hunter."

She put her hand on his arm to stop him. "Let's see how he does first. He's the one who volunteered you. Let him try by himself."

He nodded, wishing she would touch him again while acknowledging it as incidental.

As they waited while the kids said their lines, he stood close beside Sarah, smelling her perfume and wafts of her shampoo, feeling the brush of her arm against his. Pure torture. She was so close physically, but still so far out of his reach.

Before he knew it, she started reading the pink-highlighted words. "'And it came to pass in those days, that there went out a decree from Caesar Augustus that all the world should be taxed—and this taxing was first made when Cyrenius was governor of Syria—and all went to be taxed, every one into his own city.'"

Blue highlighted the next passage. His turn. "'And Joseph also went up from Galilee, out of the city of Nazareth, into Judaea, unto the city of David, which is called Bethlehem—because he was of the house and lineage of David—to be taxed with Mary his espoused wife, being great with child.'"

Sarah peeked out of a slit in the curtain. He joined her in watching the simple reenactment on their home-made stage.

Then she looked back at the Bible. "'And so it was, that, while they were there, the days were accomplished that she should be delivered. And she brought forth her firstborn son, and wrapped him in swaddling clothes, and laid him in a manger, because there was no room for them in the inn.'"

"'And there were in the same country shepherds abiding in the field, keeping watch over their flock by night,'" he read. Then they watched as Hunter acted out his part. Gregory held his breath as Hunter breezed through his lines.

Once Hunter finished, he turned and grinned toward the break in the curtain, certain that Gregory was watching and was proud. Gregory couldn't resist. He stuck his hand through the slit in the curtain and gave Hunter a thumbs-up.

"'And, lo, the angel of the Lord came upon them, and the glory of the Lord shone round about them, and they were sore afraid. And the angel said unto them, Fear not, for behold, I bring you good tidings of great joy, which shall be to all people,'" Sarah read as Gregory watched Hunter pretend to be afraid of the angel.

She had to elbow him to read his part. "'For unto you is born this day in the city of David a Saviour, which is Christ the Lord.'"

A Saviour. Born to you.

Born to me...

The reality of that statement hit him broadside. *Jesus was born to me. Even the sinner I am. Even with the dishonorable things I've done.*

Gregory took a deep breath as that thought sank in. Maybe for the first time ever. He wanted to weep. *Oh, Lord, forgive me. And thank You for removing all my sins as far as the east is from the west.*

Because of the tiny baby in that manger, I am worthy of Your love.

Sarah stared at him. Then she read, "'And this shall be a sign unto you, Ye shall find the babe wrapped in swaddling clothes, lying in a manger.'"

He realized she was staring because she'd had to finish his lines for him.

But he smiled at her anyway. He was forgiven. His slate was wiped clean before God.

So maybe Sarah would be able to forgive him, too.

He didn't want to let her down, so he jumped in with his next lines. "'And suddenly there was with the angel a multitude of the heavenly host praising God, and saying, Glory to God in the highest, and on earth peace, good will toward men.'"

Yes, glory be to You, God.

Sarah was exhausted. But so pleased at how rehearsal had gone. She'd nearly cried at how sweetly the message had come across. She knew many would be touched by the children's performance tomorrow evening.

"Okay, everyone. Put all your costumes in the choir loft. And if you forgot something today, please remind your parents to bring it tomorrow." She smiled at each child as she looked around the cluster of actors. "I'm so proud of each and every one of you. You did a marvelous job today. Practice your songs tonight, and I'll see you at six o'clock tomorrow."

She looked up and saw the treats she'd promised sitting by the door. "Oh, and pick up a goodie bag on your way out."

As she packed up her things, she noticed Gregory and the boys picking up and straightening. They seemed to be hanging around.

She decided she would have to face them. She couldn't hem and haw around all afternoon. "Well, I'm ready to lock up if you all are ready to go."

Gregory handed Hunter his keys. "Boys, why don't you go on out to the truck. I've got to talk to Miss Sarah."

As they hurried outside, thrilled to be trusted with the keys, Gregory said, "Sarah, I was wondering if I could talk to you for a minute." He looked so serious. So earnest.

She hardened her heart. "I don't really have time." She walked outside and started searching through the large key ring for the church door key. Anything to keep from looking at him.

He followed her out. And waited.

Great. Once she had the door locked, she took a deep breath and turned to leave, but he was blocking her way down the steps, and she would have to maneuver around him. Over his shoulder, she could see the boys arguing over who was going to unlock the truck.

"I'm truly sorry for what happened years ago with your dad," he said quickly, as if he knew she was about to make her escape. "That we both hurt you. But I want you to know I've prayed for forgiveness. And I'd like to ask you to forgive me as well."

She hadn't expected this at all. She knew what God said about forgiving others, but she couldn't manage it. "No. And I can't deal with this right now. Please let me by."

"I realize it might take a while. You have a lot to process." He started down the stairs, toward his truck, but then he paused, as if thinking, and then he came back up the steps. "I feel like I need to just put everything out there in the open, so there's nothing between us but the truth."

"A little late for that." Could it get worse?

He stared into her eyes, pleading. "You have to know that I never, ever used a cent of that money. As soon as I took it, I felt sick about it. I stuck it in the bank and tried to ignore it. But a few weeks later, I couldn't stand it. I took it out and tried to give it back to your dad."

"What?" She couldn't wrap her brain around it. She tried to remember if that was before he'd started dating Delia, but couldn't remember exactly how long he'd waited before asking her out.

"Your dad refused the money. He told me it was for services rendered and paid."

"Yeah, I guess so." She knew her distress showed on her face, but she couldn't help it.

"So I took the money to an accountant and had him set up a scholarship fund." He rubbed the back of his neck.

"You know, I don't really need to hear what you did with that money." She finally did the smart thing and darted around him, making sure they didn't touch at all, not caring how silly she looked.

She had to get out of there.

"There's a scholarship in your name at the high

school," he called as she hurried to the car. "Every year, it's awarded to a student who goes to college to become a teacher."

She froze for a moment. *No, don't do this.* But then she continued on.

"It was the only thing I could think to do to try to honor you with the money—to take something bad and try to make good out of it."

The last came to her as she threw herself into the car and yanked the door closed. *Lord, help me.*

Too much. This is too much.

Chapter Twelve

Sarah slipped quietly into the house but soon realized
no one was home. She vaguely remembered her mom
and dad had some sort of open house to attend—an office party. Followed by a dinner hosted at the home of
another partner in the firm.

Since her dad had been hiding out at the office, she
hadn't had to face him yet. She was still so angry with
him that she was nauseated from thinking about seeing him that night.

She went to her bed to lie down. She threw an arm
over her eyes, because they felt dry, achy. But no tears
would come.

She was too mad. Too sad.

What would her life have been like if her dad hadn't
interfered? What if he'd been kind and hadn't judged
Gregory based on his other-side-of-the-tracks address
or his bad-boy reputation? What if her dad had given
Gregory half a chance?

Would she be happily married with kids of her own
today?

No, no, no. No "what-ifs" allowed.

She rolled to her side and closed her eyes. Time for a nap. All she seemed to want to do was sleep. Just sleep until it was time to go back to Nashville. Back home to teaching. To her routine. To her Tennessee friends. To her Tennessee church family.

She groaned, because it was always so difficult to leave Magnolia after a visit.

Of course, this time, she would welcome it.

That night, after a rare, late dinner at home, Gregory got the boys bathed and tucked them into Hunter's bed.

"So, are you going to your bed tonight?" Gregory asked Chase, just like he asked every night.

"Can I sleep with you?"

"No, son."

"Can I stay here?" Chase asked.

"Hunter?"

Hunter sighed once again. "I guess."

Gregory tucked the covers up under their chins.

"Dad, did you remember to mail our letter to Santa?"

He'd forgotten all about the letter. "I'll set it out tomorrow night at Granddad's house so he can see it when he arrives."

"Okay."

"Can we pway again tonight?"

"Of course, Chase. We should make a habit of doing it every night."

Gregory opened the prayer, then Chase jumped in with a request for Santa to bring them everything they asked for.

"Yeah, that's what I want, too," Hunter said when it was his turn to pray. "And we promise to keep being good. And thank You for the Baby Jesus. Amen."

Yes, Lord, thank You for the Baby Jesus, the greatest gift of all.

Gregory kissed Chase, then ruffled Hunter's hair like he usually did. But for some reason, he didn't stop with the routine. He made a trip around the foot of the bed, to the far side, to actually kiss Hunter, even though Hunter wasn't usually physically affectionate.

When he leaned over and kissed Hunter's cheek, Hunter grabbed him around the neck and held on. "I love you, Dad."

It was like a knife to the chest. How many times had Hunter wanted to be hugged or kissed and Gregory hadn't?

He bundled Hunter in a big hug and said, "I love you, too." Then he looked over at Chase and said, "I love you, Chase."

"I wuv you, Daddy."

When Hunter let go, Gregory turned on the nightlight and left the room, the boys' soft giggles as they snuggled under the covers comforting him. Letting him know all was well in the Jones world, even if Gregory's heart was breaking over Sarah.

He and his boys would somehow be okay, with God's help.

When Gregory got to the living room, he hunted to make sure he could find the Santa letter. He figured he better also look it over to make sure he'd bought everything.

The letter was lying on his desk. A sheet of notebook paper folded four times so that it was like a note a kid would pass in school. He smiled as he unfolded it to find Hunter's kindergarten writing and spelling.

Dear Santa,
For Hunter—A whole day playing outside with
Dad by myself
For Chase—To sleep in Dad's bed for a week
For Both of us—Miss Sarah as our mom

Gregory plopped into his office chair, which rolled
backward and bumped the bookshelf.

In the first wish list, they had asked for all kinds of
toys, plus the trampoline and game system. But this
one...

For Both of us—Miss Sarah as our mom

*Oh, Lord, why this? I can't just purchase this and
put it under the tree.*

Why, after he'd tried so hard to provide the best
Christmas ever, did they have to ask for the one thing
that was impossible to provide?

Sarah heard the garage door open and close later that
night. Her parents were home.

She needed to confront her dad. And to make sure
her mom knew what was going on.

She waited in the living room. But only her dad came
in.

"Where's Mother?" she asked.

"She went on to bed. She has a headache."

"Yes, I have a headache," Katherine called from the
foyer. "But only because of your father." She walked
into the living room and glared at him. "Sarah, he finally told me, and I'm so sorry for what your father
has done. I want you to know I had no part of it. Would
never have condoned it."

An ally. *Thank you, Lord.* "I appreciate that."

Her mother raised an eyebrow at her father. "Winston?"

"I've apologized," he said defensively.

"I found out about the scholarship," Sarah blurted. "Did you know?"

He hung his head.

"Family meeting. Let's go make coffee and talk at the table," Katherine said.

They worked in silence. Sarah made the decaff coffee, Mother got the mugs, Dad pulled out the cream and sugar. All jobs they'd done a million times before.

As the coffee brewed, they sat at the table. Sarah stared at objects around the room that had always been there. Parts of her childhood.

Grandma's iron skillet that her mother still used to make corn bread. An apron hanging on the pantry door hook. An arrangement of fresh flowers in the middle of the table, something her mom had always insisted on having, whether they were cut from the yard, ordered from the florist or bought at the grocery store.

"All correspondence for the scholarship comes to you at this address," Winston said, breaking the silence. "So yes, I knew about it. But I couldn't tell you or you would have found out what I'd done."

"Gregory set it up."

"I figured as much."

As the coffeepot beeped to signal it was finished, Sarah said, "Gregory's asked me to forgive him. But I just can't."

"It'll take God's help, honey," her mom said. "Pray about it. And I'll pray, too. Because I think you need to forgive him and move on, or you'll end up hurting yourself."

"Can you forgive me?" her dad asked in a broken voice.

Somehow it seemed easier to forgive her dad. She knew he loved her and was doing his best. Even though he had been wrong in the way he went about it. "Yes, Dad, I forgive you."

Late that night, Gregory walked through the house to turn off lights and lock up. As he unplugged the Christmas tree lights, it hit him just how much Sarah had done to change their lives for the better. She'd forced him to get the tree and to decorate it. She'd put up outside lights on her own. She'd hung wreaths and put up other decorations, making the house a fun, festive place for the boys. And for him.

She'd helped the boys make gifts and to reach out to show kindness to others, helping them see that Christmas wasn't just about receiving. It was about giving, too.

And she'd encouraged them to pray, forcing Gregory to acknowledge he hadn't been leading his family in prayer like he should. And now, they were having nightly bedtime prayers.

And even though he shouldn't have fallen for her again in the process, at least when she left, his family would be in better shape. Would have their priorities straight.

And Hunter and Chase would be happier kids.

Will they still be happy once she leaves, though?

Gregory couldn't control that. All he could control was how he raised his sons. How he loved them. And he would be doing a much better job of that now that Sarah had forced him to change.

He owed her. And he would honor her by being the best dad he could be.

Starting tomorrow, he would make sure to live up to her expectations. And he would do that by returning the new game system and some of the toys. But he would keep the trampoline. They would be spending time playing outside together on it—Gregory included. And also, playing ball. And board games. Doing homework together. Church activities together.

No more working around the clock. No more pawning the kids off on his dad every single day. No, Gregory was going to get his life in order.

And since two of their Santa requests were within his ability to provide, he would figure out a way to give them those things.

The next morning, Sarah awoke and realized this was the big day. Christmas Eve. The day of the pageant.

Nervous energy flitted through her body like a massive dose of caffeine, making her feel wired, jittery.

Realization that she hadn't heard from Donna Rae added another jolt to her system. Surely with a fifth child, things should move along smoothly.

She brazenly dialed Donna Rae's cell phone, assuming she would turn it off if she didn't want calls.

"Hey, Sarah," Donna Rae said in answer to the ring.

"Well?"

"The first trip was a false alarm. But we're here now for real."

"Can you call me when you—"

"I've already had an epidural. Can you come?"

"I'll be there as quickly as I can."

Sarah got ready and arrived at the hospital within

forty-five minutes. When she walked in the room, Donna Rae and Vinny were cooing over a tiny baby swaddled in an aqua-and-yellow-striped blanket. The other kids surrounded their mom on the bed and looked as if they were in love already.

"Boy or girl?" Sarah asked.

"Girl," all the little ones shouted.

"Come meet Alice Durante," the proud dad said.

Sarah approached, and they handed the little bundle to her. "Oh, she's precious. And perfect. Such a blessing." Out of nowhere, tears burned Sarah's eyes and nose. Would she ever have a baby of her own? She handed the baby back to Donna Rae.

"Hey, gang," Donna Rae said. "I think it's time for Dad to take you back home. Come give me and Alice a kiss. And be good for Grandma tonight."

They all said goodbye, and Vinny nearly had to peel them off their new sister. They didn't want to leave.

On the way out, Vinny said, "Sarah, did you get someone to fill in for me tonight?"

"Yes, Hunter volunteered Gregory."

"Great, thanks!"

Once everyone left, Donna Rae began to feed the baby. "Sarah, what's wrong?"

"Nothing. I was just overcome by how awesome little Alice is. How awesome God is."

"No, it's more than that. I can see it in your eyes. You're sad."

Why did Donna Rae have to be so perceptive? She told Donna Rae all about how she and Gregory had fallen for each other again. But how her dad had blown a hole right into Sarah's nice little fantasy bubble.

"Oh, hon, I can't believe that happened. What did you do when you found out?"

"I said some awful things to Gregory. And to my dad. But last night Mother, Dad and I had a talk and all is well, now."

"And with Gregory?"

She smoothed her fingers over the back of Alice's head. "He apologized, told me he never used any of the money." She sat back in her chair with a sigh. "He even established a scholarship in my name at the high school."

Donna Rae gasped. "*He* set that up? I thought for sure your dad did it."

"You've heard of it?"

"Of course. I've known a couple of seniors who won the scholarship."

"This is unbelievable. No one ever mentioned it to me."

"Well, you've got to forgive the man. You love him. He loves you."

"This is starting to sound like a Barney the Dinosaur kids' song."

"Just remember you two are meant to be together. You held—"

"I know. We held hands around The Forever Tree." She pushed up from the chair. "I better go. I need to run by the church and then make some reminder calls. We had kids forget their costumes yesterday. Hunter included."

"Word of advice. Go by and pick them up. If they forgot them yesterday, there's a good chance they'll forget this evening, too."

"Are you just saying that to get me to go see Gregory?"

"Why, no!" Donna Rae laughed, but for the life of her, Sarah couldn't figure out if she was telling the truth or not.

Sarah said goodbye to Donna Rae and Alice, then she drove first to pick up the donkey tail. As she headed to Gregory's, she thought back to the night she and Gregory had held hands around the tree. He had come to her house at midnight, their regular meeting time. Usually, they talked through a window. Or she would climb outside and sit on the porch with him. Sometimes they even snuck into the woods so no one would see them.

But that night, he asked her to ride in the car with him. She was scared to death of getting caught. And just a little scared of him, period. He had such a wild reputation. But she knew the real Gregory. She knew he wouldn't take advantage of her.

And he hadn't. He'd taken her to the park in downtown Magnolia. He'd silently walked her to The Forever Tree. With tears in his eyes, the former bad boy had declared he loved her. Had asked her to hold hands around the tree so that no matter what either of their parents said or did, they would have forever love.

She'd told him she loved him, too. Then he ever so solemnly took one of her hands, walked around to the other side of the tree, and clasped the other hand to complete the circle.

"Sarah Radcliffe, I'll love you forever, no matter what happens," he'd said.

She'd been so overcome by emotion that she hadn't said anything back. Her throat had clogged and she'd just cried.

When they'd finished, he hugged her, consoled her. Kissed her silly. Until she feared she might be tempted to do more than she should. So she'd asked him to take her back home.

The next day, her parents found out she'd snuck out. They forbade her from seeing him. Demanded she break up with him. Threatened to call the police if he came over again.

She'd been so afraid that he would get arrested that she started thinking that breaking up would be best. And really, it confirmed what she'd been thinking anyway. So she broke up with him the very next day.

On Christmas Eve. Exactly...sixteen years ago.

As she pulled into Gregory's driveway, she hesitated. Would he remember?

She shook off memory cobwebs that kept trying to stick to her, dragging her back into the past.

She had to move forward. To deal with details for the play, then to have a wonderful Christmas with her parents, then to go back to Nashville and pick up the pieces where she left off.

She should probably thank Gregory for letting her hang out with his sons. They'd helped ease her grief over Peter. And seeing the three of them bond, well, that had helped even more.

She knocked on his door and braced herself. Braced herself for the pain, for the regret for what might have been.

He opened the door. And froze. "Oh. Hi." He sprang into action, stepping back and waving her through the door. "Uh, come in."

"I'll only take a minute of your time. I came by to pick up Hunter's costume. I'm going house to house to get them all at Donna Rae's suggestion. She said—"

"It's okay. I already put it in the truck, but I'll get it

for you." He inclined his head toward his office. "Have a seat. I'll be right back."

For some strange reason, she felt drawn to his chair instead of to one of the chairs facing his desk. She sat in it, then rolled up to the desk.

His desk was a little cluttered. His calendar was filled with hard-to-read notes to himself regarding…billing… potential customers…things to do before Christmas.

She chuckled when she saw his planned dates to buy a tree and to decorate and shop. All plans she'd messed up.

She spun his chair to the side. Sheets of paper sat in his printer. They looked like some kind of coupon or certificate.

She picked one up. When she read it, her stomach took a nosedive. They *were* coupons. One redeemable for Hunter to play outside with Dad. The other for a night for Chase to sleep in Dad's bed.

She looked back at the printer. There were several more copies just like the one in her hand.

The front door opened, and Gregory walked in with a brown-striped pillowcase that appeared to have holes cut in it. He held it up to show her. "We got it right on the second try. The first time I—"

He stopped short when he saw what was in her hand.

"I'm sorry. It must look like I'm snooping."

"It's okay. I was just making up some coupons for the boys. It's what they asked for on their new list for Santa." Red inched up along his cheeks as he rubbed the back of his neck.

"So they changed their requests?"

"They asked for those things." He nodded toward the coupons. "And, uh, for one or two other things."

"Well, good for them." She smiled at Gregory, surprised she felt so at ease. "So where are Hunter and Chase?"

"With Dad and Richard. They actually agreed to take them for today. Although I think Richard is putting them to work unpacking."

She couldn't help the smile that began to form. "I'm sorry. I'm afraid I've had something to do with your dad's evasiveness."

"I suspected as much."

She hopped up from his chair, suddenly anxious to leave. "I should go. I imagine you have some last-minute shopping to do."

He grinned, eyes shining, one of his most charming smiles, like the old Gregory. "Yeah, you might say that. I'm returning a bunch of stuff."

"Returning?"

"Yep. They don't need it. What they need is my time and attention. You know, those things most important at Christmas. Time with family."

Oh, Lord help me. He's dangerous when he's like this. And I do want to forgive him. But I don't know if I really can. "Yeah. I believe maybe I've said something similar before."

"Yes, I believe you did."

"Well, I'll let you go return stuff. And I guess I'll see you tonight."

He reached out as if he was going to touch her arm. But then he didn't. He put his hand in his pocket. "I'll be there at six. You can count on it."

She knew he'd chosen those words carefully. And that he meant them.

Chapter Thirteen

Gregory battled the crowds to return the toys and game system. He couldn't believe he had to stand in line to return something *before* Christmas.

But it was worth it. He felt lighter when he headed toward his dad's house to get the kids. And was happy he would be able to easily pay off his credit card bill that month.

When he arrived, Richard was with the boys in the front yard kicking a soccer ball. Gregory joined them in the game, which ended up being a tackle-Dad challenge. Before it was over, Gregory was on the ground, flat on his back, with Hunter and Chase piled on top of him. After letting them enjoy their victory briefly, he tickled them to get them off since his back was getting soggy from melted snow.

"Come on guys. Time to go home and get some dinner before the pageant."

Richard gave him a hand to help him up. "Dad said to tell you he's making sandwiches for all of you."

"Sounds great."

They all headed inside. His dad was in the kitchen

and had ham, turkey, cheeses, bread and all the condiments set out on the table. "Hey, you're just in time to eat a quick bite before you have to go to the church."

Once they'd all washed up and sat, Harry said a blessing, then everyone jumped in to make their own sandwiches. Chase and Hunter included.

"So, did a package arrive from Lindsay?" he asked his dad.

"Oh, yes. I meant to tell you yesterday. Everything's all set in that department," he said in semi-code to let Gregory know all gifts were wrapped and ready. His dad may have even assembled Chase's present.

"When's Aunt Windsay coming?" Chase asked.

"Remember, she's with Bill all the way across the ocean, going to see Bill's brother."

"Oh, yeah." He stuck out his bottom lip.

"Hey, big guy," Richard said. "You've got Uncle Richard here this year instead. And then there's the big bearded guy in red who'll be here tonight."

"Santa!" Hunter hollered.

"Santa," Chase echoed with his mouth full. "Dad, do you think Santa will bwing us Miss Sawah for our mom?"

The room got silent. His dad and brother had stopped chewing. They both stared at Gregory.

"What about Miss Sarah?" his dad asked.

"Well, it seems that Hunter and Chase have added Sarah to their Christmas list." His face flashed scalding hot.

The look on Richard's face would have been comical if Gregory hadn't been so embarrassed.

"So when did this happen?" Richard asked. "I thought you had a date with Molly."

"I did. But the boys made the list by themselves."

"So what do you think, uh, Santa is going to do?" Richard asked, controlling a smile.

Hunter and Chase were all ears.

"I guess what Santa usually does. He brings you some things on your list but not all the things on your list."

Richard raised an eyebrow. "Yeah, I remember that." He looked at his nephews. "You better be prepared, boys. Sometimes Santa just brings you part of what you ask for."

"We've been praying, too," Hunter said. "We asked God for Santa to bring us *everything* we asked for." He shrugged. "So it's gonna happen."

"Yeah. God can do anything," Chase added. He jumped out of his chair and started running around the room with his arms out like wings. "Like Superman!"

Hunter joined him in running around, acting as if he could fly.

"Sit back down and eat," their granddad said.

"I'm full," Hunter said.

"Me, too," Chase said.

Their normally indulgent granddad pointed to the back door. "Then you two go outside and play while we finish eating."

"Put your coats on," Gregory called.

As soon as they slammed the door behind them, his dad said, "What on earth are you going to do?"

"I was hoping they wouldn't remember she's on their list."

"Well, sorry, but that plan is shot to pieces," Richard said.

Hadn't he thought the same thing a dozen times? It

was Christmas Eve, and he couldn't put his head in the sand any longer. He would have to prepare himself for their disappointment. "I'm hoping there'll be enough other stuff to occupy them at least a little."

"Can you produce Molly for the boys instead?" Richard asked.

"I like the idea of Sarah for Gregory," Harry said.

The pain of Sarah's confronting him about the bribe returned in a giant wave that nearly sucked him under. He'd done well the last day or so, telling himself that everything would be okay without her. "Come on, Dad. Give me a break."

"I've seen a new side to her. Wouldn't mind having her for a daughter-in-law."

Time to escape. He didn't have the time or energy to tell them the whole story. "Well, gotta run. Thanks for dinner."

As Gregory stood, his cell phone rang. "Hello?"

"Hi, Gregory. This is Molly."

"Oh, hi, Molly," he said as he stepped into the next room.

"I wanted to remind you of my offer for you to set up your trampoline over here."

"Uh, thanks. But Richard offered to help set it up at my house after the boys are asleep."

"Oh. Okay. Well, how would you like to come over for either lunch or dinner on Christmas day? Bring Hunter and Chase, of course."

Oh, man. He needed to let her down gently. No matter what happened with Sarah, he didn't feel anything for Molly. "Um, I'm sorry Molly. I can't work that out either."

"Okay. Don't worry about it. We'll get together again soon."

He almost told her no. Still, he shouldn't rule her out. Sarah would be gone soon, and he could get back to normal. Well, almost normal. There would be a lot of changes where his kids were concerned. "Sure."

"You mean it? You want to go out again?"

"I wouldn't be opposed to it." He winced. Had he really just said that?

"Uh, Gregory. Please don't say that out of pity. Just tell me if you're not interested."

Richard stepped in the room, being nosey, listening.

"Actually, I need to be completely honest," he told Molly. "I'd rather us be friends like we've always been."

She took two audible breaths. "I understand. Thanks for telling me."

Richard stood by, rudely listening.

When Gregory hung up, he said, "Why are you eavesdropping? Are you still interested in Molly or something?"

"I treated her badly in high school, used her to make someone else jealous. And I just don't want you jerking her around."

"You're right. She doesn't deserve it. She's really nice."

"Too nice for you," Richard said as he walked back to the kitchen.

Richard was much closer to the truth than he knew.

Sarah took her time getting ready for the performance. She dressed in a red cashmere sweater. Put her pearls on. Touched up her makeup.

She wanted to look her best. And just generally wanted everything to go smoothly.

And she was anxious about all the children remembering their lines.

Face it, Sarah, you're nervous about seeing Gregory again. And you're putting on that lipstick for him.

She tried to imagine a future with Gregory in it. But every time the picture would start to form, Delia's face would invade.

Lord, I would like to leave here knowing I've done my best to forgive him so that maybe we could meet on better terms next time I come home. And Lord, I know You've commanded us to forgive. So I guess You're going to have to give me the power to do it. Please.

She met her mom and dad at the front door. "Are you sure y'all want to go this early?"

"We want to get a good seat," her mom said as her dad held out her coat, and she slipped into it.

He then held out Sarah's coat. "We don't want to miss your directing debut." He winked at her, and she felt nothing but love.

So how come she couldn't seem to feel the same way about Gregory? Why did she keep recalling Gregory's betrayal?

Maybe because she knew that her dad, though misguided, had acted out of love.

Gregory hadn't.

He obviously hadn't loved her at all. And that hurt.

"Well, the last rehearsal went great," she said. "So let's pray tonight does as well."

They made the short trip to the church. Sarah unlocked the building and her parents helped her carry everything inside, including Hunter's costume and the donkey tail.

Soon after, footsteps ran down the aisle. "Miss Sarah, look! We made a shepherd's staff."

She couldn't resist. She automatically looked behind Hunter—trying to find Gregory—before she checked out the staff. He stood in the back. Almost hesitant.

And he was staring right at her. A smile on his face. But not a friendly smile. It was something more.

She peeled her attention back to Hunter. "Oh, you did such a nice job. Did you and your dad make it?"

"Yes, ma'am."

Chase popped out from behind Hunter. "Peekaboo!"

She acted startled, then said, "And there's Chase. Did you bring your best angel smile?"

He gave her an exaggerated grin. Then he giggled as he threw his arms around her legs to hug her. "Santa's coming tonight, Miss Sawah."

"I know, sweetie. I'm sure you've both been good this year. I know Santa will be good to you."

She looked over their heads at their dad, determined to try to be civil.

But his expression had changed. He seemed…stressed.

He was probably worried again about providing enough *stuff.* Especially after returning some of it.

"Well, I guess you should both go get your dad to help you with your costumes."

They ran back to Gregory, and she didn't really have time to think about them anymore. She needed to make sure the sound system was working, that the star was ready to be lowered, and that the Baby Jesus doll was out of the manger and placed backstage.

By the time all the children finally arrived, it was nearly time to start.

At seven o'clock, parents, grandparents, church members and others from the community sat packed into the pews like sardines. A good many were fanning because the sanctuary had heated up. They even had to bring in folding chairs and *still* had people standing.

Her heart raced. Nerves like she'd never had before sent her stomach into a quivery dance. Her mouth went dry as she welcomed everyone to the pageant.

But as she and Gregory moved to their place behind the curtain, he placed his hand on her back and said, "Dear God, we ask for peace, for calm, for relief from the jitters—adults included. Please touch lives here tonight. Amen."

Then he took his hand away from her back, leaving her bereft of his warmth. "Thank you, Gregory."

Why did he have to go and be so nice?

As the kids moved into place, a sense of peace enveloped her. *Thank you, Lord. And please take away the old hurts and anger. Soften my heart.*

The children began with the nativity story. She and Gregory read their first Bible verses. Then the actors took over. When it got to Hunter's part, she expected him to jump right in like the last run-through. But he froze.

As she tried to peek through the curtain, Gregory whispered, "Cover for me." Then he tore around the end of the curtain.

She looked through the gap and spotted him crawling along the alter rail until he was right in front of Hunter. He very quietly gave him a cue. Hunter turned toward his dad and bent over as if talking to him.

Sarah couldn't hear what they were saying. But she could see Gregory. Smiling. Nodding. Encouraging his son.

After an awkwardly long silence, Hunter finally began his lines. He started off quietly, but then seemed to gain confidence.

Gregory stayed long enough to give him a thumbs-up, then crept back to the end of the curtain and dashed behind it.

She read one of his passages, but he was there for the following one.

The next time Hunter had to speak, she held her breath. But he jumped right in and got it exactly right. Gregory gave him a thumbs-up through the slit in the curtain once again. Then he grinned at Sarah, so proud, so excited for his son.

Tears practically shot out of her tear ducts. She had to wipe her eyes and search for a tissue.

Gregory found a box of tissues under the pulpit and offered one. He looked concerned. "Are you okay?"

She nodded. Then she forced her concentration back to the play.

Lord, I asked you to soften my heart. Not make it mush.

Once they finished with their reading parts, Gregory went to the edge of the curtain to watch the rest of the action and their last song. The most incredible smile lit his face.

He had been there for his boys—making sets, making costumes, cuing lines. And he had come through on every challenge she'd issued, from tree-buying to decorating for Christmas. He hadn't once failed her or his sons.

When he came back to her side, she whispered, "You know, no matter what happened between us, I have to tell you I think you're a great father."

He took a deep breath and let it out slowly. Then he started to shove his hands in his pockets.

She reached out and stopped him, took his hands in hers. "You should be proud of your sons."

He started to say something, then hesitated. "Thanks. I am."

Applause started out in front of the curtain. The play had ended.

"I guess you need to take a bow, Madame Director." He held out his hand to her.

Even as her heart thumped hard in her chest, she took hold of his offered hand, and he led her around the curtain. There wasn't a dry eye in the house.

The kids had done an amazing job touching hearts that night. Just like God had touched her heart.

Gregory couldn't remember a Christmas pageant that had meant more to him. He let go of Sarah's hand and pushed her to the front of the stage area so she could get her due. While the audience applauded for her, he slipped backstage to grab a bouquet of flowers he'd picked up earlier. The children joined in the clapping as he handed them to her.

"Thank you for all your work," he said.

Then as the applause started to wind down, he leaned close to her ear and said, "And thank you for all you've done for me and my family."

She smiled at him. "It was my pleasure."

All the crowd and noise zoomed to the background. There was just the two of them staring into each other's eyes, and some sort of…something seemed to pass between them.

"Dad! I got my lines," Hunter yelled, breaking Gregory out of their little cocoon.

"I know. You did great. And Chase…" He found his youngest son behind him. "You did great, too. You looked like a real little angel out there."

The boys clung to him, Chase reaching to be picked up.

With his sons close by, and a happy Sarah standing beside him, he felt…content.

But would the feeling last more than this one night?

Winston and Katherine walked up and each hugged her. "Beautiful job," her mom said. Then she said, "You, too, Gregory."

"Thank you, Mrs. Radcliffe."

Mr. Radcliffe held out his hand, and Gregory thought the man looked scared.

It was hard not to snub him and walk away. But if Gregory was hoping to be forgiven by Sarah, then surely he himself needed to offer forgiveness. He shook Winston's hand. "Your daughter did a great job directing."

"Thank you. We're proud of her." He looked relieved. Sheepish.

The boys cheered and peeled off their costumes.

Hunter looked at Chase out of the corner of his eye, a sneaky, mischievous gleam making his eyes sparkle. "Miss Sarah, do you think Santa will bring us *everything* we asked for?"

She leaned down and patted each of their cheeks. "How could he not?"

Oh, boy.

Richard, who'd apparently been standing behind

Gregory, leaned in and said, "I'd say there are going to be some busy little elves tonight." Then he laughed and walked away.

Chapter Fourteen

Later that evening, Sarah stood in her parents' living room with an armload of gifts. She was drained, yet energized after the play. A strange mix.

Christmas would be over before she knew it. She would return to her house. Back to teaching. Back to her real life.

She sighed clear to her toes as she placed the last couple of gifts under the tree.

Christmas sure would be more exciting with children in the house. She could only imagine how exciting Harry's house would be in the morning with Richard and Gregory and the boys. What a crowd that would be.

Well, the Radcliffes had their own version of Christmas. They'd always opened gifts on Christmas Eve. That way they could sleep in and have a leisurely brunch on Christmas Day.

Sarah's mom came into the room and sat in a chair beside the tree. She reached out and toyed with an ornament. "So, what was going on up on that stage tonight?"

"What do you mean?"

"You and Gregory."

With a whoosh, heat traveled up her neck, to her face. She was probably glowing as bright as the tree lights. "He was just thanking me."

"Maybe so. But I saw more than that."

Sarah sat on the arm of her mom's chair. "I told him I think he's a good dad."

"So what's the situation between you now?"

She shook her head. "Nothing right now."

"How do you feel about him?"

"I think I love him. But can you love someone when you haven't forgiven him?"

"Well, honey, I don't know."

"Whenever we're together, I want him to hold me, to kiss me." Her face flamed even more, but she knew she could talk to her mother about anything.

"Could just be physical attraction."

"I love his children. I love how he crawled on the floor tonight to make sure Hunter knew his lines. I love how he picks up Chase as if he weighs nothing and how he looks holding him in his arms. I love how, when he gets nervous, he shoves his hands into his pockets."

Her mother said, "Keep going," as if she were giving a preacher an *amen*.

"And I love how he turns on the charm, even though it aggravates me sometimes, because I know he only does it when he's feeling insecure."

"Have you told him how you feel?"

"Yes. But that was before Dad told me about the payoff. Now I'm not sure I can ever trust him."

"Maybe you should talk to him before you go back to Nashville."

She looked into her mother's eyes. "So if we did get together, you'd be okay with it?"

"Seems like he's become a good man. And I trust your judgment."

"And Dad?"

Her mother patted her hand. "He'll come around. But don't you worry about us. You need to do what's best for you."

That night, Gregory got the boys tucked into bed at his dad's house. Then he, Dad and Richard sat around the tree as they waited for them to fall asleep—a process that could take a while with all the excitement.

A plate of cookies and cup of milk sat on a small table near the tree. Under the edge of the cup, the "Dear Santa" letter rested, anchored by the weight of the milk because the boys hadn't wanted it to blow away when Santa whooshed down the chimney.

The weight of that letter sat heavy on him. "I need to go assemble the you-know-what pretty soon," he said to his dad and brother.

Richard kicked his feet up on the coffee table. "I'll help." He looked at his watch. "Uh, Gregory, once the you-know-what is set up, then you'll have about…oh… six hours, maybe, to get that big gift the kids really want."

"I thought the trampo—I mean the you-know-what is the big gift," his dad said.

"He's talking about Sarah." Gregory leaned his head against the back of the couch and looked at the ceiling.

"Oh, that's right."

"Yes, they want Sarah for their mom, remember?" Richard had to add.

"And to make matters worse, they've been praying for it every night," Gregory said.

"Oh, boy," his dad said, echoing what Gregory had thought earlier. After another minute or so, he said, "I'll stay here and wrap anything you need while you run to your house for the assembly."

He grinned at his dad. "I wrapped everything already."

Surprise flashed across his face before he covered it. "Well, good for you."

"He may need you to help wrap the big gift," Richard said, then slapped Gregory on the back and headed out of the room, laughing.

"I'm glad you're having such a good time at my expense," Gregory said to his retreating back.

Sarah sat in the cushy leather love seat with the lights off, snuggled under a blanket, staring at the lit Christmas tree until the twinkle lights started to blur together.

All the gifts had been opened. Her parents had gone to bed.

Mother had given her a beautiful silk scarf and a gift card from Macy's. Enough to buy several outfits.

Dad had given her a gorgeous pair of diamond stud earrings. Huge. Too huge, and probably a guilt offering.

They'd had a lovely time opening gifts. A nice, quiet night together. And her parents had loved the framed montage she'd made from scanning old photos, starting with their wedding pictures.

But something had been missing.

Gregory and Hunter and Chase are what's missing.

She slung the blanket off, folded it, then tossed it onto the back of the love seat. She unplugged the tree and walked in the dark to her bedroom.

Lord, I feel like there's this little piece of my heart

*that I'm not turning over to You. Like there's this little
bit of hurt that I'm holding onto so that I can't let myself totally care for Gregory.*

*Lord, only You can heal that hurt. Only You can
help me let it go.*

Only You can empower me to forgive him.

When Gregory and Richard returned from setting
up the trampoline, Richard headed to bed.

Gregory stared at the kitchen clock. *Tick, tick, tick.*
He knew it might take a long time for Sarah to be able
to forgive him. He had to be patient. But for some reason he felt a sense of urgency.

Probably because of the Christmas wish list.

Harry walked into the kitchen. "I'm turning in, too."

"Do you think Sarah will ever forgive me?"

"I'm sure she will. She's a fine woman. Just give
her time. She cares about you—I can see that much."

"Enough to marry me?" Whoa. He hadn't really let
himself think of that possibility, but now it was out in
the open.

A very appealing possibility.

Dad gestured to Gregory to sit at the table with him.
"Well, I guess you'll have to be asking *her* that question." He laughed. "So when are you thinking of asking her?"

"Once she says she's forgiven me."

"You may not see her again before she heads back
to Nashville."

He didn't need a reminder. It was the reason his neck
muscles felt like a pretzel. "I know. I think I'm going
over there tonight."

"Son, it's almost midnight."

"I feel like if I let her leave, then I'll miss my chance." Or lose his nerve.

"Talking things through, being totally honest, is always a good thing. But maybe you should wait till tomorrow."

He pushed up from the table. "I'll think about it."

Gregory walked outside and stared into the night sky. Stars shone brightly along with the moon. The bite of cold did him good, was kind of a kick in the rear, clearing his thoughts, clearing his mind of all the stuff that was crowding in.

He shoved out the fears. Shoved out the doubts. Shoved out the wishes of others, including his boys.

What do I want for my life at this moment? And what does God want for my life?

Sarah.

Sarah as my wife.

"Dear God," he whispered toward the sky. "Please help her find the ability to forgive me. And help us make wise decisions about our future."

Follow your heart. The thought echoed through his mind.

Follow his heart? Could it really be that simple?

Sarah was just dozing when a sound jolted her back to full alertness. Had she dreamed it?

No, there it was again. A clicking that sounded as if it was coming from her bedroom window.

She sat up in bed to listen.

Another *ping* sounded from the glass of her window.

Blood rushed through her body, and she could hear it in her ears.

But then she had a moment of déjà vu.

Gregory.

She grabbed her robe, slipped her arms inside, then tied the belt. She lifted one of the blades of the blinds and peeked out. Gregory stood down in the yard, ready to throw another pebble.

She pulled the blinds up. Then she knelt down to raise the floor-to-ceiling window.

She only opened it enough to be able to stick her head out. "What do you think you're doing?"

"I have to talk to you."

"Come back in the morning."

"It can't wait. *I* can't wait."

His claim sent her blood rushing through her skull once again. But it wasn't out of fear or alarm this time. It was thrill, pure and simple. "I'm not climbing out a window like a sneaky teenager."

"I'll come inside. Just give me ten minutes. Please?"

She sighed, because she wanted to say no. She really did. But there was no way she could resist finding out what was so urgent. "Okay. Come to the front door."

She quickly dressed, then turned off the alarm system. When she opened the door, he stood there smiling. His charming smile.

Oh, my. He's nervous.

"Come in." She showed him into the living room, hoping they wouldn't wake her parents.

"Wow. Your tree's huge."

"Yes." She reached behind it and plugged in the lights.

"It's beautiful."

"Thanks. Mother and I did it this year."

He shoved his hands into his pockets. Then pulled them out again and crossed his arms in front of him.

She wanted to cry. *Lord, are You showing me this, how vulnerable he can be?*

"I, uh, wasn't sure how long you'd be in town after Christmas, so I didn't know if I'd see you again before you left."

"I was planning on going back on the twenty-sixth."

"Yeah, that's what I was afraid of. So…well…" He shoved his hands back into his pockets.

That little place in her heart that had been cold and bitter opened up, and she imagined God reaching in to take away all the junk, then closing it with a pat. She smiled at the vision and was more than happy to let it go. "Can I interrupt?" she said before he kept on with the painful awkwardness.

"Sure."

"I need to tell you that I've forgiven you. With God's help, of course. Can you forgive me for any hurt that I've caused?"

His posture eased, and he grinned at her. "Yeah, I think I can manage that." Then he moved closer.

And closer.

When he stood right in front of her, nearly toe-to-toe, she thought her heart might burst—from love and fear.

Gregory wanted to touch her. To kiss her. To ask her to be his wife. But he had to move a little slower since he had no idea how she would react.

He put one hand on her waist. "I've been wondering if you might ever consider moving back to Magnolia to live. If you might consider teaching somewhere around here."

"Hmm. I've never thought about it before." She bit her lip. "But yes, I believe I would consider it."

"This summer would be nice. I could help you move your stuff."

"My *stuff?*" She smirked.

"Yeah, all your fine *stuff*."

"Well, thank you for that kind offer."

He put his other hand on the other side of her waist and pulled her against him. He was pleased when she placed her hands on his chest. She smiled and looked into his eyes. And this time her smile wasn't guarded. It wasn't filtered through fear or betrayal. She had truly forgiven him.

"So why should I move back to Magnolia?" she asked.

And...could it be? She looked at him as if she loved him.

He couldn't resist for another second. He kissed her, trying to show her how he felt when it was so hard to say it. When even though he saw her love, he still couldn't believe he would be lucky enough to have another chance.

She kissed him back as if pouring all her feelings into it. Which made him brave enough to speak.

He dragged his lips away from hers. Leaned his forehead against hers. "I don't want you all the way up there in Nashville." He cleared his throat. Swallowed. Then thought how ridiculous he was being. "I love you, Sarah. I think I have since I first saw you by your locker. And you had those sparkling brown eyes. So innocent. So trusting. It's a wonder you didn't run the other direction."

She laughed with tears streaming down her cheeks. "I love you, too."

Yes, there was love in her eyes.

Not the young, naive, forbidden love from before. This love seemed stronger. Forged by facing adversity, then coming out on the other side. With forgiveness.

"You know, I've been wondering what you have planned at about five a.m. on Christmas."

She swallowed. "Five *a.m.?*"

"Yep. Bright and early. Before the boys wake up and come barreling in the room."

She wrapped her arms around his neck. "I don't suppose I have any plans at that time."

"I need your help. The boys have asked for you as their mom for Christmas."

Her lip quivered. "Are you serious?"

"Yep. And isn't it amazing that they asked for the exact same model mom that I'm looking for in a wife?"

Wide-eyed, she whispered, "Are you saying what I think you're saying?"

He grinned and nodded. "Sarah Radcliffe, would you do me the honor of becoming my wife?"

"Oh, Gregory, yes. It's so perfect, I can't believe it. The perfect Christmas." She kissed him this time, her body settling into the embrace as if it remembered exactly where to go.

Sarah didn't sleep much that night. So she was only in a light sleep when her alarm went off at four o'clock in the morning.

She was so excited a buzz seemed to hum through her body as she showered and got ready for Gregory to pick her up. It was as if her system was on hyperalert. Her shampoo smelled better than ever. The cool morning air felt crisper than ever. The light from the lamp in her bedroom seemed brighter than ever. The soft yellow of the paint on the walls seemed cheerier than ever.

Her heart felt fuller than ever.

A *ping, ping* sounded on her window—louder than ever.

No, he wouldn't do that.

She burst out laughing when she saw him standing outside her window grinning. He had a potted poinsettia in his hand.

She tugged the window up. Further this time. "What on earth?"

"I wanted to bring you flowers, so I settled for swiping this from Dad's hearth."

"What a romantic."

He held his hand up to her. "Will you come ride with me?"

The same thing he'd asked her in high school the night they got caught slipping out. The night they'd held hands around The Forever Tree. "I don't know. I might get in trouble."

"I promise to behave."

She laughed. "Yeah, I've heard that before." She closed the window and hurried downstairs to open the front door.

He stood on her doorstep, grinning, with the silly poinsettia.

"So, Gregory, are you going to wrap me up for the boys to open?"

"Hadn't thought of that. I just figured I'd have you sit under the tree."

"I like that idea."

They drove to his dad's house in silence—except for the song of her heart.

Chapter Fifteen

Gregory couldn't believe this day had come. The fulfillment of all he'd dreamed about when he was eighteen years old. The completion of his family.

A Christmas he would remember forever.

When they arrived at the house, Sarah chatted with his dad and Richard as the four of them had a cup of coffee. Then they turned on the Christmas tree lights and waited. A little before six o'clock, little footsteps and squeals came from the vicinity of Gregory's old room.

Sarah clapped her hands just like a kid herself as she hurried to sit beside the tree, amongst the gifts. Her smile was the only gift he needed.

"Come on. It looks like Santa has been here," Gregory yelled.

Cheers erupted. Hunter and Chase ran into the room.

"A bike!" Hunter screamed as he focused on the gift closest to him.

"A bike," Chase echoed.

"A puzzle," Hunter screamed, and then Chase echoed.

All of a sudden Chase really looked around, and he

said, "A mom!" as if Sarah actually were a present under the tree. He ran over and dove into her lap.

She hugged him close and said, "Merry Christmas."

Hunter stopped dead in his tracks. He turned and saw Sarah. He looked scared. Afraid to hope.

She motioned him over and said, "Yes, you really got what you wanted for Christmas."

"You'll be our mom?" Hunter asked as he slowly walked her way.

"Yes."

"Every day, like when we wake up, after school, and even at night?"

"Yes, Hunter. I love your dad, and I love both of you."

His heart full to bursting, Gregory reached under the tree and pulled out a small gift. He handed it to Sarah. Then he motioned Hunter to come on over.

Hunter climbed into Sarah's lap just as naturally has Chase had.

Gregory knelt down in front of them. "Sarah, will you take me, Hunter and Chase to be your family?"

She let go of the boys long enough to rip the paper off the box. Then slowly, she opened it.

Gregory looked at his dad to make sure he was okay. Dad beamed, but seemed to have a few tears in his eyes.

When Sarah opened the ring box, she gasped. "It's gorgeous."

"It was my mother's. Dad and I would like you to have it."

"Will you say yes, Miss Sarah?" Hunter asked, so serious it nearly hurt Gregory.

His son was scared she would reject them.

She put the ring on her finger, then wrapped her

arms around both boys. "Yes! I'll marry you and be your family."

Gregory laughed, then squeezed in between his boys, wrapped them all in his arms, and gave his fiancée a kiss. "Thank you," he whispered. With his sons and the woman he loved in his arms, he had a sense of peace he hadn't felt in years. Maybe ever. He was finally forgiven and free from his past.

"Hey, I got a mom this Christmas," Hunter yelled. "I think I'll ask for a baby brother next Christmas."

The room broke up in laughter.

Gregory kissed Sarah again and said, "Maybe Santa can manage that."

At the moment, anything seemed possible.

* * * * *

A MOM FOR CHRISTMAS

Lorraine Beatty

To Jovetta Ealy, a woman after God's heart,
and in loving memory of her sons, Marco and Willie.

Acknowledgments

To Jon Young,
who shared his structural engineering expertise
with me, and who, when I told him what I wanted
to do to my hero, didn't blink, but proceeded
to tell me how to make it happen.

To Katie Lohr,
the ballerina the Lord literally placed in my car.
Her knowledge and experience with ballet and with
Ballet Magnificat added so much to Beth's story.

Dr. Brad Kennedy, DC,
who always has the perfect solution to any injury
I decide to inflict upon my characters.

I couldn't have written this book
without the three of you.

You shall have no other gods before Me.
—*Exodus* 20:3

Chapter One

The air in the enclosed stairwell reeked of age, and the timeworn wooden stairs creaked with each step. The glass in the old-fashioned door rattled in protest when Bethany Montgomery grasped the knob and pushed it open.

She stepped from the narrow staircase leading to her apartment above her mother's real estate office and inhaled deeply. Even here in the broad recessed entry of the downtown building, the air was tinged with the scent of degrading metal and aged wood. The tiny black-and-white octagonal tiles on the floor from over a hundred years ago completed the picture. Everything in her hometown of DoOver, aka Dover, Mississippi, was old. And at the moment she felt the same. Old, worn-out and irrelevant. And in need of a major do-over.

Unlocking the door to the right, she entered the office of Montgomery Real Estate, her mood sinking another level. She didn't want to be here. Not in Dover, not in the office and not in Mississippi. Her life was in New York, dancing with the Forsythe Ballet Company as principal ballerina for the last six years. She'd been living her lifelong dream, the culmination of a journey started when she was five and her mother had taken her and her sister to see a production of *The Nutcracker* in New Orleans.

Now it was all gone. Ended by a torn ACL complicated by years of overuse and damage she'd paid little attention to. Her neglect had finally caught up with her. There would be no lead roles from here on, and even a spot in the corps de ballet was doubtful. Instead she was forced to come home and work for her mother. The doctors and physical therapists had all declared her days of classical ballet over.

She refused to accept that. Others had recovered from this kind of injury and gone on to perform for years. She would be like them and she wouldn't stop working until she was on stage, *en pointe*, and once more at the top of her profession.

Beth switched on the lights, booted up the computer and scanned the small office, her gaze landing on the wall of family photos. Her throat tightened as she looked at her portrait. It was her first professional photo, and she was dressed in a white tutu, *en pointe* posed *développé croisé devant,* looking like a graceful bird. Absently she rubbed her leg, remembering the pain of the last nine months and that moment when she'd landed and heard the horrible popping sound in her knee.

Her heart dropped into her stomach, leaving a cold emptiness in its place. How was she supposed to go on from here? What was she supposed to do with her life? A sob formed in her chest, but she fought it down. She'd cried and raged enough since the accident. It hadn't changed anything and only made her feel more like a failure.

"Good morning, sweetie. I'm glad to see you up and here on time."

Beth put a smile on her face before turning to face her mother as she breezed into the office. "Did I have a choice?"

Francie Montgomery patted her shoulder before taking a seat at the desk. "Of course you do. Where you work is up to you. What you do with your life from now on is in your hands. You could open up a dance studio here in Dover."

No way. She was *not* going to be one of those failed dancers who goes home and opens up a dance school for every mother who thinks her child is the next movie star. "What I want is to dance again."

Her mother exhaled a soft sigh. "Beth, sooner or later you'll have to accept that your professional career is over. Longing for something you can't have is pointless."

"It's not over. Once I'm fully recovered, I *will* dance again. Somewhere."

Her mother came and stood in front of her. "I hope and pray that's true. But your doctors and your physical therapist think differently. You have to face the facts, sweetheart. And the sooner, the better."

It was an old argument and one of the reasons Beth had moved out of her mother's house. Though well-intentioned and motivated by love, her mom's advice had quickly grown old. Being back in the family home, where the presence of her late father lingered, had added to her distress. There was only so much heartache and sadness she could endure. With her sister, Tori, in California for an indefinite amount of time, Beth had moved in to her apartment above the real estate office to maintain her sanity.

With her mother occupying the desk, Beth moved to the front window and stared at the early morning activity along Main Street in the small town. Her mother was right. She had to face reality. But how did she begin to accept that? How did she face each day with no direction? What could possibly fill the dark, aching void left inside that ballet had always filled?

As she turned away, movement from the office across the entryway drew her attention.

Her mom had bought the entire building when she'd opened her real estate business decades ago. The ground floor consisted of two office spaces, one on either side of the entry, each with windows facing the street and each other. In the four days since she'd moved in to the apartment, she'd assumed the other office was vacant. But now a man was moving about inside. Curious, she stepped closer to the window.

He disappeared into the back room. When he reappeared, Beth strained for a closer look. Even with his back to her, it was impossible to miss how attractive he was. He had broad shoulders beneath a long-sleeved polo shirt of deep red that highlighted his muscular back as he bent and moved. Dark jeans hugged long legs. A warm trickle of appreciation oozed along her skin. Something about the dark hair curling along the nape of his neck bumped up her interest. She peered closer, hoping to catch a glimpse of his face.

"Beth, I need to show houses this morning. I don't know when I'll be back. Is there anything you need to know before I leave?"

She tore her gaze from the intriguing figure in the other office. "I don't think so. Nothing much has changed since I worked here in high school."

Her mother smiled. "True. Change comes slowly to Dover. But we're getting better. I can't wait for you to see the Christmas celebrations Gemma introduced last year."

Beth had only come home for a few days last Christmas, and had left as soon as possible. She'd been eager to get back to prepare for the London tour, and looking at the extensive decorations and events her sister-in-law had orchestrated hadn't been of interest to her.

With her mother gone, the office grew silent, allowing Beth too much time to dwell on the losses in her life. Thankfully the phone started ringing, and the next few hours passed quickly. The man next door hadn't reappeared, but she'd been unable to get him out of her thoughts.

At noon, Beth hung the out-to-lunch sign on the door, set the lock and stepped out into the entryway. She looked forward to going upstairs and hiding in her room for a while. Maintaining a happy face for the walk-in customers and a cheery tone for the call-ins inquiring about homes for sale took a toll on her emotional reserves.

She inserted her key into the lock as the door to the other office opened, and she glanced over her shoulder. Finally she would get a glimpse of the intriguing man she'd seen this morning. The smile on her face faded when she looked at him. There was something familiar about the sky blue eyes and the angle of the chin.

"Hello, Beth."

She inhaled sharply. "Noah? Noah Carlisle. Is that

you?" She took a closer look. It was him, but he was different. Very different. This wasn't the rail-thin, awkward, nerdy friend she remembered. The thick dark glasses were gone, exposing the rich blue eyes with lashes long enough to touch his brows. The planes of his face were still angled, but maturity had added a depth to his features and a sensuous fullness to his lips. Heat flooded her cheeks at the direction of her thoughts, along with a rush of delight. She reached out and gave him a hug, only to pull back when she realized he wasn't returning the gesture. In fact, he wasn't saying anything at all. There was no warmth in his blue eyes, no welcoming smile.

"I'm surprised you remember me."

"Of course I remember you." How could he say that? Her mind flooded with wonderful memories of their friendship. It had been the most important one in her life. She'd fallen in love with him, but he'd made it painfully clear he hadn't returned her feelings. Her warm recollections drained away into a dark pool of humiliation. Suddenly self-conscious, she swallowed and brushed an errant strand of hair off her cheek, attempting to collect herself. "I was thinking about you the other day."

A muscle in his jaw flexed rapidly. "Just the other day?"

What was he saying? "Yes. I mean, I've thought about you several times over the years." His eyes were hard and cold, and there was no warmth in his tone. Noah had changed in more than looks.

A sardonic grin shifted his mouth. "That often in twelve years."

Her conscience burned. She *had* thought about him,

but she'd never bothered to do anything about it. Gathering her composure, she lifted her chin. "You look good." *Good* didn't come close. The scrawny young man she remembered had grown into a dangerously attractive man.

The bony shoulders had broadened into an impressive width above a muscular chest and biceps strained at the fabric of his shirt. His clear blue eyes were more vibrant above the high cheekbones. His thick, dark chocolate hair still persisted in falling over his forehead. But it was his air of confidence that was the most striking difference. The once shy, hesitant boy now carried himself with a confident masculinity that radiated from every pore.

"You've changed."

"I grew up." He held her gaze a long moment. "I heard you were back in town."

The disinterested tone in his voice hurt. They'd been best friends. Why was he so distant and angry? True, she hadn't stayed in touch. Her career had taken all her time and attention. Surely he understood that. She refocused on his comment. "I am. For the time being."

Noah set his jaw. "Don't you think you've chased this foolish dancing dream of yours long enough?"

She clamped her teeth together and fisted her hands to keep a lid on her anger. She didn't know what his problem was, but she'd had enough. "Foolish? I'm a professional dancer with a world-renowned ballet company. I'd hardly call that a dream."

"Are you dancing now?"

The truth pierced like a scalding poker to her heart. "No. But I will be. As soon as I heal and regain my strength." Maybe if she said it often enough, it would be true.

He shook his head. "You haven't changed a bit. Still obsessed with only one thing. Being a big-time ballerina. You don't care about anything else."

"That's not true. I care about a lot of things."

Noah arched his dark eyebrows, and one corner of his mouth hiked up. "I know what you *don't* care about. Your family and your friends. How could they compete with your dreams of fame? Good seeing you again, Bethany. Have a nice life."

He pivoted and strode out onto the sidewalk, disappearing before she could form a response. Noah had always been her biggest supporter, her cheerleader. What had she done that had turned him against her? If anyone had a right to feel angry, she did. He was the one who had rejected her affections with a shrug, leaving her burning with humiliation and pain, then put as much distance as possible between them.

Up in her cozy apartment, Beth munched on a tasteless sandwich, searching her memory for some explanation for Noah's behavior. What was he doing back in Dover anyway, and why hadn't her mother told her he was here and renting space from her?

A vague memory formed of her mother mentioning something about an old friend coming back to town, but she'd tuned it out like she did most things concerning Dover.

The ugly truth forced itself into her mind. *Because keeping in touch wasn't high on your list.* Dancing had been her passion her whole life. She'd been aware that her drive had pushed most of her relationships to the side. Even her family. But to succeed, she'd had to pour all her effort and concentration into her work. And it had paid off. For the last six years, she'd been at the top of her game. *Ambiance*, the new ballet the troupe had performed in London, which she'd helped choreograph, had been the highlight of her career and put her name in the forefront of the dance world. Until one misstep had caused an injury that put her future in jeopardy. But she'd come back. She would. Somehow.

Was losing touch with Noah a big enough reason for his attitude? It didn't make sense. All she knew was that she didn't like him being angry with her. It had been a long torturous year, starting with her injury in London last winter, two surgeries and months of painful rehab in New York before coming home. She was worn down and desperately needed a friend. Noah had always been her confidant, and he'd known exactly what to say to lift her spirits.

Until today.

Noah strode away from his office and along the sidewalk, working his jaw and trying without much success to quell the anger and hurt raging in his gut. Bethany was back. He'd known that for a while. And he'd known he'd run into her sooner or later. Sooner, actually, since her mother was his landlord.

Checking Main Street for traffic, Noah jogged across to the courthouse park, making his way to Union Street and Latimer Office Supply. The chilly November wind stung, but he welcomed it. It took his mind off seeing Beth again. He had a new business to get up and running. Carlisle Structural Solutions was all he should be thinking about.

After paying for his supplies and picking up a sandwich at the DoOver Deli on the corner, Noah returned to his office and settled in the back room. The first bite of his sandwich triggered a memory—one he didn't welcome. He'd ordered the deli's special club sandwich—Beth's favorite. He'd forgotten that. He shoved the meal aside.

He'd forgotten a lot of things about Beth. Like how lovely she was. When she'd turned and faced him, his mouth had gone dry. His palms had grown sweaty, and his heart rate tripled. He was eighteen again and in love with his best friend. The years had faded away, along with the pain of her desertion and her callous indifference toward those who cared about her. All he saw was her hazel eyes that always sparkled, her kissable mouth and the way she stirred his protective instincts when she was close. The pink sweater with the wide collar added a rosy tinge to her cheeks and made her look very touchable. Her dark hair was cut in a way that made it float around her face, and when a strand had landed on her cheek, he'd had to stop himself from brushing it aside.

Then she'd hugged him, and he'd slammed into a wall of searing emotions, unable to move. She'd been soft and warm against him. He hadn't been prepared for that kind of response. He'd fought against the tender emotions, which had only brought out his long buried resentment. He'd spoken harshly, aware of the hurt he'd caused her from the look in her eyes, but unable to stop the stinging words.

Beth had severed their friendship with one quick cut and never looked back. That's when Noah realized that as far as she was concerned, nothing and no one was as important to her as her life in the dance world.

Until today, he had believed he'd recovered from his broken heart and her disregard for their friendship. But like a punctured water line, all his emotions were spewing forth. In the meantime he'd have to shut off the emotional flood and keep his distance from Bethany until she left again. Easier said than done. He was always keenly attuned to her nearness, and he'd never been able to keep her from flitting through his brain like a butterfly, touching down lightly here and there, bringing memories to life again.

He glanced around the back room of his new office. He still had a lot to do to get his engineering business up and running. In the meantime he was working full-time for the city of Dover as a building inspector. Not his first choice of jobs, but it paid the bills. Thankfully, he'd be spending most of his time conducting on-site work, and there'd be no need to interact with Beth. Besides, she'd be gone soon enough, back to the only thing that ever mattered to her. Dancing. Then life would go on as usual. And he could forget Beth. Again.

Tossing his trash in the bin in the small kitchen area, Noah locked up and headed out. He had four inspections to do this afternoon. He fought the urge to glance into the real estate office to see if Beth was there, scolding himself for his weakness. He would *not* look. Stepping onto the sidewalk, he went straight to his car and climbed in, shutting down all thoughts of his old friend, fully aware of the uncomfortable truth he'd denied for years.

Bethany Montgomery had taken root in his heart, and there was no yanking her out.

Beth rubbed her eyes, trying to focus on the listings on the computer screen. After a restless night she'd wanted nothing more than to sleep in, hide under the covers and try to forget her life was in shambles.

Her sister's apartment was perfect for isolating herself. Tori had a good eye for decorating, and she'd designed the space in soft muted tones of green and blue that wrapped around you like a warm hug. The balcony, which overlooked the courthouse square across the street, was shielded from curious eyes by large pots of evergreen vines that even in the dead of winter provided privacy.

But today her new job required her to be in the office bright and early. Her mother had a long list of showings, which meant Beth would be working alone most of the day. Not a pleasant prospect because it allowed her too much time to think.

She'd fretted over Noah's icy reception all night, but still found only one logical explanation. He hadn't forgiven her for not staying in touch. Noah didn't have a mean bone in his body, but he'd behaved like a man with a giant chip on his shoulder. A man who had been deeply hurt. But not by her. He'd never loved her. The realization still had the power to bring a sharp prick to her heart. She planned on talking to him again once he calmed down. If he did. She had enough to worry about as it was.

Shutting down thoughts of her old friend, she concentrated on sorting through the new additions on the Multiple Listing Service and the few phone messages left by locals who were putting their homes on the market. Thankfully the day passed quickly. It was early afternoon when the office door swooshed open. She looked up, expecting house hunters. Instead, a young girl walked in and slowly made her way toward the reception desk, her gaze scanning the walls as she went.

She was a cute child with golden brown hair in a

page-boy style that framed her oval face and brought out her big blue eyes. Beth guessed her to be about the same age as her niece, Abby. She leaned her forearms on the desk. "Are you looking to buy a home, or are you more interested in renting?"

The little girl giggled. "I'm not looking for a house. I'm only nine. I'm here to look at the pictures." She pointed to the wall of family portraits and photographs her mother proudly displayed.

"I see. Shouldn't you be in school?"

"Dentist appointment." The girl stepped to the desk and extended her hand. "I'm Chloe. I come in here a lot to look at the pictures when Miss Francie is here. Oh." Her eyes grew wide, and her mouth fell open. "You're her. I mean you're you, I mean—" She swallowed and pointed to the ballet portrait. "That's you, isn't it?"

Beth smiled and nodded. "Yes, it is."

Chloe's eyes grew soft and dreamy, and she clasped her hands together over her heart. "You're beautiful. Like a white butterfly floating in the air."

Her throat contracted. Never had she received such a sweet and sincere compliment. "Thank you, Chloe. That means a lot to me."

"I want to be a ballerina. I want to drift like a feather and wear beautiful costumes." She spread her arms and twirled around the office.

Beth couldn't help but smile. The child was adorable. "Well, you can if you work hard. It takes a lot of training and dedication. Do you take dance lessons now?"

Chloe stopped. Her arms dropped to her sides, and her expression sagged nearly to the floor. "No. I can't."

She spoke the words with such drama that Beth had to swallow the chuckle that rose in her throat. "Why not?"

Chloe plopped her elbows on the desk, resting her chin in her hands. "Because my dad thinks it's a waste of time, and he doesn't want me to get caught up in silly dreams."

Beth frowned and pressed her lips together. What kind of parent would tell a child such a ridiculous thing? "Dancing isn't silly or a waste of time. It is a beautiful way to express emotion. It builds muscle and teaches discipline."

"Daddy thinks it's better if I play sports. He says they build character and teach a whole bunch of life lessons and stuff."

Typical male. She could hear her brothers making the same argument. "What does your mother say?"

"Oh, she's not here. She and Daddy got divorced a long time ago. She lives in Hollywood and has her own TV show. It's called *Brunch with Yvonne St. James*." Chloe's eyes brightened, and she came around to stand beside Beth. "She's going to send me a plane ticket so I can spend Thanksgiving with her, and she's going to put me on her show, and I'll get to meet lots of famous people. I hope I can meet Dustin Baker. I love his music, and he's so dreamy."

Beth had no idea who that was, but obviously he made Chloe's little heart beat faster. "Are you going alone to see your mom?"

"Yes, ma'am. I can't wait."

Beth hadn't been addressed as *ma'am* in a long time, and hearing it now set her back. It was common, even expected, here in the South, but having it directed at her made her feel older than her thirty years.

"I've seen lots of pictures of you."

"You have?"

Chloe nodded. "Your mama talks about you a lot." She pointed to the picture wall again. "I know your whole family. Those are your big brothers, Linc and Gil, and that's their new wives, Gemma and Julie. Oh, and that's Evan and Abby." She walked toward the wall. "That's Seth and Tori, but they aren't here now 'cause Seth is in school to be a policeman and Tori is in California. I wonder if she knows my mom?"

"California is a pretty big place."

Chloe shrugged. "I wish I had a big family. It's just me and my dad. Oh, and my gram."

"I've noticed you're limping. Did you hurt yourself?"

She glanced down at her knee and shrugged. "I have Alls Goods Ladder."

"She means Osgood-Schlatter."

Beth's pulse throbbed at the sound of Noah's rich voice. She hadn't heard him come in, nor had she expected to see him again so soon. He barely gave her a glance now.

"Chloe, what are you doing here? I told you to stay in my office."

"Hi, Daddy. I wanted to see the pictures, and I got to meet the ballerina. I mean Miss Beth. Isn't she beautiful?"

An awkward silence fell over the room like a suffocating blanket. Beth kept her gaze averted as Noah placed his hands on his daughter's shoulders in a protective gesture. Noah was a father? She hadn't considered that. She'd heard he'd gotten married not long after he'd moved to California, which had added another spear to her punctured heart. Noah had never thought of her as anything other than a friend. His buddy.

She swallowed and grasped for control. "Osgood's. That's a knee problem, isn't it?"

He nodded. "She injured her knee playing soccer and then had a growth spurt, which complicated things." He squeezed Chloe's shoulder. "She's supposed to do her physical therapy exercises every day, but it's like pulling teeth."

"I hate them. They hurt and they're boring."

Beth could sympathize. "I know exactly how you feel. I had surgery on my knee, and I have to do PT exercises every day, too. It's not fun, but if you're going to get stronger and play soccer, you have to do them faithfully."

Chloe screwed up her mouth and crossed her arms over her chest. "Great. I was hoping you'd be on my side."

Beth chuckled softly. "The exercises don't have to be boring. You can listen to music—that usually helps."

"Is that what you do?"

She nodded. "I put on my favorite ballet warm-up music and pretend I'm dancing. You know dancing can help strengthen the other muscles in your legs and knees and speed your recovery."

"Really? Dad, can Miss Beth teach me to dance? I'll do my exercises if I can dance. Please?"

The deep scowl on Noah's face made it clear he was unhappy with her suggestion. "Chloe, go on back to my office and collect your things. We're going home."

"Okay. 'Bye Miss Beth."

The minute Chloe was gone, Noah approached her, his eyes narrowed and dark. "I'd appreciate it if you wouldn't encourage her to come over here."

"Why? Apparently she visits my mother frequently."

"That's different. Your mother will always be here. You won't. You said yourself you'll be leaving as soon as you're fully recovered."

She had told him that even though she knew it wasn't true. "And what does that have to do with Chloe visiting me?"

"I don't want you filling her head full of ideas about your dancing career."

Now she understood, sort of. "Is that why you don't want her to take dancing lessons? Because of me?"

"Don't flatter yourself. I want her to grow up with a practical, realistic view of the world, and I don't want her sidetracked by pointless dreams of being a dancer or an actress or any of those careers that lead to disappointment."

"Little girls need to dream, Noah. You had a few dreams, as I recall."

He nodded in acknowledgment, but his gaze still held condemnation. "But I grew up and realized that dreams don't come true."

"You're wrong. Dreams are what gives us hope and joy."

"Hope and joy?" He shook his head. "Disappointment and heartbreak. Look where your dream has left you. I want better for Chloe."

The hurt in his light blue eyes and the pain that pulled at the corner of his mouth stabbed like an ice pick to her heart. What had happened to turn the sweet, understanding boy she'd loved into an angry, closed-off man?

He held up his hands as if to ward off further discussion. "Just stop telling her dancing can help with her recovery."

"It can. In fact, ballet is being used as therapy for people with Parkinson's and a variety of other medical conditions. At the very least, it'll encourage her to do her exercises. I've been through countless physical therapy sessions over the years, and the only way to get through much of it is to make it fun. What harm can it do?"

"Harm? Next she'll want to be a dancer like you, and look where that leads."

"Where does it lead, Noah? I had a wonderful career. I achieved everything I set out to accomplish. I fulfilled my dream."

"But what did it cost you along the way? What did you give up to capture that dream, Beth? Was it really worth it?" He yanked open the door and left.

Beth clenched her teeth. She wanted to shout at him that yes, it had been worth it, but the words wouldn't come. Why? She'd always been so sure of her direction, her purpose. She'd been blessed with a gift, and she'd used it to the fullest. Until the injury had derailed her future. But she'd make a comeback. She was still working out in her old studio at her mom's house each morning. That's what she wanted, wasn't it? To dance even if it wasn't as the lead?

A small voice whispered in her ear. *Is* that what she wanted? Or was it what she was doing because there was nothing else? The last two years had taken a toll not only on her body, but also on her passion. She was still trying to sort out the shifts in her emotions from the accident. Now she was trying to swim through gelatin and figure out who she was and where she wanted to go.

Beth watched Noah walk away. Twelve years ago she'd handed him her heart, the bravest thing she'd ever done, and he'd tossed it aside. He'd gone on with his life, gotten married and had a child. He hadn't bothered to contact her, so why was she the bad guy?

She looked across the entryway to Noah's office as he and Chloe walked out. Chloe waved over her shoulder, a mischievous smile on her face. Dad may have laid down the law, but she had a feeling Chloe would find a way to come and visit her again. And she would make sure to invite her, despite what Noah had said.

Chapter Two

Noah parked the car behind the historic mansion and shut off the engine. The twelve-room Victorian home was one of the oldest in Dover. His great-great-grandparents had founded Dover, then known as Junction City, in the mid-1800s. After the great fire that destroyed many of the wooden structures, the town was rebuilt and renamed Do Over, which had evolved into Dover. The town's most prominent citizens built their homes to the east of town, along Peace Street. Only half of the dozen original opulent dwellings remained. His grandmother refused to live anywhere else, despite the home being too large for her to care for and having more room than one woman needed.

Chloe darted ahead of him onto the broad back porch and into the house. Gram was one of the reasons he'd come home to Dover. He'd been fourteen when his dad's small plane had crashed, killing him and Noah's mother. He'd come here to live with Gram and Gramps. Now that Gram was alone and getting older, he'd moved in to help her out and give his daughter a chance to know her family.

Dover would hopefully provide a new beginning for him and Chloe. Dissatisfied with the hectic pace of life in San Francisco, he'd resigned from the large engineering firm he'd worked for and decided to start his own structural engineering company in Dover. His hometown would also be a more conservative place to raise Chloe, who was growing up too quickly for his liking.

His grandmother, Evelyn Carlisle, was in the kitchen listening to Chloe recount her day. He noticed Gram was using her cane today—a sign her arthritis was flaring up again.

"I wish I could be like her." Chloe sighed loudly, a dreamy look on her face.

"Like who?"

"Miss Beth."

Noah shrugged out of his coat and draped it over the back of the chair. "No. You don't." He turned and saw a scowl on his gram's face. He probably shouldn't have said that, but he didn't want his daughter's head filled with notions of chasing fame.

"Yes, I do. She's beautiful. I wish I could see her dance. I've only seen pictures."

"I understand she is quite amazing. A very successful ballerina." Gram raised her eyebrows. "She and your father were close friends in high school."

Chloe grabbed his arm. "Really? Are you serious? You knew her? Did you see her dance? Was she gorgeous? Did she float like a dandelion puff?" Chloe spread her arms and twirled around the kitchen, bumping into the island.

"I never saw her dance." Strange how he'd never realized that until now. He'd seen her in her studio warming up, but he'd never actually attended a performance. They'd been best friends, had shared everything, but at eighteen the thought of going to a ballet hadn't been an option, even for a nerd like he'd been.

Chloe's eyes widened. "I'm sure I could find videos of her on the internet. Can I look? Please?"

Refusal was on the tip of his tongue, but the pointed look from his gram told him to give in. She wasn't above pointing out his parenting shortcomings. He really needed his own place, but he couldn't leave her alone in this big house. "You can use my tablet, but sit here at the kitchen table to search."

Chloe scooped up the device and started tapping the screen.

Gram put the finishing touches on the sandwiches she was preparing and handed him the plate. He plucked a stem of grapes from the fruit bowl and grabbed a couple of cookies from the jar before taking a seat at the island.

"I wondered how long it would take you to run into Beth again. She's been home a while now."

"How do you know that?"

"Francie told me."

He'd forgotten that his gram and Beth's mom were good friends. But then, he'd forgotten a lot about this place. He'd only been back in town a couple of months himself. "I ran into her yesterday."

Gram set her own plate of food on the counter. "Hmm. That explains why you came home hissing like a snared alligator."

"I did not."

Gram shrugged. "How does she look? Has she changed much?"

"She's too thin. But I guess she has to be. Her hair is shorter." Softer looking, and it framed her face in long curvy strands that caressed her cheeks and made him want to brush them aside and feel the silky softness. "But otherwise she hasn't changed." She still had the sweet, childlike smile that made him want to hug her. Her hazel eyes, with their sooty lashes, were still as beguiling as ever, though they held a darker shade to them now. Maturity? Or sadness?

"Chloe seems taken with her."

"Not for long. Beth told me herself that as soon as she's recovered she's going back to the ballet."

Gram studied him a long moment. "I don't think that's going to happen. Francie told me that her injury was career-ending. She'll never dance professionally as a ballerina again. She's facing an uncertain future."

The bite of sandwich stuck in Noah's throat. No. Gram had to be wrong. "Are you sure? She looked fine to me." More than fine. He shut down that thought.

"That fall she took destroyed her knee, and then there were complications."

"What fall?"

"Noah, don't you know what happened?"

He didn't have a clue. He'd made it a point not to keep track of her successes. "I knew she'd been injured, but that's all."

"Oh, it was a terrible thing. She was doing one of those big leaps and landed wrong and tore her ACL. Her mother thinks Beth is in denial over her situation. It's very sad. That child was born to dance."

That was one thing Noah could not deny. "Yes. She was." The thought of Beth never dancing again left an unfamiliar chill in his chest. As much as he resented her passion for the dance, and the way she'd shut out everyone, he knew how much it meant to her. It had shaped her entire life. How would she cope without it? What was she going to do now?

"Daddy, I found some videos. Can I watch them?"

Reluctantly, he nodded. Chloe sat beside him, and he couldn't resist glancing at the tablet as she scrolled through the selection of clips featuring Bethany Montgomery. There were dozens. "Pick three. That's all."

Chloe clicked on the one labeled Aurora's Act 3 Variation in *The Sleeping Beauty*. He had no idea what that meant, but he couldn't force himself to look away. Beth appeared in a short tutu jutting out from her tiny waist. The puffy sleeves of her costume highlighted the graceful curves of her neck and shoulders. She rose on her toes, her arms floating gracefully as she began to dance with quick, precise steps. Part of him wanted to watch. To see her passion in action. But then reality shoved its way into his thoughts. There was only room for one love in her life, and it hadn't been him. That's what he had to remember.

Pushing back from the table, he carried his plate to the sink, then headed for the room off the parlor that had once been his grandfather's office. Now it was his. He had a four-inch binder of Mississippi building codes to study. He focused on the numbers in front of him, but he couldn't fully shake the vision of Beth on the screen, moving as if gravity had no claim on her. Even in the few moments he'd watched, her joy as she performed was impossible to miss. The thought of his Beth never dancing again was a cruel twist of fate he'd never have wanted for her.

His Beth. Ha. She'd never been his, even if that's how

he'd always thought of her. He'd fallen for Beth from the first moment he'd started tutoring her in math their senior year. She'd missed several weeks of school due to illness, and when the teacher had approached him about helping her catch up, he'd jumped at the chance. They'd quickly become friends. Neither of them had fit in well at school, and their friendship had filled a void for both of them.

He'd been sullen and withdrawn, burying himself in school and video games. Beth had been the shy, pretty girl, a self-proclaimed dance geek. Her friendship had drawn him out of his lingering anger and grief over losing his parents, and had brought a new life and light to his existence. He'd never confessed his true feelings, fearing it would destroy their relationship. Deep down he'd believed a gangly, self-conscious guy like him had little chance with an elegant, talented girl like Beth.

But something had changed between them those last months before graduation. Beth had auditioned for the Forsythe Company but hadn't made the cut. She was devastated, and he'd done all he could to comfort and encourage her. The incident had drawn them closer together, and Noah had seen a new sparkle in her hazel eyes and a more intimate curve to her lips when she smiled at him. They'd touched more, laughed more and shared longing looks. He'd been certain it was love.

But he'd been wrong. She'd walked out of his life without so much as a goodbye, leaving him emotionally bleeding and giving him his first lesson in believing in dreams.

It was only later that he learned a position had opened up with the ballet suddenly, and Beth had gone to New York to pursue her dancing dream. That's when the truth had hit. Hard. In Beth's life, dance came first. Always. Friends were easily discarded, like an old pair of toe shoes. Dreams of a future with Beth were just that. Empty dreams. And dreams didn't come true. It was a lesson he would learn well over the years.

It was probably good he'd never revealed his heart. Rejecting his friendship had been painful enough. Rejecting his love would have been too humiliating to bear. For the time being, he'd stick to his plan. Avoid Beth at all costs, and when she was gone he could pick up and move forward.

But how would Beth move forward? Who would help her face the loss of the thing she loved most? An unwanted flicker of protectiveness pinged along his nerves.

It wasn't his problem. She'd made her choice, and she would have to adjust to the consequences.

"Please, Daddy, let Miss Beth teach me how to dance. I promise I'll do my exercises every day."

Noah placed the salt and pepper shakers in the cupboard after supper that night. Chloe had talked of nothing else all through the meal. "Just because Miss Beth thinks dancing is a good idea doesn't mean it is. It could make your injury worse."

Silverware clanged as Gram placed it in the dishwasher. "I think it's a wonderful idea. She needs something to encourage her to do those exercises."

Noah shut the cabinet door with more force than necessary. "Chloe is fine. She just needs to do what she's supposed to."

Gram exhaled a puff of air as she glared over her glasses. "I'm supposed to exercise for my arthritis, too, but it's uncomfortable so I don't do it. I know it'll help eventually, but getting to the 'eventually' part takes too long. Why don't you talk to Pete Jones, her physical therapist, and see what he says? Or better yet, have Pete consult with Beth about the pros and cons of letting her dance."

"Out of the question."

"Honestly." Gram faced him, a deep scowl on her face. "Would you feel the same if it was anyone other than Beth? I would have thought you'd have gotten over her long ago."

"There was nothing to get over. We were friends. It ended. I simply don't want Chloe getting silly dreams in her head. I want her to have a secure future and a job that will provide a good living. Not something like dancing that could end suddenly or never take off at all."

Gram placed the decorative candle back in the center of the breakfast room table. "Like moving to Hollywood and having your own talk show."

Noah set the tea pitcher in the fridge and shut the door. "I didn't say that."

"You didn't have to." Gram untied her apron and hung it on a peg at the end of the counter. "Have you heard from Yvonne?"

Noah groaned softly. Another sore subject. His ex-wife and her utter disregard for their child. "Not since she texted Chloe about sending her a plane ticket to come out to Los Angeles for Thanksgiving."

"Do you think she'll follow through?"

"No. And I'll have to tell my daughter yet again that her mother is too busy with her career to find time to spend with her."

"Maybe having time with Beth and learning to dance would help soften the blow."

Noah ground his teeth. "Until Beth packs up and heads back to New York without warning. Chloe doesn't need another woman in her life pushing her aside when something more exciting comes along."

"Are you so sure that'll happen? Her mother says her ballet career is over."

Noah shook his head. "You don't know Beth the way I do. If she makes up her mind to dance again, then she will. It's the only thing she really cares about."

"That's understandable. She devoted her life to being a ballerina, and I know how competitive the dance world is. She had to give it one hundred percent of her time and focus to succeed."

"No. She had to give up everything and every*one* to succeed." He glanced at his gram, intending to drive home his point, but she was looking back at him with a knowing expression and a glint in her blue eyes as if she'd discovered something delightful.

"You know, most friendships fade away after school. Why are you still hanging on to this one?"

"I'm not hanging on. She was a friend I thought I could count on, and she wasn't. The only thing I can depend on with Beth is that she'll leave." He ran a hand through his hair. "Her being back just reminds me that when it comes to women, my judgment is useless."

"Oh, I don't think so." She sat down. "You're a lot like your father was. He felt things deeply, but he didn't express them. He had a tender heart and it was easily wounded. He fell in love with your mother the moment they met. They worked together for two years before he even asked her out. He almost lost her to another guy because he was afraid to share his feelings."

"I don't have feelings. She killed those long ago."

"Beth did—or was that Yvonne's doing?"

Noah was not having this conversation. "Gram, I love you, but I'm a big boy. I can manage my own life." He strode from the room, but not before hearing a skeptical huff from his grandmother. She always claimed she knew him better than he knew himself. Unfortunately, she was usually right.

Bethany scrolled through the MLS for Dover and the nearby areas looking for a four-bedroom, two-bath ranch on ten acres. She'd tuned in Christmas music on the radio, and the mellow notes of "White Christmas" filled the air, but keeping her focus was a challenge. After a while the houses all began to look the same. She could never understand how her mother derived so much satisfaction from hunting down homes for sale and finding people to buy them. She printed out a couple of prospects, then stood and walked to the back room to get a fresh glass of sweet tea.

She was grateful to her mom for paying her to work at Montgomery Real Estate, but she'd have to find something else to do if she stayed in Dover. The thought gouged a channel across her stomach. She didn't want another job. She wanted to dance. It's all she'd ever wanted. But if she listened to her doctors and her physical therapist, she wouldn't be returning to the Forsythe Company. They felt certain with enough recovery time and continued PT she'd be able to dance, but classical ballet was not recommended. It would be too easy to sustain the same injury again.

Beth refused to accept their diagnosis. She'd heard of many ballerinas who had suffered an ACL reconstruction and went on to dance for several more years. She *would* dance again. She had to. What else was there for her? Eight to five in her mother's office? She wasn't qualified for much else. She'd given up her chance at a degree when she'd joined the Forsythe Company.

The office door opened as she came back into the front, and she smiled as Evelyn Carlisle walked in. "Miss Evelyn, what a nice surprise. How are you?"

She laid down the papers she was carrying and gave Beth a warm hug. "I'm not bad for an old lady with arthritis. It's nice to have our famous ballerina back with us. I know your mom is tickled pink to have you home. I love having Noah and Chloe with me again. Of course, I'm not one to sit in a rocker on the porch."

The woman's warm smile and zest for life made Beth smile. Noah's gram was always involved in something, always trying new things and always first to jump in to tackle a challenge. "What's keeping you so busy these days?"

Evelyn held up one of the papers. "This. I've re-opened the Dawes Little Theater, and we're having a special Christmas performance."

Beth took the large colorful poster depicting iconic Christmas events. A sugar plum fairy, children around a tree, a winter scene and the nativity. "This looks wonderful. What made you decide to reopen the theater?"

"Your sister-in-law, Gemma. She did such a fantastic job with our celebrations last year that everyone is fired up to make this year even better. I'd been thinking about starting the little theater up again, and this seemed like the perfect opportunity. We've scheduled it for the third Saturday in December. I was hoping to put a poster in your window."

"Of course. I'll put it up right away." The thought of reviving the theater sent her heart skipping. It had been a vital part of the town for years, and she'd performed in several shows. She'd been sad to learn from her mother that Evelyn had closed it because of lack of participation.

"Most of our numbers are musical. Three familiar Christmas scenes with singing and dancing. I wanted it to be happy and joyful. We've been blessed so many people were eager to volunteer to put on the show." Evelyn adjusted her glasses. "Of course, things happen. And we're about to lose a key member of our staff. Allison Kent, our dance coordinator, just received a job offer in Biloxi she's been hoping for, and she has to start immediately."

"That's too bad." Evelyn was staring pointedly, triggering an uneasy feeling in Beth's stomach.

"I thought perhaps I could talk you into stepping into her place to help us out?"

"Me?" The idea sent a swell of excitement along her nerves. Being in a theater again, performing, the excitement, the joy. Cold reality quickly squelched the feelings. She wasn't in any shape to perform, and being in a theater now would only point out what she could no longer have. "I'm not really sure how long I'm going to be here, and I promised to help my mother." She was hedging, and the look on Evelyn's face said she knew it, too.

"Since all of our performers are amateurs, Allison kept the dances simple. They're all set, and everyone knows them by heart. All you'd have to do is keep things on track."

"That's very kind of you to ask, but…"

Evelyn patted her arm. "Just think about it. We could really use your help. Oh, and I wanted to tell you I liked your suggestion about Chloe taking dancing lessons. I think it would make doing her PT exercises easier."

"Noah told you about that?"

"He did, and I told him he was being closed-minded about the whole thing."

"What does he have against it? I really can't figure that out."

Evelyn's eyes sparkled. "Oh, well, it's a long story. He's got some funny ideas about the arts that, if you ask me, he needs to get over." She scooped up the rest of the circulars. "Well, I need to get going, or I'll never get these distributed." She stopped at the door. "Oh. If you wouldn't mind, I'd like you to take a look at the scene from *The Nutcracker* we're doing in the show. Allison had doubts about some of the steps. With your professional experience, maybe you could stop by and offer a few changes to make it better?"

It would be rude to refuse. "Of course. Just let me know."

"Thank you. Oh, and would you see that Noah gets one of these posters for his office window when he comes in?"

"Of course." Beth said goodbye, then returned to the desk and sank down in the chair. It might be fun to get involved with the production. But how would she feel being in a theater, knowing she might never dance professionally again? No. It would be safer to keep her focus on her recovery.

She was doing all she could, following her doctor's and physical therapist's advice to the letter. She was eating right, getting plenty of rest and doing her exercises faithfully. Each morning she did her exercises and a full ballet warm-up in the small studio her father had built for her when she was a child. Each day she pushed just a little harder, stretched a tiny bit farther, but always wearing her brace and careful not to overdo. She believed in her heart that if she worked hard enough and long enough, she could recapture the life she had before.

But what if the doctors were right, and she was lying to herself? That question lay like a shard of ice in her chest that never went away.

She glanced out the window and saw Noah unlocking the door to his office. Picking up the poster, she followed him inside. "Your gram left this for you to put in your window. I have one, too."

He scanned the colorful announcement with a shake of his head. "She got it into her head to start the little theater up again."

"You don't sound pleased about that."

He shrugged. "If it makes her happy…"

"She asked me to help out with the dancers. Apparently her instructor is moving away."

Noah held her gaze, his mouth in a tight line. "I suppose you jumped at the chance."

"I haven't decided yet."

"Really." He rested his hands on his hips. "What's holding you back? Too busy selling real estate? Or is little theater beneath you? Going from principal dancer to small town choreographer is quite a comedown."

"That's a horrible thing to say."

"Not if it's true."

The hurt tone in his voice made her stop and study him more closely. "Noah, what happened to you? To us? We were close friends. We always supported each other. I was going to be the famous dancer, and you were going to design architectural wonders."

Noah sat on the edge of his desk, arms crossed over his chest. "I figured out pretty quick I didn't have the imagination needed to be a successful architect. I was better suited for engineering. Numbers and equations. Things that are always solid and predictable." He stood and went around the desk. "I learned to look at the future more realistically." He faced her, his blue eyes cold. "I learned a lot that year. Like who my real friends were, and who could be depended on and who couldn't."

"We used to depend on each other."

"I thought so—until you ran off to New York and never looked back. I guess friendship didn't count as much as pursuing your career."

How could she make him understand? "I had no choice. The call came in, and I had to be in New York the next day to begin rehearsing. My mom and I were running around packing, trying to make plane reservations. It was hectic."

"Too hectic to find a second to call your *friend* and share the good news?"

His barb made a direct hit. "I meant to call you and explain."

Noah's gaze searing into hers. "When? The next day? The next week? I had to find out about you joining the ballet company in the newspaper." He worked his jaw, his eyes dark. "That's how much our friendship meant to you."

"It meant a great deal to me. But I didn't think it meant much to you."

"I waited in the gazebo until midnight for you to show up. I called you a dozen times. I finally called your house and talked to one of your brothers, but all they knew was that something had come up and you and your mom had left."

Her heart sank. They'd agreed to meet that evening at the gazebo to exchange gifts. Noah was leaving for the summer semester at Mississippi State the next morning. She hadn't shown up at the gazebo because after he'd rebuffed her affections earlier in the day, she'd wanted to avoid him. It had been easy to dismiss that night amid all the rush to leave. Is that what was behind his attitude? Her failure to show up to say goodbye?

"I'm sorry, Noah, I was so busy. You know how crushed I was when I wasn't chosen after my audition. This sudden opening with the company was the answer to my dreams."

Noah worked his jaw from side to side. "And your dream trumped a casual friendship. I get it. We all have priorities, and I learned yours that night." He stood. "Now if you'll excuse me, I have work to do."

Without a word, he walked to the back office, leaving her alone, a hundred questions swirling in her mind.

Seated at her desk again, Beth replayed the events of that last day with Noah. She couldn't tell him how heartbroken and embarrassed she'd been by his rejection. It wasn't his fault she'd read too much in to their friendship. She couldn't remain friends and pretend to be happy when he found someone else.

And he had. She'd heard through her mother that he'd abruptly transferred from Mississippi State to Stanford and married a year later. Proving once and for all his heart had never been hers. Her last thin strand of hope had died. It hadn't been a misunderstanding. He truly hadn't loved her.

With her mother out of the office, Beth tried to work, but her gaze kept wandering to Noah's office. He never appeared again. He was either really busy in the back room, or he'd slipped out the back door to avoid seeing her.

A lump formed in her throat. Noah had been more than a friend. He'd been her strong shoulder, her soft place to fall. The man she'd loved. But she'd never told him that. She'd always worried that to do so would ruin the special bond between them. When she'd finally found the courage to open her heart, he'd been embarrassed and uncomfortable. He'd made it clear that the words of love she'd had engraved on the small key chain she'd given him weren't welcome.

A sudden contradiction formed in her mind. If Noah had no feelings for her back then, why was he still so upset that she'd left town without telling him? His bristly attitude and his cutting comments didn't sound like someone who had forgotten the past. They sounded like someone who still carried the pain.

What that meant, she had no idea. In the past, if she was confused about something, she would go to Noah and discuss it with him. No subject was off limits. But now, when she was so confused, he was the last person she could turn to. The realization stung.

She had to find a way to repair their relationship because being at odds with Noah hurt more deeply than she'd thought possible.

Noah's encounter with Beth wore on his nerves like a pebble in his shoe. Thankfully, his job with the city had kept him busy all afternoon doing structural inspections, but he couldn't shake the fact that he owed her an apology. He'd been rude and hurtful. What had happened, or not happened, between them was in the past. Beth had a right to live her life. Just because seeing her again stirred up old emotional wounds wasn't her fault. He needed to recommit to his original plan. Stay away. Keep his distance. Then everything would be fine.

The tension in the kitchen was as thick as soup when he arrived home that night. Gram was at the stove, stirring the contents of a pot with vigor. Chloe was hunched up in the sunroom, her thumbs flying over her cell phone. He debated which female to approach first. Gram seemed less threatening.

He moved to the stove and looked down at the contents of the pot. "So did the sauce talk back to you, or was it Chloe?"

She huffed out a breath and straightened, peering over the rim of her glasses. "Neither. Merely a run-in with that brick wall we've been living with for the last few weeks. Apparently, the Carlisle stubborn streak didn't skip a generation."

Now he understood. "Chloe won't do her exercises."

"She says she will if Bethany teaches her to dance." Gram stopped stirring and faced him. "What can it hurt, Noah? She's nine. It's not like she's going to run off and join a ballet company at her age. This thing you have with keeping her away from anything involving the arts is just plain silly."

Noah rubbed his forehead. "I'm just trying to protect her."

"From what? Exploring new things and having fun?

You can't control what your daughter dreams about, Noah. Sooner or later you have to face the fact that she's going to grow up and leave you, too. She'll make a life of her own. Denying her things she wants to do will only hasten that along, and I know you don't want that."

He knew that, but he could keep her focused on things that were more productive. Things that would instill solid values for life and a future family. He took a seat in the sunroom on the footstool across from Chloe and stretched out his palm. She sighed and handed over her phone. That was their deal. She could have a cell phone, minus internet access, and he had the right to check her call and text history. "Shouldn't you be doing your exercises?"

"They hurt."

"Don't you want to play soccer in the spring?"

"I want to dance."

"There aren't any dance schools in Dover."

"Miss Beth could show me. She's famous. She knows all about dancing."

Every word his daughter spoke poked an anthill of emotions. "Miss Beth has no time for teaching."

"Yes, she does. She told me we could practice at her studio at Miss Francie's house."

He handed back her phone. "When did you talk to Beth?"

"Gram and I stopped in to see you after school today, only you weren't there. I stayed and talked to her while Gram went to the bank."

Noah set his jaw. He'd have to have a talk with his grandmother. He didn't want Chloe getting too attached to Beth. Better yet, he'd have a talk with Beth himself and set her straight about a few things.

* * *

The next morning, Noah parked his car beside the small building behind the Montgomery home that had been converted into Beth's dance studio. Yesterday he'd been determined to tell Beth to back off and not mention dancing to Chloe. But he'd been unable to dismiss his gram's advice. Chloe was growing up, and she would strike out on her own. He didn't want her resenting him for denying her something she longed to do. But there was one other fact that wore away at his resentment. What if Gram was right, and Beth could never dance *en pointe* again?

He knew what it was like to have your dreams shattered and see the future you dreamed of go up in smoke. Beth must be suffering greatly with the prospect of never being a ballerina again. It had been her whole life.

He stepped inside the studio and found her on the small settee, her head resting on her knees. A twinge of concern hit him. As he approached, he saw her shoulder shake, which elevated his concern. "Beth, are you all right? Are you hurt?"

She jerked, lifting her head and blinking away tears. "Noah. What are you doing here?"

Taking a tissue from the box on the side table, she wiped her eyes, then rose to face him. His heart lodged in his throat. She was the essence of femininity. The black leotard and tights highlighted every feminine curve. The filmy overskirt that ended around her knees swished enticingly as she moved. Her dark hair, usually floating around her face, was pulled back into a haphazard knot at the back of her head. She looked every inch the professional ballerina—except for the sadness in her hazel eyes that brought an unfamiliar ache to his chest. He fought the sudden need to pull her close and comfort her. "You first. Why are you crying?"

She lifted her chin in a defiant gesture, only to sigh and lower her gaze, her fingers toying with strings on her skirt. "I was thinking about my daddy and how much I miss him. It's been a year already, and I still have this horrible hole in my heart."

It was not what he'd expected her to say, but he was very familiar with the emotion. "My gramps has been gone two years, and I still expect him to walk into the shop or come up behind me and squeeze my shoulder."

"Two years?" She gave him a sad smile. "I was hoping you'd say something to make me feel better." She glanced around the studio. "Daddy built this for me when I was ten. I'd told him that I was going to devote my life to dancing, and he said if that was true then I needed a place where I could practice every day."

"And you did." He remembered the hours she spent locked away. He'd count the minutes until she would step outside, put the practice behind her and become his friend. "I'm sure he was very proud of you."

She smiled, a sweet one this time that melted his insides. "He was. He never missed a performance, and he always gave me a bouquet of pink roses afterward no matter how small my part. I felt like a real princess. He was my biggest fan." She met his gaze, then set her hands on her hips. "Your turn. Why are you here?"

The determination that had driven him here had been diluted by Beth's tears. Seeing her in her element, here in the studio, forced him to understand the significance of her loss. For all his issues with Beth, he would never want her to lose the thing she loved most. Gram was right. He couldn't control his daughter's dreams. Making too much of his disapproval might have the opposite effect. And in the short term, Beth would eventually leave, and by then Chloe would hopefully have moved on to a new interest.

"I came by to tell you that if you're still willing, I think adding dance along with Chloe's PT might be a good idea."

"Really? I'd love to. In fact, I'm going to start working with my niece and her friend. Chloe can join us, and we'll have a little dance class here. It should be fun."

Seeing the joy and anticipation on her face left a warm softness in his rib cage.

"What made you change your mind?"

He didn't realize how close they stood until he looked into her eyes. He could see the gold streak in the left one. "I can't say no to my little girl."

She chuckled softly and touched his arm. "Neither could my dad."

He looked into her eyes and saw them dilate. His pulse flipped. She was so close, he caught the flowery scent of her hair. He gathered himself and stepped back. She'd always made his heart race. Her loveliness never failed to captivate him, but she wasn't dependable. There was no room in her world for anyone else. The frown on her face told him Beth clearly felt his withdrawal.

"You won't change your mind, will you? About Chloe I mean?"

He rubbed his forehead, already regretting his impulse. "No." Noah cleared his throat. "She needs to do her PT, and if dancing gets it done then I'm all for it." He pulled out a business card and handed it to her. "I have one request. Call Pete Jones, her physical therapist, and make sure you know what her parameters are and that he approves of whatever type of dancing you're planning."

"Of course. I'll be very cautious, Noah. You can depend on me."

That was the one thing he couldn't do. "Then I'll be going. Let me know when Chloe should be here."

She stared at him, a questioning look in her eyes. "Okay."

He held her gaze a moment before walking to the door. He had a bad feeling he'd just made a terrible mistake.

Chapter Three

The Sunday morning air was cool but pleasant for early November as Beth strolled through the courthouse park. Above the giant old magnolias and moss-draped live oaks, she could see the white steeple of Peace Community Church like a friendly hand beckoning her home. She'd agreed to meet her mother and family for late services today. She'd begged off her first two Sundays here, but she knew she couldn't do that any longer. Surprisingly, instead of dreading going to church, she found herself looking forward to it. She'd realized last night that worship had been one of the things missing in her life the last few years. She hadn't turned her back on God or lost her faith, but it had taken a seat high in the back balcony of her life to other things. It wasn't something she was proud of.

The front steps of the old brick church were crowded with members chatting and laughing. She wasn't in the mood to talk about her career or her reasons for being home. It was too painful a topic. Skirting the front entrance, she took the walkway along the side of the building and entered through one of the side doors. It didn't

take long to find her family. They always sat midway
up in the sanctuary. Her older brothers, Linc and Gil,
were already seated with their wives and children. Her
mother was talking to Evelyn Carlisle. Beth groaned inwardly, hoping they weren't talking about her. Too late.
Her mother spotted her and waved her over.

"Beth, Evelyn tells me that she asked you to help
with the Christmas show. That's a great idea. I think
you should. It would be good for you to get involved."

The woman laid her hand on her heart. "You would
be an answer to my prayers."

"What about my job with you?"

Her mom waved off her concerns. "Don't worry
about that. I'm used to running my business alone."

Beth forced a smile. Evelyn and her mom had skill-
fully funneled her to a point where her only option was
to say yes. "I'd love to help you out. When would you
like me to start?"

Evelyn grinned. "Wonderful. We rehearse two nights
a week and on Saturdays. We're having a board meeting
at the theater Tuesday evening. Why don't you come,
and I'll introduce you to everyone. Oh, and let's keep
this between the two of us for the time being. I want it
to be a surprise for the board."

The organ began to play softly, and Evelyn excused
herself and moved off. Beth saw her stop at a pew near
the front, where Noah and Chloe were seated. Noah
glanced over his shoulder, and their eyes met. Her heart
skipped a beat. For a moment she felt the old link between them. She wanted to go to him and ask him to
help her sort out her life. But he looked away, leaving
her adrift again. She had the horrible feeling that he
would never forgive her for leaving the way she had. She

wasn't sure she could live with that fact, because despite the years and the distance, she still cared for him. He was the best friend she'd ever had, the only person who understood her. She couldn't make that go away.

Beth forced thoughts of Noah and the past out of her mind, suddenly craving the comfort and peace she'd always found in the historic church. In her drive to reach the top of her profession, she'd lost that feeling. She was beginning to think she'd lost far more than an active faith life.

Despite her best efforts, her mind wandered through the early parts of the service. Her gaze drifted to Noah, then to her brothers. Gil had his arm draped across the back of the pew, wrapping Julie in a subtle hug. Linc held Gemma's hand, which was resting on his thigh.

A surge of longing swelled from deep inside. She wanted that kind of connection. A hand to hold, someone to depend on. For the last twelve years it had been her career, but that had failed her and set her adrift in a world she no longer knew how to navigate.

Reverend Jim Barrett's gravelly voice pulled her from her negative thoughts.

"The first commandment is 'You shall have no other Gods before Me.' Have you considered how hard it is to follow? It's the most important of the ten, but we treat it lightly. What God have you set in place of the Lord? What goal, passion, hobby or desire have you, unintentionally probably, set in place of God? What is it that you work harder for, strive for, push everything and everyone else aside for to achieve?"

A warm rush heated Beth's cheeks, making her squirm. Was he talking to her? Had he known she would be here today?

"I know we all have to do certain things to meet our goals to get that promotion or earn that raise. We tell ourselves it's so we can provide a better life for our family or for ourselves. But the problem lies in the definition of better life. If you're ignoring your family, your friends and your God, then how can that make anything better? Ask yourself what is your goal really costing you? People, jobs, dreams will all fail you. Put Him first always, and He'll take care of the rest."

Beth stood for the final hymn, her mind replaying the things she'd heard. Had she done that? Had she pushed aside those she loved in her drive to achieve her lifelong dream? The answer wasn't hard to find. She had. A sour feeling formed in her stomach. The buzz and push of people making their way out of the sanctuary pressed in on her. Her mother was talking to a friend. Her brothers and their families had exited the pew on the other end, leaving her a clear path to the side door. Quickly she made her way to the side aisle, but before she could reach the door she heard her name called. Chloe hurried toward her.

"Daddy says I can take dancing lessons from you. When can I come?"

Noah stepped forward, resting his hands on his daughter's shoulders and looking absurdly handsome in a dark suit and crisp white shirt that contrasted pleasantly with his sun-darkened skin. The sky blue tie lying against his chest made his eyes even bluer. But the deep scowl on his face said he still had strong reservations about the situation.

Ignoring the wince of discomfort his look caused, she looked at Chloe. "I was thinking we'd meet twice a week on Tuesdays and Thursdays, right after school."

Chloe frowned. "Not every day?"

"No, that's not good for your muscles when you're starting out. Even I have to take some downtime. And I have a surprise for you. My niece Abby and her friend Hannah are going to come, too."

"Really? Cool. Abby's here today. Dad, can I go find her?"

He nodded, giving her a loving smile before turning his blue eyes on her. She knew exactly what he was going to say. "Yes, I spoke with Pete and he's all for the ballet lessons with a few exceptions. But those are things she wouldn't be learning for a few months anyway."

"What time will the lessons be? I need to work it into my schedule."

"You plan on watching the entire hour?"

"Yes."

"I wish you wouldn't. It's not good for Chloe if you're hovering all the time."

"I want to make sure nothing happens."

Evelyn joined them, giving her grandson a light swat on his shoulder. "Noah, stop behaving like an overprotective father. Beth is a professional, and I'm quite certain she knows what she's doing."

Beth stifled a smile at the resigned look on Noah's face. "Thank you, Miss Evelyn, for the vote of confidence. I'll take good care of all the girls."

Noah set his jaw and made an excuse to leave. After he stepped away, Evelyn slipped her arm in Beth's and walked her toward the side door.

Evelyn pulled her a little closer. "We have some things to discuss, dear, and now that you're part of the little theater we'll have plenty of time to catch up."

Beth wasn't sure what she meant exactly, but she liked the idea. She had a feeling there was a lot more to Noah's attitude than she knew. They'd been close back then, and she'd been able to sense his moods—except for the day she'd given him his graduation gift and he'd handed it back. Figuratively, of course. She had to find out why he was still holding an old grudge.

Maybe by accepting Evelyn's offer, she could learn more about Noah's attitude and find a way to repair the damage from the past.

Beth couldn't remember the last time she'd been this anxious about anything. Not even her first solo performance as principal ballerina had tied her stomach in this many twisted knots. She scanned her small studio again. It was cleaned up and ready for her first students. Abby, Hannah and Chloe would be arriving soon for their first class.

Beth had conferred with Pete Jones a few more times about things she wanted to teach to make sure she fully understood Chloe's condition. He'd offered to work with her, too, if she needed any help with her ACL rehab.

She exhaled a long sigh, clasped her hands together and glanced for the tenth time at the clock, fighting the churning sensation inside. For most of her dancing career she'd been the student, attending daily classes and rehearsals. She'd helped other dancers in her career, but they'd been professionals seeking advice. She'd never taught beginners, especially children. What if she was too technical? What if she pushed too hard or became impatient? What if—

"Aunt Beth, they're here." Abby charged through the door, all smiles.

"Hi, Miss Beth." Chloe followed behind, and Hannah brought up the rear.

"Hello, ladies. You look excited."

Hannah giggled. "We're not ladies. We're girls."

Beth tapped her shoulder. "You are young ladies who are going to learn the first few positions of ballet."

Chloe clapped her hands. "On our toes?"

"Not yet. You have to work up to that. Put your things over there and we'll get started."

Beth's new sister-in-law, Julie, stopped at her side. "Thank you for doing this. Abby and Hannah were so excited on the way over, I thought my eardrums would burst."

"I have to admit I was nervous about this at first, but I think it'll be fun."

"And much needed."

"What do you mean?"

"Abby has wanted to take dancing for a while, but the only school near here is in Sawyer's Bend. I've been reluctant to let her attend there. I've heard some disturbing things about the kind of dance moves they teach."

Beth looked to her sister-in-law for an explanation.

"A lot of the moms here in Dover have pulled their girls from that school. At the last recital Hannah was in, she looked like a pole dancer. Her mother was furious."

Beth was well aware of the suggestive movements popular in today's world, though she couldn't imagine teaching some of them to children. "I had no idea that was happening."

"How do you teach your daughter Christian values and modesty when the world tells them it's okay to dance like a stripper? Maybe you should think about opening up a school here. I know dozens of mothers would love to sign their children up if they knew they didn't have to worry about inappropriate dances."

Julie waved goodbye, and Beth focused her attention on her students. But her sister-in-law's suggestion began to churn in the back of her mind.

"Okay, ladies, let's get started. First we have to stretch out all our muscles."

She noted with interest what each girl had decided to wear. Abby had chosen black tights, leather dance flats and a purple-and-black leotard. Hannah wore bike shorts and a tank top. Chloe proudly wore traditional pink tights and a leotard with a net tutu to match.

Hannah chuckled. "You don't need a tutu to practice, silly."

"I don't care. I want to look like Miss Beth, and that means I have to have a tutu."

"But she's not wearing a tutu today," Abby pointed out.

Beth chuckled and gestured to her all-black dance ensemble with a knee-length wrap skirt.

"You wear what makes you comfortable. And today I'm comfortable looking like a teacher. First we warm up."

Watching the girls' excitement as she introduced simple steps and explained various movements chased away her lingering nerves. They were sweet and eager to learn. She'd take her cues from them and use this first class as her barometer to gauge how she would proceed.

An hour later the girls were pulling on their jackets and gathering up their things. The warm glow filling her chest as she watched them brought a smile to her face. Teaching these girls had been more enjoyable than she'd ever expected. Their energy and enthusiasm had filled her with joy. The idea of a dance school didn't seem like the end of the road, but a possible new bend in it.

Abby and Hannah waved and hurried out the door. Chloe stood at the barre pretending to be on her toes as she waited for her father to pick her up. A flash of light and a soft squeak filled the studio as the door opened and Noah strode in. In his leather jacket, which showed off the breadth of his shoulders, and faded jeans that hugged his muscular legs, he bore little resemblance to the tall, skinny boy she remembered. He grinned in her direction, his blue eyes soft with affection. Her pulse hiccupped. It quickly stilled when she realized his warm welcome was directed at his daughter and not her.

Chloe ran toward him and gave him a quick hug, chattering about what she'd learned. He gave Chloe a pat on the shoulder. "I'm glad you had fun. Why don't you wait in the car? I want to talk to Miss Beth for a second. I'll be right there."

Chloe waved and smiled before walking outside.

Noah finally settled his clear blue gaze on her, and her pulse jumped again. Something in his attitude raised her defenses. "She did very well. In fact, I know you don't want to hear this, but she's a natural. I don't think you'll have any problem getting her to do her exercises now."

"That's good. I just want to make sure she doesn't get any ideas when it comes to these dance classes. I don't want you glamorizing your profession, making it appear all fun and games."

Beth set her jaw and crossed her arms over her chest. "I will always answer her questions honestly. I won't sugarcoat anything, but I won't lie about the enjoyment and satisfaction, either."

"I don't want her lured into thinking fame is something she should chase after. It only leads to disappointment and ruins relationships."

She shook her head. "I never chased the fame, Noah. You know that."

A muscle flexed in his jaw, and his eyes narrowed. "Not you. Her mother. How can a husband and child compete with Hollywood celebrity?"

Stunned, Beth could only watch as he spun around and walked out. Had his wife walked out on him and Chloe? She knew he was divorced, but she'd never thought about what had brought it about. Is that why he was so against anything connected to the arts? It explained a lot. She wanted to ask him what had happened, to help her understand his animosity. Hurrying to the door, she opened it as his car disappeared around the bend in the drive.

This is what had been the strength of their relationship—the ability to help each other through hard times. Noah needed someone to talk to, to work out his anger. It wasn't all about her after all. He'd been hurt deeply by his wife's betrayal.

But first they had to get beyond their own past.

Noah tried to pay attention to the conversation going on between his gram and Chloe as they ate supper that evening, but they were talking about Beth, the last thing he wanted to hear. He was trying not to think of her, but he'd found that to be difficult. Gram had fixed his favorite—roast beef with homemade noodles—but he was barely aware of eating any.

He blinked and tried to pick up the thread of the conversation. He knew it had something to do with the first dance class earlier today, but all he could think about was the joy on Beth's face when he entered the studio. Chloe had been bubbling over with excitement, but Beth's expression was one of pure delight. Her hazel eyes had sparkled, and her smile was brighter than morning sunshine. He'd been caught off guard by the emotions swirling up from deep inside. All his old feelings came roaring back. He'd reacted by blurting out the truth about Yvonne. He hadn't intended to, but sharing his concerns with her was as natural as breathing.

He'd forced himself to listen to Chloe and keep his eyes away from Beth. He'd slammed his defenses into place. He couldn't forget that she was driven and focused and had only one agenda in her life. One that didn't include family and friends.

"Noah. Noah. Yoo-hoo."

He jerked his head up. Gram was staring at him. "Sorry. I was thinking about…work. What were you saying?"

Gram peered over her glasses. "I was reminding you that there's a board meeting for the little theater this evening. Your presence is required."

Chloe groaned. "Does that mean I have to go, too? Those meetings are boring."

"Maybe so, but you can't stay here all alone. You can use my tablet while you wait."

A mischievous grin appeared on her face, putting a sparkle in her eyes. "Can I watch videos of Miss Beth?"

He still didn't like the idea. The more she watched the clips, the more time she spent with Beth, the greater the risk of her latching on to a dream that could only bring heartache and disappointment. But he couldn't keep her a baby forever. "Okay, but I'm going to put your spelling words and your study guide for the test on Friday on there, too, so you can spend part of the time looking at those."

A half hour later he pulled out of the drive for the short trip to the little theater. For a man who vowed to steer clear of any artistic endeavors, he found himself hip-deep in them. First his gram sweet-talks him into taking part in her renewed theater project, then Beth comes back to town and gets Chloe involved in dance classes.

He really needed a nice steel rod to insert into his spine. Either that, or he had too many women in his life. Problem was he loved them too much to turn down their pleas for help.

Except Beth. He couldn't deny he felt something, but he was absolutely sure it had nothing at all to do with love. It was merely an emotional muscle memory being reawakened. It would settle back down soon enough.

Noah opened the back door of the old building to allow his gram and Chloe to enter. The board usually met in a small room at the back. He never had much to add to the proceedings. His lack of creativity put him at odds with the other members, and only reminded him of high school and being the misfit. The only time he'd felt he belonged was when he'd become friends with Beth. But he did it to please his gram, and he tried to act as the practical, business-minded member.

He stepped into the cramped space and froze.

"Miss Beth." Chloe darted between the members and into Beth's arms.

Noah stared at Beth, his emotions tilting between surprise and dread. What was she doing here?

His gram hurried toward Beth, too, patting her cheek and smiling before directing her to be seated. In his stunned state, he waited too long to choose a seat and ended up having to take the chair next to Beth. He leaned toward her slightly. "Why are you here?"

"I'm taking Allison's place. You?"

"I'm on the board." She met his gaze with an insincere smile that created a kink in his chest.

Gram was sorting through her papers, and Chloe had curled up in a chair in the corner, busily tapping away on his tablet. He had a feeling she was watching videos of Beth again.

"Good evening, ladies and gentlemen. We have some new business to go over, and I want to get right to it before we address the other issues. Beth, my dear, would you stand?"

Her chair squeaked as she moved to rise, and Noah reached for the back to pull it away.

He didn't want to look at her, but he couldn't help it. Her smile was warm and genuine now as she touched each member with her gaze.

"I'd like you to meet our new dance coordinator, Miss Bethany Montgomery. I'm sure you all know some member of the Montgomery family. There are a bunch of them here in Dover." She paused as the members chuckled. "And you may know that Beth is a professional ballerina. She's home now and has graciously agreed to take Allison's place."

His gaze traveled around the room as the board gave Beth a round of polite applause. Gram looked delighted. Smug, actually, which raised a flag in the back of his mind. She then introduced the other board members: Shelby Durrant, who owned a small stationery shop on the square, Todd Newsome, the new president of the bank and David Atkins, an attorney.

"I'm sure her knowledge and expertise will add another level of excitement to our humble production," Gram said after she had introduced everyone and turned back to Beth.

"Thank you all," Beth said. "I'm looking forward to being a part of the *Christmas Dreams* musical."

"Noah, dear. Why don't you show Bethany around and introduce her to everyone. I'll fill you in on our discussions later."

Trapped, he had no recourse but to agree. With a stiff smile and a wave of his hand, he gestured her to precede him. Once outside the small room, he stopped, only to have Chloe bump into him from behind. "Where are you going?"

"I want to look around, too."

"Not happening." He took her hand and marched her to the steps along the side of the stage. "See those nice comfy seats? Pick one, open your homework and get busy."

With a barely stifled groan, a roll of her big blue eyes and a dejected droop to her shoulders, she stomped down the wooden steps and threw herself into a seat, scowling at him above the tablet. Anticipating her next comment, he pointed at her. "Homework. No videos." It earned him another glare.

A soft snicker to his left drew his attention. Beth was covering her mouth with her fingertips, her eyes bursting with amusement. "What?"

"I thought you said you couldn't say no to your little girl?"

"Not all the time." He faced her. "What changed your mind?"

"I missed the theater. I thought it would be good to help out and keep busy."

"You don't have enough to do with working for your mom and teaching dancing?"

"Teaching only takes two hours a week. And I don't work full-time at the office. That leaves a lot of free time. Even with daily workouts."

"So what happens to this show when you're all healed up and you run back to New York?"

The teasing smile that had lit her eyes suddenly vanished, and the hazel color shifted into the dark brown spectrum. "I'm not going anywhere for a long time. I have three, maybe four months of rehab yet to do before I'll be cleared to dance, so you can stop stressing over that. I'll be here to finish the performance."

"Good, because it would break Gram's heart if you just disappeared one day."

"Noah, I left here suddenly because an incredible opportunity came my way. I apologize for not keeping in touch afterward, but frankly, I didn't think you'd care one way or the other. You transferred to another college and got married. Your life went in a different direction. So did mine."

Why would she think he hadn't cared? He opened his mouth to ask when someone tapped his shoulder. He glanced around to see the director of the show at his side.

"Is this our new dance teacher?" She gasped, before letting out a high-pitched squeal. What was it with women that they had to screech when they were happy? Chloe did it all the time.

"Beth Montgomery. Please tell me you're replacing Allison."

"Jenny Olsen. Oh, it's so good to see you. Yes, I am. You?"

She held out her arms. "I'm the director of this extravaganza."

Noah tamped down his irritation while the women went through another round of squeals and giggles. He'd forgotten that Jen and Beth had been friends since grade school. As soon as he could get a word in, he made his escape. "Now that you two have been reunited, I'm going to get back to the board meeting. Jen, I'm sure you can give Beth the tour."

Jen linked arms with her old friend and waved him away. "I'd love to."

He watched as the women walked off, knowing his Plan A to keep his distance from Beth was toast. Beth glanced over her shoulder at him, a taunting smile on her face. She was enjoying his discomfort, and he had his gram to thank for this. Pivoting, he started back to the stage, pausing only to remind his daughter to finish her homework.

He had to come up with a Plan B. Fast. He was already having a hard time with Beth working next door. Now he'd have to deal with her at the theater for the next several weeks, as well. Maybe she'd leave soon.

No. Then the show would suffer. And Chloe would be upset.

Rubbing his forehead, he sent up a prayer for strength and guidance in dealing with the three females complicating his life.

Chapter Four

Beth moved to the large mirror leaning against the wall in her bedroom, taking a few deep breaths. Tonight would be her first rehearsal for the Christmas show, and she wanted to make a good impression so she'd pulled on her best dark jeans, low-heeled boots that ended right above her ankles and a sophisticated dark green cowl-necked jersey top with a diagonal insert.

She frowned at her reflection. She was overdressed for a little theater practice. Tugging off the tunic, she slipped on a simple gray crew neck sweater and draped a loop scarf over her head. Better. At least in Mississippi she didn't have to wear a bulky winter coat and hat. Clothes usually gave her confidence. Not tonight. Now she was wishing she'd thought things through more.

Learning Noah was on the board of directors of the little theater had challenged her decision. Judging from his expression when he'd walked into the room, he'd been blindsided, too. She grinned as she remembered the look on his face, like a man who'd been dumped in the lake and suddenly realized he couldn't swim.

She was treading water, as well. The more she was

near him and the more they talked, the more she remembered how much his friendship mattered, and how he'd given her a sense of belonging she'd always missed. As much as her family loved her, and she had no doubts that they did, she'd always felt different. Her siblings were all extroverts—she was the only introvert in the clan. Noah had made her feel that being different was the perfect way for her to be.

Taking a deep breath, she put on her earrings and squared her shoulders. How bad could it be? It's not as if Noah was involved with the production. Besides, in a few weeks it would be over, and she needed something to fill her time beyond working in the real estate office. Once she got past this first meeting, everything would be fine.

Her gaze landed on her tablet as she reached for her purse, sending a thread of shame through her mind. Noah's comment about his divorce had spurred her curiosity. She'd caved to temptation and looked up Noah's wife online. Apparently the stunning blonde had exploded on the news scene like a rocket, going from weekend reporter on a network affiliate to being an anchor to having her own talk show in less than three years. What had disturbed her, however, was that there was no mention of a husband or a child in her bio, only the celebrity aspects of her life. No wonder Noah was so against Chloe getting ideas about anything concerning performing. He was probably afraid Chloe would want to follow in her mother's footsteps.

Noah was a black-and-white thinker, and knowing him, he'd obviously equated her leaving to become a professional ballerina with his wife doing the same to become a TV personality and concluded that keeping

Chloe away from the arts was keeping her from heart-break. But that didn't fully explain why he was so angry with her. She hadn't left a husband and child behind.

She locked the door and dropped the key into her bag, striding down the sidewalk along Main Street. The little theater was only a block off Peace Street, an easy walk from her apartment. The parking lot was full when she arrived. Making her way up the concrete steps at the back of the old two-story brick building, she stepped inside and her concerns melted away. This was her world. She took a deep breath and went in search of Jen.

Shorty Zimmerman, the theater manager and insurance agent, informed her Jen was backstage. Beth made her way down the aisles, taking time to appreciate the surroundings. She'd been too busy meeting cast and crew the other night. The theater looked the same as she remembered. Old, small and in need of major re-modeling. It wasn't designed as a theater originally. It had been coaxed into the role with leftover seating and other materials from a variety of sources, one of which was the old Palace movie theater on Church Street. She hated to think of that grand old structure decaying away, but no one had stepped up to preserve it. Supposedly a full restoration was too expensive. Not to mention Dutch Ingles owned it and the building next door, and the old miser refused to sell or donate the theater. But old or new, a theater had a certain atmosphere about it that revved up her excitement.

Jen hurried toward her. "Are you ready for this madness?"

"I think so."

"It'll be fun. You'll see." She handed her a piece of paper. "This is our program. Three acts. The first focuses on the secular aspect of Christmas—pop songs, presents and the like. Act two is family-oriented, with carols, a short scene from *The Nutcracker* and 'White Christmas.' Act three is about the real reason for the season—hymns, a nativity and a scripture reading."

"It sounds wonderful. You've included something for everyone."

"Beth." Jen touched her arm gently. "I didn't have a chance to mention it the other night, but I heard about your injury. I'm sorry. I know how much dancing has always meant to you."

Beth's heart swelled with warm affection. It would be good to have a friend to talk to. She hadn't realized how much she missed that. "Thank you. It's been a long, painful recovery."

"Do you think you'll be able to go back to ballet?"

A few days ago she would have snapped out a firm yes, but at the moment that seemed more like a hope than a certainty. "I'm not sure."

"Well, if anyone can make a comeback, it's you. You're the most committed, dedicated person I've ever known."

"I have to admit I'm nervous about this rehearsal."

"Don't be. Everyone here is sweet and eager to please. They are looking forward to working with you. Allison designed the dance numbers and the costumes, and everyone has learned their steps. Basically you'll just have to oversee rehearsals and keep them on track until the show. I think for tonight you can just find a seat, watch the numbers and then we'll go over any questions or concerns you might have."

Jen's enthusiasm lightened Beth's mood as she found a seat in the sixth row, where she could see the entire stage. Pulling out her tablet, she swiped to the note app and turned her full attention to the performers.

The numbers were charming and engaging, but she saw room for improvement both in the dances and the scenery. With a little effort she could easily bump up the show to another level and make it sparkle. She wasn't sure how Jen would take to her ideas, though.

When the rehearsal was over, Jen motioned Beth forward and introduced her to the cast. Beth made the appropriate speech of reassurance and encouragement.

Jen dismissed everyone then faced her. "Did you have any suggestions or questions about the numbers? I saw you making notes."

"I do." Beth ran through some of her thoughts about changes to the choreography and expanding the scenes to amp up the excitement. Jen nodded thoughtfully, and Beth braced herself for pushback. She didn't want to complicate things. She was here to help and not to cause trouble. If Jen didn't agree with her suggestions, then she'd leave things as is.

Her friend released a long, slow sigh. "I'm so glad you said that. Allison did her best, but I felt the numbers lacked that element of excitement. They seemed flat and boring to me. Do you think you can fix them?"

Relief and anticipation swirled inside her chest. "I believe I can. Do you have the time and money to add to the sets and maybe a few new costumes?"

"Absolutely. Miss Evelyn is fully committed to this show, so money isn't an issue. We can certainly add to the sets if our carpenter has time. We won't rehearse over Thanksgiving, so that leaves only three weeks until we open." She pulled out her phone and typed in a text message. "I love your ideas, Beth. I think you're exactly what we needed for this production. We all want it to be a worthy addition to the holiday celebrations. I know we're all amateurs, but I'd like this to be as professional as possible."

"Hey, Jen, what's up?"

Beth spun around at the sound of Noah's smooth voice. "What are you doing here?"

Jen glanced at her. "Oh, didn't I tell you? Noah is our set builder. Anything you want constructed for the numbers, he'll make it happen."

Beth wasn't sure how she felt about that. Being around Noah was already stirring old emotions. She didn't need any more exposure to this new, compelling version of her old friend. "I'd forgotten you were handy with a hammer."

"Thanks to the insistence of my grandpa." He raised an eyebrow, and his blue eyes held a challenge. "I'm the go-to guy. Whatever you need built, fixed or scrounged up, I'm the one to call."

"Beth has some ideas to spruce up the show, and she might need a few props built."

Noah looked like he'd sooner swallow nails. "Give me a sketch, and I'll see what I can do."

Jen was called away for a phone call, leaving them alone, a painfully awkward silence hanging between them, like actors who had forgotten their lines. If her presence here was going to create tension, then maybe she should bow out. "I had no idea you were so involved in this production."

"Like I said, it's hard to say no to the women in my life. Gram asked me to help out."

"If this is going to be uncomfortable, I'll quit."

Noah looked surprised. "I never said that. I'm sure

the show will benefit from your knowledge and experience."

The performers had drifted out, and the stagehands were putting their gear away. When the bank of lights over the stage shut down, Beth draped her purse over her shoulder. "That's our cue to leave. Say hello to Chloe for me."

"Sure." They walked to the back door, exiting with a few stragglers. After saying good-night to Shorty, they stepped out into the small parking lot. Beth searched for something to say. "It was like old times. We helped your gram with a couple little theater shows, as I recall."

Noah shoved his hands into his jacket pockets and rocked back on his heels. "That was a long time ago."

He was shutting her out. It was a feeling she was well acquainted with. Being different. Not being included in groups. But it had been Noah who'd given her a place to belong. They'd both been oddballs; it's why they'd grown so close. But now *he* was the one closing the door.

She blinked and turned away, not wanting him to see how hurt she was. "Yes, it was. Good night."

Folding her arms around her waist to ward off the night chill, she started toward home. Would she always feel like the outsider? The one who didn't fit? Not with her family, not with her school friends, not even with her coworkers. The only place she fit was on stage. And that was closed to her now, as well.

Noah watched Beth walk across the parking lot and down the sidewalk toward her apartment. He'd caught a glimpse of the moisture in her eyes, and he'd quickly regretted his harsh words. Being close to Beth brought out the worst in him. She'd stepped in to help, and he'd behaved like an ungrateful jerk. A quick glance around the deserted street raised his concern. It was a full block to the town square, and the building where she lived stood at the far end. He couldn't in all good conscience let her walk alone. After tossing his things into the back of his car, he jogged to catch up with her. "Hey. You shouldn't walk home alone."

She stopped and faced him. The light spilling from the corner streetlamp danced on her dark hair and made her eyes shine.

"It's only a block, and there are plenty of street-lights." She pointed to the one on the edge of the square. "Besides, Dover is the safest place on earth."

"Maybe, but I think I'd better see you home."

She chuckled. The sound washed through him like sparkling water.

"You sound so formal and polite. Evelyn would be pleased. But seriously, I'll be fine."

Noah took her arm and steered her forward. "Nope. I want to make sure you get home safely."

"Thank you."

They walked in silence, and Noah searched for a topic that didn't touch on their past. Sadly, there were none he wanted to bring up. Finally Beth spoke.

"I have a confession to make. I looked up your for-mer wife on the internet."

He wasn't surprised. He knew she'd be curious. "No problem. I looked you up, too."

He'd learned enough about ACL reconstruction to know that Beth's dream of returning to dancing was a slim one.

"You did?"

"Chloe wanted to see some videos of you performing."

"Oh." She sounded disappointed.

"I didn't realize how serious your injury was. I'm sorry."

"Thanks. Other dancers have made a successful comeback. I could, too. I don't give up easily."

"I remember." Nothing came between her and her desire to dance. "Did you find all the answers to your questions about Yvonne?"

"Some. What disturbed me was that there was no mention of a husband and child in her bio."

A strangled chuckle escaped his throat before he could stop it. "That's because a family didn't fit with her image. Her manager wanted to present her as free and unencumbered."

"I'm surprised she agreed to that. It seems so cold and heartless." She stopped. "I'm sorry. That was a very thoughtless thing to say."

He looked at Beth. Even in the faint light, her hazel eyes were filled with sympathy. The Beth he remembered, even when obsessed with her dancing, had carried a heart for others. For the first time, he wondered if perhaps she still existed beneath the professional drive. He hoped so. He'd like to spend time with her again.

"But true. She wasn't always like that. We met in college my sophomore year. She wasn't like anyone I'd ever met. She was outrageous, impulsive and exciting. She showed me a way of life I'd never known before. I was looking to make a change, and she made it happen."

The boy he'd been hadn't been enough for Beth, so he'd decided to reinvent himself, and Yvonne had been his teacher. Yvonne had changed the outside of him. She'd encouraged him to work out, taught him how to present himself. She'd given him a total makeover, down to hairstyle and wardrobe. Unfortunately, clothes could only make the man to a point. While he looked confident and polished on the outside, on the inside he was still the same misfit with thick glasses who never belonged. Except with Beth.

"She sounds amazing."

"It all happened fast. We fell in love, got married and then Chloe came along. Everything seemed possible. We were going to school, working and raising our daughter. After graduation, she got an offer from a big network affiliate in San Francisco, and I hired on with a prestigious engineering firm. All our dreams were coming true."

"Then her career took off?"

He nodded. "An overnight sensation."

"And she just left? How could she do that?"

"I believe her reasoning was that she couldn't make us happy if she didn't first make herself happy."

Beth slipped her hand in his, sending a jolt along his senses. He told himself to pull away, but her fingers felt good entwined with his. The old habit of baring his soul to her took over. "Truth is, she left long before she walked out the door. I stayed in San Francisco so Chloe could see her mother from time to time, but those times eventually became never. When Gram got sick last spring, I decided to come back home."

"Chloe told me her mother is going to send her a plane ticket to visit for Thanksgiving."

Noah shook his head. "Never going to happen. She makes plans with Chloe all the time that she never keeps."

"Poor baby."

"Chloe keeps dreaming that one day her mom will come and get her, and they'll go on wonderful adventures together."

"Is that why you don't want her to dream? Because dreams don't always come true?"

"Dreams set you up for heartbreak." He could sense Beth gearing up for an argument, and he was thankful that they'd reached the apartment. He waited while she fished out her key and unlocked the door.

"Thank you for walking me home. You were always such a gentleman. It was one of the things I liked most about you."

He wanted to ask if there had been other things she liked, but thought better of the idea. "Thank my gram. Any good manners I possess are her doing."

"Good night, Noah. Be careful walking back to the theater."

He grinned and held up his arm, flexing the muscle. "Never fear. I can handle it." That earned him a bright smile. He walked away, acutely aware of Beth's eyes on his back. He took his time walking down Main Street. Dover at this time of night was quiet and still, and he let the peacefulness ease some of his concerns. The tension between the two of them had been uncomfortable. But like it or not, he'd have to work with her for the next several weeks. He'd given his commitment to helping his gram with her dream, and he wouldn't let her down.

The hair on the back of his neck tingled and he stopped, cautiously glancing around. Was someone watching him? Slowly he scanned the darkened storefronts, the shadowed paths through the park. He looked behind him and his gaze traveled to the balcony above his office, the one in Beth's apartment. He saw her, lean-

ing over the iron railing, her head sticking out from behind one of the vine-covered posts. He started to raise
his hand, but looked away and started walking again.

Why was she watching him? To make sure he reached
the theater safely? Or was there something more?

Beth took the hand of her older brother, Gil, seated to
her right, and the smaller hand of her niece Abby on her
left. Closing her eyes, she listened to the soft tone of her
mother's voice as she offered grace over the meal. Her
mind filled with a rush of memories of family dinners
here in the old house. Back then it had been her father
saying the blessing, his deep voice strong and reverent,
giving thanks for all they had and for each other. The
memory filled her with familiar warmth and a deep,
aching sadness. Even after a year, her father's presence
lingered within the walls. It probably always would.

Beth ate in silence, letting the chatter of her family
fill the air. Linc and Gil were each happily married to
wonderful women. Linc and Gemma were expecting
their first child. Beth had bonded with her new sisters-
in-law quickly, and she found her new nephew, Evan,
a joy. Having her niece, Abby, back in the family was
another blessing. Her family had grown in the last year.
Everything was changing—in her world, too.

After dinner Beth joined her mother in the kitchen
to clean up.

"So, how are things going with you and Noah? Are
you getting caught up?"

"Not really. I don't think he's interested in catching up."

"Why?"

She shrugged. "He's angry with me for not staying

in touch, which doesn't make sense because he didn't stay in touch with me, either."

"You did leave suddenly." She shook her head. "That was a crazy time."

"Even crazier when I got up there. I remember waking up one day, and it was September and I had no idea where the summer had gone."

Mom nodded, folding the dish towel slowly. "You went from amateur to professional literally overnight. That's a huge life change."

"That's what I told him, but he was upset that he had to learn about my job with Forsythe from the *Dover Dispatch* and not me."

"He was your closest friend. I would have thought you'd have found time to share your good news with him. It's important to stay in touch with loved ones."

The melancholy tone in her mom's voice tugged at her heart. "I stayed in touch. I called. I came home."

Her mother took a long moment to reply. "It would have been nice to hear from you more often. I understood that your life would be hectic, and I knew you had to devote all your efforts toward succeeding, but your dad and I missed you. We felt a little abandoned at times."

Beth flipped back through her memory, sorting through the years. She could see now where she'd kept putting off coming home to visit, postponing phone calls. "I didn't intentionally cut you out of my life, Mom. Honest."

"I know, but it reached a point where the only time we heard from you was when you told us about your next performance. All I'm saying is that I can understand Noah's position."

Why did everyone blame her for not staying in touch? "The phone rings both ways."

"Yes, it does. I'm sorry if I sounded judgmental. Since your father has been gone, I do a lot of thinking back on things I wish I'd done differently. It's been a difficult year."

Beth moved to the window and stared outside, avoiding eye contact with her mother and hoping the subject was closed. The last few years of her life had been difficult for her as well, but she couldn't share the reasons with her mother. Not yet anyway.

"I'm glad you decided to help with the Christmas show. Now you can stop trying to stay in dancing form and focus on something else. Who knows. It might be the beginning of a whole new career for you."

Her mother's comment had stirred a dark pool of anger and grief. "Mom, I know you mean well, but you don't understand. Dancing has been my life since I was five. It's what I love. It's the most important aspect of who I am. You don't know what it's like to lose the thing that gives your life meaning and purpose."

Her mom came and took her hand, pulling her down beside her on the little bench beneath the window. "Bethany, I know better than anyone what you're going through. I've lost the person who gave my life meaning and purpose, the man I shared my life with and the father of my children. We were supposed to grow old together. We were going to travel and do all the things we couldn't do with five children. Now I'm struggling to learn to live alone, and figure out who I am without him by my side. It's hard, Bethany. It's painful. Some days I don't even want to get out of bed. But I can't shut down. I have to move forward no matter how difficult it is."

Beth's chest ached, and she swiped tears from her face. How could she have been so thoughtless and cruel? She'd been so focused on her own pain, she'd become blind to anyone else's. "Mama, I'm so sorry. I didn't mean to hurt you." A sob made its way up her throat. "I'm sorry." Her mother pulled her into her arms before she could move.

"I know. I understand how devastating this situation is for you, but we'll get through it. Together." She pulled a napkin from the table and gently dabbed at the tears on Beth's cheeks. "You're so much like your father. Strong, determined and fully committed to whatever goal you set. But sometimes that commitment makes it hard for you to see when it's time to let go."

"Is that even possible?"

"Not entirely. But when I look around at what the Lord has added to my life after losing your father, I have to be in awe of His blessing. In the last year Gil brought Abby home to us and added Julie to the family. Linc gave me Evan and Gemma." She brushed the hair off Beth's forehead. "And I have my little dancer back home again. If you let Him, the Lord will open new paths for you. But you have to let go."

With her throat tight with remorse and sadness, all she could do was nod. Her mother was right. She had to accept the truth and let go. But she had no idea how to do that. What if she let go, and there was nothing out there to grab hold of?

Chapter Five

Beth took her time walking to rehearsal Thursday night. She'd forgotten how pleasant November could be in Mississippi. She needed only a light jacket to protect from the cool wind. Back in New York, she'd be bundling up and digging out gloves and boots.

Nervous excitement bubbled in her rib cage as she neared the little theater, but her confidence ebbed and flowed. With the aid of videos of the performances Jen had sent her, she'd worked up simple steps and movements that would enhance each number. She hoped the dancers could pick up the changes quickly and wouldn't find the routines too complicated.

Her nervousness vanished over the next hour when the cast welcomed the additions she'd created. They admitted that Allison's routines were too simple, and they were eager to learn more to make the show better. After working out a new rehearsal schedule for each cast, she went in search of Noah to discuss her ideas for new props.

Other than a glimpse of him coming and going in the

office, she hadn't seen him since he'd walked her home the other night, and she hadn't been able to get the incident out of her mind. His concern for her safety had shifted something inside her. She understood he was just being a gentleman, but there'd been something romantic about walking beside him along the dimly lit streets and saying good-night at her door. She groaned inwardly. Hadn't she learned the hard way that romantic gestures were worthless?

Learning about Noah's wife had given her insight into his attitude and his heart. Noah was a family man, a man who planted his roots deep into the ground. He'd spoken often about his parents and how someday he wanted to have a family of his own so he could recreate the happy life he'd known before their deaths.

In a way, they were very much alike. She was determined to excel in her career, and Noah was unshakable in his desire to provide a solid foundation for his daughter, even staying in San Francisco in an impossible situation for his daughter's sake. He'd moved home to help his gram. He was an admirable man, a man who would do anything for those he loved. But if betrayed, he would be a hard man to deal with.

She found Noah in the back of the building, talking with Shorty. He smiled when he saw her. The first genuine smile he'd given her since she'd seen him again. The way his lips tugged to one side when he smiled sent a trickle of warm appreciation along her nerves. His smile hadn't changed one bit, but the body around it had. *Gangly* had been a good description of the boy she remembered. Now the only word that came to mind was *hunk*. Her cheeks flamed, and she glanced down at the sketches in her hands to compose herself.

"What have you got there?" Noah patted Shorty on the shoulder and came toward her.

"Some ideas for new props."

He took them from her hands. "You didn't waste any time, did you?"

"There's no time to waste. Besides, I'm anxious to get started. I think this show can be one of the highlights of the weekend."

He held her gaze a moment as if reassessing her, then his clear blue eyes warmed, unleashing a sudden uneasiness. She pointed to the first sketch of a full-sized staircase: six steps with railings and a wide landing at the top. She shifted to his side to explain her idea and immediately regretted it. He smelled like he'd just stepped from the shower. The scent of soap and musky aftershave entwined around her senses, making her want to lean in close and inhale the tantalizing scent deep into her lungs.

"I thought a staircase would make that *Night Before Christmas* scene more homey and highlight the family Christmas theme. Stairs and fireplaces shout family, don't you think?" She looked up at him and her heart thumped. He was still staring at her. "Anyway, the tricky part is I want it to look like a staircase on this side, but on the other side I want it to be flat so it can be painted to look like a nativity backdrop for the next scene. That way we can simply turn it around, and we won't need two separate pieces."

"Clever. I like it."

"And it needs to be on wheels so we can move it around. Can you do that?"

"Sure. It'll take a little figuring, but it shouldn't be hard."

"Good. And about the Christmas tree. It's in all three acts, but it's too small. It needs to be twice that size and with more lights, and it has to be on a dolly so we can move it."

"The dolly I can help you with, but the tree is out of my area of expertise."

"I'll talk to Jen about that."

Noah shook his head, crossed his arms over his chest and looked down at her, making her aware of the muscle he'd acquired. His biceps and broad chest strained the fabric of the cotton shirt he wore. She looked up at him, thinking how the top of her head would nestle perfectly under his chin. She blinked and took a small step back, bracing for some sharp remark.

"I'm not sure bringing you on board was such a good idea." He leaned toward her. "I remember how you get. You charge forward like a little race car, dragging everyone behind you like tin cans on a string."

"I get excited."

"I know. It's what made being your friend so much fun." His smile grew tender, then abruptly vanished as if he was regretting the memory. "I have a feeling I'm going to be spending all my free time in the workshop."

She exhaled. "It'll keep you out of trouble."

His eyes suddenly darkened, and he pressed his lips together. "I think it's too late for that."

He walked off, calling out over his shoulder as he went. "I'll get right on this."

What did he mean about it being too late? Too late for them to repair their relationship? Spinning on her heel, she walked off. How was she supposed to make sense of anything with Noah when he hid behind that wall of resentment all the time? Every now and then he'd peek over the top and reminisce about their past. Then he'd duck down again.

Her mom's comments pushed into her mind, sending a feeling of shame along her nerves. In chasing her dream, she'd allowed all her relationships to fade away. It hadn't been a deliberate decision, but friendships hadn't seemed as important as becoming the best artist in the company. The one relationship she'd succumbed to had ended in disaster, and left her questioning every aspect of her life and career. She'd responded with even more determination and buried herself in her dancing, driving herself mercilessly. And now she was paying the price.

How did you balance the desires of your heart with the dedication to achieve your goal, and still find time to stay connected to those you loved? Was that even possible?

She could balance on the tips of her toes. She could pirouette and execute any number of precise moves with only the smallest part of her shoe touching the floor. But she'd never learned to balance her life.

With effort, she brushed the troublesome thought aside. She had new things to occupy her mind, and she liked it. Teaching the girls and working with the Christmas show provided a measure of satisfaction she hadn't experienced since her accident. That was a lot to be thankful for.

Sawdust flew around his head as Noah pushed the two-by-six through the table saw. The workshop behind his grandma's house had been his grandpa's domain. It's where Noah had learned to work with his hands. Gramps had been proud of his grandson's intellectual acumen, but he'd also wanted him to have a knowledge of basic handyman skills. Gramps had been a real estate developer by profession, but he'd been raised on a farm and worked his way through college as a carpenter. He'd headed the local Habitat for Humanity program in Dover and insisted Noah volunteer as often as possible. Noah had balked at first, preferring to have his nose in a book or a computer, but he soon realized that the special time with his gramps and helping people achieve a home of their own gave him a connection that meant more.

Noah switched off the saw and removed his safety glasses. The woodworking tools hadn't been touched in the two years since Gramps had passed, and it had taken Noah days to get them in order again. He'd resisted getting involved with the little theater when Gram had approached him. Being on the Board of Directors was one thing; getting involved with the actual production was something else. Now it had brought him even closer to Beth, which was the last thing he wanted. The harder he tried to keep his distance, the more they were thrust together.

"It's good to see this workshop in use again. Your granddad spent a lot of time in here. It was his therapy."

Noah grinned at his gram as she entered the shop. "I keep expecting him to look over my shoulder and point out my mistakes."

"He wanted you to do a good job." She stopped at his side. "What's this for?"

"Beth wants some new props built."

"I felt sure she'd bring new life to the show. Allison did her best, but she lacked vision. How is Beth getting along with everyone?"

Noah met her gaze. "Don't you mean how is she getting along with me?" His gram shrugged, a small smile on her lips.

"I always liked her."

"I did, too."

"Past tense?"

He sighed and slid on the safety glasses again. "She's doing a good job. Everyone likes her, and they like the changes she's adding. Your production is in good hands."

Gram patted his back. "Give her whatever she wants."

Noah sent another board through the saw, then shut it down again. What did Beth want? When he picked up Chloe from dance class, Beth was glowing with delight. At the theater, she vibrated with energy as she worked with the dancers. One thing he'd realized was that Beth's obsession came from her love of dancing. Yvonne's obsession sprang from an insatiable need to always be the center of attention. Yet in the back of his mind, he kept hearing her say she'd dance again—in New York. Not Dover.

Could she ever be content in a small town? He shook off the dangerous notion. No matter how strong his resolve to keep his heart protected from her, his heart had other ideas. The more time he spent with her, the more he thought about her. Their lives had become so intertwined that he had little chance to keep his distance.

Chloe had started to talk about Beth more than her mother. Another danger to avoid.

He stared at the wood he'd cut. All he could do for the moment was make Beth happy. The show had to succeed for Gram. Beth was something he'd have to deal with along the way.

Right now he had an appointment to inspect a house before he picked up Chloe at Beth's studio. Thank God for his inspector's job. It was the one time he could honestly say he didn't think about Beth. But the minute he stopped working, there she'd be again.

He *really* needed to get that under control before he ended up falling for her again.

Beth turned off the music and faced her students. "Good job today, ladies. I can't believe how quickly you're learning."

Hannah giggled. "That's 'cause it's so fun. I like you better than my other dance teacher."

Chloe nodded, a big smile on her face. "You're the best teacher ever."

Abby gave Chloe a friendly shove. "She's the only one you've had, silly."

The girls giggled as they gathered up their things. A horn honked, signaling that Julie had arrived to pick up Abby and Hannah, who lived next door to each other. "Remember, ladies, point those toes."

Abby and Hannah linked arms and chanted as they walked away. "Point your toes. Point your toes."

Chloe was standing at the barre trying to get her leg up on it, which made her look like a very awkward ballerina. The child was determined to learn, pushing for more and more new steps. Beth had to constantly remind her to be careful of her knee. "Chloe, why don't you practice your *demi pliés* while you wait. You might hurt yourself otherwise. I've already asked my brother to install the lower barre for you girls to use. It should be done by next lesson."

Chloe sighed and nodded, grasping the barre and placing her heels together.

Beth's cell chimed, and she hurried to pick it up from the back room. "Hey, Noah." Her heart fluttered at the sound of his voice.

"Could you take Chloe home for me today? I'm on a job site, and I won't be able to get away for another hour or so."

"I'd be happy to."

"Gram has a garden club meeting today and isn't answering her phone. I appreciate this. I'll make it up to you."

"No need. Friends help each other out."

There was a long pause before he responded. "Right. Thanks again."

Beth changed quickly into street clothes. Chloe talked nonstop on the way home. Evelyn's car wasn't in the drive when they arrived, so Beth went inside to stay with Chloe until she returned. She didn't have long to wait.

"What a nice surprise." Evelyn gave her a warm hug. "I was going to call you when I got home. I wanted to talk to you about something."

"The show?"

"No, something else. Let me fix you a glass of tea and we'll sit and talk."

Beth joined Evelyn in the small sunroom at the back of the house. "I've been telling my friends how you've helped Chloe, and we were wondering if dancing could help some of us with our arthritis and other issues. Phoebe—she lives next door and we've been friends since high school—mentioned some chair dancing that she'd read about online? She's in a wheelchair now, but she used to dance and she misses it."

Surprised at the request, Beth took a moment to consider it. "Dancing can be a huge benefit to older women. I'm sure I can do a little research and come up with something that would be fun for you."

"And my friends?"

"Of course, but my studio is small. There's barely room for me to work with the girls."

"Phoebe suggested we could meet at the senior center. There's plenty of room on the second floor, and we all spend time there off and on anyway."

"That's a good idea. I'll look into it and see what we could set up."

Evelyn smiled and patted her hand. "I can't tell you how glad I am that you came home to Dover. You have a lot to offer this town. I know you miss your career, but you could do so much here."

"Thank you. I'm still trying to figure out how to move forward without my dream, but I'm truly grateful for you getting me involved in the Christmas show. It feels good to be working again, even if it is on the other side of the stage." She rose and moved to the door, Evelyn close at her side.

"You know dear, the good Lord doesn't give us only one dream for our lives. He has a whole mountain of dreams and gifts He wants to give us. You simply have to hold out your hand to receive them."

She was starting to believe that. A few weeks ago she had despaired that nothing could fill the void left by her dancing. But now she woke up each morning looking forward to teaching others to dance. Was this the new dream the Lord was giving her? Or was she settling for what she could get?

A sudden desire raced through her to call Jen and

talk things over the way they used to. It had been a long time since she'd had a real friend to share with. The women in the troupe were nice and she had made several friends, but the atmosphere was too competitive for really deep and lasting relationships. It was a part of her life that had become barren over the years, and she hadn't even noticed.

But even though she and Jen worked well together at the theater, and it felt as if they'd never been apart, she couldn't ignore the differences in their lives. Jen was a happily married working mother. How could she possibly understand the position Beth found herself in now? The thought brought tears to her eyes. Her past and her future were colliding in the present, and she didn't like it one bit.

Noah waited as Beth made her inspection of the moveable staircase he'd built. He'd painted and stained the steps and railing, but he'd leave the nativity backdrop in the hands of Eric Dobbs, the high school student who was the set designer and artist.

"Noah, it's perfect. Exactly like I imagined it. Thank you."

His shoulders eased with relief. He hadn't realized how much he wanted her to like his work. He wanted to please her. "Good. I'll start on the tree dolly next, but I wanted to finish this first since it took longer."

She smiled and lightly touched his arm, heating his skin and causing a miss in his heartbeat. He started to lay his hand over hers, but Jen joined them and he stepped back.

"This is awesome, Noah. It's going to make a huge statement in this number."

"It was all Beth's idea."

"I'm not surprised. This show is going to be so much better. You are a real blessing. I'm so glad you came home."

"I'm happy to help."

"Could I impose on you two to get us a bigger tree? Noah, I know you're building a dolly so we can move it, but that tree needs to be at least ten feet, don't you think?"

Beth nodded. "I'll take care of it."

Jen frowned. "Do you have a truck? An artificial tree that large, even boxed up, won't fit in a car."

"I don't, but my brothers do. I'll get one of them to take me shopping this weekend."

Jen shook her head. "Is there any way you could go sooner, like tonight or tomorrow? The clock is ticking, and we don't have much time to get these new changes in place."

"Why don't Beth and I go over to Sawyer's Bend tomorrow afternoon and pick one up?" Noah suggested. "I'm sure one of the big box stores will have a tree that size."

Noah studied Beth's expression. Apparently she wasn't too fond of the idea of going with him on the errand.

"You don't have to drive me. Linc and Gil both have trucks I can borrow."

Her hesitance spurred his amusement. "Nope. I'm the property guy, remember? But I need your artist's eye to pick out the right tree. Unless you don't want to go." He watched her internal debate reflected in her eyes and knew the moment she decided to accept.

"I do. Thanks for offering."

"Good. We can grab a bite to eat on the way." He felt like he'd just won a battle. For what, he didn't really know.

The soft look of longing in her eyes struck a chord. Did she long for the old camaraderie the way he did? He'd told himself to keep his distance, that renewing their old relationship could only end badly. But he found himself looking for ways to be close to her. Apparently he was incapable of learning some lessons.

"That would be nice. Like old times."

A cold rush of reality doused his good mood. Old times that had ended in heartbreak. The memory of when he realized she had cut him out of her life was like a thorn that never left his side. She would leave again. Maybe not today or next month, but she would, and he'd be left behind again. Only this time his child would be hurting, too.

"Not like old times. Those are over forever."

The look of hurt that flashed through her eyes tightened his throat, but he forced himself to walk away. He couldn't avoid Beth, but he sure could keep his protective shield in place.

Noah opened the door of his Silverado the next afternoon, placing his hand under Beth's elbow to steady her as she climbed into the large vehicle. As she settled into the cab, she suddenly realized that she was trapped in a small space with Noah. Not the ideal situation, given the tension between the two of them. She watched as he slid behind the wheel and fastened his seat belt. It was a good-sized cab, but cozy enough that she could catch a whiff of his aftershave and sense the warmth of his body. Yesterday this had seemed like a good idea, but now she realized she should never have agreed to this excursion.

Noah started the engine then glanced over at her. "I checked online, and it looks like Cost Saver Market should have a ten-foot tree. We'll stop there first."

"I appreciate you doing this."

He grinned, his blue eyes filled with a friendly glint. "I like shopping for Christmas trees. It's my favorite time of year. I'd prefer a live tree, but that wouldn't work for the show."

"No." At a loss for topics to discuss, she clasped her hands in her lap, listening to the strains of "Hark! The Herald Angels Sing" coming from the truck's radio.

"You're doing a great job on the show. And it looks to me like you're having a good time."

"I am. It's more fun than I expected." Another lull in the conversation lasted for nearly a mile. They used to never lack things to talk about. Now, every subject threatened to open up an old wound or a door better left closed. She started when Noah suddenly spoke up.

"Can I ask you something? What did you mean the other day when you said you didn't think I'd care if you left town?"

She stared out the window. This was not what she wanted to discuss, especially trapped in a vehicle with no way to escape. Then again, maybe it was time to face the past and clear the air. "Because that's how I felt."

"Why would you think that?"

The memory of that day and the humiliation burned inside. How could she explain that he'd broken her heart without admitting she'd been in love with him? "You made your feelings very clear when I came by your house that afternoon. I knew you were embarrassed by my gift. You tried to let me down easy, but I was so humiliated I just wanted to run back home."

"What are you talking about?"

She sighed and closed her eyes briefly, fighting the old pain that was reforming inside. "The graduation gift I gave you that afternoon."

"You mean that key ring with the odd shape?"

He hadn't even noticed the symbolic nature of her present. He was rubbing salt into her open wounds. "It was a stylized heart. I had it engraved on the back."

"You did? I don't remember seeing that."

Beth jerked her head to look at him. Was that possible? Had he not read the words that had taken her hours to compose, words that revealed her deepest emotion? "Then why did you act so nervous and uncomfortable?"

"Because I didn't have your gift ready. We weren't supposed to exchange them until that night in the gazebo. I hadn't wrapped your present and I was still working on my speech. You threw me a curve when you showed up without warning in the middle of the day. Wait. You had that thing engraved? What did it say?"

Beth bit the inside of her mouth. She couldn't tell him now. It would put them both in an uncomfortable position. She tried to choose her words carefully. "It was just a BFF kind of sentiment. You were leaving for Mississippi State the next morning, and we wouldn't see each other much over the summer. I wanted to make sure you didn't forget me. Our friendship was very important to me. But after your reaction, I thought you were anxious to leave Dover. And me."

He glanced over at her, his brow furrowed, his blue eyes clouded. "No. Never. I cared about you very much.

I was worried we'd drift apart, too, so I was writing a speech to give you along with your gift. I just never got the chance. You were gone the next morning, and I had to no idea where or why. When I found out you'd joined the Forsythe Company and never bothered to tell me, I figured…" He stared straight ahead, his jaw flexing. "It doesn't matter what I figured."

Beth studied his profile, outlined by the truck window. He'd never read her heartfelt message, and she'd misinterpreted his reaction to her gift. They'd cleared the air, but nothing had really changed. She'd still left without telling him and shut him out of her life. He would never know she'd offered him her heart, and he'd never said he cared for her beyond friendship. The damage had been done.

What now? Could they rebuild their relationship? Could he accept it was all a misunderstanding and forgive her? She'd hurt him deeply, and she couldn't go back and fix that mistake. And it wasn't just her abandonment that he'd endured. Yvonne had further dismantled his belief in women and in love. All he'd ever wanted was a family, and his dream had been shattered.

"I'm sorry, Noah. I waited too long. I didn't mean to cut you out of my life." She held her breath, hoping for some words of encouragement, a peace offering.

"We can't go back and change the past. But we can learn from it."

What did he mean? "Can we call a truce? For the good of the show." She watched a muscle in his jaw flex.

"Sure. Why not? For the good of the show."

Any hope she might have had for their relationship floated off like a feather in the wind. His cold, flat tone of voice spoke far more than his words.

* * *

Beth pressed closer to the glass in the front window of the real estate office, straining to see all the activity taking place around town. Trucks with elevated buckets and platforms carried men who were attaching lights to the facades of every old building. Others were hanging Christmas drapes across the streets while a crew scurried around the courthouse square setting up the traditional nativity and other lighted shapes. The entire downtown was filled with workers. "I had no idea there would be so many lights put up around town."

"There are twice as many this year. I get giddy just thinking about it. I know you weren't here long enough to see what Gemma accomplished last Christmas, but I think in a few years Dover might become one of the must-see holiday attractions in the state."

"I have to admit, we're both looking forward to the big lighting ceremony."

"We?"

Beth cringed. She'd have to watch her tongue around her mother. She gave a nonchalant shrug. "Noah and I were talking about it on the way home from buying the tree yesterday. The streets were blocked off so we had to take the back way to the theater."

"How nice. Maybe you can watch the grand lighting together. It's really quite spectacular."

Time to change the subject. "Do you know where Tori keeps her holiday decorations? I think I'll put up a tree this year and maybe string some lights along the balcony."

"There's storage space in the back of the guest bedroom closet, but you'll need help getting it out. Maybe Noah can help you."

Absolutely not. "I'm perfectly capable of getting stuff out of a closet."

"Normally I would agree. However, some of the boxes are heavy, and you don't need to be putting extra stress on your knee. It wouldn't hurt to have a pair of strong arms around."

No, it wouldn't hurt, but those arms wouldn't belong to Noah. They'd been getting along nicely since their truce had been declared, but while he'd lowered his wall, it was still far too high for her to climb over.

"I think we should go all out for the storefront-window decorating contest this year, too. I did the bare minimum last year, and Noah's office was vacant. Maybe you and Noah could come up with something to coordinate both windows."

Beth rolled her eyes. "Mom. Don't try to play matchmaker. I'm not looking for any kind of relationship, and I'm sure Noah isn't, either. Especially with me." She muttered that last part under her breath.

"Well, I don't know why not. You two were thick as thieves in high school. Besides, he's a very attractive man, in case you missed that. Evelyn swears women stop in their tracks and stare at him when he walks by. But he never even notices."

Beth had no doubt about that. With his broad shoulders, touchable, wavy dark hair and those blue eyes that could melt your insides with one glance, he was the ultimate masculine package. The icing on the cake was that he had no idea he was handsome. She felt sure that in his mind, he was still that skinny, geeky kid no one paid any attention to. It was a trait that made him all the more appealing.

Beth shook her head to dislodge the thought, but

her gaze drifted to the office window next door. She stopped and caught her breath. Chloe had her arms wrapped around Noah, her head pressed against his chest as he patted her back. Beth moved to the door to get a closer look.

"Mom. Something's wrong." Without a second thought, she hurried over to Noah's office.

"Chloe, are you okay?" She touched the child's shoulder, her gaze locking with Noah's. His eyes darkened as he shook his head, and a muscle in his jaw flexed rapidly.

Chloe shifted her head against her dad's chest and looked at Beth with tearful, sad eyes. "I didn't get a ticket, and tomorrow is Thanksgiving."

Beth's heart sank. Her mother had let her down. "Oh, Chloe, I'm so sorry."

"Is everything all right?"

Beth glanced over her shoulder as her mother joined them, but before she could explain, Chloe broke from Noah's arms and plunged into Francie's.

"I can't spend Thanksgiving with my mom."

"Oh, sweetie. I'm so sorry."

"I was going to meet Dustin Baker and all kinds of famous people. Now it'll be an old boring day with just Dad and Gram."

Noah's mouth pinched, and his brow furrowed. Her heart went out to him. She felt certain he knew Chloe didn't mean what she said, but it probably stung at any rate. How could a dad and grandmother compete with the rich and famous in Hollywood? But maybe she could soften the blow a little bit.

She caught her mother's gaze. "How about Thanksgiving dinner with a not quite as famous ballerina and her family?"

Her mother's face brightened with delight at the suggestion. "That's a wonderful idea. Why don't you and your dad and grandma come and spend the day with us? You already know Abby and Evan. We play football in the afternoon, and we have the dogs running around and all kinds of fun things to do." She stroked Chloe's hair and looked at Noah. "Please. We'd love to have your family join us. We have plenty of room and more than enough food."

Noah considered the idea. "That's very kind of you, but I think Gram already has some food prepared."

"Just bring it with you." She set Chloe away from her and smiled. "Will you come, Chloe?"

She wiped tears from her cheeks and looked over at her father. "Can we? Please?"

Beth grinned at the resigned look on Noah's face. She knew he probably didn't want to spend the holiday with her, but it's not like they'd be alone or anything. They'd barely have time to talk.

"I'll have to check with your grandma, Chloe."

Francie waved off his concerns. "Leave that to me. I'll give Evelyn a call right now and arrange everything. Thanksgiving is more fun with lots of family. Since you're my renter, that qualifies you. Besides, we'll be a couple members short this year. Tori is still in California, and Seth is a newly minted Houston police officer, so he's working."

Francie took Chloe's hand and went back to the office, leaving Beth with Noah. He was worrying his bottom lip with his finger as if rethinking the idea.

"I'm sorry her plans didn't work out."

"I knew they wouldn't, and I tried to prepare her, but she won't listen. Once she gets an idea in her head it's hard to get it out."

"Family trait, huh?"

"Yeah. I guess."

"I hope I didn't make this awkward for you with my invitation. Mom's right, though. We're used to having a full house for the holiday, and we're short this year. You'll be our fill-ins."

"A fill-in family. Should I be honored or insulted?"

She tilted her head. "That's up to you. I just wanted to cheer Chloe up. She had her heart set on going to see her mom."

"We don't always get what we set our hearts on. You should know that better than anyone." He paused and took a deep breath. "I didn't mean to sound judgmental. It never gets any easier."

"This happens a lot?"

"Too many times to count."

She reached out and touched his arm. "I'm sorry. For both of you." His blue eyes softened with affection, sending a sweet warmth curling through her rib cage. It was the look she'd seen in his eyes frequently those last few months before they'd graduated. The one that had convinced her he was secretly in love with her the way she was with him. "I'd better get back. Is it okay for Chloe to stay with us for a while longer?"

"Sure. I'll finish up here and then come get her."

At the door to the real estate office, Beth looked back to see Noah rubbing his forehead before placing his palms on the desk and bowing his head. How many times had he been forced to endure his child's disappointment? She'd known a lot of disappointment in her life and it had been deeply painful, but experiencing Chloe's had hurt in a way she'd never known before. What must it feel like to be a father?

On the heels of that thought came one from her own conscience. How many times had her family been disappointed when she canceled a trip home or failed to remember a birthday?

She couldn't go back and fix the past, but she knew she didn't want to be that out of touch with the people she loved ever again. Seeing the sadness in Chloe's eyes held up a mirror to her own failures.

And she didn't like the picture it revealed.

Chapter Six

Noah had never experienced a Thanksgiving dinner like this one. He'd agreed to spending the holiday with the Montgomerys in a moment of weakness and had been regretting his decision ever since. Even reminding himself it was for Chloe's sake hadn't helped ease his anxiety.

His grandparents had always celebrated with quiet formality, in a solemn and dignified fashion. He'd expected the Montgomerys to be the same. He'd anticipated being on edge and feeling awkward in the midst of a family gathering with no connection to his familiar traditions. But Beth's family was boisterous and funloving. While the table was set with fine china, silver and crystal, the atmosphere was relaxed and casual, and it was obvious they enjoyed being together.

It reminded him of holidays growing up with his parents. Being surrounded by this large family renewed his hopes that he could give his daughter a complete family one day.

He took another bite of the melt-in-your-mouth cornbread dressing Beth had prepared and tried not to moan with delight. He had no idea Beth could cook, even though her mother had touted her skills before the Thanksgiving dinner.

He glanced around the table at the Montgomerys assembled for the holiday meal. Gram was seated next to Francie, and the two women giggled and chatted between bites like teenagers. They had been friends for a long time, but after they'd each lost a spouse, they had a deeper bond now.

Beth's brothers were clearly crazy in love with their new wives. Her sisters-in-law were beautiful women— Gemma a stunning strawberry blonde with sparkling eyes, and Julie a lovely brunette with a megawatt smile. But neither could hold a candle to Bethany's serene, elegant beauty. Maybe it was her years of dance training that gave her the graceful carriage, or maybe she'd been born with it and that's what had made her such an exceptional ballerina. Either way, she was the most fascinating woman he'd ever met, a unique combination of femininity and strength.

He glanced at Beth. How had she lived in New York away from this kind of support for so long? She'd always claimed that she didn't fit in here, but she looked relaxed and happy to him. She caught him looking at her and smiled, making his mouth suddenly dry and his palms sweaty. He hated the way his body reacted whenever she looked at him or touched him. He'd strengthened his defenses today, but when she'd opened the door to the Montgomery home with her welcoming smile, they'd tilted like the Leaning Tower of Pisa. The dark slacks she wore emphasized her long legs, and the soft teal top with the scooped neck showed off the graceful curve of her shoulders. Earrings with tiny stars bobbed around her chin, adding even more sparkle to her pretty eyes.

All in all, he was glad he'd agreed to come today. As close as he and Beth had been, he'd never spent any time with her family. Her older brothers had been away at college or working for the family business. But he'd been welcomed today with handshakes and smiles. They'd inquired about his new business, and offered to pass his name along to the architects they knew. They said they would do whatever they could to help him get established.

A giggle drew his attention to his daughter. Mostly he was glad he'd come because of the smile that was now back on Chloe's face after a long night of tears. She and Abby were seated together talking nonstop, waving forks in the air to punctuate their conversation. He marveled at the resiliency of his child. Time after time, her mother let her down, broke promises and failed to follow through on plans. Chloe would cry, but then get back up, convinced that one day her mom would come through. She shamed him with her faith and loyalty. Unfortunately, he knew that loyalty had its limits.

His gaze drifted immediately to Beth. Where were her loyalties? With her career, or with her family?

The tapping of metal on glass drew everyone's attention. Gil stood. "Before we have our dessert, we have an announcement to make."

Abby jumped up. "Can I tell? Please? I've waited *forever.*"

Gil chuckled and reached down to take his wife's hand. "Go ahead, sweet pea."

Abby clapped her hands and bounced up and down. "I'm going to be a big sister."

The room erupted with cheers and laughter, and questions were flung at the couple. Beside him, Beth remained silent. Her smile was forced, and her hands gripped her napkin tightly. He watched as she closed her eyes briefly. When she opened them, her attitude had changed. She stood.

"Now we're really ready for dessert. Let's celebrate with Mom's pecan pie."

Noah glanced around the room. Everyone was preoccupied and didn't seem to notice the strain in Beth's voice. He rose and picked up his plate, following her to the kitchen.

He found her standing at the counter, pie cutter in hand but not moving. Her shoulders were slumped as if she was too weary to proceed. He stopped at her side, fighting the urge to pull her into a hug to comfort her. "Are you all right?"

The sadness in her eyes when she looked at him pierced every nerve ending.

"What's wrong?"

"Nothing. I'm fine."

"I know you're not. Talk to me."

"I think you might have been right. I did pay too high a price for my career." The mellow tones of classical music intruded. She pulled her phone from the small pocket on her top and looked at the screen.

"I have to take this." Turning her back, she disappeared from the kitchen.

When the pie had been served and she hadn't reappeared, Noah went looking for her. Gil directed him to the office off the foyer. She was curled up in one of the leather chairs, legs tucked beneath her, staring out the window. Her cell phone was still clutched in her hand. "Beth."

She glanced up and saw him, and the worry in her eyes pricked his throat. Something was wrong. He considered leaving her alone. If she needed his help, she could ask for it. But he couldn't leave her alone like this. Slowly he moved toward her, taking a seat in the chair next to her. When she didn't withdraw, he braved a question. "Bad news?"

"Maybe. Probably." She chewed her bottom lip and clutched the phone to her chest. "A friend called from the ballet company. There's a rumor that a new artistic director is coming in, and she's going to void all our contracts and renegotiate."

"Can she do that?"

"It's happened before. My contract is up in February. I was hoping to be back by then, but I won't be ready to perform again for several more months, if then."

"You're their star. Surely they wouldn't let you go. Don't you have an agent or someone that can handle this for you?"

She shook her head. "Most ballet dancers don't have agents. And I'm an injured star who hasn't danced for nine months. The rumor is Noreen Andrews is taking over, and she's never been one of my fans."

He wanted to reach out his hand, but she was so closed off, he doubted she'd accept his sympathy. He searched for something comforting to say. "You should check with your attorney. Maybe you should resign and cut your losses."

She nodded, wiping a tear from her eyes. "But if I do that, it means it's truly over. I'm done. I'm not ready to accept that."

Noah set his jaw. Now he knew where her loyalties were. She was still focused on getting back to her other life. "Do you really think you can get back to the level you were once at? Honestly?"

"Yes. Other dancers have overcome this type of injury. I can, too."

Small shards of ice cut across his insides. He stood. "Well, knowing how obsessed you are, I'm sure you'll be back onstage in no time."

He pivoted and walked back into the family room, where Linc and Gil promptly drew him into a game of football on the front lawn. He welcomed the diversion. Physical exertion was exactly what he needed to work off that big dinner.

But he knew he was lying to himself. He needed to work off his anger and disappointment in Beth. She would never, *ever* change.

With the real estate office closed the day after Thanksgiving, Beth used the time to begin decorating the windows for the upcoming contest. She'd been dragging her feet on this project, mainly because her mother had wanted her to do Noah's window, too, so they'd match. After yesterday, she doubted Noah would welcome her invading his office to put up Christmas decorations. Each time she thought they'd made progress toward restoring their old friendship, something would drive them apart again. Usually it involved her career.

Thanksgiving with the Carlisles had gone well, though not as she'd expected. She'd counted on her large family to act as a buffer between her and Noah, but his presence had instead been an electrified magnet, drawing her attention to his every movement. He seemed to enjoy all the hustle and bustle, but there'd been times when he'd looked a bit overwhelmed, even melancholy. When they'd taken their places at the table, the tension between them had intensified. They'd ended up on one corner of the long table, making it impossible to avoid eye contact or bumping knees. After the third apology, she'd given up.

During the blessing, Beth had taken Noah's hand, his touch sending little jolts of awareness up her arm and swirling around her heart. When the prayer ended, he'd clung to her fingers a long moment before letting go. She looked into his eyes, searching for an explanation, but he only smiled and looked away, giving her hope that he might be ready to forgive her.

Then the phone call about her contract had come, and now she was on his bad side again. He'd tried to comfort her and she'd raised her defenses, declaring she would dance again and pushing him away. She'd taken his advice, however, and made an appointment to talk to the family attorney, Blake Prescott, to go over her contract.

Hopefully, working on the window would keep her mind off her troubles. Locating her sister's stash of Christmas decorations was easy. Getting them out of the narrow crawl space behind the closet was something else. Nothing was heavy, just awkward, and she was concerned about twisting her knee. She made a mental note to call one of her brothers to get the boxes out. She'd managed to retrieve one container filled with craft ribbons and other items, and she maneuvered it down to the office.

The old building's display window consisted of a raised platform, a common feature in the past as a means to showcase merchandize. It was a charming touch, but it made it awkward at times to hang posters and other things. She used to worry that her mother would forget about the twelve-inch rise and would lose her balance. Now that worry was for her own safety.

Opening the lid, she rummaged through the carton, silently thanking her sister for being so organized. Every item was neatly packaged and labeled. However, now it was up to her to create some kind of holiday design out of the bits and pieces. She'd never been as good at that as Tori. There was an abundance of white paper and red ribbon. She fingered the items, trying to jump-start the long-dormant creative part of her brain. The white paper reminded her of the church steeple of Peace Community rising above the trees. A memory surfaced of her and Tori making piles of paper snowflakes and trees to hang around the house. The thought made her smile. It might actually be relaxing to sit and cut out paper shapes.

After pulling up her playlist of Christmas music, she selected an album then settled in, folding and cutting various designs, large and small. Her mother had told her there was a small white artificial tree in the back storage room of the office. The more she worked, the more her ideas grew. And so did her satisfaction. The window might not win an award in the contest, but it would be attractive.

She was securing the last red ribbon to the corner of the window when someone tapped on the glass. Chloe smiled and waved. She waved back and went outside to join her. Noah was there, causing her to come up short. For some reason, she'd expected Chloe to be with Evelyn.

He looked ruggedly handsome today in a plaid button-up shirt in soft colors, faded jeans and a sleeveless zip-up vest that made his shoulders appear impossibly broad. She couldn't tell from the closed expression on his face if he was still irked with her, so she turned her attention to the little girl. "What do you think?"

"I love it."

"I still have to decorate the tree and add lights." She stepped back and examined the arrangement. Overall she was pleased. It could use a touch of greenery and maybe a contrasting color, too. Something to make it all pop, but she'd tackle that later.

"Where did you get the big snowflakes, Miss Beth?"

"I made them."

Her eyes widened. "Can you teach me?"

Beth laid her arm across the child's shoulders. "Of course. It's easy."

"And can we do our window the same so we'll match?"

Noah stepped forward. "Chloe, I'm sure Miss Beth doesn't have time to do our window, too."

A bubble of perverse glee caused her to smile. It was nice to shove the rigid Noah off his foundation sometimes. "Actually, my mother has asked me to do both windows, so it's not a problem."

"Can I help? I like decorating."

"Of course." She ignored the deep frown that had formed on Noah's brow. "We can do it now if it's all right with your father."

Chloe nodded enthusiastically. "Is it okay, Daddy?"

"Do I have a choice?"

She and Chloe glanced at each other before turning to face him. "No."

Their simultaneous response sealed the deal. They shared a smile, linked arms and went back inside the office.

Beth eased her conscience by remembering Noah's declaration that he couldn't say no to his child. This time it had worked to her advantage.

Noah leaned back in his office chair, pinching the bridge of his nose. He'd decided to work while Beth and Chloe decorated the front office window. With several reports due and calculations to make on a few structural situations, he had plenty to keep him busy. His new plotter, the large printer he used for blueprints, had been delivered and needed to be set up.

The office was quiet at the moment. Beth had taken Chloe to the store to pick up more decorations for the window. They'd run out of paper and red ribbon. He'd welcomed their departure to focus on his work, but found the office strangely lonely with them gone.

He'd chosen to work here in the back office as they went about their business, but it had been hard to concentrate. The wide opening in the wall between the spaces made it easy to see and hear customers as they entered. But it had the opposite effect when two females were decorating a Christmas window. They'd worked quietly, but the soft giggles and happy chatter had distracted him. After the huge disappointment Chloe had suffered thanks to her mother, he was glad the holiday weekend was providing some enjoyment for her. He just wasn't sure how he felt about Beth being the source.

Watching them work together had unleashed a flood of warmth and longing deep inside of Noah. Chloe was missing out on having a woman in her life. Gram was great, but the age difference sometimes became an issue. Beth was young, enthusiastic and close in age to Chloe's mom. Though Yvonne had always been more concerned with her own enjoyment than her child's. There were times when he seriously considered marrying again to give his daughter a mother. But he couldn't get beyond the knowledge that he'd failed twice.

Rising, he walked into the front office and stopped. The room had been hit by a craft tornado. Tiny slivers of white paper littered the desk and floor like confetti. Ribbon in various lengths curled on every surface. Instead of being irked, he chuckled at the mess. Chloe was having fun. That's all that mattered.

Suddenly the pair entered like a burst of energy, laughing and cradling bundles of items for the window. He frowned at the large assortment. "I don't think there's room in that one window for all this stuff."

"Some of it's for Beth's apartment, Daddy. She can't reach the boxes in the closet so she bought some new things."

He looked to Beth for an explanation.

"My sister has all her Christmas decorations shoved in the back of her closet, and they're too heavy for me to pull out." She gestured toward her knee. "Normally it wouldn't be a problem, but I don't want to risk it right now."

"I'll pull it out for you. You should have just asked." What was he saying? When had he become her rescuer?

"Oh, that's all right. I'll get one of the boys to come by."

"Don't be silly. I'm right here. Besides, it's the least I can do to thank you for decorating the window." She smiled, and his heart dipped into his stomach.

"Thanks. We'll do that as soon as we're finished here."

Working was pointless. He gave up and offered himself as the token tall person to fetch the things too high for them to reach. When the window was done, there remained an empty spot that begged for a tree.

"Is this where our tree will go? Do I need to go buy one?"

Beth set her hands on her hips, her mouth puckered into a thoughtful—and adorable—grimace. "Not sure yet. A white tree to match the one in our window would be the obvious solution, but I'd like to see what else I can find."

"So are you done?" He studied the window. White paper snowflakes bobbed in the air along with red streamers. They'd cut out shapes to look like snowdrifts and taped them to the bottom and edges of the window like a frame. He would never have thought of using simple paper and ribbons to decorate.

"For now."

Chloe nodded. "We need an accent color. We've decided that it should be aqua."

Noah had no idea what they were talking about. Aqua? That wasn't a Christmas color.

Chloe reached into one of the larger sacks and pulled out a figure of a peacock in hues of aqua. "This is for Miss Beth's window, and she's still looking for one for ours."

"Maybe my sister has something in her closet."

"Now's as good a time as any to find out." There he went again, volunteering his help when there was no need. Beth looked as surprised as he felt.

"Thanks. Give me a few minutes to put this stuff away and straighten up the office."

Noah watched her go, suddenly aware that she'd taken a considerable amount of energy with her when she left. His office didn't seem nearly as bright and cheerful without her.

"Daddy, I love Miss Beth. Isn't she wonderful?"

She was something. He just hadn't decided what yet. He cleared his throat, which was unusually tight. "She's a very nice lady." Beautiful, strong, compassionate— and determined to leave Dover. "Let's clean this up."

A half hour later, Noah pulled the last box from the crawl space in Beth's closet and stood. There was no way, with her injury, she could have done this on her own. He was glad he'd been here to help. He placed the plastic container near the others in the living room.

Chloe dashed in from the balcony. She'd been watching the vendors arriving in the square for the grand lighting kickoff this evening. "Wow, that's a lot of boxes. Can we open them now?"

Noah picked up her jacket and tossed it to her. "It's time to go. I'm sure Miss Beth would like some time to sort through these things on her own."

Chloe slipped on her jacket, glancing over her shoulder at the balcony. "Are you going to watch all the lights come on tonight?"

"Of course. I'm looking forward to it. I think it's going to be spectacular."

Chloe bit her lip, an impish smile lifting the corner of her mouth. "I think your balcony would be the best place to watch from."

"Chloe." Now his daughter was playing matchmaker, too. Or was she simply looking for more time with Beth and a perfect vantage point to see the lights? Either scenario was not good.

Beth must have read his reluctance because she slipped an arm across Chloe's shoulders and gave him a challenging smile. "I think you're right. Why don't you come back this evening? I'll fix supper, and we can watch the lights come on together. Wouldn't that be fun?"

No. No way. He was spending too much time with Beth as it was.

"Please, Daddy. That would be so totally cool."

He sighed. He had a sturdy spine and it worked to perfection, except when his little girl made those puppy dog eyes, and her voice went up three levels, and she asked him for something she really wanted. Then those healthy vertebrae turned to jelly. Gram was going out to dinner with friends this evening, so he'd been looking at ordering pizza. If Beth's cornbread stuffing was any gauge, she would probably serve a tastier meal than he'd been planning.

"Fine. What can I bring?"

"Nothing but yourselves."

They started for the door, but Chloe stopped and spun around. "Do you need any help with supper? I help Gram all the time."

Noah froze. "Chloe, it's not nice to invite yourself to people's homes."

"I'm not. I'm offering to help. That's different."

Not in his view, but when he saw the grin on Beth's face, he knew he was licked.

"Chloe, you are just full of good ideas today. I'd love to have your help. In fact, it's nearly time to start preparing anyway. You could stay, and your dad could supervise."

Talk about being ganged up on. How was a guy supposed to stay strong when he had two beautiful women working against him? "You can stay, but I'm going back to the office to work. That window-decorating session cost me some time."

Beth helped Chloe remove her jacket. "Fine. You do that, and we'll call you when everything is ready."

Noah opened the door and headed down the stairs. As he entered his office, he felt the silence in a way he hadn't before. Worse still, he was looking forward to the meal and to watching the lights go on all over downtown. He wanted to see that childlike sparkle in Beth's eyes. The thought of seeing his daughter and his friend experience the grand lighting filled him with joyful anticipation. He sent a quick text to his gram explaining the change in plans, knowing she would be smiling happily at the turn of events.

As he stepped into his office, the delicate snowflakes and ribbons in the window fluttered, reminding him of the video he'd watched last night of Beth. Red reminded him of her strength and determination. White conjured up all her feminine traits. How could the thing he admired most about her be the thing that kept them apart?

He owed Beth a debt of gratitude for helping to lift Chloe's spirits and forget about her mom's broken promise. But he worried he was trading one bad situation for another. Beth still had every intention of returning to dancing, which meant the heartbreak would be deeper when the dance world lured her back.

He was standing in a bed of wet cement, and it was hardening around him faster than he could pull himself out.

The bell on his office door chimed, and he looked up to see a slender middle-aged man enter. "Can I help you?"

The man gave him a quick once-over with piercing dark eyes. "You the engineer?"

"Yes, sir. Noah Carlisle." He extended his hand. "What can I do for you?"

"Harvey Kramer. I'm remodeling a house out on Old Agler Road, and I need an engineer to check things out to make sure the changes I want to make are possible."

"I can help you with that. Have a seat and tell me what you're looking at doing."

Noah sent up a grateful prayer. Nothing better to take his mind off Beth and Chloe than his first client. This was something he understood and could control.

Chapter Seven

Beth slid the casserole dish into the oven and closed the door, double-checking the temperature before setting the timer. Anticipation over the meal with Chloe and Noah bubbled up, making her feel lighter than she had in a long while. She loved to cook, but with little free time and no one to cook for, she'd rarely taken the time.

Making one small adjustment to the fall-themed place mat she'd put at Noah's place, she scolded herself for being so particular. He'd never notice the table decorations. Not the way she'd noticed him as he'd wrestled the boxes from the tight storage space. Every masculine movement had captivated her attention. The muscles in his arms and back had flexed appealingly as he'd tugged the boxes from the deep space. His jeans had stretched tightly over his thighs as he stooped to place them on the floor. He'd caught her staring more than once, but she dismissed her interest as the need to make sure he didn't miss any boxes or break anything fragile.

The truth was, she liked watching Noah. She liked the little groan in his throat as he hoisted a heavy box.

She liked the way he had to repeatedly brush his wavy hair from his forehead. She liked many things about him. But she shouldn't.

Chloe came in from the balcony for the tenth time, her impatience growing. "There sure are a lot of people down there. When did you say the lights will go on?"

"Seven o'clock. You still have an hour to wait."

They'd worked together, making the chicken-and-mushroom casserole and preparing fresh rolls. Chloe proved to be an entertaining and helpful assistant. Now they had to wait forty-five minutes before they could eat.

"Can we look in the boxes now?"

"Sure. In fact, let's start with this big one because I'm hoping there's a garland I can drape over the balcony railing." As expected, a large garland was coiled neatly in the bottom. Bright gold bulbs were intertwined among the long faux evergreen strand and accented with lights and strings of beads. It would look lovely draped along her balcony rail. The next box they opened held tabletop decorations her sister had collected.

Chloe hummed along with "Frosty the Snowman" playing in the background before pulling out a sturdy snow globe with a white church in the center. She shook it to set the flakes in motion. "I love Christmas. It's so pretty and happy. I think it would be fun to spend each Christmas in a different place so I could see how other people decorate."

"That would be fun, but if you're away for the holiday, you won't be with your family."

"I'd take them with me. It's only Gram and Daddy."

Beth chuckled softly as she tried to envision wrangling all her family members in one direction. But they'd never leave the family home at the holidays. A sharp stab of regret pricked her heart when she thought about the many Christmases she'd missed and could never recapture. This Christmas would be one she would cherish because it would be one she fully embraced. "I couldn't do that. There are too many of us."

Chloe nodded. "I wish my mom would come home for Christmas." She shook the globe again, watching the mini snowstorm.

Her melancholy tone pinched Beth's conscience. Chloe's disappointment from the last holiday was still so fresh. "I'm sorry you weren't able to go to see her over Thanksgiving."

Chloe offered a small smile and a shrug. "She's very busy and very important. That's why she forgets about me sometimes." She shifted and looked Beth in the eye, her smile confident. "But she loves me. I know when she sees me again, she'll remember how much she misses me, and then we'll spend more time together and go places and have adventures."

Beth forced a smile. From what she'd learned from Noah, Chloe's hopes would likely never be realized. She wanted to hug the little girl close and try to explain the behavior of adults, but she had a feeling Chloe's belief was too strong to be swayed by truth. Eventually she'd have to come to terms with her mother's indifference. She prayed Noah would handle that time carefully.

Noah arrived just as the timer dinged on the casserole. They worked together to get the food on the table, and Noah gave the blessing.

Beth was thankful that Chloe's excited chatter prevented any conversation between her and Noah. She liked looking across the table and seeing Noah there.

Mostly she liked the feeling of inclusion that being together created. It wasn't too different from the feeling she had when she performed. If someone had told her she could have that feeling outside *pointe* shoes, she would have scoffed. But here she was, in her sister's apartment with an attractive man and his adorable daughter, feeling more like she belonged than she had in a long time.

"Beth."

She blinked and looked at Noah. "What?"

He grinned. "You wandered off for a moment. I was complimenting you on your casserole. I never knew you were such a good cook."

"Thank you."

Chloe twisted in her chair and looked out the front window. "Is it time yet?"

Noah checked his watch. "Almost."

"Why don't you two go out on the balcony while I clean up? By then it should be close to seven."

Noah stood but he didn't follow his daughter outside. He picked up his plate and carried it to the sink.

"You don't have to do that."

"Oh, yes, I do. If my gram found out I didn't help clear the table, I'd be in the doghouse for a week."

"Well, I'd hate to see you forced to endure that horrible fate."

He laughed, causing her to study him a moment. "You're in a good mood."

"I am. While you were preparing the meal, I was landing my first private client. He's restoring an old house out on Old Agler Road, and he needs an engineer to go over the place."

"That's wonderful. Congratulations."

"Thanks. It's a small start. Hopefully once I get connected with a few local architects, I'll get into the commercial business deals. That's what I really enjoy."

Beth glanced at the clock. "Oh. It's almost time." The temperature had dropped, and the lightweight sweater she wore wouldn't provide much warmth. She lifted a throw from the sofa as she headed for the balcony, but Noah took it from her, opened it and gently draped it around her shoulders. His arm lingered awhile, making her aware of the warmth of him and the nearness.

He looked into her eyes as if searching for something. His arm urged her forward.

"Beth."

Her name was a whisper, soft and caressing. She knew what he was asking, and she raised her head in response.

"Daddy, look at all the people. And there's the carriage going by."

They pulled apart and joined Chloe on the balcony as she leaned over the rail, watching the crowds of visitors milling around in anticipation of the grand lighting event.

Beth allowed her gaze to scan the square, chasing the moment with Noah to the back of her mind. "Mom told me this was a big deal, but I had no idea. I can't remember ever seeing so many people in our little town."

"I hope it's worth it."

She opened her mouth to scold Noah for his negative comment, but saw the twinkle in his blue eyes and gave him a playful punch in the shoulder instead.

Suddenly, the streetlamps, storefronts and other usual lights in the square blinked out. The crowd hushed in anticipation. Then in an instant, the lights flashed on in a dazzling display of color, illuminating the entire square. The courthouse glowed with tiny lights from the dome to the pillars on each side. The historic gazebo was awash in white lights. Large standing displays in different colors dotted the park. Every storefront, from sidewalk to roof parapet, was ablaze with twinkling Christmas lights. The oohs and aahs went on for several minutes before changing to loud applause and shouts of approval. From speakers above the crowds, Christmas carols filled the air.

Beth wiped tears of delight from her eyes.

Chloe exhaled a soft sigh. "Daddy, it's the most beautiful thing I've ever seen."

"I'd have to agree."

"I didn't expect it to be this spectacular and moving. Gemma told me she wanted the lights to reflect the glory of God's arrival here on earth. I think she succeeded."

They watched in silence for a few moments, gazing in wonder and appreciation at the glory of it all. Noah placed his arms on the railing, bringing his shoulder into contact with hers, making her acutely aware of his warmth and the heady scent of his aftershave.

"Daddy, can we walk around and see the lights up close?"

"I think that's a good idea. Don't you, Beth?"

He was asking her to join them. How could she refuse?

"Awesome." Chloe whirled around and started inside, but stopped to plug in the garland they'd placed on the railing earlier. "We forgot to turn it on. Now it's perfect. Did the lights in the office windows downstairs come on?"

"They should have, provided the timer worked correctly."

Beth slid the throw from her shoulders, only to find Noah there to take it from her. His fingers grazed hers. And she looked into his eyes.

"She's right. This was a perfect evening. The food, the lights, the hostess." He reached out and gently skimmed her cheek with the back of his fingers. "Christmas lights become you."

She held her breath, anticipating his next move. Was he going to kiss her? She hoped so. She couldn't deny her feelings much longer. She'd had feelings for Noah since she'd met him, but what she'd felt back then was a crush. What she was feeling now was grown-up attraction, and she wasn't sure what to do with it.

"Come on, Dad, let's go."

The moment shattered. She set aside her concerns and decided to go with the flow. All she wanted was to walk amid the millions of lights with Noah and Chloe and enjoy the moment. She'd deal with reality tomorrow.

Noah let the noise of the drill drown out his conflicted thoughts as he attached the locking casters to the bottom of the platform he'd built for the large Christmas tree in the show.

He'd retreated here to the workshop right after breakfast, hoping the project would stop the persistent loop of memories that played in his mind. He'd almost kissed her. Twice. His emotions were still firing on all cylinders from his time with Beth last night. His pulse still beat erratically whenever he thought of how close he'd come to kissing her on the balcony.

He'd gotten caught up in the girls' anticipation for

the big display of lights, and they hadn't been disappointed. Chloe had been thrilled. Beth had been awestruck, and the glow of the lights along the front of her building had bathed her in a soft light that sent a quiver of attraction along his nerve endings. She was beautiful. Not in a stop-traffic way, but she possessed a sweet and pure loveliness that lingered in your mind forever. Her big hazel eyes drew a man in. Her thick brown hair fell in soft curves to her shoulders, drawing attention to her rosy cheeks and pretty mouth.

He'd wanted nothing more than to take her in his arms and taste her lips. In all the time they'd known each other, he'd never kissed her. Not even a peck on the cheek. If it hadn't been for Chloe's interruption he would have, and if the look in her eyes was any indication, she wouldn't have minded.

It was a good thing he hadn't acted on his impulse. Who knew what kind of Pandora's box of complications that would have unleashed? The evening had chipped away areas of his heart that he'd plastered over long ago, allowing that old dream to break free. Sharing a home-cooked meal in the cozy apartment, laughing with Chloe and watching Beth's delight in everything his daughter said, had filled him with sweet contentment.

Yet instead of following his common sense and going home, he'd agreed to walk around the square. They'd wandered beneath the canopy of lights, marveled at the twinkling storefronts and sipped hot chocolate in the gazebo as they watched the people milling around.

The wind had picked up, putting a bite in the air. He'd taken Beth's hand to keep her warm. He'd wanted the connection. He'd known it was risky but he'd done it anyway, like touching an electrical wire, knowing you'd be injured, but unable to stop yourself. When had he become a masochist?

Pulling off his safety glasses, he pinched the bridge of his nose. Why was it so hard for him to acknowledge the truth? Being with Beth, holding her hand and sharing the brilliant scene with her, had made him feel whole and complete. The only thing that had ever come close to matching that was when he'd held Chloe in his arms for the first time.

"Noah, dear. How's it coming?"

He jerked his thoughts together as his grandmother entered the shop. "Good—the dolly for the tree is done. I just need to paint it, then I can haul it over to the theater."

"I can't thank you enough for lending your skills to my little project."

Noah had to smile. There was nothing little about Gram's projects. Ever. "My pleasure."

"Will you come with me to the storage shed? I have something for you."

Noah followed Gram out back to the old wooden building, waiting while she unlocked the weathered door. Musty air whooshed out of the darkness. The room probably hadn't been opened since Gramps died. He pulled the dangling string to turn on the light, scanning the cluttered interior. "What are we looking for?"

Gram glanced around a moment, then pointed to the section on the right. "There it is." She picked her way toward the dust-covered shapes.

When she pulled the cloth away, he smiled at what was underneath: the scaled-down village pieces his gramps had made for the front lawn decades ago. "What made you think of this? I didn't know these little build-ings were still here." His granddad had constructed nearly a dozen miniature Dover buildings and placed them in the front yard. Each building stood between two and three feet high, with the church being the center-piece. Lit from within, the display had been a charming depiction of a Victorian Dover Christmas.

"I've thought about putting them out again, but it's too much trouble for me." She sidestepped to the piece that was taller than the rest. "I thought with a little freshening up, this might look really nice in your of-fice window."

"The church." Noah lifted the church from amid the other buildings and set it near the door so he could get a better look. Other than a few loose trim pieces and several missing shingles, it was in good shape. "Needs a little attention and a paint job."

Gram touched the steeple. "Sort of like each of us. We need to examine our faith life and make any repairs we've been neglecting." She looked at him.

Was she trying to tell him something?

"Do you think Beth would like it? She has the tree in her window, and you could have the church as your centerpiece. I'm hoping the lights inside still work."

Beth would like it. He had no doubts. "Thanks, Gram. I'll get it in shape this afternoon and take it in tomorrow."

"How's the new client working out? You haven't mentioned him in a few days."

Noah scratched the back of his neck. "He's proving to be a challenge. He likes shortcuts and quick fixes. He's not a fan of adhering to building codes."

"Don't you let him get away with anything."

"I don't intend to. My first priority is to keep people safe. Even if they don't realize they need safety."

He carried the church back into the workshop and set it on the bench, his gaze drifting to the tree stand. His workshop was being taken over by projects for Beth. His gram may be the source of the work, but the one who had to be pleased was Beth. And he wanted to please her.

He was doomed. That cement he'd stepped in had hardened, and he'd need a jackhammer and a lot of determination to chip his way free.

Beth stepped inside the senior center on Church Street and took a deep, fortifying breath. Today was her first dance class, and her stomach was fluttering as if a swarm of butterflies were inside. She'd checked with Pete and gone over her routine. He'd approved it, but he'd advised her to go slowly and keep in mind the limitations of her older students.

Her gaze scanned the room for Evelyn, but it was the familiar face of Millie Tedrow she saw first. The former librarian had introduced her to many wonderful books. When Beth hadn't been dancing, she'd been reading.

"Bethany my dear, you look wonderful." She came toward her, arms outstretched. "We are so excited about your class. Evelyn is already upstairs." She led the way through a space filled with comfy couches, recliners, game tables and a big-screen television. To the rear was a large gleaming kitchen and eating area.

"This place is amazing."

Millie stopped in the back beside a staircase and a small elevator. "It is. Lots to do. The lower level is an activities room, and upstairs is the craft and exercise space. There's an apartment on the third floor that the director, Greta Rogers, lives in. We're not open round-the-clock, but it's good to have someone on the premises at all times."

"Greta was very helpful in organizing this dance class." Beth followed the woman up the stairs, pleased to see she hadn't taken the elevator.

"She was sorry she couldn't be here today. She wanted to meet you in person."

On the second floor Millie walked through a narrow hallway past bathrooms, then into a large open space with wood floors and large windows looking out onto the square. Nearly a dozen women smiled and waved as she entered. Evelyn hurried forward.

"We can't wait to get started."

The next forty-five minutes flew by. Evelyn introduced her to everyone, and Beth took a few minutes to learn about their dance backgrounds and what they hoped to accomplish by learning to dance. She took her time demonstrating simple basic steps of tap and ballet, keeping a close eye on the exercise. Today's class had been designed for ambulatory seniors. If there was enough interest, she'd look into starting a chair class for those who weren't able to stand for long periods of time and those in wheelchairs.

Everyone was eager and willing to try each move. A couple of ladies teased her about the tights and leotard she'd worn today. She explained that the outfit made it easier to see how they were supposed to stand and move.

"I hope we don't have to get some of those things to wear," one woman joked.

A heavyset lady chimed in. "I don't mind getting them, but I could never get 'em up."

Beth joined in the laughter. It didn't take long to see the potential for smaller, more diverse classes. The varying levels of ability and interest would be challenging, and the thought fueled her energy. If this dance class took off, she could see bringing in another instructor to help. It was an idea she'd like to present to the center's director.

"Great workout. We'll slowly build up to doing more as we go."

Echoes of conversation bounced around the high ceilings as the seniors drifted out of the room. Some grumbled, some claimed they felt better already and a few decided they didn't like to dance at all. None of that discouraged her. She knew if they'd really enjoyed it, they would return. The most amazing part of the afternoon was how much *she* had enjoyed the class. She couldn't wait to tell Evelyn and thank her for the suggestion.

But when she glanced around the room, her gaze landed on Evelyn's grandson instead. Noah stood at the edge of the room, one shoulder resting against the doorjamb, arms crossed over his chest and one hip cocked in a purely masculine pose. Her mouth went dry. Sometimes she wished he'd stayed skinny. This attractive, mature version had way too much heart appeal.

"You looked like you were having fun."

He came toward her, a small smile lighting his blue eyes. A soft sigh escaped her throat. He'd always had the most knee-weakening smile. Whenever he'd flash that row of white teeth, it would bring out a deep crease on one side of his mouth. She'd always thought he looked very roguish. Like a tall, dark pirate, or a dangerous sea captain. But she'd been reading a lot of historical romance novels back then.

She cleared her throat. "I was. Are you here to learn to dance?"

He shrugged, the twinkle in his eyes flashing. "That's an intriguing idea."

Their eyes locked, trapping the breath in her throat. Was he imagining the same thing she was? The two of them in each other's arms, waltzing in the starlight?

"Oh, my." Evelyn dabbed at her neck with a towel as she walked over to them. "I'd forgotten how strenuous dancing could be. Just those few steps had me huffing." She patted her grandson's arm. "But all this exertion is more fun when you do it with friends. Speaking of fun, we're going to decorate the center's Christmas tree tomorrow, and we could use some assistance. Even putting ornaments on trees isn't as easy as it used to be. You two would be a big help."

Beth suspected some matchmaking tactics at work here. Noah would never refuse his grandmother, and she couldn't turn down a plea to help these sweet people. "I'd love to." She looked at Noah and raised her chin, daring him to refuse. She allowed a small smirk to lift her mouth, and she stifled a giggle at the resigned look in his eyes. He was aware of the maneuvering taking place.

"Sure. What time?"

"Afternoon, then Chloe can help, too."

Beth's affection for Evelyn tripled in that moment. She was doing what Beth couldn't—finding more ways for her to be with Noah and Chloe.

Noah glanced over at his grandmother as he drove her home after exercise class. The small, self-satisfied smile told him all he needed to know. "What are you up to?"

She faced him, her expression one of pure innocence. "Excuse me?"

"Don't try your mind tricks on me. You keep finding ways to put me and Beth together. You need to stop. There is nothing between us, and there never will be."

"Oh, I'm sure of that."

"What does that mean?"

"Well, you are a down-to-earth, no-nonsense kind of guy, like your father, and Beth is a sprig of spring flowers, a dandelion puff on a warm breeze, a sparkle of sunlight on the water."

Noah shook his head. "And she disappears when the dancing muse summons her."

His gram waved off his words. "Noah, you are assuming way too much. Have you talked to her about that time?"

"Actually, we have. The bottom line is her career was more important than our friendship." *And she didn't love me.*

"That sounds more like Yvonne than Beth. Did you ever tell her how you felt?"

"No. There was no point."

"If you never told her, then how can you hold her responsible for something she didn't even know about?"

"We were talking about your clumsy attempts at matchmaking."

"Were we? When? Oh, look. We're home. Thank you for picking me up, dear. I'm going to get supper started."

Before he could respond, Gram was out of the car and hurrying to the porch. For an old lady with arthritis, she moved fast. He sat in the car a moment. Gram was right about one thing. Beth was all the things she'd mentioned. He was acutely aware of it whenever she was near. Watching her work with the seniors had lifted another layer away from his emotional barrier. She'd been gentle and considerate as she helped them with their movements, completely shattering the image of the indifferent woman he wanted her to be. If she was cold and callous he could dismiss her easily, keep his wall of doubt intact. But if she was the warm and caring woman he remembered, then he was in danger of falling in love with her again.

Gram was right. How could he hold her responsible for his feelings? Yes, she'd broken his heart, but he wasn't the first guy to be rejected. Yes, she'd ignored friends and family after she left home, but he was guilty of the same neglect. When he'd moved to California, his grandparents had frequently complained that he rarely called or came home to see them. He'd been busy, starting his career and his life. Could he blame Beth for doing the same thing?

But what about when she left? And what about Chloe? After Thanksgiving with the Montgomerys decorating the windows and the lighting event, she was in love with Beth. She'd even ordered a poster of Beth to put on her bedroom wall.

He had to remember it was his job as her father to protect her from getting hurt. She was getting too enamored of Beth. It was time to pull back and put some distance between them. Once the show was over, he'd put an end to the dance lessons and sign her up for more soccer. She should be ready to play indoor soccer for the winter. That should give her plenty to focus on.

Yet deep down, he knew it wasn't that simple. Chloe gave all of her little heart to those she loved, and her trust, as well. He used to be that way. A couple of classes at the school of hard knocks had cured him. Now he realized he wanted to love and trust again.

Except the risk was too high. He couldn't face another rejection.

The afternoon light was already fading, casting downtown Dover into dull shadows. Usually the early darkness of winter dragged Beth down, but nothing could diminish her excitement today. She'd started decorating her apartment last night, placing many of her sister's lovely items around on shelves and end tables. She'd even added a few of her own touches with candles she'd picked up the other day. For the first time in years, she was embracing the holiday and looking forward to helping the people at the senior center decorate their tree.

Strange how she'd been surrounded by the extravagant holiday displays and events in New York City for years, but she'd hadn't experienced this kind of childlike excitement since she was little. Or the growing sense of satisfaction. Since her first class with the seniors, she'd received a dozen calls telling her how much fun they'd had and how they couldn't wait for the next class. They were all looking forward to the tree-decorating party today and never failed to remind her to bring Noah along.

Picking up her purse, she locked up and went next door. She noticed the addition to the window immediately as she entered Noah's front office. He was seated at the desk, but she strode past him to the display window.

"Where did you find this precious church?" She stroked the roofline, then bent down to peek in the small windows that had been painted to look like stained glass.

"Gramps made it. He had a whole village of houses and buildings he'd put on the front lawn for Christmas. Gram thought it would look good in the window."

"I remember that little town. I used to wish I could shrink down like Alice in Wonderland so I could go inside each building. This is the perfect touch for our windows. Does it light up?" She spun and smiled at him, only to receive a deep frown in response.

"It will. I have to pick up a bulb."

He lowered his gaze as if not wanting to look at her. She tried to ignore the sharp twinge in her throat. "Perfect. We might just have a chance at winning a prize in the window-decorating contest this weekend."

Noah shifted in his chair. Something had made him very uncomfortable. Her? She didn't understand him at all. The mixed signals were driving her crazy.

"Are you ready to help decorate the tree?"

"Sorry, but I have to work. I have a stack of inspection reports to finalize."

She moved toward him, only to see him brace. What had she done now? "Noah, your gram and the seniors are counting on you to help."

He avoided looking at her and shuffled the papers on his desk. "There should be plenty of people there."

Beth stepped to the edge of the desk, her fingers resting on the top instead of around his neck, despite her temptation to put them there. "What about Chloe?"

"Gram picked her up from school. They should already be at the center. You'd better go on."

"Noah, what's bothering you? Have I said something

or done something to upset you? If so, I'm sorry. I can't fix it if you don't tell me what's wrong."

He looked at her with eyes filled with a strange mixture of sadness and confusion. "It's not you, it's—" He paused for a second, then inhaled a deep breath and squared his shoulders. "Like I said. I've got work to do."

His tone said the subject was closed. "Fine." She strode to the door, then spun around. "You know you're letting Chloe down the same way her mother does. You told her you'd help decorate, but at the last minute, you're backing out. For *work*. How can you justify disappointing her this way?"

Noah didn't meet her gaze. He stared resolutely at the papers on his desk. With a loud huff, she pulled open the door and left.

Men. They said one thing but did another. When would she learn that lesson?

Chapter Eight

Noah's office door closed with a sharp click, leaving him in silence to confront things he'd rather avoid. Like the way his emotions were constantly swinging between his need to protect his daughter and his growing feelings for Beth. He should have anticipated Beth stopping by. He should have known she'd want to go together.

He gazed at the wooden church in the display window. He'd been ridiculously pleased that she liked it. And pleasing her had become one of his goals. But alongside that emotion flashed a warning sign, reminding him to maintain a clear distance and protect his heart.

Since she'd come home to Dover, he'd been forced to adjust his opinions of Beth and view the past through a more mature lens. Nothing was as cut-and-dried as it appeared. He shouldn't have interpreted her sudden departure as a personal rejection. And he should have tried harder to find out the truth. But his ego had been bruised, and he'd made assumptions. He hated to think he'd been that shallow and selfish, but at eighteen he'd thought he understood the world. Now, at thirty-one, he knew better. Though he still wasn't clear how his confusion over her gift had given her the impression he didn't care about her.

His cell buzzed, and Chloe's picture appeared on the screen. "Hey, princess. Everything all right?"

"Daddy, where are you? Gram and I are here, and so is Miss Beth. It's time to decorate the tree. Hurry up or you'll miss it."

Noah rubbed his forehead. How could he spend time with Beth, knowing the constant exposure would only peel away another layer of his heart? Their truce should have made being with her easier. Instead it had only increased his longing to reestablish the friendship they'd once had.

No. He needed to stick to his plan. Steer clear and keep his distance.

"Sorry, but I have to work today. You and Gram have fun, and tell me all about it over supper tonight."

The disappointment in his daughter's voice as she said goodbye spilled like hot lead along each of his nerve endings.

After hanging up, he rested his elbows on the desk, hands fisted against his mouth as waves of guilt crashed against his mind. Beth was right. He was doing what Yvonne always did. Putting a job before family. Something he swore he'd never do. And not because he loved work, but because he was afraid.

Shoving away from his desk, he snatched his jacket from the back of his chair, locked up and headed across the courthouse park to the senior center. Warmth and the mouthwatering aroma of fresh popcorn greeted him as he stepped inside. The large tree in front of the window was surrounded by people when he arrived. It looked like his skills wouldn't be needed after all.

Chloe spotted him and dashed across the room full tilt, throwing herself into his arms and knocking him backward. He scooped her up and held her close. At nine she was too big to hold, but he relished the feel of her in his arms, hugging his neck.

"Daddy, I'm so glad you came."

"Me, too, princess."

"Come on, we need your help with the extra lights."

Beth turned as he approached the tree, and the smile on her lovely face wiped all doubts from his mind. This is where he wanted to be. Working beside her and his daughter.

The sweet melody of "I'll Be Home for Christmas" that had been playing when he came in gave way to "Little Saint Nick." He chuckled as some of the seniors started to move to the upbeat tune and sing along.

"Chester Floyd, get your hands out of the popcorn." Gram wagged a finger at the stocky gentleman. "That's for stringing on the tree."

Beth's soft laughter drew his gaze to her. Her smile was bright and mischievous. "Let that be a lesson to you. No munching the decorations."

"I'm glad I'm not Chester."

"Daddy, you need to hang this up 'cause you're tall." Chloe hurried toward him, her hands overflowing with a pile of popcorn garland. It took him a moment to locate the end, then he tucked it in the back of the tree near the top and slowly draped it across the branches.

"It's so pretty, Daddy. Isn't this fun?"

He looked down at his child. The dreamy glow in her blue eyes was the most beautiful thing he'd ever seen. Beth stepped to Chloe's side and slipped her arm across her shoulders, a happy smile bringing a pink flush to her cheeks. He was glad he'd changed his mind and come. Sharing Chloe's and Beth's delight was too precious a moment to miss for work.

While the next strand of popcorn was being assembled, he and Beth began removing the lids from the boxes of ornaments stacked on a table. He watched her face fill with delight as she opened each box. She looked happy and content. But for how long? She caught him staring and held his gaze, smiling deep into his eyes.

"I'm glad you changed your mind about coming."

"You were right. I was behaving exactly like Yvonne. I swore I'd never let her down."

"You know that's an impossible goal."

"Yeah. But a father can dream."

She faced him, raising her eyebrows. "Oh. So you *do* have dreams. I knew it."

He smiled, taking the bulb from her hand and letting his fingers brush against hers. What would she say if he told her he was living a dream right now? Being with her and Chloe, performing a holiday ritual like a normal family, was a dream he'd held since his parents died. But she knew that already. He'd told her long ago. Did she remember?

Beth lifted a glass ballerina ornament from the box. "Oh, how sweet. Chloe, look what I found." She hurried over to the tree, and he watched the two of them search out the perfect spot to hang the ornament, leaving him to second-guess his decision. Had he just made another big mistake by coming to help? In making Chloe happy in the short term, and sharing more time with Beth, he may have set them both up for a bigger disappointment down the road when she left.

How was a father supposed to know what was right?

* * *

Beth watched the dancers as they went through their steps for the scene from *The Nutcracker*. Allison had chosen the scene when Clara receives her gift and combined it with a few more iconic Victorian holiday scenes.

When the music ended, Beth moved up onstage. "Great job, everyone. Now remember, we'll be practicing every night between now and the performance. I know that's a lot to ask, but we all want this show to be the very best. It'll all be worth it when you hear that applause. And speaking of that, while this is a performance, remember that we are also trying to show not only the earthly joy of Christmas, but also the joyous miracle of Emmanuel. God with us. Here as a human baby. So when the applause starts, remember it's not only for you, but for Him, as well. Take a break, and we'll run through the final number one more time."

Beth looked over her notes, jotting down a few thoughts on how to improve the number. A swell of happy satisfaction rose up through her body, bringing a smile she didn't try to hide. She was beginning to think Miss Evelyn was right about God having more than one blessing in store for each of His children. Taking this job had already blessed her in ways she never could have imagined.

"I'd like to speak with you, Miss Montgomery."

She looked up as Beulah Jenson approached, with a tearful girl in tow. Her daughter, Mindy, was dancing the role of Clara in the *Nutcracker* segment. If there was one sour note in the show, it was Mrs. Jenson. The woman found fault with every direction Beth or Jen gave, and tested her self-control to the limit.

"I'm afraid your practice schedule is too strenuous for Mindy. From here on I'll only bring her to the important rehearsals."

Beth struggled to keep the irritation from her tone as she spoke. "Mrs. Jenson, Mindy has a key role in this production. She needs to be here for each rehearsal in case we have to make any changes."

"If you ask me, there are far too many changes. You may be a professional, but Mindy isn't, and I don't appreciate the way you work her beyond her capabilities. The routines were perfectly fine until you showed up and complicated everything. I think it's best we let her part be taken over by her understudy."

Beth blinked. Was she serious? "She doesn't have an understudy. This is a little theater production, and the performers are here because they want to be."

"Well, we no longer want to *be*." She whirled, grabbed her sobbing daughter's hand and marched out.

Beth clutched her notes to her chest. Great. One of the main performers had quit. Mindy was hardly the best dancer, but she knew her part. Beth's confidence sagged. She thought she'd been doing a good job. Everyone was tired, but no one had balked at the extra practices. "What am I going to do now?"

"Don't worry about it." Jen came and stood at her side. "I've been expecting this from the beginning. Stage mother."

"I'm sorry. I guess I'm better at performing than directing and choreographing."

"You're great at both. Don't let her get you down. Beulah has a reputation for being difficult."

"That doesn't solve the problem of losing our Clara."

"No, but we'll think of something. Maybe one of the older girls could take the part?"

Beth stared at the stage, mentally running through the routine and reimagining the sequence. Excitement sent her pulse racing as an idea began to form. "What about three Clara's?"

"What?"

"I've been teaching Chloe and my niece and her friend basic ballet. What if we had the three girls dance the part together? They already know some easy steps. We could dress them alike, pick up two more small nutcrackers and present them as triplets."

Jen nodded. "It might be cute. See if you can set it up."

A squiggle of excitement zinged along her nerves. She was certain Abby and Hannah would love the idea. Chloe, too, but she wasn't sure how Noah would react. Giving Chloe dance lessons as incentive to do her PT exercises was a far cry from actually performing on-stage. "I don't know if Noah will like the idea. He may not want Chloe in the show."

"Why not? His gram is putting it on."

Beth frowned. "It's complicated. But maybe I can get his gram on our side. And make sure he knows we're in a difficult position with the show only a week away."

Jen squeezed her hand. "If I remember correctly, you can be very persuasive when you set your mind to something. We make a good team. I look forward to the next production."

Beth looked at the warm smile on Jen's face, her memory flashing back to when they'd shared so many happy times. "I must confess I'm enjoying this more than I thought I would. My life has been so set in one direction that I'd forgotten how much fun other things can be, and how important old friendships are. I'm sorry I failed to keep in touch over the years."

"Don't be silly. It's what happens after school. We all go on with our lives. I thought about you often, and I'm so proud of what you accomplished. The friendship never went away, Beth. It was held in a special place in my heart, waiting to be dusted off and polished up again."

Beth gathered up her belongings, wondering if her friendship with Noah could be polished up, or if it was simply too late. The truce had eased the tension between them, making it easier to be together. But Noah still carried his shield at his side, ready to raise it without warning.

She knew he was trying to protect himself from being hurt again, but how could they ever move forward if he didn't drop his guard? Maybe he didn't want to. Maybe she was indulging in wishful thinking again. Wanting him to care because she did.

She knew he was attracted to her. The sparks between them were too strong to ignore. But was that mere chemistry, old emotions stirred to life again? Or was it something more? Something that could become real?

She grabbed her tablet and made a few notes about the changes she had to make. She had no time to worry about what Noah did or did not feel.

Noah set the screw in place, pressed the trigger on the drill and drove it into the wood. A second screw secured the table leg in place. He tightened the other screws before setting the small table upright, confident it wouldn't wobble during the *Night Before Christmas* act.

He straightened and removed the drill bit. Despite telling himself not to, his gaze sought out Beth, who was standing in the aisle talking with the mother of one of the children. He forced himself to look away and gather up his tools. His feelings for Beth were growing each day. He still couldn't bring himself to believe that Beth would stay in Dover. Given the chance, she'd dance her way out of his life at the first opportunity.

Yet he knew she was enjoying teaching the girls and working with the seniors at the center. He'd seen her gentleness toward his gram and the others in her class. Here at the rehearsals, she glowed with energy and enthusiasm, and he was confronted hourly with his daughter's adoration for Beth.

She had a lot to offer their small hometown. Her heart for others was evident in everything she did. That was the Beth he remembered. The one that still called to him from the far recesses of his mind. But was it enough? Could teaching others to dance take the place of doing it herself? Could she ever completely let go of her lifelong dream?

"Noah, do you have a moment?"

He spun, nearly bumping into the object of his thoughts. "Sure." She was holding her tablet. He frowned. What did she want constructed now?

"I need one more rather large prop, and I was hoping you could throw it together."

Why did everyone think that building things was just a matter of throwing some lumber together? "You do realize that the show is next week."

"I know, but we've had a change in one of the numbers. Mindy Jenson pulled out—or rather, her mother pulled her out. Which means I have to restage the number, and I had an idea."

He didn't even try to hide the groan, but he tempered it with a wary smile. "What is it?"

"I need a giant nutcracker."

"What?"

She hastened to explain. "It doesn't have to be elaborate or anything, but it needs to be about eight feet tall and about three to four feet wide." She rotated the tablet so he could see her sketch.

The design looked like an actual nutcracker with tubular arms, a tall hat, full body and long legs ending in boots on a platform. "Beth, that would take weeks to construct, not to mention the time to figure the angles, the amount of wood and other materials."

"I thought you were a structural engineer?"

"I am."

"So make a structure."

Her eyes twinkled, and he realized she was teasing him. "Very funny. Now what do you really want?"

"A big nutcracker, but it can be a one-dimensional flat one. Eric will paint in all the details, but it's an important prop because it'll be the one your daughter will be dancing around."

"What are you talking about?"

Beth clutched her tablet to her chest like a protective shield. "Since we've lost our Clara, I'm going to replace her with three Clara's. Abby, Hannah and Chloe."

Not what he'd expected. He shook his head. "I don't know about that."

"As you pointed out, we only have one week until opening night. I'm improvising. Besides, I know the girls will love the idea. Please consider letting Chloe be in the number. It's only one performance, not a life-long contract."

She had a point, but what if she got a taste of performing and liked it? He met her gaze, trying to ignore the hopeful glint in her pretty eyes. He knew once his daughter heard the idea, there'd be no way he could tell her no. "All right." He pointed to the tablet. "How soon do you need it?"

"The sooner the better. Thank you, Noah. For letting Chloe dance and for the prop. Is it all right if I call her now?"

"Sure." He nodded, then watched her hurry off. He needed to figure out when he'd lost control of his life.

Chapter Nine

Noah stared at the sketches Beth had emailed him of her nutcracker idea. One, a complicated three-dimensional one. The other, a simple flat one in the shape of a nutcracker. With so little time left until opening night, he really didn't have time to do more than cut out the shape and get it back to the theater so Eric could paint it.

However, what he wanted to do was surprise Beth with the giant nutcracker she'd teased him with. He could imagine her shock and delight when he brought it into the theater. Ideas on how to create it had started forming in his mind from the moment she'd suggested it. He'd worked out a simple design, but he'd have to rely on Eric to make it look realistic.

He had plenty of lumber, and the rest he was hoping to find in the storage shed. When it came to building materials and supplies, Gramps had been a pack rat. He believed sooner or later he'd find a use for all the things he'd saved.

Pulling the shed key from the hook beside the door, he let himself in, heading toward the large assortment of poles, pipes and other odd-shaped pieces. After selecting a small plastic box, several lengths of PVC pipe and a bucket, he set them beside the door. As he reached for the string to turn off the light, a small wooden object caught his attention. His treasure box.

It was the size of a shoe box. His gramps had built it for him as a Christmas gift when he was ten. He and his parents had been living in Florida at the time, and he'd been fascinated with pirates and wanted a place to keep his valuables. Over time the box had held a variety of important items. His throat thickened as he thought about the last items of value he'd placed in the box. Slowly he raised the lid, his gaze zeroing in on the small white box in the middle. Beth's graduation gift to him. His hand shook as he reached for it. What had she written on the back? She claimed it was nothing but a friendly sentiment.

The oddly shaped emblem on the key ring glinted in the light when he removed the lid. Nestled upon the white batting inside was what he could clearly see now was a heart, shaped as if it had been gently tugged to one side, distorting its shape. He swallowed against the dryness in his throat, then flipped over the charm, his breath catching as he read the words engraved there.

Noah, every time you touch this you'll be touching my heart. Love, Beth

Love? He read the words again, trying to understand. The sentiment was from someone who cared—deeply. Not a casual friend. Had she cared? Had she loved him?

His gaze landed on the other small box in the chest. The gift he'd selected for her. Beneath the blue box was a faded paper. His speech. The one he'd never gotten to deliver.

Noah gripped the key ring in his palm, wrapping his fingers around it and feeling the sharp edges dig into his skin. What did he do now? Did he tell Beth and ask her what she meant? Did he dare hope that she'd been confessing her love for him that day? Or was he reading too much into a few simple words?

Even if she'd meant the words, even if she'd given him the gift and revealed her feelings, when the call from Forsythe had come she would have gone anyway. Dancing had been her whole life then. Still was.

He didn't have the energy to try to figure it out now. Shoving the key ring into his pants pocket, he gathered up the materials and headed back to the shop. Working with his hands was a good way to sort out his thoughts and come to a decision.

Or even better, avoid one.

The sun was barely up the next morning when Beth switched on the lights in her small studio. Sleep had been impossible. Dark and disturbing dreams had awakened her several times during the night, leaving her shaken and filled with a chilling sense of abandonment. Her body ached, and the thought of doing her exercises and ballet warm-up dragged her down. She didn't have the energy for either. But she would do them just the same.

She pulled off her jacket and changed into comfy pants and a tank top before starting her physical therapy exercises. She ran through them with ease, then moved to the mirrored wall, intending to begin her ballet warm-up. She stopped, a hard knot lodging in her throat as she stared at her reflection. Why bother? Her life as a professional ballerina with the Forsythe Company had ended with a swipe of a pen.

She'd met with Blake Prescott yesterday, the family attorney, and gone over her contract, ultimately deciding to terminate her association with the ballet. She had nothing to gain by holding out the last two months. It was a scary prospect, and she suspected her decision was the cause of her nightmares. She had no idea what she would do going forward.

But for now, she would go through her ballet warm-up. It's what she did when she hurt or was lonely or confused. She danced. Some people sought solace in a bar. She found it at a different barre.

Pushing the play button, she started her favorite CD of praise music. The familiar songs gave her a measure of comfort, and allowed her to reconnect with the artist she'd once been. The opening strains washed over her as she grasped the barre and prepared, acutely aware of the alignment of her hips, legs and turnout. Slow *tendu*. First position. *Demi plié* and stretch. Four-count *relevé*…

The warm-up was so engrained into her muscle memory that it had become a struggle to hold back from throwing herself into it fully. Her knee wasn't ready for a *grande plié*, but she was close.

At thirty years old, she was well aware she was entering the last phase of her career. She was also aware of the younger dancers waiting in the wings, eager to jump into her place. She refocused on her warm-up. *Plié, eleve*, point toes, front, back, side, change position. It was as natural as breathing. She raised her arm, letting it float on the air with the music as she stretched. It felt so familiar, so right. She missed it so much.

An hour later, drained yet exhilarated, she downed several gulps of water and smiled at her reflection. She'd pushed it a little more today. The pain was easing with each workout, and she felt herself growing stronger.

Fueled with confidence, she decided to try a little center work. Stepping to the middle of the room, she balanced, positioned her arms and raised her right leg out to the side, only to wobble and lose her balance. Three more tries only led to frustration. The sense of lightness and control she always experienced was missing, replaced with a feeling of clumsiness. Nothing was the same anymore. Not her body, not her proficiency level, not even herself.

Taking a moment to collect herself, she started toward the small sofa, her gaze landing on the pair of worn pink *pointe* shoes hanging on the wall. Gently she took them in her hands, overcome with poignant memories. They were her last pair before she'd left for New York. The ones she'd worn as she'd practiced for her audition to the Forsythe Company. She'd danced her very best, but it hadn't been good enough. Until another position had opened up, and her prayers had been answered and her dream realized.

Beth sank down onto the small sofa, her fingers stroking the worn satin. She'd left Dover with wings on her feet. She'd worked harder than anyone, rising through the ranks from corps de ballet to demi-soloist and eventually principal dancer, achieving everything she'd set out to.

Noah's question reverberated in her mind. But what had it cost her? A friend who felt rejected. A mother who'd needed to hear from her daughter, a family she'd barely seen since she was eighteen. The memory of

Chloe's sorrowful expression when her mother had failed to live up to her promise surfaced. Is that what her mother and father had experienced? Sadness and disappointment?

Leaning back against the cushion, she clutched the shoes to her chest as stark realization forced its way into her mind. This wasn't about dancing, this was about her. The truth about her life was coming to the surface, forcing her to confront her sins and shortcomings.

When had she become so indifferent to others' feelings?

She knew the answer. It had been that night she'd left Dover. Realizing Noah didn't love her had shaken her foundation. From then on, becoming a professional dancer had changed from being a dream to a necessity, a way to prove her worth to herself and to him.

Once she left Dover, her life had been all about becoming the best dancer she could be. Living her dream. She had shoved everyone aside in her drive to succeed. There'd been moments when she'd looked up and realized she was alone. No close friends, a family far away, no special someone. But then the dance would call, and she'd plunge into it and forget everything else.

Her dad had always stressed faith first, but she'd never really understood what he'd meant. She was beginning to now. She was coming to see that she'd placed things in her life in the wrong order. A swell of shame and regret formed deep inside. Her life was out of balance.

Her mom was right. She'd been holding on to something that was never going to happen. She had to change. If she didn't, she'd end up chasing everyone in her life away—again. She didn't want to lose Noah or Chloe. They'd become too much a part of her life now.

Did she have the courage? She couldn't do it alone.

She looked at the middle of the room. A few moments ago she'd tried to balance on her good leg without support. It should have been easy. But her body was out of balance, too. She needed the barre to steady her. And she needed something more than her own determination to balance her life. She *had* to reset her priorities. Put God first. His hand should be what she grasped for security, not the wooden beam against the wall.

Lord, forgive me. I don't want to be that person. Help me find a way to reconnect with those I love and balance my life. I want You first in my life.

Her dream was over. She had to face it. God gave her what she dreamed of, but He never said it would last forever.

Clutching the shoes to her chest, she grieved the passing of a dream.

Beth stood onstage the next night, staring in disbelief at the giant nutcracker Noah had delivered that evening. She'd been expecting a flat in the shape of a nutcracker. Instead he presented her with a three-dimensional eight-foot version, complete with tall hat, round arms and legs, and a square wooden body on a rolling platform. The sections were a mismatch of materials, but Eric could transform it into a spectacular sight. "When did you do this? It's amazing."

He grinned, his eyes bright with pride. "I realized it wouldn't be all that difficult to make a large one if I used PVC pipe for arms and legs and kept the body square. Once I started, it took on a life of its own. Of course, Eric will have to use his skill to make it look like an actual nutcracker."

"You put so much work into this. Thank you. This is going to transform the entire number."

He shrugged, his expression revealing his embarrassment. "Well, it is my daughter's shining moment after all."

Unable to contain her delight, she slipped her arms around his neck and gave him a kiss on the cheek. As she pulled away, her attention landed on his mouth, only inches from hers if she shifted just a bit. Heart pounding, she moved her hand from his shoulder to his jaw. It was warm and strong and slightly scratchy from end-of-day stubble. She dared to look into his eyes and saw her own desire reflected in the blue depths.

It hit her then that they were standing in the open, where anyone and everyone could see them. She swallowed, tucked her hair behind her ears and stepped back. "Thank you, Noah. It's amazing."

"I'm glad you like it." He held her gaze a moment, searching her face. "You've changed."

She frowned, glancing down at her outfit. What was he talking about?

"You look different. Your eyes aren't shadowed anymore. Your smile isn't restrained. What happened?"

Was her transformation so apparent? But then, Noah would notice things like that. Perhaps this was the opening she'd been waiting for. The time to have a talk about what really had been going on in her heart back then. "You're right. Something has changed. Maybe we can talk about it after rehearsal?"

"I'd like that. I have something to tell you, too. And I have some questions."

Questions? That dimmed her mood a bit. But once they sat down and talked it out, she knew things would be better, and hopefully they could admit the attraction between them and move forward. After all her soul-searching the other night, there'd been one more truth she'd had to face and accept. She loved Noah. Always had. Always would.

A knot formed in her abdomen. What about now? Was she just seeing what she wanted? Was this attraction only on her part?

Beth carried the warmth of Noah's touch with her the rest of the rehearsal. Their relationship had changed over the last weeks. Working together on the show and the props had eased them back into their comfortable friendship. More importantly—and disturbingly—the attraction between them had heated up. Her heart was already in danger, but now the sparks between them were zinging whenever they were close.

Noah stopped at her side, his smile warm and affectionate, his blue eyes filled with tenderness. "May I walk you home?"

"I'd like that."

Outside, Beth pulled her coat a little closer. The weather was unusually cold for southern Mississippi. Thankfully the forecast called for a warm-up tomorrow. She didn't mind the chill, especially when Noah took her hand in his.

"Thank you again for the wonderful nutcracker. It's amazing."

"This is an important holiday event. A guy shouldn't skimp when his three favorite women are involved."

"Three?"

"Gram, Chloe and—" He squeezed her hand. "You."

She couldn't misunderstand the tone of affection in his voice or the look in his eyes. Now would be a good time to tell him about the inscription. But where did she start? "I'm glad you let Chloe do the number. She's very excited, and she's working very hard to learn the routine."

"She practices at home all the time. Every time I turn around, I'm running into her."

"You're a great dad, Noah." Inhaling a fortifying breath, she plunged ahead. "Have you ever thought about getting married again?" She sensed his surprise.

"No. I don't think I'm very good at the marriage thing."

"I don't believe that. Any woman would be blessed to have you for a husband. You're a good man."

"Charlie Brown."

She chuckled and moved closer to his side. "Well, you are."

"What about you? Why haven't you taken the plunge? I'm sure you had plenty of chances. You must have had guys falling at your feet wanting to date the beautiful ballerina."

A shadow settled over her happy mood. This wasn't the topic she wanted to discuss, but maybe it was time to share that heartache with him. "There was a man. His name was Ivan and he was a guest dancer from Russia, very charming and sophisticated. We started dating. I was head over heels in love with him, and I got carried away with my emotions. Everything was fine until I told him I was pregnant. Then he moved on to the next girl and the next city and left me to deal with a miscarriage all by myself. I never saw him again."

Noah stopped and faced her, pulling her into his embrace. "Oh, my Beth. I'm sorry you had to go through that alone."

Beth allowed the warmth and protection of his arms to soothe her, wishing she could turn to him with her worries every day. His Beth. That's all she'd ever wanted to be.

"What about your family?"

"I couldn't tell them. I was too ashamed. I was still trying to figure out what to do when I lost the baby."

Noah gently set her away, looking deep into her eyes. "Is that why you left the table so suddenly on Thanksgiving Day after Abby announced the new baby?"

She nodded. "I'm happy for them, but it only reminded me of the big hole in my own life. Sorry to dump this on you."

They'd stopped at the apartment door. Noah tilted her chin upward as he looked deep into her eyes. "Don't be. I'm glad you told me. You used to tell me all your deepest secrets."

She touched his lips with her fingertips. "That's because you always understood. I wish we'd been friends then. I was so scared and alone."

"You deserve so much better."

"I'm not so sure." She touched her leg. "My injury wasn't entirely an accident. I'd been pushing myself beyond my limits since I lost the baby. I didn't know what else to do. I didn't want to tell my parents. Then Dad died suddenly, and I couldn't tell Mom, so I buried myself in my career. It's all I had. Sometimes I think that's all I am. A dancer."

"You're wrong. You're more than a dancer. Yes, you devoted yourself to your art, but when you came out of that studio you were always doing things for others. Remember we served meals at the community Christmas dinner? You helped with a habitat house and collected toys for the kids at Christmas. And now you're teaching the people at the senior center, working with the theater and teaching Chloe and her friends. You have more to offer than a brief time in the spotlight."

His support touched her deeply, and gave her hope for their relationship. "Do you think so? Because you were right. Something has changed, and I want to tell you about it. Can you stay for a while? I'll fix coffee."

"Make a big pot. We have a lot of things to discuss."

Up in her apartment, Beth poured a cup of coffee, mentally rehearsing what she would say to Noah. As she set his mug before him, the doorbell chimed. *Who could possibly be stopping by at this hour?*

"Are you expecting someone?"

"No. It's too late for Mom to come by, and the boys never come here unless invited." Moving to the security screen that allowed a view of the door below, she frowned when she saw a man standing there. He turned his head. She inhaled a quick breath. What was he doing here?

She glanced at Noah. "It's a friend from New York." She buzzed the man in and waited at the top of the stairs as he walked up, conscious of Noah standing protectively at her side.

"Who is this guy?"

The man obviously overheard because he reached the top of the steps, pulled Beth into a bear hug and announced, "This guy is the man who's going to change her life."

Beth saw the muscles in Noah's jaw flex rapidly and his lips press into a hard line. She shoved her guest away, putting distance between them. "Kurt, what are you doing here?"

"I was passing through and wanted to say hello." He stepped close again and draped an arm across her shoulders. She moved out of his reach. The man had always been far too touchy-feely for her liking. "No one just passes through Dover. It's not on the way to anywhere."

"You telling me? It's barely on the map. Seriously, I'm on my way to New Orleans and I wanted to see you in person."

"How did you find me?"

"Seems everyone in this town knows who you are."

Beth became aware of Noah standing close, as if to protect her from an unknown threat. "Noah, this is Kurt Townsend from the Forsythe Ballet Company. Kurt, Noah Carlisle. An old friend."

The men nodded. Neither one offered a hand to shake. Beth gritted her teeth. Of all the times for Kurt to show up. "You could have called, given me some warning."

Kurt struck an arrogant pose and winked. "What? Are you too busy in this burg to have time for a colleague and very close friend?"

She blushed at the suggestive smirk that appeared on Kurt's face. He was deliberately taunting Noah. "I am busy, as a matter of fact."

"I only need a few minutes, then I'll be on my way." He faced Noah. "But I need to talk to you alone."

Noah shifted slightly toward her. "Do you want me to stay?"

She rested one hand in the center of his chest, surprised at how hard his heart was beating. He was genuinely worried about her. The thought softened her anxiety and gave her great comfort. "I'll be fine. I'll see you tomorrow."

Noah gave Kurt a hard stare, then placed a light kiss on her lips as if staking his claim before guiding her to the door. "I'll call you later."

She nodded, waiting until she saw him go down the steps and outside before closing the apartment door and touching her fingers to her mouth. He'd kissed her. Why? Had it been a warning to Kurt or merely a way to reassure her that he'd be there if she needed him. Her heart tightened. She wanted to believe he'd kissed her because he cared, but she had to be careful and not read too much into it. That would be foolish.

Right now she had to deal with Kurt.

Beth stepped into the kitchen to see Kurt drinking from Noah's coffee mug. Irked to the limit, she took the mug away, dumped out the liquid and faced him.

"Who was that guy? A local farmer?"

His snobbish attitude rankled. "He happens to be a structural engineer."

"Really?" He glanced around her rooms. "So how can you stand to live here? I mean, this apartment is huge, but this town is off the grid. Nice tree."

He pointed to the pencil-thin Christmas tree she'd put up. She really didn't care what he thought. "I'm actually very happy here. I like being home again."

"Well, you won't be happy here for long. I guess you heard about the shake-up in the company? Noreen taking charge and all that. So I'm out, and I couldn't be happier. I'm starting my own dance troupe. I've been offered the artistic director's job with Dance Unique. They have new backers who plan on turning it into a first-class company, and they've given me carte blanche to hire the personnel. I want you to come on board as the choreographer. Your name alone will shoot us to the top."

The offer was too good to be true. "Kurt, I appreciate you thinking of me, but I'm not nearly ready to go back to dancing full-time, and classical ballet is probably over for good."

"I know that, but hear me out. I think you'll be excited. There's only one hitch. I need an answer by Christmas."

Beth listened as Kurt outlined the details of his plan but made no promises. She breathed a sigh of relief when he finally left.

Curled up on her sofa, she thought through his offer, excitement building as she thought about the possibilities. She could reclaim her dream and the life she'd worked so hard for. The timing was perfect. By the time the new company was ready to perform, she'd be fully recovered. They would be focusing on other forms of dance and reaching out to young people. The idea was intriguing.

The money and the job security were enticing, too. An opportunity to create new ballets and new choreography was something she loved. She should have refused him immediately, but she told him she'd think it over. A month ago she would have jumped at the chance to leave Dover and go back to work in the dance world. Now she was hesitant. All because of Noah. Yet until she knew how Noah felt, she'd be smart to keep her options open, wouldn't she?

Beth grabbed a pillow and hugged it close. But hadn't she just decided to put her life in balance? Could she do that if she went back to New York? She'd started reading her Bible again and had even signed up for a women's bible study in the New Year.

She wanted to scream in confusion. Kurt's offer appealed to her ego. Why did God do this? She'd finally accepted that her dancing was over, she'd let it go and was turning her energies toward new dreams, then He dumps this big opportunity in her lap as if reminding her what her true dream was. What was she supposed to do? Was God saying don't let go? Was she walking away too soon? She'd been at peace with her decision, but now she was questioning that choice.

If only the Lord would give answers to her prayers in a loud voice, or write it across the sky. How were you supposed to know what God's will for your life was?

What she wanted was to talk it over with Noah, but she knew what he'd say. At the very least, she wanted to hear his voice. She'd told him she'd call. He was probably worried. Had he been protective because he was a gentleman and Kurt had posed a threat, or because he cared? He had kissed her before he left.

Her heart lodged in her throat as she waited for him to answer. She smiled when she heard his smooth voice. "Hi. It's me."

"Everything okay?"

"Yes. Kurt is obnoxious but harmless. I'm sorry he ruined our talk."

"Yeah. Well, I'm glad you're all right."

His casual response triggered concern. She'd expected him to bombard her with questions. Something in Noah's tone was off. "Are you all right? Is something wrong?"

A heavy sigh was her answer. "Yvonne called. She's

coming in tomorrow to spend time with Chloe. She wants to see her in the *Christmas Dreams* show."

"Oh." No wonder he was distracted.

"I need to go. Can we talk tomorrow?"

"Yes, of course." She hung up, her mood sinking. She'd been hoping for a word of comfort from Noah, but now she longed to comfort him. She knew how worried he was for Chloe. With her mother showing up, so did the potential for another heartbreak for the little girl. That was far more important than her own silly problems.

Tonight her prayers would all be for Chloe, and that this time, Yvonne would stay true to her word.

Noah poured his fourth cup of coffee and spooned in sugar and a splash of creamer before returning to his desk. He didn't like working in the front office. The expanse of windows made him visible to everyone who passed by, which would be great if he was a merchant trying to sell goods. Not so much when he was promoting an engineering business. But right now, he needed to be visible, and an empty room said closed not open. Working out front had snagged his first private client, albeit a very difficult and frustrating one. Still, he'd be glad when he could land some commercial jobs, hire a receptionist and move his desk to the back room.

But that wasn't what had him sucking down caffeine like a student on an all-nighter.

He couldn't shake the image of Beth wrapped in the arms of the irritating Kurt. The man's possessive attitude still made his blood boil. He'd held Beth in his arms as if he had a right, and the smirk on his face begged to be wiped off with a fist. He'd only left because Beth had assured him she would be fine, but he'd been tormented by the man's remark about changing Beth's life. Had he come to lure her back to the dance? This made him wonder if there was more to their relationship. He knew what was eating at him. Jealousy. He had no right to feel that way, but there it was.

Unfortunately, by the time she'd called him to say she was okay, he'd barely listened. He'd been too distracted by the news of Yvonne's visit. Chloe had texted her mom the moment she'd learned of her starring role in the Christmas show, and her mother had responded in her usual way, promising their child that she would come to the performance, film it for her TV show, then take her to New Orleans for a long fun weekend.

He'd tried to prepare Chloe to be disappointed, but she wouldn't listen. She went up to her room and started to pack, leaving him dreading the huge letdown sure to come. Yvonne was due in town today. She planned to stay through the Christmas show tomorrow night, then she and Chloe were going down to New Orleans for a few days of shopping and to take in the Christmas events.

Please, Lord, don't let Yvonne let my little girl down again.

His ringtone drew his hand to his cell phone in his pocket. Gram. "Is she here?" He'd wanted to wait at the house, but he had a heavy load of inspections today and another go-round with Kramer at the old house.

"Yes. She picked Chloe up a few minutes ago. They're going up to Jackson to shop then have dinner at the Lady Banks Inn. Chloe is super excited."

"And Yvonne?" There was a long pause before his gram answered, putting a knot in his chest.

"Her usual busy self."

Noah rubbed his forehead. Translation—Yvonne was preoccupied with her cell phone and probably wouldn't spend much time actually talking to her daughter. "Did she seem happy to see Chloe?"

"She made a grand show on her arrival."

"I'm sure she did."

Gram tried to reassure him that everything would be fine before she hung up. He wanted to believe her, but he sent a few more pleas heavenward just in case. Leaning back in his chair, he rubbed his bottom lip, trying to quell the churning in his gut. He pulled the key ring from his pocket and studied it. He'd wanted to talk to Beth last night about the words she'd put on the back. But Kurt had interrupted them, and now Yvonne was intruding, as well.

Light tapping on his door pulled his attention away. Beth pushed it open, her hazel eyes narrowed in concern.

"Are you okay?"

Quickly he shoved the key ring into his pocket. Now was not the time to discuss it. "Yeah. As good as I can be, I guess."

"Did she come?"

"Yes. They're going up to one of the malls in Jackson to shop."

Beth moved closer, biting her bottom lip. "I hate to ask this, but will Chloe be safe with her?"

Her concern for his child touched him deeply. He took her hand in his, squeezing it gently. "Yes. Yvonne would never do anything to hurt her child. In her own way, she loves Chloe." His words did little to ease the troubled frown on Beth's face. "Don't worry. She won't try to kidnap her. That would interfere with her glamorous life. She's not going to go off and forget about her, and if something does come up, she'll bring her home. It's not Chloe's physical well-being I'm worried about. It's her mental state."

"She wants her mom to love her."

"I don't know how many more times she can be shoved aside and rejected."

"She's a hopeful little girl. She believes in the goodness of others. But I worry, too. Then I remember that she has you, and I know she'll be all right. I think her security in your love allows her to maintain her hope that her mom will change."

"Thank you. I needed to hear that. I feel pretty inadequate at times. I don't know much about little girls. I'd be totally lost without Gram."

"Noah, I adore Chloe. If there's ever anything I can do, please don't hesitate to ask. I was a girl once, you know."

He remembered. Vividly. "So you were." Their gazes meshed, setting off tiny sparks along his skin. The image of Kurt holding Beth flashed across his mind, forcing him to retreat. "So, what did your friend have for you that will change your life?"

She looked down, hooking a strand of hair behind her ear. A sure sign she was reluctant to share.

"He had a job offer."

Noah's heart chilled, releasing all the old fears and hurts. "I see. So when do you leave?"

"I haven't given him an answer yet. He needs to know by Christmas."

He wanted to fight to convince her to stay, but like Chloe, he'd come to realize he couldn't make others behave the way he wanted. "You do what you think best. I want you to be happy." He shuffled the papers on his desk, surprised to find he really meant what he said. "I need to get to work."

Her eyes were wide and slightly moist as she nodded and turned to leave. "I have to get back. The phone is ringing. Will you let me know how Chloe is if you hear from her?"

"Sure, but I don't expect to. She'll be too busy to think of her old dad."

"Shopping will do that to you. Pushes everything else out of your mind."

"If you say so."

As soon as Beth left, Noah gathered up his work orders for the day, slipped them into his leather folder then went out the back door to his car. He'd told Beth the truth when he said Yvonne would take good care of Chloe, but he never could completely let go of his concern. Work was a good diversion, provided he could concentrate long enough to get the job done. He hated having to share his child. Even with her mother.

But for some reason, he didn't mind sharing her with Beth.

Chapter Ten

Beth took her time walking back to her apartment Friday night, enjoying the glow of the lights. She'd met Jen at the Magnolia Café for a meal and a little girl time. They'd ironed out a few details for the show the next day and spent the rest of the time catching up. There was never time to talk at rehearsals, and they were both eager to restore their friendship. The longer Beth remained in Dover, the more settled and secure she felt. But she couldn't totally dismiss the opportunity Kurt had offered. She'd prayed about it, but still had no clear answer.

If things between her and Noah were different, her choice would be so much easier. But at the moment, she had no idea where their relationship stood. She knew he cared for her, but to what extent? One minute he was placing kisses on her lips, the next he was pulling away.

Kurt's offer was to blame for part of that. She had to make that decision before she could move forward, but her emotions were tilting up and down between the choices like a child's seesaw. Her desire to dance was still strong, but so was her growing contentment here in Dover.

Pulling her keys from her purse, she stepped into the recessed entry of her building. Movement in the shadows stole her breath. She froze, her heart pounding.

"Miss Beth."

As her eyes adjusted to the low light, she saw Chloe seated on the floor, her back to the apartment door, her knees drawn up to her chest. Fear for her own safety shifted to fear for the little girl. "Chloe, sweetie, what are you doing here?"

"Waiting for you."

Beth opened her arms, and the little girl scrambled to her feet and into her embrace. "Chloe, what happened?"

Her little hands were chilly despite the thick jacket she wore, and Beth held her closer as she began to cry. She noticed the small rolling suitcase beside her.

Quickly, Beth hurried her upstairs to the apartment and settled her at the table. "I'm going to make you some hot chocolate, and then you can tell me what happened."

"She had to go back."

Beth slid into the chair, taking Chloe's hand in hers. "Your mom?"

Chloe nodded, wiping fresh tears from her cheeks. "She got a call when we were at the mall, and she was mad that she had to bring me all the way back here."

Beth clenched her teeth to prevent herself from voicing her anger. "Why here? Why didn't she take you home?"

Chloe's blue eyes glanced downward. "I told her Dad and Gram were at a meeting and weren't home. I told her you were."

"And she just dropped you off without making sure I was home?" Beth struggled to understand that level of irresponsibility.

"I told her I had a key 'cause you were my teacher."

"Oh, Chloe. Why didn't you want to go home?"

"'Cause my dad would be all mad and stuff. He never wants me to go with Mom. She was going to film the *Christmas Dreams* musical, and interview me for her TV show, and then we were supposed to go to New Orleans." Tears rolled down her cheeks. Her mouth puckered into a pitiful frown.

"I'm so sorry." She held her close a moment before retrieving the hot chocolate from the microwave and urging Chloe toward the sofa. After settling her in under the fleece throw, she gave her the mug. "I need to call your dad."

"No. Please don't. I don't want to go home. I want to stay here with you."

"Chloe, he'll be worried. Won't your mom call him and tell him she had to leave?"

The guilty look appeared again.

"I told her he had his phone off, and it wouldn't be on until late because of his meeting."

"Oh, Chloe, I know this is hard for you, but I have to call him. He loves you, and he'll be frantic."

"Okay, but please can I stay here with you? I can't talk to him about Mom, and I can talk to you. Please don't make me leave."

Beth paused with her cell in her hand, torn between the pitiful pleas coming from the little girl and her responsibility as an adult. "Chloe, I have to call him, but I'll see if he will let you spend the night with me. We can talk all night if you want, but tomorrow is the big show. You need to get some sleep so you'll be ready for the *Nutcracker* number."

"I promise I'll sleep and then go home in the morning."

Beth stepped into the bedroom to make her call, bracing herself for Noah's shock and anger. She wasn't disappointed. He was furious.

"I knew agreeing to this weekend was a mistake. I try not to get too involved because Chloe loves her mother. But this is the last straw. I'll be right over to get her."

"No. I think you should let her stay here with me tonight. She wants to talk, and since I'm a neutral party it'll be easier for her to open up to me. We've become close, and the fact that she asked her mom to bring her to me tells me she trusts me." The silence bothered her. Would he refuse?

"Yeah. You may be right. Let me know what happens, okay? And, Beth, tell her I love her."

Her heart warmed at the tenderness in his voice. "Of course. I told her you'd come get her first thing. Tomorrow is going to be a busy day so we both need our sleep, and we need to get to the theater early."

"Beth, thank you. I'm sorry she was dumped on your doorstep, but I'm grateful you were there to take care of her. I appreciate what you're doing. I'll make it up to you somehow."

"I adore Chloe, Noah. And all I need is for you to be my friend again, and trust me when I say that I won't hurt Chloe."

"I know. Beth, when the show is over we need to talk. I found the key chain, and I read what it said."

"Oh."

"I think there are things we should have said to each other a long time ago."

What did he mean? Was he going to remind her that he hadn't cared then, and he still didn't? That was something she'd think about later. Right now Chloe was her first concern.

Her little roommate was standing at the French doors leading to the balcony when she returned to the living room. She went to her, draped her arms over the slender shoulders and held her close. "The lights are beautiful, aren't they?"

Chloe nodded. "I wanted my mom to see them."

The wistful tone in her voice dragged Beth's heart down to her stomach. "I'm sorry, Chloe. I know you're disappointed."

"Why does my mom like her job better than me?"

Beth turned the little girl around and hugged her. "Oh, sweetie, I don't think she does. But I think she's so happy in her job that she forgets what's important."

"How can she forget me? I never forget her."

Beth steered the child to the sofa and pulled her down beside her, covering them both with the soft throw. She picked up the remote that controlled the lights and switched them off, leaving only the glow of the Christmas lights outside to illuminate the room. Sometimes it was easier to talk in the dark.

She hugged Chloe to her side while she gathered her thoughts. "I don't know your mother, so I don't know what her reasons are or what she dreams about. But I do know that some people are good at loving and some aren't. And some people have big dreams they work very hard to achieve. It becomes the most important thing in their life, and they'll do whatever it takes to make that dream come true."

"Like your dream to be a ballerina?"

The simple question pricked her conscience. "Yes. I worked hard and my dream came true, but I had to give up a lot of things along the way. Like friends and vacations and a lot of other things that at the time didn't seem as important as learning to be a better dancer and practicing to stay in shape. I even forgot about my family along the way."

"You forgot Miss Francie?"

"I didn't forget who she was, but I forgot to call her. I forgot her birthday. I forgot to come home to visit, and that made her sad."

"Do you think my mom's dream is to be on TV?"

"Maybe right now. Your mom is trying to be a success, and along the way she's forgetting what's important. The sad part is one day she'll realize she missed all these adventures with you, but it'll be too late. You'll be all grown up and maybe even have a little girl of your own. But I'm sure she loves you. I loved my mom even though I didn't think about her much. I just lost track of the priorities."

"Maybe I should call her and tell her how much fun we could have."

"You could."

Chloe snuggled closer. "But it wouldn't matter, would it? She always breaks her promises. Daddy tells me not to count on her when she promises things, but I want them to come true so much."

"Of course you do."

"Miss Beth, do you think God would be mad if I stopped loving my mom?"

Beth rested her head on Chloe's, feeling her pain as if it was her own. "I think He might. He doesn't stop loving you just because you make a mistake. But maybe you could look at this in a more grown-up way. Sooner or later, everyone lets us down. A mom, a job, a friend. God is the only one who never fails us. The next time your mom sets up a visit, be excited, be happy, but hold a little caution in your mind, too. Maybe you won't be so disappointed then."

"I guess my mom won't ever be the way I wish she was."

"I don't know. Maybe someday. But for now, you concentrate on the oodles of good things in your life. Your gram, your dad who adores you and your friends. You can have plenty of adventures with them."

"And you, too?"

"Of course. We're having a huge adventure with the Christmas show."

"I wish you were my mom, Miss Beth. We'd have way cool adventures together."

She blinked away sudden tears. "Thank you, Chloe. That's the nicest thing anyone has ever said to me. I'm glad we're friends. And I'm glad you came here tonight. I want you to make me a promise, though. You need to talk to your dad about tonight and what happened with your mother."

"Okay, but he'll say the same old thing. 'Don't get your hopes up when your mother calls.'"

"Will you the next time?"

Chloe sighed. "No. She might be good on TV, but she's not very good at being a mom."

"But your dad is very good at being your father, don't you agree?"

"He's the most phantasmagorical dad ever." She grinned. "And he's handsome, too, don't you think?"

"I wouldn't know about that. We'd better get to bed, or you'll be the Clara that falls asleep and never wakes up for her dance."

Tucked in bed with Chloe sound asleep beside her, Beth's thoughts went to Noah. He was a fantastic father and a disturbingly handsome man. But it was his heart she'd fallen in love with all those years ago, and his heart had captured hers again.

It's why she'd engraved her feelings on the back of the key chain. She'd been too shy and insecure to say the words back then. But now he'd read them, and he wanted to talk. Why?

She wanted to believe what her eyes and her senses were telling her whenever she and Noah were together. She wanted to believe the light in his eyes was for her, the tender smile for her and the gentle touches for her.

In that moment she realized that Noah was her new dream. Noah and Chloe and a future together.

But what if she was wrong?

Nothing, not even her most triumphant role with the Forsythe Company, came close to the elation coursing through her tonight. The cast was taking its third curtain call. The audience was on their feet. The little theater's production of *Christmas Dreams* had gone on without a hitch. Her dancers hadn't missed a step. Her heart was so full, she wasn't sure she could contain her joy.

Jen came to her side and gave her a quick hug. "We did it. I can't believe how well it all went."

Beth glanced at the crowd, only now starting to leave

as the cast made their way off the stage. The shouts of joy and laughter filled the old building. Cast members hugged one another and shared high fives. The children ran to greet proud parents, who were waiting to congratulate them.

"Miss Beth."

She saw her three students hurrying toward her, their flouncing costumes rustling as they came.

Hannah grinned up at her as she tugged the bow from her hair. "We didn't forget a step."

Abby laughed. "You almost messed up on that turn."

"Almost."

Chloe slipped her hand into Beth's. "We got lots of applause."

"That's because you were so adorable. I'm so proud of you girls. Of everyone."

Chloe hugged her, which drew the other two into a group hug. "We love you, Miss Beth."

Abby nodded. "I'm glad you're my aunt. This was so cool."

Hannah nodded. "Can we do this again?"

Noah came to her side. "You might have to. Judging by the response, once word spreads about how awesome the show was, you might have to give another performance."

He opened his arms and gave Chloe a big hug.

"Did you like me, Daddy?"

"You danced liked a professional. You were beautiful. I was very proud." He handed her a small bouquet of white miniature roses. "These are for you."

Gram joined the group. "My little princess. You were amazing." She smiled at the others. "Y'all stole the show."

Hannah spotted her mom and darted off with a wave. Abby spun around when her dad called her name and hurried to join him and her mom.

Beth looked at Noah. He was looking at her with such warmth and tenderness she couldn't breathe.

"Thank you. I know I've had my concerns about Chloe getting caught up in this dance thing, but I've never seen her so happy. She really loves to dance. You are a very good teacher."

"It's easy when the students are so eager."

Gram took Chloe's hand. "Let's get you out of that costume, and then we'll go celebrate."

Gram had arranged a wrap party at the senior center for all the cast and crew.

Noah turned to Beth. "You're coming to the party, aren't you?"

She wanted nothing more than to extend this night as long as possible. She did want to celebrate. With him. "Of course."

"You two go on. We'll meet you there."

"Guess that's our cue to leave." Noah touched her arm lightly. "Would you rather walk or drive?"

"Let's walk. I want to savor this feeling and stroll through the lights of town."

Outside they took their time along the sidewalk, crossing to the park. The town was filled with visitors, making it hard to stay close. Noah took her hand. The lights were on in Dover, creating the sensation of walking inside a lovely snow globe. Without the snow, of course. "(There's No Place Like) Home for the Holidays" filled the air, elevating her good mood up another level.

The atmosphere was electric with lingering excitement. Everywhere they turned, people were talking about the show. Three times on their walk across the park, Beth was stopped and congratulated on the event. By the time they entered the senior center, Beth's heart was soaring.

Evelyn and Chloe were already there. Gram hushed the crowd and came forward, motioning her and Jen to her side. "We contemplated several ways to thank you for your hard work and dedication. We had a long list of gifts we could purchase to express our appreciation. In the end we realized nothing we could buy could truly demonstrate the depth of gratitude we feel. So we're giving you our hearts instead. Thank you. Both."

The three Claras stepped forward and handed each woman—Evelyn, Jen and herself—a large bouquet of roses. Beth's vision was blurred with tears, but she could see hers were pink. Her favorite and exactly like the ones her father always had given her after a performance. That had to be Noah's doing.

The applause was peppered with shouts for a speech. Jen said a few words. Beth tried to remember all the people who'd helped, but her emotions were so close to the surface she gave up, muttering a soft thank-you before hugging the flowers close and thanking the Lord for this blessing she'd never expected.

Noah watched from the sidelines as Jen and Beth each gave a short speech of appreciation. Beth glanced over her shoulder in his direction when she spoke of the talented painters and carpenters who had added so much to the production.

Noah leaned against a post, watching his girls enjoy the wrap party. Gram was in her element, accepting the adoration and gratitude of the cast and crew. Chloe was laughing, huddled with her friends, giggling and screeching in happiness.

His Beth was glowing from the triumph of the production. Her smile lit up the room, making her eyes sparkle. She glided around the room, speaking to everyone with gracious sincerity. Many times he saw her tug Chloe to her side and speak to her. His chest expanded with happiness, threatening to crack his ribs from the pressure.

When the party began to wind down, Gram came over to collect Chloe. "Are you coming?"

"Shortly. My truck is still at the theater, and I want to make sure Beth gets home safely. It's late."

Gram patted his arm in approval, a knowing smile brightening her eyes.

Beth gave his daughter and Gram a hug, then looked in his direction. His heart warmed ten degrees at the affection in her hazel eyes. As she came toward him, he couldn't help but admire her grace and the way her red dress swished around her knees. She was the most beautiful woman he'd ever known. There was a sweetness about her that drew him to her, made him want to keep her close to his side and never let her go.

He looked into her eyes and saw that her exhilaration had given way to fatigue. She'd worked hard on the *Christmas Dreams* show. She needed a few days to rest and recharge.

"You ready to go?"

"Yes. I've suddenly lost all my energy."

"Then I'd better walk you home to make sure you don't fall asleep on your feet." He draped her fringed shawl over her shoulders, noticing that the little sparkles woven in the threads matched the sparkle in her eyes. Outside, the glory lights were still on downtown, flooding every nook and cranny of the square in a soft, dreamy glow. The crowds had thinned, and they took their time walking home.

"I want to add my congratulations to all the others. The show was amazing. You and Jen deserve all the praise."

"I don't know about that. We didn't do it alone, you know. Besides, like I stressed to my dancers, this was for Him. He's the one who came to earth."

"Point taken. Nevertheless, I'm proud of you and I'm glad you asked Chloe to be in the show. She's beyond happy."

"I'm so glad. She appears to have bounced back from last night."

"I think so." He took her hand. "I can't thank you enough for taking care of her. I'm just sorry she didn't feel she could come to me when her mom had to leave."

"She was angry and confused, and I think all she wanted was to talk to someone."

"She could have talked to me."

"Normally, but you would have been so furious at her mother, you might not have listened to Chloe."

He had to admit she had a point. He would have exploded. "I called her mother, and there's going to be some changes made. I can't put Chloe through this again. I just hope she understands."

"I believe she will. I think she finally realized that she can't make her mother change to fit her wishes. I tried to explain about dreams, and how easy it is to lose track of the important things in life. I think she understood some of it, and hopefully she'll be more cautious the next time her mother calls."

"It's hard being forgotten by people who are supposed to care. You feel like you don't matter." He saw her wince, only then realizing how she might have taken his statement. It hadn't been directed at her. He pulled her a little closer. "I'm glad she had you to talk to. That she trusted you with her feelings."

"I'll always be there for her. I'm afraid your daughter has stolen my heart." Stepping into the shadows of the entryway, she smiled into his eyes. "Thanks for walking me home."

"Speaking of hearts, we need to talk."

Even in the dim light he could see the worry darken her eyes. "All right. We can go upstairs if you'd like."

He thought about the cozy atmosphere in her apartment, the sense of home he'd experienced there. Being alone with her while feeling the way he did wasn't a good idea. "No. That's playing with fire. This will do fine." He slipped his hand into his pocket and pulled out the key chain. "I want to know what you meant. 'Every time you touch this you will be touching my heart. Love, Beth.'"

She tugged her shawl closer, avoiding his eyes. "Noah."

"Did you mean it?" His heart thudded fiercely in his chest. He searched her face, longing to hear confirmation of his suspicions.

"Yes. At the time, I had a huge crush on you."

A crush? Not what he'd hoped to hear, but it was a start and he pushed ahead. "What about now?" That's what he had to know.

"What do you mean?"

"How do you feel about me now?" She took so long to respond, his throat tightened. He was fearful of having misread all the signals and the sparks between them. She met his gaze, the connection melting them together as if they physically touched. Her hand came up to rest on his cheek.

"I think my crush never faded."

Pulse racing, he pulled her into his arms and kissed her with all the stored-up emotion he'd carried for years. He wanted her to have no doubts about his feelings. She slipped her arms around his neck, burrowing her fingers into his hair and sending his mind spinning. Kissing her was everything he'd dreamed of, and it filled him with a sense of home. For the first time since losing his parents, his heart was whole again.

He ended the kiss, holding her against his chest, inhaling the sweet floral scent while his chin rested on her silky hair. He trailed his fingers through the strands along her temple. "If I'd read this inscription that day, everything would have been different."

"Would it?" Her words were muffled against his chest.

"Yes, because I would have given you my gift even if it wasn't wrapped."

"You never told me what it was."

"A promise ring. I wanted you to be connected to me while I was at college. I wanted you to know how I felt."

"How did you feel? I was never sure."

"I was in love with you. I had been from the first day, but I didn't figure I had a chance. Not against your passion for dance."

"I guess we were both too afraid to admit what we were feeling. So what now?" She slid her arms around his waist. "This thing between us, where do we go from here?"

He held her closer, finding a peace in her closeness he'd never experienced before. "Take our time. See what happens. It's not just my heart involved now. I have Chloe to think about, too."

"You know I would never hurt her."

"I know." He tilted her face upward and kissed her again, overcome by a longing to never let her go. When he broke the kiss, he gulped in air and stepped back. "You'd better go on up."

She touched his cheek. "Good night, Noah. Think of me tonight."

"I always do."

He forced himself to turn and walk away, but stopped at the edge of the entryway. "Beth, if I'd told you how I felt that day, would you have stayed?" He wasn't sure why he'd asked the question and wasn't at all sure he wanted to hear the answer.

She held his gaze a long moment, then shook her head. "No. I would have chosen to dance. I didn't understand what I was giving up. I won't make that mistake again."

It wasn't the answer he'd hoped for, but it was one that gave him hope. And for now that was enough.

Chapter Eleven

Beth snuggled deeper into the covers, reliving Noah's kiss once again. She'd gone straight to bed, not wanting anything to diminish the feeling of euphoria and bliss still lingering in her senses. The tenderness in his kiss and the gentle way he'd held her had carried her away on emotions she'd never imagined. In his arms she found the sense of belonging she'd always craved.

She recalled again the sweet sensation of his kiss. So much had been revealed in that kiss.

Neither of them had declared their feelings outright, but the kiss had sent their relationship in a new direction—one she was eager to pursue. Was it possible to have a future with Noah? Could they move beyond the mistakes of the past and find a future together here in Dover? She prayed that was true because Noah was the only one she wanted to share her life with. The only one who knew her faults and her failings, and loved her in spite of them. He was her perfect partner.

Bright sunlight woke her the next morning. She'd overslept but got up feeling happier than she had in a long time. Her dreams had been filled with images of her and Noah dancing together, around and around, holding each other close, lost in their happiness.

She poured another cup of coffee and curled up on the sofa. For the moment it was still a dream. She had things to do today. Her first order of business was to call Kurt and tell him she wasn't interested. She wasn't sure why she'd taken so long to decide. The more she'd considered his offer, the more the truth had risen to the surface.

The thought of returning to a full-time dance career, with the constant stress and pressure, had brought a knot of tension into her chest. Since coming home she'd been sleeping better, eating better, even to the point of needing new clothes. She greeted each morning eager to start the day.

Looking back, she could see her passion for ballet had started to wane long before the failed romance and the miscarriage. She'd just been too committed to realize it. She'd had her time in the spotlight and she'd lived every aspect of her dream.

Kurt had said she wouldn't be happy here for long. But he was wrong. She wanted different things now. A line from one of her favorite show tunes came to mind: "The gift was ours to borrow." She'd been given the gift of dance and had used it to the fullness of her ability. Now it was time to let someone else use their gift.

And she would explore a new gift and a new direction. She placed the call to Kurt, who did his best to change her mind, but in the end he was surprisingly supportive.

Relieved and buoyed with anticipation, she opened her laptop, logged on to the local MLS and pulled up the commercial listings, searching for a place to open her dance school. She wouldn't tell Noah just yet. She'd wait until it was all settled. That way he'd know for certain she was staying in Dover, and he could depend on her not to run off again.

Financially she was in pretty good shape. She'd been so busy working that she'd spent very little of her earnings, and money went a lot further in Dover than in New York.

She scrolled through the handful of properties, stopping on several possibilities. There was plenty of rental space available, but she preferred to own. A small knot formed in her stomach. Becoming a business owner was a big step. She had no idea what was involved in starting a dance school, or the necessary legalities. Would she need to be certified? Bonded? It wasn't simply a matter of getting a loan; there was also marketing and advertising to think about. The thought set her mind spinning. She pursed her lips and leaned back on the sofa.

Was she ready? Was she capable? All she'd ever known was dancing, and a large part of that consisted of other people telling her what to do—how to stand, hold her head, position her arms, feet, hips, neck.

She forced the negative thoughts away. She was getting ahead of herself. First she had to find a suitable place. Then she could take her time working out the rest.

Her gaze landed on the address of a familiar building. Miss Barker's School of Dance. Her old teacher. She'd taken lessons there three times a week until she'd started private lessons in Jackson. The picture showed a very old, run-down structure. Was this a sign? A nudge from on high that she could step in and restore the school? She searched the screen for the owner and saw that the property was represented by a local bank.

Logically, she should work with her mom on this purchase, but she wasn't ready to share her plans. She wanted to prove to her family and herself that she could take charge of her life, and go in a new direction. But if she mentioned her idea to the family, she'd be buried in advice and far too many helpful good intentions. She knew how quickly a plan like this could fall apart. She'd already had one career dream crumble. She wasn't eager to lose another one. Once things were finalized, she'd make the announcement.

Tiny fingers of doubt crept along her nerves. Was she a fool to consider opening a dance school? She thought of her three little ballerinas, and the ladies at the senior center. No. Dover needed a place for children to learn to appreciate the dance, and a teacher who would make sure they were taught modest moves.

What would Noah think? Would starting a business in Dover finally assure him she wasn't going back to the stage?

That was her prayer, because if it didn't, then she had no hope of ever convincing him.

Noah pulled his truck to a stop in front of Kramer's dilapidated old house, his mood sagging when he recognized the owner's vehicle sitting near the back. Kramer had asked him to come by and check out a few structural issues he'd uncovered during demolition. This was the last place Noah wanted to be this morning. His thoughts were still bouncing back to last night and the kiss he'd shared with Beth.

He didn't put much trust in dreams, but last night, holding Beth, he'd seen his old dream reforming in front of him. A wife, a family and a home of his own. His dream was giving Chloe the kind of security and completeness he'd known, but lost.

They'd both danced around actually admitting they loved each other. She'd said her crush was still there; he'd confessed to loving her in the past. But they'd agreed to explore their feelings. That was a long way from the timid, insecure kids they'd been long ago.

Yet part of him remained wary. There was a lot of scar tissue to deal with.

"Carlisle."

Noah glanced up to see Kramer waving at him. He climbed out of the truck and joined him. His first client was proving to be more trouble than he was worth. Noah had thought about walking away, but the guy was the type to make his displeasure known to anyone who would listen, and bad word-of-mouth could kill his business before it even got off the ground.

"Glad you're here. I need you to look at this floor and tell me why it's sloping."

Noah followed him inside to the back of the house, but stopped before they entered the old kitchen. The wall that had separated the rooms had been removed. A closer look revealed that another wall had been torn down, too, and a quick glance upward triggered his alarm. "When did you take these walls down?"

"A few days ago. I need to get some of this work done if I'm going to make any money on this flip."

The statement unleashed a flare of anger in Noah. Kramer was trying to take a beautiful old home filled with fine craftsmanship and turn it into an open-concept hollow shell. But that wasn't his concern. "You should have checked with me first. You've taken down a load-bearing wall. Didn't your carpenter know that?"

"I didn't ask him. I did this myself to save some change."

Noah gritted his teeth. "That second floor is already sagging." He pointed to the obviously bowed joist above them. "You'd better shore that up before the entire second level falls down." He glanced around the space for something to shore up the beam, but could only find two-by-fours, which were not nearly strong enough to support the weight.

"I'll do that, but first look at this floor." He walked into the kitchen area and bounced up and down. The floor beneath his feet moved. "What's going on?"

Noah stooped down. The boards were clearly soft and probably rotten, but it was the supports beneath that concerned him. "Not sure until I can pull up some of the boards and get a look at the foundation."

Kramer grunted. "Great. I can't afford any more major hits. Are you sure about this?"

"Like I said, I'll have to get under the house, but it's a safe guess that either your joists aren't large enough or they're rotted out. It could also mean your piers have sunk into the ground."

"Meaning what?"

"A new foundation. We'd have to pour a concrete pad, set a new pier and put in stronger joists. Then beef up the floors, and maybe add metal leveling supports and stabilize the house from sinking into the ground more."

"Can you get under there now?"

"Not today. But I'll come back tomorrow and take a look. In the meantime, you need to get this ceiling stabilized. If you want this whole space open, you're going to need an I beam."

"You said a fifteen-foot beam would be plenty strong enough."

"That's when you were only removing one wall."

"Look, can't we work something out? Do we really need to be so picky? I mean, you're a building inspector, too, aren't you?"

Noah kept a tight hold on his anger. "Yes, but since you've hired me as your engineer, I won't be doing the city inspection on this house. We have building codes for a reason, Mr. Kramer, and if you want to continue to remodel this house, you'll have to meet them." He glanced at his phone. "I have another appointment. I'll try to get back out here tomorrow to look under the house. In the meantime—" he pointed to the sagging ceiling "—get that shored up."

Kramer's rude comment hung in the air as Noah walked away. He couldn't wait for this job to be finished. It wasn't the first time he'd been asked to let something slide to hold down costs, but he wasn't going to pass on something that could fail down the road. It was his responsibility to make sure structures were safe and compliant with current codes. If something he signed off on failed, then he would be held responsible.

Beth gripped the phone tighter in her palm as a violent wave of heat coursed through her veins, and blood pounded in her ears. Her hopeful excitement when she'd seen the name of the bank on an incoming email had deflated like a punctured tire when she'd read that the inspection had failed and she couldn't move forward with her application. She'd immediately placed a call to the loan officer, Burt Valens. "What do I have to do now?"

"I'm afraid there's nothing to be done on that property. The inspector recommended the building be condemned. It's not safe."

"But can't it be fixed? Restored or whatever?"

"I'm afraid not. Mr. Carlisle reported the structure was too far gone to redeem. I suggest you select another property. We'd be happy to process your application at that time."

"Thank you." Beth could barely speak around the anger clogging her throat. Noah. He'd done the inspection on her building and condemned it. The place looked rough. She knew it would need fixing up before she could open her studio; that's why she'd asked for an inspection. But condemned? No way.

She set her jaw. This had nothing to do with the condition of that building. This was about Noah's stubborn refusal to believe she wasn't going to suddenly walk out of his life. He didn't trust her, and this was his way of getting back at her. He was making her pay for something his ex-wife had done.

Glancing over at his office, she saw him moving around. Time to have a long overdue talk. Striding across the entryway, she yanked open his office door. He spun and looked at her, his dark brows pulled down into a fierce frown.

"Why did you do that?"

He swallowed. "Do what?"

"Condemn my building? I can't believe you'd carry a grudge this far. How dare you deliberately sabotage my future that way?"

Noah held up his hand and came toward her. "Hold it right there. I have no idea what you're talking about."

"Miss Barker's old building on Liberty Street. Your inspection caused me to lose a loan from the bank."

"You're the potential buyer? Why? What do you want with that run-down place?"

She wasn't ready to tell him that. "That's not important. You deliberately condemned that building."

"Beth, that building isn't safe. My report was based on facts and a thorough inspection. The place is ready to fall down. Besides, I had no idea you were the one wanting the inspection."

"I don't believe you. I'm positive my name was on the work order. You are determined to make me pay for leaving."

"No, I'd never do that. You know me better than that."

"I thought I did, but now I realize I don't know you at all." Furious, she whirled around and stormed back to her office, too upset to think clearly. Noah followed behind, clearly determined to explain himself.

"Beth, I want to know what's going on. You owe me an explanation."

"Don't put this on me." She crossed her arms over her chest, breathing rapidly. "You're afraid. You've built this steel wall around your heart so you won't have to risk getting hurt again. You use me and Chloe and anything else you can think of to keep yourself protected. I thought I saw that wall coming down and you opening up. Until Chloe's mother messed up and Kurt appeared, and now you're diving behind that wall again and shutting everyone out."

"You're wrong."

"You forget who you're talking to, Noah. I know you better than anyone. I know what you're most afraid of. I know how much you want a family again. A place to belong. Just like I do." With some of her anger spent, she took a deep breath and met his gaze. "We found that place in each other, but we were too young and naive to understand what we had. We were the right people. It was just the wrong time."

Noah ran a hand through his hair before resting his hands on his hips. "I didn't do this to hurt you. I didn't even know you were the one trying to buy the place."

"Then change your report."

"I can't do that. The building is too dangerous. I won't say it's safe when it's not just to make you happy."

Noah rubbed his forehead, then lowered his head and stared at the desk. Beth waited for him to continue. His shoulders braced. He reached over and picked up the printed boarding pass lying on the desk. His jaw flexed rapidly as he read the destination. "New York?"

His eyes were the color of an angry summer sky. She hastened to explain. "Yes, I'm going to—"

He waved the paper at her. "Your friend's offer was too good to pass up."

"No. That's not why I'm going."

"But you are going."

"Yes, but if you let me explain—"

The door swished open and her mother hurried in. "Beth, I need that list of properties for the Andersons. I forgot to put it in my phone before I left. Hello, Noah."

"Francie." He sent a glare at Beth, tossed the paper back onto the desk then walked out, leaving a heavy tension in the air.

"Did I interrupt something?" Her mother cast a puzzled look in her direction. "What's wrong?"

Beth could barely speak around the pain and hurt clawing at her throat. "Noah condemned my building. And then he saw my boarding pass for New York." She sank into the desk chair, wiping tears from her eyes. "He thinks I'm walking away again."

Francie frowned. "You're leaving?"

"Yes, but I'll be right back. I'm due for a follow-up visit with my doctor in New York, and I decided to go right away and get it over with. Noah stormed out before I could explain, and I'm sure in his stubborn, distrustful way, he thinks I'm going back to work."

"And this building thing. What's that about?"

"Oh." Her guilty conscience swelled. "I was going to wait to tell you until it was all finalized, but I put an offer in on Miss Barker's old building, the one where I took lessons. It's for sale, and I thought it would be a good place to open my school." She shrugged. "Sort of carry on in her honor."

Her mother nodded. "You want to open a dance school. Here in Dover? I thought that was the very last thing you wanted to do."

She nodded. "It was, until I started teaching the girls and working with the seniors and helping with the show. Now it sounds like a good idea."

"I think so, too."

"But Noah did the inspection on the building and recommended it be condemned."

"Good for him."

"Whose side are you on?"

"His, in this case. Honey, I know that building. The owner lives in New England someplace, and he has no intention of fixing it up. He's only interested in the ground it sits on. How had you planned on paying for it? You sold the land your father gave you when you moved to New York."

"I know, and I don't regret it. But I'm in good shape financially. I can afford to do this."

"Why didn't you come to me about this?"

The hurt tone in her mother's voice scratched across her conscience. She should have thought things through better. "I wanted to accomplish it on my own, to prove to everyone I'd changed."

"I admire your intentions, but if you'd told me, I could have saved you a lot of trouble. If you really want to open a studio, I have several places better suited that wouldn't need much to get them ready. Or you could rent a place until you get up and running."

"I'd rather own."

"Okay. Scoot over."

Her mother pulled up another chair to the desk and quickly pulled up three locations on the computer. Beth took one look at the two-story property, with its blue paint and dark blue awnings, and knew it was perfect. "That's the one. Do you think I can afford it?"

"We'll make sure of it." She hit the print button and pulled the sheet from the printer.

"When do you go to New York?"

"Now. I need to leave for the airport in a few minutes. I have an appointment first thing tomorrow morning. I had just printed out my boarding pass when the bank called and I found out Noah had done the inspection on my building and condemned it. I accused him of doing it deliberately to hurt me."

Her mother frowned, studying her closely. "Do you really think Noah would be so vindictive? Not to mention unethical."

With her shock and anger fading, Beth realized she'd overreacted. "No. He's too honorable to ever do something like that. I was upset. I guess I was lashing out at him without thinking."

"Maybe you'd better go explain things to him."

"No. I think we both need to cool off. I'll talk to him when I get back tomorrow afternoon. That way he'll know for sure I'm staying here."

At least she prayed he would understand. Once this final checkup from the specialist was done, she could cut the last tie to her past life, and turn all her attention toward the future.

Please, Lord, let that future include Noah and Chloe.

Chapter Twelve

Noah gripped the steering wheel with more force than necessary. New York. Beth was returning to New York. All her talk about staying in Dover was just that. Talk. Apparently her friend Kurt had convinced her that coming to work with him was too good an opportunity to pass up.

What hurt even more was how she'd accused him of deliberately sabotaging her building inspection. How could she think he'd be so underhanded? And if she was so upset that he'd nixed her building, why was she going back to New York?

He glanced out the window at the open country along the highway. Maybe he should have taken time to ask her. But the scalding shaft of pain in his chest had released all the old hurt from her walking away long ago. Instead, the anger had churned inside him all night, robbing him of sleep and darkening his mood all day. This was his last stop. Maybe then he could deal with Beth's defection and try to move forward.

The green-and-white sign for Old Agler Road flashed

by, signaling he was nearing the old Victorian house. He was in no mood to deal with Harvey Kramer today. The man had no concern for his own safety or that of his crew, and balked at every regulation he had to adhere to. If Kramer had his way, he'd ignore building codes altogether.

If he hadn't promised Kramer he'd be here to check out the foundation problem, he'd turn around and have it out with Beth. Even if that meant going to New York to confront her. She'd left him so confused, he wasn't sure which way was up. All he knew for certain was that he didn't like being at odds with her. He didn't want to lose the connection that was reforming between them. The kiss they'd shared still had the power to warm his blood and send his heart pounding.

Flipping the turn signal lever, he eased the truck into the long, narrow driveway leading to the old home. It wouldn't take long to get under the house and identify the problems, but convincing his client to make the necessary reconstruction might take a while.

Kramer met him at the front door. "I hope you can come up with a quick and cheap solution to this floor issue. I'm losing time on this deal."

Noah followed him into the large kitchen on the northeast side of the house, noticing Kramer had ripped out cabinets and appliances in his haste to remodel. The man's impatience was also evident in the pulled-up floorboards, which now exposed the joists below. He also noticed the sagging ceiling had been braced. Unfortunately he'd done so with a few two-by-fours, which were far too weak to do the job safely. Noah pointed to the already bowing lumber. "You need to use two-by-sixes to hold that up."

Kramer waved him off. "I'll get around to it. It's all I had. So what about this floor?"

Noah flicked on his flashlight and examined the exposed wood beneath the floor, then began taking a few measurements. "I don't like what I'm seeing, but I'll have to get under the house to know for sure."

"Fine. Do it. I need to get the project on track before I lose my shirt."

Noah shook his head and went back to the truck, pulling out his blue coveralls and the tools he'd need to do a thorough foundation inspection.

A quick glance at the sky told him a rainstorm was on its way. He'd better get started. But between his truck and the opening to the crawl space, his thoughts reverted to Beth. He didn't want her to leave Dover. But how did he get her to stay? She'd gone to New York— but was it for good, or a quick trip to work out the details of a new job? He should have at least asked her before storming off. He'd considered calling her, but each time he'd lost his nerve. How could he convince her she needed to stay here with him and Chloe? Could they even compete with the life she'd once had?

Zipping up the coveralls, he flipped up the hood and got down on his knees. Thankfully the crawl space was reasonably spacious and allowed him plenty of headroom. He belly-crawled toward the corner, examining joists and foundation pilings as he went, not pleased with what he was seeing. When he reached the opening Kramer had made, he pulled out his tape measure and the flashlight again. Thunder rolled through the sky.

The floors definitely needed more joists to bring it up to code. The current ones were too small, and a couple were completely rotten. Rolling over, he scooted to the next pier block, which had sunk down nearly three inches into the poor soil. He took a couple pictures and made a few more measurements before preparing to crawl back out. As he maneuvered past another pier, he noticed a joist riddled with termite damage. How had he missed that? Simple answer—because he'd been constantly distracted by thoughts of Beth. He'd had to take each measurement twice because he couldn't keep the numbers in his head.

A closer look at the wood revealed the entire section was paper-thin. It could collapse at any moment. Time to get out of there. He stashed his tools in his belt and started forward on his stomach.

A loud snap sounded from overhead. Thunder? He reached forward, his feet digging into the soft dirt below the house. A loud crash. The house shook. A crack. Sudden weight pressed on his back, robbing him of air. Pain sliced into his thigh.

There was another rumble, then a blow to his head… then darkness.

Beth ducked in to the entryway, escaping the pouring rain, then stepped into the real estate office, unable to keep the smile from her face. Her mother glanced up. "Welcome home, sweetheart. How did it go?"

She placed her small suitcase and purse in the corner then sat down. "The doctor said I'm healing better than expected, and he even thinks I'll be able to do a little pointe work in time. Nothing long-term, but I might be able to dance a little."

"That's wonderful news. You must be excited."

"I am, but that's not the only thing that happened. On the plane back, I sat with Katie Lorman. Remember her? We studied ballet together."

"I do. How is she?"

"Fine. She's working and dancing with Ballet Magnificat in Jackson, and she's asked me to join the staff working with the trainees. It's part-time, so I can still have my school and work with the ballet, too. Maybe even perform with them at some point." She didn't mention the one part of her plan that was still unsettled. Noah's place in her life.

Her mom held up her finger. "Speaking of your school, I did a little more digging on that blue building you liked." She tapped the keyboard then angled the computer so she could see. "It's on south Church Street, and it's in great shape. I looked it over this morning. Wood floors, lots of windows. It was an office complex, but it could easily be reconfigured to suit your needs."

Beth scrolled through the photos of the interior, her excitement growing. "It's adorable."

"I've already been in touch with the owner, and he's very motivated. And you won't need to worry about an inspection. He's already had that done, and I have the paperwork. In fact, I've started the purchase papers, too, and talked to Todd at the bank. All you have to do is take a look at the property, and we can get moving on it."

"You sound more excited about my new business than I am."

"I guess I am in a way. I like having you back home."

Beth wrapped her mother in a tight hug. "Thank you. I'm glad to be home, too." The reality of her decision landed on her mind, triggering a rush of insecurity. "Mom, I've never started a business before. There's so much to think about, so much I don't know."

"Don't worry. I know exactly what to do. I'll walk

you through every step. We'll come up with a business plan and get everything lined up."

The phone rang, and her mother answered. Beth looked at the photos again, mentally assigning each space to a part of her dance studio.

"Evelyn, what's wrong? Yes. She's here. She just got back."

Beth's heart seized when she saw the look of horror on her mother's face. "Yes. I will." She scribbled something on the notepad. "I'll notify the prayer chain."

Fear gripped her lungs. "Mom? What is it? Chloe?"

"No. Evelyn has been trying to reach you for the last half hour. Is your phone dead?"

She nodded. "I forgot my charger at the hotel."

Her mother took her hand. "It's Noah. He was doing a foundation inspection, and there was an accident."

Blood iced in her veins. "Is he—" She couldn't bring herself to ask the question.

"The house collapsed, and he's trapped underneath. The rescue squad is trying to get him out now, but it's a slow process. They don't want to cause another collapse."

"I've got to go. Where is he?" She took the paper from her mother. She recognized the road. The house belonged to Noah's first client, the difficult one.

"Maybe I should take you."

"No. I'm fine. I've got to go."

Her heart pounded so hard as she drove out of town she feared she couldn't breathe. Sweaty palms made gripping the steering wheel difficult. Fear like crashing waves ebbed and flowed in her stomach. A thousand questions darted through her mind. What if she lost him? Where was Chloe? How much of the house had collapsed? Why wasn't he more careful?

The answers didn't matter. She had to be there with him. He needed her. She needed him.

The pouring rain caused her to miss the driveway, and she lost precious time turning around. Fire and rescue trucks were parked next to the old Victorian, which was still standing. In her mind she'd imagined a pile of rubble. She grabbed her raincoat from the back and slipped it on as she hurried toward the activity, her feet sloshing on wet earth. She wanted to call his name, but he'd never hear her above the rain and thunder and the shouting of the workers. She looked around for a familiar face.

"Beth." Evelyn hurried toward her, wrapping her in a tight hug. "I'm so glad you're here."

"Where is he? Is he all right?"

Evelyn kept an arm around her waist as she walked her toward the back of the house. That's when she saw the corner of the house sagging awkwardly and a heap of rubble on the ground. "Oh, no. Is he under there?" Her heart beat in an unnatural rhythm, as if one chamber had shut down.

"Yes. They're working to get him out. All I know right now is that he's alive."

Beth glanced around at the men coming and going, walking slowly as if there was no urgency. "Why aren't they working harder? They have to get him out of there."

Evelyn patted her arm. "They're working as fast as they can. They don't want to trigger another collapse, and the rain is making things difficult."

Beth's barely controlled emotions gave way. Tears poured down her cheeks, and a sob burst from her throat. "He has to be all right. I can't lose him now. I love him. Please, Lord, not now." She found herself in

Evelyn's strong embrace as she cried, holding on to the woman tightly.

"Let's go sit in my car and get out of the rain. We can see everything from there. The chief promised he'd keep me updated."

Beth resisted moving. She needed to be right here when he came out. She wanted him to know she was here. "No, I'd better wait."

Evelyn pulled her around and urged her toward her vehicle parked a few yards away. Inside the warm, dry car, Beth was able to take a steady breath and think a little more clearly. "Where's Chloe? Does she know?"

Evelyn shook her head. "She's with friends. They were going to the movies in Sawyer's Bend. I'm not going to call her until we know something for certain."

After a half hour, Beth couldn't sit another moment. She got out and moved as close to the activity as she could. It was silly, but standing here in the rain, near Noah, made her feel like she was doing something. Lending moral support by her presence.

The next half hour saw progress. The firemen had shored up the area and were now under the house tending to Noah's injuries, but there was still a lot to do before they could safely remove him from the small space. He was unconscious.

Cold and wet, she returned to the car to wait with Noah's grandmother.

Evelyn took her hand, rubbing it to restore warmth to her skin. "You're freezing."

"I didn't notice." She laid her head back, closing her eyes. "He has to be all right. He has to be."

"That's what I'm praying for."

Beth squeezed Evelyn's hand. "I'm sorry. I should

be trying to comfort you. I know you're as worried as I am."

"We both love him, don't we?"

"I always have. Life just got in our way."

"It happens." They sat in silence for another forty-five minutes, then Fire Chief O'Brian tapped on the car window.

"We're bringing him out now. He's still unconscious, but he's stable. He has a leg injury, and probably some cracked ribs. We're taking him to Magnolia County Hospital in Sawyer's Bend. You can meet us there."

"Can I see him?"

"He won't know you're here, but I guess it won't hurt."

Beth squeezed Evelyn's hand before getting out and hurrying toward the house. The rain had eased up. She stopped when she saw the men carrying the stretcher. She got as close as they would permit. Her heart was a cold lump in her chest. Noah had a wide brace around his neck, and his right leg was wrapped in thick covering. She ached to touch him to prove to herself he was alive, but she wasn't allowed that close. She had to settle for whispering his name and telling him she loved him.

She waited until the ambulance started off before getting into her car. Evelyn had left, probably to go get Chloe. Her impulse was to start the car and race to the hospital. But common sense prevailed. She took a moment to calm herself, then called her mother before she headed out.

By the time she arrived at the hospital, Noah was in surgery to repair damage to his leg, and all she could do was wait for Evelyn. Since she wasn't a relative and no one would tell her anything about his condition, she sought out the chapel. Her mind was so clouded by fear that she couldn't form a coherent prayer so she sat silently, knowing the Lord would understand her pleas.

She knew now that loving Noah and Chloe was more fulfilling than any starring role. She wanted to spend the rest of her life with them. She'd prove to him somehow that she'd never leave again. She'd stay by his side until he regained consciousness. She wanted to be the first person he saw when he woke up. Maybe then he'd understand that he was her obsession.

Noah fought his way through the gray fog of pain and confusion. He hurt, but he couldn't pinpoint where exactly. Thinking made his head throb. Something heavy was sitting on his chest, making it hard to breathe. He tried to move, only to regret it when pain shot through the right side of his body.

He heard his name being called. A soft feminine voice. Beth? He struggled to clear his thoughts, but the gray fog swirled around him again, drawing him down into darkness.

When he opened his eyes again, his vision was blurred. He blinked and glanced around, trying to grasp where he was. A hospital. He recoiled as the memory rushed back. The house. It had collapsed on top of him. He'd been too preoccupied with thoughts of Beth to notice the danger.

Beth. Was she here? He started to raise his head, only to wince and drop back down on the pillow.

"Noah. Oh, praise the Lord."

Gram? He closed his eyes to ease the ache and drifted off again.

"Daddy? Please wake up."

His vision was clear when he opened his eyes the next time, and he could process thoughts easier. "Chloe?"

Her little face held a bright smile. She leaned over the side rail and grasped his arm. "Daddy. You're awake."

He squeezed her hand, but his gaze searched the room. "Beth?"

"She's not here. She's talking to someone about a new job. I'll go get Gram."

Before he could speak, Chloe darted away, leaving him with a new ache that twisted deeper into his core than any physical pain. She'd left. The job had won. His gut kicked, stirring up the old sediment of resentment. When would he learn?

"Noah. Oh, my dear boy, it's so good to have you back. You had us worried."

He tried to force a smile for her sake but failed.

"How do you feel?"

"I'll survive." He'd survive his injuries. But not Beth's defection. "Has she left?"

"Who?"

"Beth?"

"No. She's right here. She's on the phone. I'll go get her. She'll want to talk to you."

"Don't bother. I know what she'll say."

"You're not making sense. Maybe I should call the nurse." She reached for the call button.

"Chloe told me Beth was taking a new job. I know all about it. There's nothing I need to say to her. I knew she'd never stay in Dover. Once that friend offered her a job, I knew she'd jump at the chance. I can't depend on her to hang around."

He glanced up as someone stepped close to the foot of the bed. Beth. His heart swelled with affection. She was the only thing he wanted to see when he woke up, and his muddled brain had dangled her image in his mind repeatedly. But she'd been smiling, and she wasn't now.

"You'll never change, will you? I could start a dozen dance schools here in Dover, and you'd still be waiting for me to walk away."

"Dance studio?" What was she talking about?

"If I miss your call, or if I leave town for some reason, your first thought will always be that I've left again. Well, I'm done, Noah. I won't live like that."

Tears were seeping from her eyes. "I'm glad you're going to be all right."

He reached out to her, but she spun and walked out. "Beth."

Gram pressed him back against the pillow, her stern expression clearly revealing her distress. "Honestly, you are the most blind, closed-minded man I ever knew. Worse than your granddad and your father. I'll have you know that young woman has been here at your side from the beginning. She stood in the pouring rain while they dug you out from under that house. She's been here at your bedside around-the-clock the last two days, refusing to even eat. Her mother brought her food because she was afraid you'd wake up while she was down in the cafeteria. Francie had to bring her fresh clothes."

"Gram."

"I'm not finished. Beth loves you, and if you don't come to your senses, you're going to lose her again. You listen to me. I know you're protecting your heart from being broken again. But that's not your job. You're not strong enough to do that alone. You're supposed to give your heart, all of it, to the Lord so He can heal it and return it to you able to love again."

Noah knew she was right. It was the one thing he'd never been able to turn over to God because he feared he'd be opening himself to disappointment and failure again.

He loved Beth. He'd made a mistake and jumped to conclusions because she hadn't been the first thing he'd seen when he'd awakened. Now he had to fix the mess he'd made. "Gram, call her, tell her I didn't understand. She'll listen to you."

"Not on your life." Gram shoved her hand into her purse and pulled out her phone, laying it firmly on his chest. "Do your own dirty work."

Chloe had come to the side of the bed and frowned at him. "Daddy, Miss Beth isn't like Mom. She loves me."

Gram took Chloe's hand. "Even your daughter sees more clearly than you do. We'll be back later. The doctors say you can go home tomorrow, and I have to get the house ready. Come along, Chloe. Let's leave your father to stew in his own sour juices awhile."

"What does that mean?"

"I'll explain on the way home."

Noah stared at the cell phone a long while before finding the courage to call Beth. It went straight to voice mail. Four more tries brought the same result. He left messages, but he was beginning to fear Beth would never listen to them.

It hit him then that she might leave Dover after this. And it would be entirely his fault this time.

Beth strolled through the lower rooms of her new dance studio. Things had moved quickly, and she'd signed the papers first thing this morning. Her mother had handled all the details and greased some wheels along the way. Beth had wanted to be involved with every aspect of her new venture, but she'd been too concerned about Noah to leave the hospital.

That was proving to be a pointless endeavor. She'd stayed by his side every moment, but all he could see when he woke was that she wasn't there. His first re-action had been to assume she'd left again. She'd done all she could to convince him. Now it was time to let go and move on.

Turning her attention to the building again, she stepped into a small room at the back that held a sink and small fridge. She could expand this to accommo-date a full kitchen. She would be spending many hours here now. Retracing her steps, she went back to the front of the store. The room on the left would be her office, and with a little remodeling she could have two large rooms downstairs and two upstairs. It was all working out perfectly. All that remained was to complete the business paperwork and decide on a name for her new dance school. She was undecided between Bethany's School of Dance and Montgomery's Dance Academy.

Hopefully the countless details of setting up her school would keep her mind off Noah. The thought of him never failed to send a spike of pain into her chest and moisture to her eyes. He'd called repeatedly, and left messages begging her to talk to him. As much as she longed to, she knew it was futile. She had to find a way to let go before she went nuts.

The bell sound on her cell phone was a welcome interruption—until she saw the name on the text mes-sage. Evelyn. Her heart ballooned into her throat as she read the words. Noah needs you. How soon can you get here?

Please, Lord, let him be all right. What had happened? Had he relapsed? Fallen? The drive to Noah's was only a few blocks, but it felt like forever. She hurried to the front door and didn't bother to knock. "Evelyn." She went into the front parlor and stopped. Noah was coming toward her, moving slowly, his hand clutching a cane. He looked pale but better than he had in the hospital. The chambray button-up shirt he wore matched the blue of his eyes. Eyes that were bright with affection and curiosity.

"Beth. What are you doing here?"

She scanned his tall frame, searching for something wrong. The bandage was still on his temple where the board had struck him, but it was smaller today. Otherwise he looked fine. A bit pale but solid. Strong. "Evelyn said you needed me and to come right away."

Noah frowned then nodded slowly. "I see. She's right. I do need you."

Beth took a step backward. Obviously Evelyn was trying to get them to work out their differences. But it was too late. "You look perfectly fine to me. I have to go." She whirled, but Noah called out to her.

"Please don't leave. I can't chase after you in my condition. Won't you take pity on a guy who has no sense, who let fear rule his life for so long it might have cost him the only woman he's ever loved?"

She closed her eyes, willing herself not to rush into his arms.

"Forgive me. Gram told me how you stayed with me through all this. I think I knew that on some level because the only images I remember during that time were of you. When I woke up and you weren't there I—"

She heard him take an unsteady breath. Were his ribs

hurting him? She faced him, the love in his eyes making her breath catch.

"I wanted to crawl back into the dark and never come out."

He took a few slow steps toward her, never taking his eyes from hers. "Beth, please forgive me. I don't want to lose you again. I love you. Chloe loves you. We belong together."

"How can I trust that you won't always think I'll leave?"

"Because I heard about your dance school and your position with Ballet Magnificat. But mostly because I'm going to love you so much you'll never want to go anywhere else but in my arms. Beth, you're my family. You're where I fit."

Her tears blurred his handsome face. She swiped them away and met him in the middle of the room. "And I fit with you."

He wrapped her in his arms, letting the cane fall to the floor with a thud. She held him close, too close. He grunted. She'd forgotten about his ribs.

"I'm sorry."

He shook his head. "No. It's worth the pain to hold you close." He kissed her tenderly, cradling her face in his palms. "Marry me."

"Yes. Oh, yes." She kissed him before sliding her arms around him and snuggling close to his chest. She wanted to stay here forever. "When?"

He chuckled. "Are you in a hurry?"

"Oh, yes. We've waited too long to find each other again."

He stepped back and pointed to the cane on the floor. "Let's sit and talk about it."

After handing him the cane, she slipped an arm around his waist to steady him, and to feel his warm presence. She sat on the arm of the chair, her hand holding his, unwilling to let go.

"I thought you'd want a big wedding with all the trimmings."

"No. Not big. Fast."

He laughed and squeezed her hand. "Lady, you make a man feel like a king. All right, when do you suggest?"

She took a moment to orient her dates. "Christmas Eve?"

"That's only three days away. Are you sure?"

"What about Christmas Eve eve, would that be better?"

Noah pulled her down and kissed her again. "Today would be perfect, but I think there are a few legalities to take care of." He captured her mouth again, kissing her with all the love and promise she knew he held in his heart.

"Gram. I think they made up."

Chloe's voice drew them apart. Beth stood, taking a place behind him, her hands resting on his broad shoulders.

"Are you getting married now?" Chloe's tone was filled with hopeful excitement.

"Yes. We are."

"Oh, Daddy." She threw her arms around his neck and squeezed. "You've given me the best present ever. A mom for Christmas."

"What's this I hear about wedding bells?" Gram joined them, her smile wide and loving. "I knew if I could just get you two knuckleheads in the same room, it would all work out. So when is the wedding?"

Beth bit her lower lip. "Christmas Eve."

"Oh, my. Then I need to get busy. It'll be too late to get the church. We'll have the ceremony here. Thank goodness I had the house professionally decorated for the holidays. I'll call Francie about food. But you'd better talk to her first. I know she'll be thrilled at the news."

"Wow. A wedding right here. That's so cool." Chloe gave Beth a hug. "Miss Beth, is it okay if I call you Mom?"

She glanced at Noah before answering. "Yes, but do you think your mother will be okay with that?"

"She won't care. She always wanted me to call her Yvonne anyway."

Gram gathered Chloe away to start making preparations, leaving them alone again.

Noah rose to his feet again and tugged her into his arms. "There's just one more thing I need from you."

"Anything."

He touched his wounded leg. "You helped Chloe and Gram. Do you think you could teach me to dance—to help with my leg, of course?"

She laughed and caressed his face with her palm. "I would love to teach you to dance. In fact, I have the perfect studio. All it needs is a name."

Noah kissed her lips, letting his finger trace a path across her lower lip and up her chin. "I was thinking Carlisle's School of Dance sounds nice."

"I think it sounds perfect."

* * * * *

Get 4 FREE REWARDS!

We'll send you 2 FREE Books plus 2 FREE Mystery Gifts.

FREE
Value Over
$20

Both the **Love Inspired®** and **Love Inspired® Suspense** series feature compelling novels filled with inspirational romance, faith, forgiveness and hope.

HARLEQUIN
PLUS

Announcing a **BRAND-NEW** multimedia subscription service for romance fans like you!

Read, Watch and Play.

Experience the easiest way to get the romance content you crave.

Start your **FREE 7 DAY TRIAL** at www.harlequinplus.com/freetrial.